THE BLIND MIRROR

ALSO BY CHRISTOPHER PIKE

PUBLISHED BY TOR BOOKS

THE COLD ONE

THE LISTENERS

SATI

THE SEASON OF PASSAGE

THE BLIND MIRROR

CHRISTOPHER PIKE

A TOM DOHERTY ASSOCIATES BOOK
NEW YORK

TOR®

THE BLIND MIRROR

A Tor Book
Published by Tom Doherty Associates, LLC
175 Fifth Avenue
New York, NY 10010

www.tor.com

TOR® is a registered trademark of Tom Doherty Associates, LLC.

Library of Congress Cataloging-in-Publication Data

Pike, Christopher.
    The blind mirror / Christopher Pike.—1st ed.
        p.   cm.
    "A Tom Doherty Associates book."
    ISBN 0-312-85895-7
    1. Artists—Fiction.   2. Separation (Psychology)—Fiction.   3. Missing persons—
Fiction.   4. California—Fiction.   I. Title.

PS3566.I486B55   2003
813'.54—dc21

2003040215

First Edition: May 2003

Printed in the United States of America

0 9 8 7 6 5 4 3 2 1

For Abir

THE BLIND MIRROR

ONE

Time to land. For most, the sensations and sounds of a descending plane signal a fresh start or a familiar homecoming. Logic dictated as much. You were either coming or going. Yet when David Lennon tried to place himself into one of the categories, he failed. For some reason he felt lost between the cracks.

He opened his eyes; he did not remember closing them. He assumed that meant he had slept. A robotically smiling flight attendant patrolled the aisles. Buckle up, she said, landing at LAX in twenty minutes. Her blond hair was stiff as straw, her lipstick the color of orange soda. She probably liked her job as much as he had enjoyed the meal she had served at the start of the flight. He had wanted to throw up after eating it but there had been a line to the toilets.

Reaching for the seat belt, David heard a bone in his back pop. His spine was stiff, his thoughts as dull as the blood his brain soaked in. He felt like he had just awakened from a nap in a box.

"How was your sleep?" the man on his left asked.

David had the window, the guy the aisle. They had spent six hours together and had not exchanged a word. David had been engrossed in a novel he had to read for a cover he planned to paint over the next two weeks. The man had been studying what appeared to be textbooks, in between tapping on a silver laptop and talking into a cell phone the size of a pack of cigarettes.

"Good," David replied, lying. The man was fifty, tan and athletic, dressed in a gray suit, eyes to match—although they had an intensity David found disconcerting. He appeared professional, rich, confident of his place in the world.

"You were snoring," the man said, and offered his hand. "Dr. James Rean."

"David Lennon," he said, shaking his hand. "Really? I don't usually snore."

"How would you know?" Dr. Rean asked.

What a question. "What kind of doctor are you?"

"A medical doctor. A surgeon, actually." He added, "I specialize in transplants."

David was intrigued. Once upon a time he had dreamed of being a doctor. He was addicted to ER reruns, the dozen patients being wheeled in every week, their cries for help, the instant miracles—the power those people in white had, even if they were only high-priced actors. Of course he had no aptitude for science, could only paint and draw.

"Heart? Liver? Kidneys?" David asked.

"Livers, for the most part. But I have done a number of kidney transplants."

"I didn't think doctors did that—crossed over, I mean. You must have had a lot of training."

"Endless years. I work out of Miami."

"My parents live in Florida—in Setter. I have flown into Miami many times. What brought you to New York?" Their flight had originated out of Kennedy.

"Old friends. I'll be attending a medical conference in Los Angeles." Dr. Rean paused. "How about you?"

"I'm from California. Have you heard of Lompoc? It's a small town on the coast, about three hours north of L.A."

"Never heard of it."

"Don't feel bad. It's the sort of place—when you leave for any length of time, you try to forget it."

"But it's on the water. It must be nice."

"It's *near* the water. Between the city and the beach, you have six miles of flat farmland. They grow strawberries, grapes, watermelons. Plus you've got Vandenberg Air Force Base north and south of the town. They shoot off missiles there. The worst thing is the prison at the edge of town. The place has a white-collar penitentiary as well as jails for hard-core criminals." David added, "It's not really a tourist town."

"Did you grow up there?" Dr. Rean asked.

"Yes. I was born there."

"How long were you in New York?"

"Two months. It was largely a business trip. I'm an artist. I do book covers, when I can get them. The last eight weeks I've been trying to build up my contacts."

Dr. Rean raised an appreciative eyebrow, nodded to the bulky manuscript tucked in a pouch in front of David's seat. David had been reading Marcy Goldberg's *Vampire of My Heart* when he had dozed. Fortunately, he'd had the presence of mind to collect the four-hundred-plus Xeroxed pages and put them aside. Not that he remembered the actual act—the nap had completely thrown him off. Did he have a nightmare? He had a vague memory of something unpleasant.

"Is that an assignment? I saw you reading it earlier," Dr. Rean asked.

"Yes." David touched the manuscript. "It's a horror novel."

Dr. Rean brightened. "I love horror. Is that what you specialize in?"

Just like a doctor, David thought. Expected everyone to specialize.

"No. Never done horror before. Don't even read the stuff."

"What's it about?"

David hesitated. "It hasn't been published yet. I don't know if I should be talking about the plot."

"It's not a patient, is it?"

Was Dr. Rean mocking him? David was not sure. At the same time he did not like to be rude. "It's a long story, and we'll be landing soon," he said. "I don't think I could do the story justice in just a few minutes."

Dr. Rean smiled smoothly. "I'm impressed. You're what—twenty-five?— and you're doing book covers for big-time publishers."

"I'm twenty-eight, thanks. To tell you the truth, this book is a big break for me. For the last three years I've been stuck doing romance covers—the bronze guy holding the helpless woman, her breasts half hanging out of her dress. It's gotten so boring, the same theme over and over again. But the publisher says this novel could be a best-seller. They paid a lot for it."

"Do you already have a *theme* for your cover?"

"No. I haven't finished reading it. But I have to hurry. The publisher gave me a tight deadline."

"Any ideas?"

"No. The publisher didn't really give me any ideas either. That's unusual with a book they've paid a lot for. Usually they don't give you that much room to maneuver. But on this book I think they were all stumped. They want to see what I come up with."

"I'm sure you'll have to read the book a few times before it sinks in all the way," Dr. Rean said in a reassuring tone, perhaps the same one he saved for patients who had incurable diseases.

David felt himself withdraw. The man was friendly enough—he was going out of his way to make conversation—but David imagined a smirk behind his smile, a sparkle of condescension in his eyes. They were green as well as gray, moss growing on rocks, not warm at all.

"I plan on doing that." David shifted uncomfortably and glanced out the window. Five minutes from touchdown, L.A. raced by like a den of confused zoning commissions. The new skyscrapers made the old buildings look like bottom feeders. He hated big cities—he had hated New York, even more than Lompoc. Odd how he had run off to the Big Apple to heal from his relationship with Sienna Madden. He must have wanted to prolong the pain.

They dropped into overcast. A jar went through the length of the fuselage, and the view was wiped away, sparing him further opportunity to dwell on L.A.'s shortcomings. Dr. Rean continued to talk. He enjoyed an audience, even when it wasn't looking at him.

"The biggest problem we have in the transplant field is finding the organs in time," he was saying. "The national bank only supplies one heart for every four that is needed. With kidneys and livers the percentages are better; nevertheless, I have dozens of patients in the hospital where I work who just waste away in bed waiting for that magical call."

David felt obligated to turn and face the guy. After all, he was talking about a sensitive subject. Yet, once again, he felt Dr. Rean's concern was not genuine, that he was merely mouthing a spiel he had said many times before.

"Is there nothing to be done?" David asked.

"I suppose we could place people who come in for surgery into comas and harvest their organs when they're napping." Dr. Rean chuckled as David blinked in surprise. The doctor added, "You never saw the movie or read the book? *Coma?*"

"I'm afraid not."

"A great story, although ridiculous. It could never happen in reality." Dr. Rean glanced over at him and smiled. He had very white teeth, very small—dentures made for a child, perhaps, or maybe he simply had an odd collection of genes. He added, "You really should read it, after you're done with your vampire novel, that is."

"How did you know it was about vampires?" David asked.

"The title is printed on the top of every page."

"Oh." True, very true.

The conversation died right then. David returned to the dismal view and Dr. Rean laid his head back and closed his eyes. He passed out after a couple of deep breaths, and he snored as well.

The plane landed minutes later. The doctor roused quickly. Seated near the front, they were off in minutes. Dr. Rean handed him his card as they walked into the passenger lobby.

"If you're ever in Florida, give me a call," Dr. Rean said. "We can have dinner."

"Sure." David gave the card a glance—Miami address, some sort of life extension clinic—before slipping it in his back pocket. He knew the chances of his ever calling the good doctor were zero.

Outside the terminal he ran straight into mid August; hot and smoggy, New York City seen through a three-thousand-mile-long telescope. He was surprised to find himself looking forward to reaching Lompoc. At least there he knew half the people by their names. It was not a tourist town, but at least it was home.

His car was in lot C, long-term parking. Five bucks a day, times sixty, a nice wad of cash. He was having to count it these days. The four-walled box he had rented in New York had cost fifty a day, but it had been only a block from a Jewish deli that made turkey sandwiches so delicious it made him think every day was Thanksgiving.

Two months of dirt covered his windshield. Wiping it with a T-shirt yanked from his suitcase, he coughed on the dust. The girl at the exit smiled in sympathy when she asked for the three hundred dollars.

"Been gone a long time?" she asked.

"It feels like years," he said.

Ten in the morning—the freeways were kind. In half an hour he was out of Los Angeles and heading north toward Santa Barbara and Lompoc. Driving fast, the radio blasting, he thought of the former more than the latter. Sienna had lived in Santa Barbara, in the dry hills behind the city, in a small guest house on a wide ranch. But he would not stop there on the way up, he told himself. *There* was empty: here, there and everywhere—one big fucking galaxy minus the stars. Maybe it had been a mistake to come home. He missed her as much as the day he had left.

No, he missed her as much as the day *she* had left.

"Got to go, David. Don't ask why."

The Beatles, "Yesterday," came on. He turned to the news.

Santa Barbara appeared an hour and ten minutes later. David kept his foot on the gas, didn't even look at the exit that led to her place. She was not there, she had moved out. Gone home, wherever that was. He knew the city but not the address.

Driving north, Lompoc did not follow automatically. One had to turn west off the freeway, head through a hilly cow valley that should have led to the ocean in seconds but which seemingly went on forever. The California coast had a bump right there. Lompoc had been built on the tip. But not on the water, Dr. Rean. Why hadn't they built it on the water? No one knew, it was one of those mysteries no one could bother to solve. Leave the ocean views to the cabbages and the strawberries.

The valley ended abruptly and he was home sweet home. First came the old side of town, then the older end. The only relief from the forties and fifties was to head north toward the new mall and dust-free fast-food joints. His house was that way, a couple of miles. But he turned west and drove toward the beach instead. He wanted to see the water.

Lompoc was thirteen thousand strong. It took only three minutes of driving to leave it all behind. The cabbage and strawberry fields greeted him with flat indifference. The prison was to his north—too far away to see clearly. As he closed on the water, Vandenberg AFB grew on his right and left, encircling the coastal area like a real estate deal gone bad. He could see little of the base: a couple launch towers; a handful of coffin-shaped barracks; and steel-toothed fences. You had to have barbed wire to shoot super-secret military rockets into outer space.

In reality the base was not bad, not when you actually got onto it. David had taken a tour of it while growing up. The men and women in their neat uniforms always looked handsome, and there were few sights as far-out and patriotic as a good old red, white and blue missile lighting up the night sky before vanishing into the great unknown. Yet the sight had never inspired him to join up. He had an instinctive distrust of authority, or else he just didn't like being told what to do.

The main beach came up quickly. What a delight the town took in water sports. Here it was a hot August day and there were twelve people on the sand, less in the water. The reason was said to be the tides. Treacherous was too kind a word for them. When the surf was big you were pulled every which way but toward the shore. As a lifeguard, seven years ago, he had saved a girl from drowning. She had been eight then, Mary Pomus, a pretty little thing, with so much wet hair he had almost choked on it trying to get her to the beach. That had been his proverbial fifteen minutes of fame. The paper had put him on the front page: LOCAL HAS THE HEART OF A LION—never mind that lions were lousy swimmers. For a month he'd eaten free at McDonald's.

David parked and got out, wiping the sweat off his brow. The sky was a blazing blue, the sea a cauldron of foam and glare. Another big day and no surfers around to talk about it. The locals always went ten miles south to Jamala. There, the tides were almost as bad but the spot had spectacular cliffs and vast stretches of undisturbed sand. Hemmed in by the base, Lompoc's beach was claustrophobic. He saw two families with their kids, a bunch of teenagers playing Frisbee. The place bored him, he was not sure why he had come.

Ah, but there was mystery and magic only a mile north, if one had the guts to make the journey. It required a hard walk along a rocky railroad track, over a dizzy bridge and into dangerous base territory. Yet if a person kept his head down, and immediately veered into the sheltering sand dunes after the hop across the bridge, it was possible to elude the dreaded BP— Vandenberg's base police. David knew from experience how little senses of humor those guys had. He had told Sienna as much the last time they had come here.

That had been the last time he had seen her.

"Got to go, David. Let me go."

"So that is why I came here," he said to himself as he started walking north in the ankle-twisting gravel that shored up the rusty railroad track from the inevitable California earthquakes. *Talking to myself a lot these days,* he thought. Bad sign.

Five minutes later he ran into an old friend, Charles Beard.

What a history they had: Charlie, him, and Billy Baxter. They had met as kids, and in high school had run track together: Charlie in the mile, Billy in the two mile, and David in the half mile. Of course Billy could beat them at any distance. He had the devastating kick, won all the trophies—not the least of which was Rachel Bronson, the cutest girl in the school, sweet, blond Rachel. David had used to look at her sexy smile and think that Lompoc still had a few surprises left to show him.

Billy had lived for Rachel and the races. Up until Rachel seriously burned her face when her house caught fire. What a horror that had been. Three months later, after three failed surgeries to restore her looks, Rachel had committed suicide by opening her veins in her bathtub. Then Billy had settled into a depression so dark and deep that none of them had guessed the depth of it until the night they graduated from high school and Billy drove his car down to this very beach and drank a quart of Bacardi rum and wrote an incoherent note and put a gun in his mouth and pulled the trigger.

Standing where he was, in the center of the railroad track, David could see Charlie on his left, thirty yards away in the direction of the water, and the secondary beach parking lot on his right where Billy had made his last toast. It was only then David realized he had dreamed about Billy on the plane.

Charlie stood and shouted. "Hey, David! You're home!"

David waved and stepped down the embankment toward Charlie. "What the hell are you doing wearing that red flag on your back?" he asked.

He loved Charlie—everyone did, including his wife of six years, Karen, who had left him six months ago with their two daughters, Maggie and Mona. Why did she leave? Because he's a fuck-up, Karen replied when asked.

Charlie had been an athlete in high school and also the campus stoner. While the rest of them liked to get high on weekends, Charlie loved to sneak off every day at lunch and smoke a joint the size of a cigar. Then he would wander over to McDonald's with a case of munchies so huge he would order enough fries to grease the engine of his thrice-rebuilt Chevy van, which he drove red-eyed and fearlessly all over town.

He got better in his twenties, especially after he and Karen got married.

When he had his first daughter, Maggie, he told David he was giving up pot forever. Unfortunately, the night Mona was born, he was in jail on his third DUI, and David could see in Karen's eyes—when *he* was holding the infant in place of the father—exactly how it would end.

She left, no one could blame her, and Charlie had freaked. Word had it that he was still freaking. David had not spoken to him since leaving for New York. They were not the friends they once were. It had been Billy who had brought them together. High school memories could only function as so much glue.

But David hugged him when they got close; it was still great to see him. Charlie brought back plenty of memories, more good than bad.

"When did you get back?" Charlie asked. "Missed you, man."

"I just drove into town. Haven't even been home. I missed you too."

"So you came to see me right away?" he asked.

"Sure."

"Shit! You didn't even know I was out here."

David gestured to Charlie's plastic red jacket; it was more an abbreviated poncho, designed for visibility, not warmth. "So you guarding the beach or what?"

Charlie nodded. "It's a cool job. Almost nobody comes out here, and when they do I just have to tell them to go to the other lot. I can read and play my guitar all day."

"Since when did you start to read?"

"I knew you were going to say that. I read a lot these days."

Charlie did not add, *because the apartment is empty*. For all his wild ways, he had class, and seldom sought out sympathy.

"Why does the beach need guarding?" David asked.

"We've got an endangered bird living in the sand dunes. The government says it needs to be protected. They've cut the main beach down to half a mile. Right now, standing where you are, you could get hit with a ticket for a thousand bucks."

"I bet you pocket half of that."

Charlie laughed. "They don't even let me write the tickets. I have to call some teenage megabitch in town if someone won't listen to me. She races out here on her bike. Hey, tell me about New York! You split without giving me a call. I didn't know you'd left until Karen told me."

"Who told her?" David asked. At least Charlie must be talking to his ex.

David worried about him being alone. Charlie was a people person, he needed company to stay sane. Whereas David could hole up in his house and paint for a month and talk to no one. He hadn't known anyone in New York.

"I don't know. Reverend Pomus, I think," Charlie said.

Reverend Pomus was the father of the girl he had saved from drowning. They'd had breakfast just before he'd left town. The minister had encouraged him to go; he had thought the trip would be healing.

"Sorry. I didn't know I was going until the last minute. I had fun, there's so much creative energy in that city, with all the artists and musicians and writers. Every morning I would ride the subway to Central Park or Greenwich Village and just walk around and look at all the people. It's a zoo there, but it was inspiring as well."

"So you goofed off the whole time?"

"No. I met with tons of art directors. Setting up appointments was easy, but getting jobs was next to impossible. There's so much competition. I literally had to make fifty copies of my portfolio. That set me back a thousand, but I had to leave it everywhere I went. I concentrated on book publishers, and guess what? I got the cover of a potential best-seller!"

Charlie was happy for him. "You're on your way, man. Remember what I used to say in high school? One day the whole world is going to see your paintings."

"Well, let's see. I still have to do the painting, and they still have to accept it."

"They'll love it, I have faith in you." Charlie patted his shoulder. "When you're rich and famous, will you still talk to me?"

"I don't talk to you enough now. So tell me what's happening with you? How are the girls?"

"The girls are great. Mona had her fifth birthday last week. She's so cute! She got up on her chair before we cut the cake and sang 'God Bless America'!" He shook his head in amazement. "She looks so much like her mom."

"Is Karen all right?"

Quick answer. "Sure. Sure."

"Are you two talking?"

"We talk plenty." Charlie backed off a step and glanced north, in the direction of the hills and the sand dunes. David followed his gaze. The only base building visible was the security building—the BP lighthouse—up on a dry grassy mound, about a mile away. Charlie added, "They've tightened security."

"You think I have to turn back? The BP don't care about jerks like us."

Charlie gave him a hard look. "That's what you think."

The seriousness of his expression surprised David, and he took a moment to study his friend more closely. Ordinarily Charlie was a scarecrow on speed, but he had lost another ten pounds since David had seen him last. The bones in his jaw were visible when he spoke. His dirty-blond hair was long and scraggly, seldom combed, and his blue eyes were tinged with red, although probably not from drugs this time—maybe from lost sleep, worrying about Karen and the kids.

David had to ask himself, though, why Charlie had been willing to accept a job that required him to sit a mere hundred yards from where Billy had committed suicide.

"Why are you making such a big deal out of it?" David asked.

Charlie held up his hands. "Just trying to save you the fine. The BP hassle everyone who crosses the bridge. But you do what you want to do."

There was an edge to the conversation, when it should have been casual— two high school buddies running into each other at the beach. He wondered if he was missing something. He looked around, uneasy, at the churning water, the parking lot where Billy had sprayed his brains onto the ceiling of his red Toyota. The sun was hot on the top of his head, he felt dizzy. He imagined he had lost weight as well, his appetite had shrunk since Sienna had left. It struck him right then, how all three of them, high school buddies, each in their own way, had had their lives ruined by women.

Yet that was not fair. Rachel had been a jewel, Karen was a great mom to the girls, and would probably take Charlie back if he could learn to act normal all week long. And Sienna had had her reasons for leaving.

The only problem was she hadn't shared them with him.

Had she met someone else? David had to force himself to consider the possibility, yet he didn't believe it. Maybe it was vanity but he felt he had what it took to hold a great woman. His talent was real, people gushed over his work, and he was beginning to make decent money. Lots of girls around town considered him a catch. He had wit, he was handsome, he knew how to dress and brush his teeth. Like Charlie, he was tall and thin, but had a lot more muscle on his shoulders and arms. He worked out regularly, did the treadmill and weights. His parents had both been attractive—he had lucked out with a blend of their best features. His wavy brown hair and starry eyes made him a sensitive soul, while his firm jaw supposedly showed his inner strength. Whatever, if a woman's standards weren't too high, he was considered babe material.

David squeezed his friend's hand. "I'll talk to you on the way back," he said.

Charlie nodded, accepting his decision to keep walking. "I haven't had lunch yet. Maybe I could sneak off for an hour. We could go to Baker's Square. They have the best burgers."

"You buying?"

"Sure. You just got that big cover, it can be a kind of celebration."

"That would be fun," David said honestly. It would be good to catch up.

They shook hands and he continued on his way.

The bridge stretched over an inlet that fanned into a lush marsh, with grass as tall as a man and a multitude of ponds that drew birds by the flock. The bridge was high, only solid in intervals—wherever there was a railroad tie. David knew from experience that it was best to keep his head up while crossing the bridge. Looking down between the oily boards made his head spin. Yet he had to glance down occasionally to keep from tripping.

The real scare was to have a train appear while walking across the bridge. That had happened once in high school, with him and Billy. Common sense said they should have heard it coming a mile away, but the blasted thing could have fallen out of the sky. One second they were talking about nothing and the next they were being chased by a dragon.

Of course Billy, with his great leg speed, tried to outrun the train and get off the bridge before it reached them. There was no discussion between them—he just bolted, leaving David in a quicksand of panic. Yet his lack of decisiveness made the decision for him. The bridge was enclosed on both sides with a rusty web of bars. There was no way he could jump into the water, which was too shallow anyway. As the train grew behind him, he was forced to hug the metal scaffolding and pray the monster did not have a stray bar sticking out. One whack in the guts, he knew, and the birds floating in the marshes would have had an early dinner.

Yet in retrospect, it was the intelligent thing to do. Trains passed over the bridge all the time and never sparked the railings. Nevertheless, as the train ripped by, inches from his back, he felt as if he had made the worst mistake of his life. He could only hang on and pray.

Out the corner of his eye, though, he saw Billy running. His friend was determined to beat the train, even if it cost him his life. Their races were often decided in fractions of a second and this one was no different. Only at the last instant did Billy reach the end of the penned-in metal tunnel and dive off the side and into the rocks and grass.

The feat impressed David, at the time. He complimented Billy on his boldness. But later he thought his friend had been foolhardy.

David reached the end of the bridge and stepped back onto the gravel. Shielding his eyes from the glaring sun, he glanced behind but could not find Charlie. The BP were more his concern now. Technically speaking, he had just stepped onto base property. The sooner he got away from the track, and lost in the sheltering dunes, the safer he would be.

The sandy slopes were taller here, more primitive, roped with water-fat ivy and dry, clawing bushes. It was one of the most isolated spots on the entire coast. Unless there was an intruder, the BP had no occasion to visit the beach. David knew for a fact that none of the regular Air Force personnel came here to sun themselves. Hiking to the beach in a straight line from the base was difficult—the area was strewn with a veritable forest of driftwood.

As David left the railroad track and labored through the sand toward the water, he half expected a dinosaur to lift its head over the dunes. He was one mile from his car and he could have been on another planet—Mars of a million years ago, maybe, when coppery seas filled the red valleys and wine-colored canals zigzagged across the lonely plains. He'd had a telescope as a child, and had always been fascinated by Mars.

He remembered Mars had been high in the sky when he had made love to Sienna, that last night, the two of them cold and naked beside a fire they were forced to keep tiny for fear of the base police. He had pointed out the red dot to her. Preoccupied, probably because she was about to dump him, she had not responded.

He continued north, trying to stay below the line of the dunes, not sure where he was going, or else knowing all too well. One sand dune looked pretty much like another, night or day, but he had an eerie confidence he would be able to spot the one where they had held each other. It would be wrapped in light and darkness, love and pain, and he would see it and his heart would stop and the pain of the last two months would finally cease.

Then, he did see it, the spot, and his heart almost stopped.

The decomposed body of a woman lay half buried in the sand.

TWO

Two cops, two witnesses. The policemen had separated them to talk. Standard procedure, they explained. Funny how, from the start, David felt as if he were a suspect.

The younger cop, the deputy, Max Fields, was talking to Charlie. Max had been a freshman in high school when they were seniors, and there were not many pleasant things that could be said about him. He was obese, carrying three hundred pounds on a five-foot-six-inch frame. With his sleazy grin and beady eyes—distrustful of everyone he met, except the blind mom he still lived with—he looked like a computer-generated nerd. When David had first seen Max walking out to the beach—alongside Charlie and Sheriff Lyle Stanton—he had been grinning. For Max this was the most exciting thing to happen in Lompoc in a long time. What probably made it even better for him was the fact that David Lennon was involved. Max had been their water boy on the track team, and he had resented the fact that everyone on the squad was thin and fit. Even as a freshman, Massive Max had liked his doughnuts.

Sheriff Stanton was another matter, one of the good guys, a man who was not only great at his job, but who was smart enough not to brag about it. He had been Lompoc's chief police officer going on twenty years. He'd been in 'Nam, Special Forces, and still had the rock-hard posture and Brillo-pad haircut. His face was heavily lined, sunbaked, and he chewed tobacco with something akin to religious fervor. Yet no one ever saw him spit the stuff out, and how he did that was a minor mystery.

David had gone to school with his son, Steve, who had gone on to play first-string tackle for USC. Word had it that Steve was now a big-bucks criminal lawyer Back East. Stanton was not above bragging about his kid. The man seldom talked about himself, however. He didn't care about the light offenses that kept the majority of small-town cops in pocket change. A dozen times he had caught Charlie smoking marijuana and had let him go. On the other hand, it had been Stanton who had busted him for the DUI that had kept Charlie absent from the birth of his daughter. Sheriff Stanton was fair but could be hard—not a man to get on the wrong side of, especially when it was a matter of life and death.

"I've got to ask you some questions," Sheriff Stanton said, pulling out a tiny tape recorder that he hooked onto his belt near his gun.

"Is that necessary?" David asked, nodding to the recorder.

"I hate them as much as you but they do make life easier." He paused. "Are you nervous?"

"No," David lied.

They stood near the water, not far from the body. David hoped the roar of the surf would drown out the recording. Of course he was nervous with that dead woman and her half-exposed skull staring at him. He tried not to stare back. In reality, he had examined her less than two seconds.

When he had found the body, he had immediately run back to Charlie, and his friend had gotten on the cell phone to the cops. But while waiting for the police to show, they had barely talked. Then, feeling an obligation to guard the body, David had hiked back to the woman, while Charlie had waited in the parking lot. The cops had talked to Charlie on the hike up from the lot, and David wondered what his friend had told them. Charlie had a habit of exaggerating.

Stanton reached down and pushed the RECORD button. The offshore breeze had died and the whirling north wind had transformed what was left of the surf into soup. The sheriff's voice came out low and raspy.

"August fifteenth one-thirty P.M. Sheriff Lyle Stanton talking with David Lennon in regards to the unidentified female found murdered on Lompoc Beach."

"She was definitely murdered?" David asked. Stanton had examined the body for twenty minutes after he had arrived, Max gawking over his shoulder the whole time. The sheriff had explained that he had already called for a medical examiner in Santa Barbara. It seemed Lompoc did not have its own expert. David could not recall the last time he had read about a murder in town.

"Yes," Stanton said. "She was murdered."

David shook his head. "God."

"Let's begin. What brought you out here this afternoon?"

"I wanted to go for a walk. I was on a plane all morning, flying back from New York."

"Why were you in New York?"

"Business."

"For how long?"

"Two months."

"Did you fly into LAX?"

"Yes."

"What time did your plane land?"

"Ten this morning."

"You drove straight up here?"

"Yes."

"What time did you get back to town?"

"Around twelve-thirty."

"What did you do then?"

"I told you, came out here for a walk."

"You came straight here?"

"Yes."

"You didn't go home first?"

"No."

"Why not?"

"Jesus, what is this? That woman's been dead forever. I didn't have anything to do with her. I just found her is all."

Stanton raised a hand. "I'm not saying you're involved. We have to ask these questions. Often the person who finds a murder victim is the one who murdered them. And you have to admit this place is out of the way." He added, "I just want to know what brought you here."

"I wanted some exercise."

"I spoke to Charlie. He said he tried to stop you from walking this way but you insisted on coming here."

"He didn't exactly try to stop me. He just said he didn't think it was a good idea."

"Did he explain about the Western Snowy Plover quarantine?"

"Yes."

"Did he explain that this beach is technically the property of Vandenberg AFB?"

"Look, Sheriff, give me a break. I grew up in this town. I know this place belongs to the base. But you know guys like us sneak over here all the time."

"I didn't know that but let's let that pass. What about the bird?"

"What about it?" David asked.

"The Western Snowy Plover is an endangered species. There is a stiff fine for disturbing it in its natural habitat. This area is off-limits even to base personnel. Charlie says he explained all that to you and yet you still insisted on coming this way. Why?"

"Charlie is full of shit."

"He didn't explain these things to you?"

"Not in those words. To be blunt, I was not thinking about the bird or the base. I just wanted to go for a walk along the beach and that's what I did. End of story."

Sheriff Stanton did not look like he agreed. He'd seen plenty of action in Vietnam, had killed people and won medals. He did not blink as he glanced at the body, perhaps thinking that the corpse looked like it had been decomposing for about two months. The same thought had occurred to David.

"It's Charlie's job to warn people away from here," Stanton said. "By ignoring him, you put his job in danger."

"I should have thought of that, I'm sorry. Are we done?"

"No. Have you been to this spot before?"

"Sure. I have come to this beach many times. I used to lifeguard near here. You remember."

"No. I mean have you come to this spot recently?"

"No . . . I've been in New York."

"Before then—before you left for New York—did you come here?"

David was tempted to lie. He was tired and hungry, and he had the beginnings of a nasty headache growing in the temple region. More than anything he wanted to grab a quick sandwich and go home and lie down. The situation was getting more complicated with each question. Worse, he was beginning to feel guilty—and for what? He sure as hell hadn't done anything wrong.

Yet he would be taking a chance lying to Stanton about his last night with Sienna. He had told Reverend Pomus about the breakup, and Stanton and the minister talked. Actually, everybody in town talked—Lompoc was a washing machine set on a permanent spin cycle.

"I came to this beach before I left for New York," David said.

"To this exact spot?"

"I'm not sure. It was late at night."

"What night was that?"

"You want the date?"

"Yes."

"I don't know."

"How long was it before you left for New York?"

"The night before."

"Do you have your ticket from that flight?"

"Maybe in my bag."

"So you might be able to figure out the exact date you were here?"

"I might."

"What time of night were you here?"

"Around midnight."

"How long were you here for?"

"An hour. Maybe two."

"Were you alone?"

David hesitated. "No."

"Who were you with?" the sheriff asked.

"My girlfriend."

The sheriff looked like the question-and-answer session might have just gotten interesting. "What's her name?" he asked.

"Does that matter? I would rather not bring her into this."

"Her name is important."

"Sienna Madden."

"Did I meet her once? That skinny woman with the long brown hair? At the mall? About six months ago?"

"Yeah. We were getting ice cream. I introduced you guys."

Stanton nodded. "Pretty woman. So you were both here that night for an hour or two. What were you doing?"

"Hanging out. We went for a swim, built a fire . . ."

The words were no sooner out of his mouth when he realized his mistake. Stanton glanced once more in the direction of the body. David followed his gaze. Ten feet to the side of the body were the scattered remains of burnt driftwood.

"Did you make the fire here?" Stanton asked.

"I told you, I'm not sure." David added hastily. "She has blond hair."

"What?"

"That dead woman. She was blond. Sienna is a brunette."

"I'm not saying this woman is your girlfriend." The sheriff added, "How's Sienna doing?"

"Fine."

"You two still together?"

"No."

The sheriff's interest level kept increasing. "You broke up?"

"Yes."

"When?"

"Before I left for New York."

"That night?"

"Yeah."

"Why did you break up?"

"I don't know. You know how women are. She dumped me, what can I say?"

"Did you two fight?"

"No."

"She just said she wanted to break it off and that was that?"

David fumed. "My relationship with Sienna has nothing to do with this situation. I'm not answering any more questions."

Stanton was sympathetic. "I hate asking them, David, believe me. But look at it from a cop's perspective. Your own words put you here two months ago. I don't know how long this woman has been dead, but it could be two months. And you can see how isolated this spot is."

"You're contradicting yourself. A minute ago you said that you didn't think this body had anything to do with Sienna."

"That was before you told me you broke up with her."

David got pissed, raised his voice. "Are you accusing me of something?"

Max and Charlie looked over, and Max grinned. Stanton took a step closer and spoke in a confidential tone. "Don't get excited, David. You can see how this looks the same as me. To clear your name quickly, I'm going to have to talk to Sienna."

David looked away, at the water. "Whatever."

"I need her number."

"I don't have it."

"Why not?"

"She moved away, I don't know where she is."

"You have no idea?"

"Nope."

Stanton shook his head, spoke in a gentle tone. "I have known you all your life. You went to school with my son. I used to go to all your track meets. We've always had a healthy relationship. For the record, I don't think you killed your girlfriend. But you have to help me out here. I need to talk to Sienna to verify that she is all right. Furthermore, since you have admitted to being here recently, I need skin and hair samples. You can give them back at the station. This is to protect you."

"How exactly does that protect me?"

"You were here with your girlfriend two months ago. There's a remote possibility that some of your hair or skin is still here."

"It could be on the body?"

Stanton hesitated, nodded. "It's possible."

David snickered. "So much for our healthy relationship."

Stanton tried another approach but David would have none of it. He agreed to give the skin and hair samples at the station—that was it. No more questions. Stanton said that Max would meet him in town in thirty minutes. Great, David thought, now Max got to poke around his body.

The body. Before leaving the beach with Max, David studied what was left of the woman. A bag of bones, enough rotting skin attached to give rise to a dozen nightmares. One eye was just gone, a hole into a lost world—probably the victim of a hungry seagull. The other eye was a mass of dry pulp. Black specks crawled around the socket—what was left of the eye had attracted the attention of a colony of ants. Her right jawbone was clearly visible, tapering into the immortal anger of a skull's bared teeth. No clothes, she had been killed naked, or else murdered and then stripped. Her entire front looked like it had been opened and disemboweled. Finally, her hair—long stringy lumps, matted with sand, but definitely blond, not simply bleached from the sun.

David looked away. Enough, it was not Sienna.

THREE

The station turned out to be less hassle than David feared. Max was on his best behavior. Stanton had probably told him to keep his mouth shut. The deputy took the samples—Charlie got pinched as well—and they were out in ten minutes. David was tired, he no longer felt he had a right to yell at his old friend. After all, Charlie *had* tried to warn him. Standing in the police station parking lot, Charlie said he still wanted to go for burgers.

"Stanton said the medical examiner and his team would be out there by now. I don't think I can go back to work. They can stand guard over the fucking birds." Charlie chuckled. "I'm not sure I still have a job."

David felt guilty. "Sorry I didn't listen to you about crossing the bridge."

"It's like you told them, we used to go there all the time. Anyway, that girl might have rotted there another two months if you hadn't spotted her. The way I look at it, you did her a favor."

"I was a little late to be doing her any favors."

"I wonder who it was."

"Can't be anybody local. They would have been reported missing, and Stanton said he hadn't heard about anyone."

"She was a blonde?" Charlie asked.

"Yeah."

"How tall?"

"I don't know, hard to tell the way she was balled up."

Charlie shook his head. "It's sad, the way her life was cut short."

David wondered how old she had been. "Yeah. It was."

"Still want to go to Baker's Square?"

"Sure."

The restaurant was at the new end of town, beside the mall and a half dozen other fast-food joints. Lompoc was not a basin for fine dining. The place was always jammed, as was Carrows across the street. People saw Baker's Square as a treat, a step up from Denny's. They saved to go, a big occasion, the local economy was that lousy.

They got a booth in the corner, ordered double cheeseburgers and Cokes. Then Charlie's cell rang. Stanton wanted him back at the beach. Charlie figured the news could only be bad. He got his food to go.

"Man, if I lose this gig, I won't have enough to take care of the kids," Charlie said.

"Karen's not working?"

"She's doing twenty hours a week at Rite Aid, but gets paid shit. Anyway, she should be at home with the girls."

"If the cover gets accepted, they send me five grand. I could help you out until you get something else."

"I don't want your money. Let's see what happens." Charlie patted him on the back. "Good to have you back."

"Thanks. Take care of yourself. Blame me if you have to."

Charlie left and eventually David's food came. He had the waitress dig him up a newspaper. Eating alone, he couldn't enjoy his food unless he had something to read. He was one of those guys who read the labels on the milk cartons and drew letters in spilled table salt.

The burger was good, he ate with relish, his mood picking up. He had to focus on the positive. The incident with the dead girl was a terrible tragedy, sure, but it was a cold world. She was dead and there was nothing he could do for her. His career was what mattered. His Sienna pain would fade the more he kept busy. It could take six months, a year, he would just have to gut it out. There was nothing he could do anyway, she had wanted to go. And he had not lied to Stanton, he had no idea how to reach her.

David was finishing his burger when Julie Stevens entered the restaurant and took a nearby booth. She was one of those high school fantasies that his brain never seemed to tire of, despite repeated late-night visits. She'd been a cheerleader, and of course he'd never had the nerve to ask her out. Back then she'd dated a football player named Nick Meyers—Stonehead—who to this day worked in the lumber section at the local Home Depot—the same job he'd had in high school. Bring up Julie around Nick and he'd get all misty-eyed. David always felt sorry for the guy, like the best years of his life ended the second he got his high school diploma. If he remembered right, Julie had dumped Nick that same night.

Julie was blond and blue-eyed, tan as the summer sun. She dressed like she was always heading to the beach: blue jeans, plain white shirts; and her long hair was all over the place. She didn't care about makeup. She had a raw sensuality, a great ass—a burger without the bun, as Charlie used to say—and a smile that hinted at plenty and promised nothing. Back in high school, watching her from the bleachers and feeling small, he had thought that kissing Julie would be the equivalent of having full-blown intercourse with the rest of the cheerleading squad combined. Sadly, he'd never had the nerve to ask any of those other girls out either.

Julie sat and ordered, opened a paperback and did not look up. If he risked saying hi, she might not remember him. They had barely talked in high school. Humiliation was a real possibility. Yet the very thought annoyed him. Here it was ten years later and he was still in the stands, talking to himself. He decided to say hello.

Right then she looked up, saw him and smiled.

"Hi, David," she said.

"Julie. What are you doing?"

"Getting a late lunch. Have you eaten?"

"Yeah. But I'm contemplating dessert." He added casually, "Want to join me?"

"Could I? I hate to eat alone."

"Sure," he said.

She moved quickly, settling into the seat across from him, her hair brushing the top of the table. She was a dirty-blonde, could have been a brunette in the right light. Looking at her, he tried to find lines around her beautiful eyes and failed.

"I haven't seen you in a while," she said.

"I've been out of town."

"For three years?"

"Well, it's not like we're in the habit of calling each other every week."

"Whose fault is that?" she asked.

"Mine. A popular jock like me, it's hard to keep up with all the chicks."

"Hey. You mocking my cheerleader past?"

"I wouldn't think of it."

"You know, I used to go to all your track meets and cheer."

"You went to cheer for Billy Baxter."

"I used to cheer for all you guys. Don't you remember?"

He honestly did not remember because it honestly had not happened. But he did not wish to be rude. "Sure. I remember you shouting my name on every lap. You were my inspiration. You looked great then." He added, "You look great now."

"Thanks. I've been going through hell lately."

"What's wrong?"

She shook her head. "Everything. Just lost my job at Macy's, which I know doesn't sound like much. But I had worked my way up and was in charge of all of women's wear. The way I got canned—I don't even want to go into it, I'll just get all negative. Let's just say I'm not going to get a glowing recommendation for my next job, and that sucks. I need a good recommendation to get anything in this town."

"How long were you there?"

"Five years. I feel like I wasted a chunk of my life."

"Have you thought of leaving town?"

"I have nowhere to go." She gestured. "Then there's my dad, he's disabled. He can hardly dress himself. I'm all he has."

"Does he know you lost your job?"

"He hardly knows my name."

"Alzheimer's?"

"Yeah. He's a pillowcase."

"I'm so sorry. I wish I could help."

"You're probably the only one in town who feels that way. And I know you're not just saying it. Back in high school, I used to think you were chivalrous."

"Come on, Julie. You never thought about me at all."

"I did, you just never noticed."

She was stroking him but he was still flattered. "How long have you been out of work?" he asked.

"Three weeks. I've done a dozen boring interviews. My big fear is that I end up at Rite Aid. They pay awful—I'd have to supplement my income stealing Vicodin and selling it on the streets."

"I hear Charlie's wife, Karen, is working there."

"I heard they split up."

David shrugged. "It happens to the best of us."

Julie's eyes widened. "Ain't that the truth? I just got dumped."

"Really?" Another impossible-to-imagine scenario. Guys didn't just walk away from girls like Julie. She was no dummy, though, she knew what he was thinking.

"You remember someone who never existed," she said. "All that rah-rah stuff—it had nothing to do with me. It was an act, I was going through the motions. I hated being a cheerleader. Anyway, high school stardom has a short half life. Believe me when I say I just got dumped. His name was Terry Haven, and he told me two days after I got fired from Macy's that he wanted to go back to his old girlfriend. We were together two years. It just came out of left field."

"Were you happy in the relationship?"

"I thought I was. You must have seen the two of us together."

"No." The few times he had seen her, she had always been alone. "Was he in contact with the old girlfriend the whole time?"

"That's the big fear, isn't it? I don't know. He seemed really sincere, I wanted to marry him." She added, "But now he's fucking her and not me."

He shuddered at the brutality of the line. "Does he live around here?" he asked.

"No. That's one plus. There's no chance of running into them." She added, "He lives in Santa Barbara. So does she."

Just the mention of the place. "What's her name?"

"I don't know, Susan something. I guess she was the love of his life and when he saw a chance to go back to her, he went." Julie wiped her face, maybe at a tear—the damn things, always showing up at the worst times. "I'm really going through it, I'm sorry I'm such a mess." She finished wiping her face and forced a smile. "How about you?"

Misery loved an audience. But he didn't feel like talking about Sienna, not in a public place, not with a woman he hardly knew. Instead, he steered the conversation to his trip to New York, the big cover he had won. Julie seemed to listen with interest, asked a number of questions about what it took to put a cover together. After a half hour he realized how comfortable he felt, that he was rambling away. He had to stop himself.

"I shouldn't talk about how well things are going for me when you just got fired," he said.

"Why not? Why should I bring you down?" Julie was munching on a grilled cheese, drinking a cup of black coffee. She continued, "It makes me feel good to know someone from our class is living their dreams."

"I wouldn't go that far."

She touched his hand. "Hey, you want to go to a movie tonight?"

He had not seen a movie in months. "Sure. What time?"

"I'll check the papers. But let me pick you up. I hate for people to have to meet my dad, the shape he's in. I never know what he's going to do. Where are you living?"

"Out on Backford, in the Wasteland." The Wasteland was the old section of town. David liked the area, the laid-back vibe, the huge spaces between the structures, the funky neighbors. He was able to get a tiny house for half the cost of a new condo near the mall.

David gave her his address and phone number. She promised to call when she had pinned down the time. Leaving for a job interview, she leaned over and kissed his cheek. "It's great to see you again. I take it as a good omen," she said.

"Maybe you should wait and see how our date goes."

"Just buy me popcorn and I'll be happy."

Julie left and David ordered his pie. He'd been talking too much to eat. Waiting for the dessert, he realized he was happy, that he was smiling. It had been a long time.

FOUR

Still, he did not go home, not right away. It was as if he had an allergy to the place. He told himself that he needed groceries, stopped at the store across from the Baker's Square, loaded up. Then he took the super-long way home, swung out toward the prison, drove alongside the north end of the base, then, finally, passed the church where Reverend Jake Pomus preached. Why he stopped *there*, of all places, he didn't know. He just pulled into the lot, turned off the engine, got out. It was not like he felt the need to pray.

David had trouble defining his spiritual life. In a glib mood, he would tell people it was because he did not have one. He did not adhere to an organized religion; however, he did believe in God, or at least in some kind of super-natural force. He was fond of buying New Age books, on all subjects: UFOs, reincarnation, channeling. He would read them cover to cover, and when he was done he would launch into a heated internal argument of why everything the author said was ridiculous. It was a ritual with him.

The next week he would be at the bookstore again, buying another weird title. He was a fanatical agnostic, if such a thing was possible. Yet in all his pain over Sienna, he had not once prayed to God to bring her back, a significant change from the time he had lost Billy. Back then, he had been at Reverend Pomus's church every day. And the man had done a great deal to comfort him.

Pomus's church had an unusual design: a tall three-sided pyramid with so much glass for walls that David supposed the air conditioner felt like it was in hell every day during the summer. The glass was tinted dark brown—it collected dust like the homeless. The minister was forever having to hose down the outside. With a central altar, and no distinct front or rear, the interior was a maze. Going to church, you were forced to look at your neighbors and worship at the same time, not an easy thing to do.

As David approached the church, he ran into Herb Domino. Herb was trimming bushes, and David had to stop and blink. Normally Herb did not work—he was a salesman, a trader in illegal pharmaceuticals to be exact. He pretty much supplied the whole town. David had gone to high school with him as well, and even then Herb had been a successful entrepreneur. It was said by those who knew that Herb had turned more teens onto drugs than all the *Brady Bunch* reruns combined. David hated to admit it, but the rare times he bought pot, it was always from Herb. And Charlie, of course, was a regular customer.

Herb had money, he was an investor. He rode the Internet stocks up, then stood aside, rolled a fat one, and watched them fall, while he poured his money into real estate. He owned five homes, rented them out to respectable families. The most amazing thing about his true-life American dream was that he had never been busted. Stanton had tried and failed to get to him, for over a decade now. David just didn't understand it.

"Hey dude," Herb said when he saw him, setting aside a pair of clippers with monster blades. Herb called a lot of people *dude*, as well as *babe*. He did not read the thesaurus in his spare time. It was hard to say whether he was a shrewd businessman or a fucking idiot. He sure looked like an idiot. He dressed like a dope addict, and make no mistake, he was his own best customer. A redhead with a million freckles, he had green eyes so dull they could have been microwaved peas.

Yet, for all of that, the *babes* liked him. They liked his porous cranium, loved his herbal medicines. Really, Herb's pot was always a sound investment. Three hits and all the stars in the sky turned into galaxies.

"What the hell are you doing?" David asked.

Herb nodded to the chapel's bushes. "Cleaning up, I like to help out."

"So you volunteered for this?"

Herb was too cool to be offended. "It's not like I need the money." He added, "Heard you were back in town."

"Who told you?" A stupid question, Herb heard everything. The guy shrugged.

"Heard about that body you found."

David almost fell over. "Fuck!"

Herb grinned. "Can't tell you my source," he said.

David pointed to the church. "Does Pomus know?"

"Sure. He told me ten minutes ago that he hoped you'd stop by."

"Why?"

"He's worried about you."

"I found the woman, I didn't kill her. What else have you heard?"

"Nothing much."

"Come on, Herb."

"I'm telling you the truth."

"Did you hear that I was a suspect?"

"I heard Stanton drilled you pretty hard." Herb added, "That bastard."

"Stanton asked the standard questions. God, I can't believe this got out so quick."

"What do you expect? This is Lompoc. A dead body is almost as exciting as a new drive-thru. Speaking of which, you need anything?"

"Yeah. A publicist."

"Can't help you there." Herb paused and frowned. "Do you owe me money?"

"No. I used a coupon last time, remember?"

Herb laughed. "Hey, it's good to have you back, dude. You come see me sometime, we'll break out the bong."

David shook his head. "I need all my brain cells these days."

He went inside. The cool air was a welcome greeting, so was the stillness. Plus there was a fragrance in the air, a type of incense he could not place but which nevertheless smelled familiar. But except for Jesus on the cross, and Mother Mary over in the corner, the place appeared empty. Perhaps Pomus had already gone home. As quickly as he entered, he decided to leave.

A deep voice stopped him in his tracks.

Reverend Jake Pomus was not a classic Holy Roller: too intelligent for the cliché, too subtle in the ways he combined the Bible and history, philosophy and science. Indeed, his arguments in favor of grace and forgiveness were amazingly persuasive. Yet he could throw a tantrum, when it suited him. He scared David on occasion. Nevertheless, David had run to him for advice the day after Sienna had dumped him. Old habits died hard, and that, in a nut-shell, was what David feared was the sum of his religious convictions. When he went to church or talked to the minister, he did so because it was famil-iar. Not a rationale, he imagined, that would get him into heaven.

Pomus was not merely a large man, he was imposing. His massive head was an attic trunk—it collected scraps of people's lives as far back as the *old* days. Yet he was not old himself, less than sixty, maybe a lot less. He had one of those fleshy faces that age could not get a handle on. His gray eyes too, were so bright, they bore past any wrinkles, turned them into an afterthought.

Pomus had also gone to their high school races, probably more often than Julie. He could quote times from specific meets, splits even, describe their expressions when they had crossed the finish lines. His memory was unnatu-ral; he knew the town's history inside out. Christ, he was a big part of it. A street had been named after him, over in the old section of town.

"David. You're back, great." Pomus walked toward him, his suit coat open and flapping, gave him a hug. The minister had put on a few pounds over the last few years, but he still wore the same dark brown suits. His grip belonged to a bear—David took a few seconds to recover from it.

"Good to see you, sir. Yeah, I just got back into town."

Pomus gestured for him to pull up a pew, sat beside him, breathing heav-ily. For all his appearance of robust health, Pomus's lungs did not sound well, wheezing like traffic at rush hour. The man could sweat a river, often dab-bing his enormous face with a red silk handkerchief. He did not look uncom-fortable, though, especially not here. The church was his ship, and if the Lord Jesus Christ filled his sails, Pomus damn well decided which direction the rudder turned. When David did approach him for advice—which was more seldom these days—he did so carefully. Pomus liked being the boss, never mind the fact that David had saved his daughter's life seven years ago.

"You look well," Pomus said, checking him up and down. "Have you had any contact with Sienna?"

"None since I left."

"How's the heartache?"

David shrugged. "It's still there, needs more time."

"But the distance helped?"

"Sure." No need to point out it stopped helping the instant it was removed. "New York was good to me."

As he had done with Julie, David changed the subject to his work, the places he had seen in the Big Apple, all the time worrying about the two half-gallon milk bottles he had in his car. He did not want to talk about Sienna. He tried to be concise about the trip, but Pomus was a detail freak. As usual, the minister listened closely, often nodding his head with approval. He asked a lot of questions about the book, trying to get an idea of what David planned to paint, and David finally had to admit he had not read it all.

"I only got the assignment when I was about to leave New York," he said. "I read the first few chapters on the plane."

"Could it be a best-seller? That would do wonders for your career."

"I'm not a fan of horror, but I like it. The publisher paid enough for it. The story has a melancholy mood, it sucks you in. I'll try to capture that mood in my cover."

"You can do it, perhaps now more than ever. Terrible as this is to say, a broken heart often liberates a torrent of creativity." Pomus paused. "I'm sure you don't want to hear that."

"It's probably true. I want to bury myself in my work, keep my life simple."

Pomus leaned back in the pew. "I didn't want to bring this up, not now," he said.

"You talked to Stanton?" David asked.

"He didn't call to tell me about it. He's not a gossip. But I'd already heard about it from someone else, and inevitably we ended up discussing the body you found." Pomus paused. "He sounded concerned about what you told him."

"He put me on the spot, like I had done something wrong."

"Stanton's not like that. You must have said something to get him going."

"I told him that I was out there two months ago with Sienna. That's not a crime."

"Actually, it's a small crime but we'll let that pass. You have to understand that Stanton is on your side. You know him, he's a man of high integrity. But he told me you were elusive when he questioned you, and that bothered him. You can't do that with him—he's the sheriff."

"He was asking me personal questions, like what Sienna and I were doing there that night."

"David, he's a cop, he's been around. You and Sienna are adults, there's nothing to hide. He knows you two were having sex. Who cares? I mean, it's a sin outside of marriage but the world is full of sin, and Jesus can forgive them all. What you have to do is put Stanton's mind at ease. Let him talk to Sienna."

"I don't know where she is."

"Stanton said you told him that. Call her family, find out. Better yet, let Stanton contact the family. That way you don't stir up your pain."

"I don't know her family. She never spoke to me about them."

"That's odd. Do you know what state they live in?"

David hesitated. "No."

Pomus frowned. "You're going to have to track them down."

"The dead woman's family has to be tracked down. Sienna is irrelevant, I'm irrelevant. Stanton treated me like a criminal. I'm not doing anything to help him."

Pomus was disappointed. "That's a poor attitude. Stanton's not asking a lot, and he's been a friend to you guys for years. I'm sure Charlie wouldn't appreciate hearing you say that."

"Why the hell is he working out there anyway?"

"I don't understand."

"You know. Billy shot himself out there."

"Charlie has the girls to support. He has to take whatever kind of work he can find." Pomus gave him a look. "The question could be turned around, you know. Why did you bring Sienna out there?"

He flushed. "That was different. We hiked a mile away from the parking lot."

"To the spot where you found the body?"

David felt as if his day was going in circles. "Yeah. To that spot."

FIVE

Finally, he went home, and when he got there, he wondered why he had waited so long. The place was an absolute nothing: an oversized box, tossed onto a dirt lot that had emotional issues with growing grass. But he had lived there five years, done some of his finest work inside its four walls, and the house actually smelled like him. Stepping inside, bags of groceries in hand, he drew in a deep breath and sighed. It was as he had left it: clean, simple— and if it was just as lonely as it had been that chaotic morning two months ago, then that was reality and he would have to live with it. Time would fill it once more, he told himself. He would.

Putting away his food, he listened to the messages on his machine. There were three—he had been picking them up from New York. The first was from his parents, wanting to know if he had gotten home safe. The next was from Julie. She had already checked out the movie times, was going to pick him up at seven. He didn't have to call her back unless that was a problem.

The third message almost stopped his heart. Sienna.

"Hi, David. I feel stupid leaving this message. I'm sure you don't want to talk, not after what I did. I can't tell you how sorry I am about that. But I was thinking about you, and I heard through the grapevine that you were back home. I mean, I don't know how to say this, I miss you. Yeah, I miss you a lot. Is that a bad thing? You probably think it is, that I don't have the

right. Anyway, I hate these machines, but if you had answered I probably would have hung up. Just hearing your voice on the machine made me tremble, but made me happy too. Real happy, David. I'm in the middle of a big transition right now, so I don't have a permanent number. But I promise to call tomorrow . . . Miss you, honey. Love you."

David sat on the floor, he had stopped breathing. The reflex to draw in air had simply left; it did not matter. Sienna loved him, she was thinking about him. Two months in New York; it could have been two days or two centuries. The effect of the call wiped it all out. Listening to her message, he had felt her voice inside his soul. Strange as it might sound to another—because he had thought about her constantly since she had left—but he had not realized until that moment how deeply he had missed her.

His answering machine had a clock. She had called twenty minutes ago, while he was talking to Pomus. If he had come straight home after lunch . . .

He played the message again, a third time, trying to find a word, an inflection even, he had missed. Sienna's voice was unusual: very young, but tinged with mystery and loss. Yeah, she was not faking the pain in her tone. She missed him!

"Shut the fuck up," he told himself. The anger came out of nowhere, or perhaps it came from everywhere. Every part of his life she had ruined when she had walked out on him that night. What she said was true, she did not have the right to call him and say such things, not after what she had put him through.

Then he listened to the message a fourth time, swung again, was happy she had called, felt nothing but joy at the possibility that they might get back together. Then the happiness and the anger both fled and he felt anxious, and that emotion did not leave. Either way, he realized, if he ran to her or simply ran, he would have no peace of mind. So in the end he was screwed. He had been screwed from the moment he had met her.

When had that been? Six months ago. Half a spin around the sun.

Starbucks, coffee and a muffin, close to closing, the place thinned out, the lights low. Just him and a book and nothing earth-shattering happening in his life. He did not see her sit across from him, just looked up and she was there, and still the earth did not shake. But he liked her, immediately, and that was unusual for him. It was not just her obvious prettiness, but the way she held herself, her shoulders wrapped in a sweater so soft and white it could have belonged to an infant; the graceful turn of her head, her long hair melting in the gentleness that surrounded her. He thought her vulnerable, not to him or other guys, but to life itself. There was an expectant quality to her that hung so close to her head it could have been doom.

Her lower lip quivered as she too picked up a paperback and tried to focus in the poor light. Did the story she read frighten her? It gripped her quickly, that was for sure. Seeing her concentrate on her book, David sensed invisible forces that could sweep from around fate's bend and take her away before her story could be told. He felt anxious, and she was only a stranger.

"Hi," he said. She looked up, did not smile, yet her eyes lingered. A fair face, green eyes, long dark lashes. She was thinner than she should have been; and it added to her mystery. Pale though, ghostly, a cat who did not know how to count to the storied nine. She wore a long green-and-white pleated skirt—Catholic school—but no white socks, only skinny long legs. Pretty, sure, but was she beautiful? No, she was just different.

"Hello. Do I know you?" she said.

"No. I just . . . said hi." He cleared his throat. "What are you reading?"

She gestured with the book. "A murder mystery."

"I love mysteries. Especially when I'm able to figure them out."

"Really? I'm the opposite. I always think the best mysteries are the ones I can't figure out."

"That's okay with me—as long as the author plays fair."

She was interested. "What is fair?"

"The author has to give enough clues that the mystery can be solved. I don't like stuff coming out of left field at the end of the book."

"But is that realistic?" she asked. "Life is not like that."

"I don't read mysteries for reality. I read them to escape."

"A good reason." She paused. "Are you sure I don't know you?"

"Why do you ask?"

"You look familiar."

"I have one of those faces."

"Which kind is that?"

"The bland kind. I blend in at crowded malls and amusement parks. Did you grow up in Lompoc?"

"No, I'm from the East Coast." She added, "I live in Santa Barbara now."

"What brought you up here tonight?"

"A lecture, at your public library."

"What was it about?"

She smiled, finally; he thought she should smile more often. At last, the earth did move a little. "I don't remember, it was so boring," she said.

The Starbucks was closing. They went elsewhere, had more coffee, talked. He did most of the latter; it was hard to get information out of her. But he did learn that she was new to Santa Barbara, escaping an East Coast relationship that had ended badly. She was a schoolteacher who was not sure she wanted to teach. Her family had money, but she did not like *their* money. It was poisoned, she said, and did not explain why. She sounded lost, he thought, perfect. That was the romantic in him. Later, he was to realize lost people were masters at leading others astray.

He fell in love, spent the next six months with her, night and day. If she was not in love with him, she played the part well. Then she just walked. "*Got to go, David. Don't ask why.*" He was not given a chance, it happened so quickly. That night, two months ago, when he had finally returned home, he had been cold and shaking, a piece of seaweed in his hair, sand in his pants, a nightmare burning inside his skull. But the blood was on her hands. She had not given him any warning.

Now she called and said she missed him. God help them both.

He had two and a half hours until seven o'clock and his date with Julie. He had planned to take a nap but now sleep was out of the question. He didn't want to just pace the floors, he would go nuts. He glanced at the manuscript, *Vampire of My Heart*, and wondered if he would be able to concentrate. It was worth a try.

His read on the plane had been unsatisfying. Publishers, he knew, preferred that a cover be designed with the beginning of the book in mind. For that reason, he decided to start again from page one.

I awake in the evening like so many other evenings, and I know something is different. The sun burns through a crack in my curtains, red and fading, and dust floats in the air like orange stars lost in a stuffy void. The silence is pervasive, filling the house, whispering with the thoughts of the dead. Lying on my bed and staring at the covered windows, I think of those gone by, of those who still live, and, finally, of those who are neither dead or alive—such as myself. For I am what is usually called a vampire, although I dislike the term and the tales that have gathered around my kind. Yet many are true, and I am in fact very old, much older than mankind cares to remember. However, it is only this evening that I feel physically old.

Yes, it is a thing of the body, this difference. Standing, I stretch naked in the center of the room and let the evening light fall on my chest. The sun does not burn me, although I have an aversion to bright light, as do my partners in immortality. There is something lacking in my exercise, a fluidity. I do not suspect illness—I have never been sick—but I feel weaker than I should, and wonder if I have gone too long without feeding. I have not drunk blood in three months, and have not killed in much longer.

The hunger of youth no longer torments me. Nothing does, neither circumstances nor my own thoughts. I have had them all before. The tape plays and I watch and listen. There is nothing else to do. I cannot die, I know, I have tried. We all have.

Yet that is not to say I don't care. I do not want to die. Suicide was a passion of my youth, and now I have come to a vague peace with my own reality. I exist, I will go on existing, whether it is natural or not. For that reason, I decide to leave my house and find a victim. But before I go I take my knife, my favorite knife, that I usually keep under my pillow. Yet I doubt I will need it . . .

A bookstore, the sun already set. I stand in the aisles and stare at the brightly colored titles, occasionally picking up a novel, fanning through the pages and memorizing every word in an instant. My memory is not a product of genius, but of cellular integrity. Perhaps, though, with so much to remember, I have grown wise. I am not sure and I do not care. Really, I seldom think about myself at all.

A man approaches, I saw him when I entered the store and have been waiting for him. Forty, handsome, he does not wear a wedding ring, or the burden of a serious relationship. His breath smells of dinner, a hasty hamburger and soft drink, and his gray eyes are not as confident as the rest of his unshaven face. Naturally my beauty intimidates. He sees a tall, thirty-year-old blue-eyed blonde with bronze skin and lips so red they hint at many hungers. He wants to touch me, but he is a gentleman. There is a gun in his coat—I smell the gunpowder—but he carries it as if it were a wallet. A police officer, I think, not the best type to kill. Yet I like him, want to touch him as well, so a police officer it will be.

"Hi," he says, pointing to the book I hold. "What are you reading?"

A glance at the cover, the biography of General Patton, a person I once met, during the Great War, but whom I let live, for the sake of the world. I never liked those Nazis, so few gentlemen among them. I show the man the book.

"I like war stories," I say, a truth.

He nods. "I hope I'm not bothering you."

"No. I am alone."

My openness surprises him; he falls into a stutter. "I'm sorry, I don't ordinarily walk up to strange women in bookstores," he says.

"Am I strange?"

"No. But you're . . . very attractive. You must hear that a lot."

"Not so much these days."

"Why not?"

"I don't get out much."

"Do you live around here?"

"Some distance, not far. You?"

"I live four blocks from here." He adds, "I'm a cop."

"Are you a good cop?"

He smiles. "I can't be bought, if that's what you mean. Hey, would you like some coffee?"

"Yes. I love coffee." Another truth. Blood is not my only source of nourishment. Yet it is the only thing that truly satisfies.

We go to a place, I have what he's having. We sit in the corner and share a pastry. He talks more than I do; he is nervous. I do not go out of my way to soothe him; rather, I let my eyes linger on his face. He feels my power, that there is something not right about me. That does not excite him as much as he might have imagined. Humans are fascinated by the unknown, but only from a distance. Up close—say in my immediate presence—is another matter. There are no boundaries with me. The floor can drop away in an instant. It is not a comforting feeling.

Yet he does not want to lose me. I am too beautiful, and I am kind to him. When he jokes, I laugh and touch his hand. My skin feels normal, as long as my fingers do not linger too long on any one spot. Otherwise, a human begins to feel the strength behind my hands, even if I don't wish it. They feel the coldness of a statue, something that cannot die. If I stop and hold his hand for any length of time, he will not invite me back to his place.

Later, though, we go there.

He lives alone, he is not rich. He shows me his things. A carpenter in his spare time, he has built a desk where he sits at his computer, an entire bed-room set that is his pride and joy. He is a good man, modest, but that will not affect my decision to feed on him. And because he is a policeman, and will wonder at the mysteries of this night after I leave, he will have to die.

How does that make me feel? It should not make me feel anything. During my first centuries as a vampire, I struggled endlessly with the moral consequences of my hunger. It was the reason I tried to destroy myself—the first time. But moral arguments can be indulged by mortals, not vampires, not when the years never end. It is not that immortals feel they are above the debate, we simply know that many of the choices we make in this world will never be resolved in the presence of a caring conscience, only accepted in the harsh light of reality. Nor does it matter that such a light also hurts our eyes, worse in many ways than the sun's light. When we need blood, we take blood.

Tonight, though, looking into his expectant expression, a face that will soon cease to breathe, I feel sorrow. He sees my mood change, worries.

"Is something wrong?" he asks.

I force a smile. This difference is not just in my body, I realize, it has invaded my mind. There is weakness inside. I have to feed, but I do not want him to be the one to pay for my weakness. Who then? An evildoer? They are no easier to kill. Indeed, they have so much regret as they die, it is often worse to kill them. Better the innocent, one can always hope they leave for a nicer place.

"Kiss me," I say.

We kiss for a long time, standing in the middle of the floor, before we move to his bed. Since I am going to kill him, I do not deny him sex. I feel he deserves it, but that is also a feeling I have not had in a long time. He tries to help me with my clothes but he is clumsy, and I end up stripping him bare. My own I take off more carefully. He has a nice body, thin and strong, and I let him climb on top of me, and enter me, and it is soothing to feel him inside, and not have to fake the sounds of pleasure. Still, I am caught in the thought—*he will be dead soon.* Why does it bother me?

When we are done, he lies beside me in the dark, tells me how pretty I am, how much it means to him that we met. The words go deep inside when they should float on my frozen surface. Suddenly, I must sit up, look down at him. He touches my long hair, drinking up his vision of my body.

"What are you thinking?" he asks.

"You don't want to know."

"You're not going to tell me you're married, are you?"

I consider. "I was married, when I was young."

"Tell me about it."

Foolish to speak of Ash, but I do anyway. "He was a high priest in a church I belonged to. I was very much in love with him." I add, "It is because of him that I am still alive today."

He frowns. "Did he save your life?"

"In a manner of speaking. He made it so that I could not die."

He grins. "What was he, some kind of magician?"

"He was an alchemist."

He stops grinning. "I'm not sure what you are talking about. Are you still in love with this man?"

"That is an interesting question. I have asked it myself many times. Do I still love him? I hate what he did to me, I know that. You see, the change he put me through, it cannot be reversed. So in a sense I have to hate him. But I must love him as well."

"Why?"

"Because I still think about him each day, and I have not seen him in a long time. That fits a description of love, don't you think?"

He sits up, beside me, touches my face. "Have I caught you at a bad time in your life? Is that what you are trying to tell me? Is tonight all we're going to have?"

I nod. "Tonight is all we can have."

"But . . ."

"Shh." I put a finger to his lips, a strong finger. Literally, he is unable to reply. I do not need my knife. With my other hand, I take his hands and squeeze them together, and now he cannot move either. He struggles a bit, surprise growing in his eyes. Coming closer, I stare deep into his eyes, they are really very lovely.

"I am not what you think I am," I say. "There are no words to describe me, but if you must, you can call me a monster. I came here because I need your blood. I am going to take it now, then leave. But when I do, you will be dead, and for that I am very sorry. I know you do care about me, and in a way that is confusing to me, I care about you. But that feeling will not stop me from taking what I need."

Only then does he feel the full power of my grip, and he tries desperately to escape, but I have moved my hand from his lips to his throat. With a sharp nail, I slice open his neck, and let the blood pour over his chest and onto the sheets. The wound is severe; he cannot get out a scream. Still, I do not bend to drink, I cannot stop staring into his eyes, so much pain and confusion; the entire life swept away in seconds. Seeing him anxious to speak, I staunch his wound and lean close so that my long lashes touch the tears on his face.

"Yes?" I say.

The words are sad. "I could have loved you."

Sitting back, I shake my head. "Only what you saw, not who I am."

I drink his blood, and he dies in my arms.

The phone rang, David set aside the manuscript. Julie.

"You didn't tell me you found a body at the beach!" she said.

He sighed. "Who told you?"

"The whole town is talking about it. Why didn't you say something?"

"I didn't want to spoil your lunch."

"What did she look like?"

"Julie. She had been dead two months."

"Yuck. Look, I'm sorry to bother you, I just found out and I had to call. Are you upset about it?"

"No, not really."

"Good." She added, "I still want to go out tonight."

"With the serial killer?"

Julie giggled. "People are saying you're a suspect!"

"God."

"Hey, this is big news, and you were always Mr. Proper."

"That is not true. I am as disgusting as everyone else."

"I hope so! Hey, I'll pick you up at six-thirty instead of seven. There's a special movie I want to see. Okay?"

"No problem. What's the movie?" he asked.

"It's a horror flick, something about an invading virus. I like stuff like that. I read that the special effects are great."

"That's all that matters."

"Good-bye, killer!"

David smiled as he hung up. His earlier gloom had definitely fled. The call had not upset him. Indeed, the whole situation with the body might give him a few months of celebrity status, like when he had saved Mary Pomus from drowning. He was looking forward to his date more than he had realized. Ironically, Sienna's calling had spiked his enthusiasm for Julie. He felt he was going out on the date with less damage. Silly, of course, that one call could make such a difference, but there it was. He indulged a brief fantasy in which Sienna returned to Lompoc and found him in bed with Julie.

"That will never happen," he muttered. The hard truth—and he hated to admit it—was that he would drop everything to get Sienna back. He knew he would be waiting all day tomorrow for the phone to ring.

Who had told Sienna he was back in town?

She didn't know anyone here, except him.

David returned to the manuscript, knew what was coming next. On succeeding nights, Cleo—curiously, the author did not reveal her name until the second chapter—seduces two more men, drinks their blood, and kills them. Her compulsion to feed is driven by her continuing sense of weakness, and her amazement at her feelings for her victims.

On the fourth night, Cleo picks up a woman, a lesbian, and takes her back to her place, something she seldom risks. The encounter goes badly for Cleo. Her victim is a martial arts expert and Cleo is weaker than ever. Even when she finally has her victim subdued, the taste of blood makes her sick. She vomits, something she has never done before. She ends up strangling the woman to death, and then bursts out crying.

David found the author's style unusual. In a way he was surprised the book was going to be published, although he admired the work. The plot was a series of snapshots—no scene was ever developed. Cleo went here and there, met people, killed them, moved on. Her life was a montage—events were viewed from a distance. Cleo said as much—she did not act, even in the midst of activity, she merely played a role. The overall effect was disconcerting. But perhaps the tone would change as she got more human.

Nevertheless, he suddenly had an idea for the cover. He was almost ashamed to admit what it was, because it involved Sienna. Four months earlier, they had visited an old Catholic cemetery in Northern California that overlooked a rocky portion of coast. Sienna had posed for him on the tombstones. She had been in an exhibitionist mood—unusual for her—and had stripped down for several shots. There was one picture in particular—he riffled through his desk to find it—that had her straddling a tombstone and wearing nothing but her open blouse. In the photo, her pubic hair was visible but that would be easy enough to erase. Also, it would not be difficult to make Sienna's brown hair blond.

The picture was only half the idea. Once he had the basic painting complete he imagined he could make the ground beneath the tombstone transparent, and in the midst of that place a glowing vision of the ancient continent Cleo came from. He assumed her home was Atlantis, although, once again, the author was circumspect about revealing the name. It was as if the author disliked having to attach labels. Anyway, he thought, the top portion of the painting could be dark and despairing, while the bottom glowed with golden light—symbolic of the fact that everything that really mattered to Cleo was in the past, buried.

"It's an idea," David said to himself, growing more excited about it. Sienna was pale to begin with. Make her lips a dark red and she would look like a vampire, never mind that Cleo spoke of herself as bronze. Skin color was nothing, a detail. Sienna had the large haunting eyes and Cleo's solemn expression. Really, he could not have paid for a better model, or conceived of a more seductive pose.

David popped the photograph in his camera lucida, pulled out fresh paper. Through a series of mirrors and lenses, the camera lucida—or *Lucy*—projected the picture onto the paper, making it any size he desired. Many artists felt that using the machine was cheating, but he was not one of them. The device greatly speeded up his work. All his romance-novel covers had been created using photos of models fed through his Lucy. Also, when his painting was complete, he could scan it into his computer, use his Adobe software to add fire to her hair and a supernatural shimmer to the lost continent.

"It could work," he muttered, drawing with a charcoal pencil. Naturally, at this early stage, he was only outlining, but already he had an idea of how the lost continent could be portrayed: bronze pyramids set in rows alongside a series of canals; sky touching palm trees; silver sailboats far out on the sea. They were just ideas, he knew—he hoped that later in the book Cleo described her homeland in detail.

Time flew, he lost all track of the hour. The knock on the door startled him. He glanced at the clock: six-thirty. Julie and his big date, and he hadn't even showered. Throwing a towel over his drawing and turning off the light in his Lucy, he got the door.

"Hi guy," Julie said. She had not dressed up, but had changed into white pants and a red top. And she had washed her hair; it smelled like lavender. "Did I wake you?" she asked.

"No. I was drawing. When I work, I always get a glassy-eyed look. Hey, do I have time for a quick shower?"

Julie checked her watch. "As long as we leave here in ten minutes."

He swung the door wide open. "I only need half that," he said.

The shower felt great. He took a cold one, the fatigue of his travels went down the drain with the soap bubbles. He had brought his suitcase into the bathroom, and he changed into clothes he had washed in New York the night before. Already Manhattan seemed like a dream.

When he came out, Julie was studying his drawing. But she had not turned on the camera lucida. She did not know what he was sketching from. Julie pointed to his drawing.

"Who is she?" she asked.

"She might be the beginning of my new cover."

"But is she someone real?"

Obviously Julie did not understand what the Lucy was, that there was a photo inside. He quickly crossed the room, picked up the sketch, moved it away from the machine. "She's real to me," he said.

Julie laughed. "You artists and your models. Tell me who she is."

He hesitated. "Her name is Sienna."

"Is she from around here?"

"No."

"Just a friend?" she asked.

He set the sketch on the couch. He wanted to cover his work with something, but ended up doing the opposite, letting his gaze linger on Sienna's face. Drawing feverishly, he had not paused to study what he had created. Now he was stunned. His sketch had already transcended the original photograph. He had caught a look she had not shown that afternoon in the cemetery, an expression he had only seen that night she had left him alone on the beach.

The woman in his drawing was still seductive, but her face was devoid of hope. Even with her smile, her despair seeped through the lines like black ink spilled from the unconscious. Given the subject matter, the overall effect might have been called perfect. A lost and lonely vampire? He had found his model for Cleo, he was sure now, and he had discovered his theme for the cover. Instead of an ex-girlfriend, the love of his life, he had drawn a living shell.

"Yeah. She's just a friend," he said.

SIX

They went to the new theaters in the new section of town. David still felt nostalgic about the old ones. Growing up as a kid, with his pals Charlie and Billy, he remembered the times they had searched all over town for dusty bottles they could trade in for a few cents, scraping together a dollar for the afternoon matinee. Then again, the seats in the old theaters swallowed your ass whole, plus the sound stunk. He supposed nostalgia was a thing best enjoyed from a distance.

David bought the tickets for *Infected!* Julie insisted on getting the popcorn and drinks. Half the reason David went to a movie was for the popcorn. He liked it plain and hot, salt, no butter. Julie shared his taste. They each got big bags, and Cokes tall enough to keep them up half the night. Julie was already dropping hints that she thought he was cute: touching his arm at odd moments, letting her hair brush against him. He had to admit she looked good. Now if he could just stop comparing her to Sienna they would both be fine.

Julie had to go to the bathroom; she left him holding the goods. She was gone a minute when he spotted Karen Beard, Charlie's ex, with another guy. Holding hands in fact, with their own bags of popcorn. The sight did nothing to cheer his heart.

Karen was half Mexican, half Swiss, with a round friendly face. She wore her brown hair straight, down to her butt. Short, she was a tad overweight, but had great tits—he thought she was sexy. For a time, as a teenager, he'd had a crush on her; they used to hang out a lot. But when Charlie had asked her out, he had stuffed the feeling. He figured she had done the same. She always stared at him too much whenever they met.

Her date was older, forty, a nice-looking guy in a suit. But he was stiff, obviously not homegrown, unsure how to behave when surrounded by barbarians. He had prep-school manners; his thick blond hair looked like it had been molded in place.

Yet the moment David spotted them, the guy left for the bathroom. Karen caught him staring at her; he walked over slowly. They hugged briefly and she gave him a quick peck on the cheek.

"Charlie told me you were back," she said. "I'm glad. But don't do that again, David, go away without calling."

"I didn't know I was leaving, I just got on the plane." He glanced in the direction of the rest rooms. It was not hard to read his mind.

"My mom's watching the girls, not Charlie," she said.

"What's his name?"

"Duane." She added, "I'm not sure about him."

"But you like him?"

"Yeah. I moved out, you know, a long time ago."

"Hey, I'm not saying anything."

She spoke seriously. "Don't say anything. Charlie doesn't know, but I'm going to tell him."

David nodded to the crowded lobby. "Better tell him soon."

"I know." An awkward silence. "I heard about that body you found."

"I've got to be more careful where I dump my victims."

"Don't joke. People are talking."

"I'm glad they have something to talk about."

"You're not in trouble, are you?"

"No. Don't be ridiculous."

"Charlie got fired," she said.

"What? Really?"

"Stanton told him when he went back to the beach. Don't blame yourself, it was a shitty job."

"But he needs the money."

"He still has his night job, at the gas station."

"I didn't know he was working two jobs."

Karen looked sad. "He's trying to get me back. He never stops."

"Does he stand a chance?"

Karen shook her head. "I really don't think so."

"I could talk to him for you."

"No. Not about that. I mean, you just got him fired."

"And you don't want me to feel guilty?"

Karen smiled. "I saw you two when you came in. Julie Stevens? Did you do heavy drugs in New York and damage your brain or what?"

"What's wrong with Julie?"

"Well, she was a cheerleader in high school, remember? She walked around with a megaphone stuck up her ass. We used to despise people like her."

"I never despised her. I kind of liked her, actually."

"You liked her tits. She's so self-absorbed. Does she still talk about herself constantly?"

"No. She's grown up since then, been through some hard times."

"Girls like Julie Stevens don't know what hard times are."

"Because of her tits?"

"Exactly. They act as insulation. I'm just saying you deserve better."

"What about Duane?"

"What about him?" she asked.

"He looks caste conscious."

"Nah. Daddy's money just fucked him up a little. He'll grow out of it."

"When his gray hair turns white?"

"He's not that old."

"What do you guys talk about?"

"Everything. Politics." Karen giggled. "He's always using words I don't know."

"Does he talk during movies? Explain things to you?"

She nodded. "Yeah. Don't sit behind us."

"Got ya. Julie might bump him with her tits and then we'll both be out in the cold."

Karen stopped smiling. "It's good to see you, David. I've missed you."

"Same here. But . . ."

"You're worried about Charlie?"

"Sure. He's no Rock of Gibraltar."

"Not like you."

"Don't be fooled. I feel more like a snowman these days."

She was gentle. "What happened with her?"

Karen had seen him around town with Sienna. They'd had coffee together once. Neither woman had liked the other. For some strange reason, Karen had asked Sienna tons of questions about her past. Karen had thought Sienna was a liar, and Sienna had thought Karen was jealous of her.

David shrugged. "We broke up."

"She hurt you."

"Shit happens."

"What happened?"

"She dumped me, okay? You were right about her. She was an asshole, a cold bitch. She just split and didn't explain why."

"That's why you went to New York?"

"Yeah."

"Why didn't you call me and tell me?"

"Who wants to listen to stuff like that?"

"I would have listened. David, you're still hurting. You don't look well."

"I've been traveling all day. I get home and I stumble on a corpse and the local sheriff—who is supposed to be my friend—thinks I killed her. I've had an awful day. How am I supposed to look?"

"It's not that, it's Sienna. It's eating at you, I see it."

"Yeah. But don't tell me Julie Stevens is not going to help things."

"Whatever gets you through the night. I don't give a damn about Julie. Screw her brains out if it helps. As long as you know she's no better than popping a pill. People don't really change. Julie's still shaking her ass in front of a crowd. She just wants attention."

"You said that about Sienna."

"No. I said Sienna was dangerous. Look, David, you're a smart guy, you're talented, you're cute. But you don't know how to pick them. You're a pain magnet." She added, "You let me get away."

"I seem to recall you married one of my best friends."

"Only because . . ." Her voice trailed as she glanced over her shoulder. "Damn. Duane is coming."

"Sounds like a movie title. I won't make a scene if you don't."

"Will you call me later?" Karen asked.

"Not later tonight."

"That's not what I meant. Call me tomorrow."

"All right. Have fun with Duane."

"Have fun with Julie. Don't catch anything."

Julie came out of the rest room and they went inside the theater. It appeared Karen and Duane were seeing another flick. David looked for them during the previews but couldn't find them.

The movie turned out to be great, much to David's surprise. Naturally, the virus was from outer space, embedded in a wandering meteorite that had crash-landed on Earth centuries ago. Once it infected people, they turned into flesh-eating monsters. Only they did not become zombies. They still had their wits about them, and plans to take over the world. All that stood between them and their goal was a twenty-year-old chick with an attitude. At the end she became infected, but she managed to keep enough of her personal identity to destroy the monsters. The final scene was tragic but satisfying. Julie grabbed his leg no less than five times.

Afterward they went to a bar, in the old section of town—Chubby's, where the new rules against smoking were already obsolete. Chuck Warner, the owner, put them in the corner away from the smoke and music. Julie surprised him by lighting up a cigarette. He did not know she smoked. Really, he knew very little about her.

They ordered tacos and beers. Chubby's had great food at any hour. David was not much of a drinker but while waiting for dinner, Julie put away two shots of tequila.

"Does that go with beer?" David asked as she choked on her second drink. Laughing, she shook her head, gestured to Chuck for another round.

"The only thing that goes with tequila is Mexican food. Do you want a shot?"

He was feeling reckless. "Why not?"

They were both drunk before their food arrived. Now the music came out of the walls, and it had legs. The heat inside his gut was a slow burn; it melted away the day's tension. He figured he should drink tequila more often. Julie was asking him more about the book he was working on. He had to think a minute to remember the plot.

"It's about Cleo the vampire," he said, talking loudly. "She's messed up. She's so old she's forgotten how to feel. But what's happening in the book, I think, is she's slowly turning back into a human. She's losing her power and getting all weepy whenever she kills someone. Drinking blood makes her want to puke. I'm at a part where she's just going to visit an old friend, Hector, who's also a vampire. These creatures are like twenty thousand years old. A long time ago Hector was in love with Cleo, but she dumped him."

"Why the fuck did she dump poor Hector?" Julie asked, giggling.

"Because she was still in love with Ash—the dude who turned her into a vampire. But he died when Atlantis was destroyed, or they say he died, I don't know. I keep thinking he's going to show up later."

"So you haven't finished the book?"

"No."

"Why the fuck not?"

"Everyone keeps asking me that."

"Who else asked you?"

"This guy on the plane, Reverend Pomus, and now you."

"What guy on the plane?"

"I don't know, he was a doctor. He cuts people up for a living and puts in fresh parts. He was trying to be friendly but I didn't like him."

"Why didn't you like him?"

David leaned over the table; it was littered with shot glasses. "Why do you keep asking me questions?" he asked. She looked better drunk than sober, her cheeks flushed. He would kiss her good night, he vowed.

"Because I like listening to you talk! Hey, now you're asking me questions!"

He sat back, belched. "Sorry."

"I saw you talking to Karen before we went into the movie. What did she say?"

"She said you were a bitch."

"Fuck her! What did you say?"

"Nothing."

"You didn't defend me?" Julie asked.

"I defended you. She just doesn't like you is all."

"I don't like her. She dumped Charlie for no good reason. He's a cool guy."

"What do you know about Charlie?"

"Nothing much, he's your friend."

"Have you ever gone out with him?"

"No. He's been like married forever."

"Okay. Just checking."

They left the bar at midnight, staggeringly drunk. The drive home was an adventure. Julie ran a light and made two wrong turns. Then she parked so close to David's car that he had to get out on her side. It was hilarious, the two of them tumbling over each other, out into the driveway.

"You want to come inside?" he asked. "I can make coffee."

"I think I better," she said, helping him up.

At home on a Friday night with a beautiful woman. He put on coffee and the sweet aroma filled the house but they never got to drink any. Julie suddenly kissed him, hard, and in that instant he stopped hurting over Sienna and kissed her back.

That was only half true. Suddenly a part of him—no more sober than the other parts—felt that Julie was no different than Sienna. With her tongue in his mouth and his hand on her nipple, he felt as if he had stumbled onto a clown's stage, where everything was familiar and nothing was forbidden. He didn't care, he told himself. Flesh was flesh, as long as it was sweet and soft, and it didn't cause him any pain.

Yet old agonies stood waiting. He did not understand why—pulling Julie down, taking off her clothes—he suddenly felt love. Not a mere stir of affection but a tidal wave of longing. For Julie Stevens? He hardly knew her and that did not seem to matter. The intensity of his feeling grew as he slipped inside her. The emotion altered his room. His bed was an altar, the alcohol in his blood a sacrament. Of course, he was drunk, he didn't know what he was doing, but it seemed as if he could not stop saying Julie's name, even as he heard Sienna calling to him from somewhere nearby. He heard her over a roar in his brain, the same kind of roar the waves made late at night along the beach.

SEVEN

He awoke to a ringing phone, the sound never so unpleasant. Bolting upright in bed, wincing in the morning light, his hangover felt like a tumor in his brain.

Nobody else in his bed, Julie was gone. She had said something about an early job interview. Amazing that she had been able to sneak out without waking him. Maybe that was her on the phone. He picked up.

"Hello?"

"David?"

"Sienna?"

"It's me. But before you say anything, I can hardly hear you. I'm on my cell, at the airport, JFK. Are you there?"

He could hear flights being announced, an overall fuzz. But her voice sounded pretty clear.

"Yeah, I hear you. What are you doing at the airport?"

"What?"

"Why are you at JFK?"

"I'm coming out to California. My plane leaves in a few minutes. I should be on board but I wanted to call you. I need to ask you something."

"What?"

"What?"

"I said 'what?'" he said.

There was a forever pause, during which time he heard the roar of a plane. It sounded like she was on the runway, not inside the terminal. He recognized the flight being announced in the background. It was the same one he had caught heading west twenty-four hours earlier. The coincidence shook him almost as much as her voice. She sounded good, though, excited.

He didn't know what to think. His back was hurting from all the sex he'd had with Julie. She must have woken him up five times. "*Just give it to me, baby.*" And he had, from every angle.

"Do you want me to come out there?" Sienna asked. "If you don't, I understand. What I did, that night, it was cruel. I've missed you so much! I'm heading to California on business anyway, and I thought if you wanted me to drive up, I would . . . David?"

"I'm here, yeah."

"What?"

"I said, yeah, come."

Another long pause—he did not know if she had heard him. Her flight was being paged, so he thought, the friendly skies calling out the last call. Why was he telling her to come?

"You want me to come?" she asked, shouting.

"Yeah."

Her phone cracked and hissed. "I'll come then, I want to see you. Let me call you tonight, when I get settled. I have to see some people in Orange County. They're picking me up at the airport . . . David?"

"I'm here." He added, "I can pick you up."

"No. Don't. Let me call, okay?"

"Can I call you?"

"What?"

He almost shouted. "Give me your cell phone number." He wanted a way to reach her—for normal personal reasons—as well as to get Stanton off his back. If the sheriff could call her, just once, it would end the questions. Unfortunately, the static on the line was awful.

"What?" she shouted back.

"Can you hear me?"

"Not really!" A long crackly pause. "I love you, David!"

"Okay! I love you, Sienna!"

He lost the connection. It didn't matter, the damage was done. Sienna driving to Lompoc. Sienna apologizing about her cruelty. Sienna saying she loved him. Somehow, he could not take it all in. She had chosen a great time to ask him to make a life-changing decision: background buzz and her flight tugging on her cape. Not a coincidence, he was sure. She always did stuff like that, stacked the cards in her favor. In reality, she had not given him a chance to say no to her question.

"She's fucking with me again," he said. He didn't care, that was the scary part. Get real—he was dancing for joy inside. And his conscience—that was not breaking a sweat either. He had no reason to worry about Julie. She was a nice girl, but one night of sex did not constitute a relationship. He owed her nothing but the truth, and he would tell her that the first chance he got.

Wait a minute, slow, he thought, *no reason to burn the cheerleader bridge.* He would tell Julie about Sienna when he was *sure* he had Sienna back. That way he couldn't lose.

"Yeah, right," he told himself angrily. He was already lost. What was he going to do all day except wait for the phone to ring? He could have six months of that, and then nothing in the end. He wished he could call Sienna back and take back the "I love you." She had forced him to say that as well. You couldn't very well answer an I love you with anything else.

Someone knocking on the door. He went to answer, realized he was naked, pulled on sweats. The last person in the world he expected to see was Sheriff Stanton, but there he was, fresh as a morning headline, standing in the sun like an armed uniform all dressed up with no one to hassle. David's head continued to ache. Stanton had on dark glasses and an ominous expression.

"David? I hope I didn't wake you. Do you have a minute?"

"Yeah." He was not in the mood to invite him in. "What is it?"

"We have a problem."

"By 'we' do you mean me?"

Stanton sighed. "Don't start, David, I am serious. We need to talk. That body we found yesterday—that woman was definitely murdered. A preliminary autopsy has been performed. The murder was a ritual killing. Do you know what that is?"

"Something satanic?"

"Yes. The woman was cut open, her internal organs were removed, and her intestines were arranged around her in a particular pattern."

"What was the pattern?"

"I would rather talk about that at the station. You need to get dressed and come down. There's an FBI agent who wants to question you."

"An FBI agent? In Lompoc?"

"He flew in early this morning. With ritualistic killings, we're required to notify the FBI. His name's Krane, and he's tough. I'm warning you ahead of time, don't fool with him."

"I answered all your questions yesterday. I have nothing to add."

"Krane and I have read a transcript of that conversation. You brought up more questions than you answered. At the station, be prepared to be grilled." He added, "You might want to bring someone with you."

"Like the Easter Bunny?"

"Damnit David! You need to think about a lawyer."

"Like I'm going to find myself a lawyer at this time of the morning."

"You could ask to postpone your statement."

"You just told me to hurry down to the station!"

"You know everything you say can and will be used against you."

"Sounds like you're arresting me."

"Not at all. I'm just saying you better think twice."

"You're wrong, Sheriff. Guilty people have to think twice. I can say the first thing that comes to mind because I am innocent." David went to shut the door. "Tell Agent Krane I'll be there in an hour."

Stanton put his foot in the door. "Half an hour. He's a busy man."

"An hour. I want to have breakfast."

Stanton gave him a hard look. Even through his dark glasses, it was easy to read. David didn't care, he might take two hours to get to the station.

He showered and dressed and drove to a coffee shop in the new section of town. He ordered bacon and eggs, coffee—the perfect antidote for a hangover. He read the paper as he waited for his food. The story about the dead woman was on the front page, but his name was not mentioned, although they had a Charlie quote, "She looked *really* dead." Stanton had also been interviewed—he said the police had no leads. There were no details about the condition of the body, no mention of satanic cults. David did not find the article interesting.

He was halfway through breakfast when Herb Domino and Mary Pomus walked into the coffee shop. David did a double take. Mary had been eight when he had pulled her from the sea; she was now fifteen, and looked like a corpse. Her outfit was Goth-black: white powder and mascara, chains and nails. What was the world coming to?

Herb could have slept in his clothes, his scraggly red hair played huggies with his eyebrows. He looked exhausted, but then again, he never looked fresh. But he waved to David as he came in, and they walked over and sat down. David did not like to think they were dating. It was difficult to see Mary—the cute button he had risked his life to save—and not feel disturbed. Her lipstick was Purple Haze—he was sure it glowed in the dark. She smiled and reached over and touched his hand.

"Uncle Davy," she said. "You're staring at me."

"I haven't seen you in a long time."

"Because you never look at me when I walk by."

"No. I just haven't seen you."

She chewed gum, stared straight ahead. The diameter of her pupils worried him. He hoped Herb had not given her anything to expand them. The hope was sort of vain, though, he figured. Herb was a walking syringe. Why did Pomus let his daughter hang out with him? Maybe the minister did not know.

"I see you all the time," Mary said. "But I missed you when you went to New York. Are you back to stay?"

"Yes."

"Did you have fun there?"

"Sure. Worked a lot, though. How are you doing?"

She popped a gum bubble, continued to hold his hand. Her fingers were cold. "Having plenty of good times. Are you still seeing that girl?"

"What girl?"

"That one I always saw you with."

David hesitated. "No."

"Good. I didn't like her. She smelled funny."

He paused. "Did you meet Sienna?"

"We met her here a few times," Herb said. "She'd come here for breakfast. Didn't she tell you?"

The few nights Sienna had spent with him—they had usually slept at her place—she had always left early, always anxious to get back to Santa Barbara. She had never liked Lompoc.

David shrugged. "What did you guys talk about?"

Mary giggled. "How great you were in bed."

David took his hand back. The conversation was unsettling. To think Sienna had friends in Lompoc she had not told him about, particularly these two. "I can't imagine her talking about our sex life," he said dryly.

Herb nodded. "She was a pretty woman, intelligent. I liked the way she smelled."

"That's because your nose is snorted out," Mary said, before asking David, "Still think about her?"

"What if I say yes?"

"I'd tell you to stop!"

"Mary, do you think you're old enough to give me advice about my love life?"

"Yes." She jumped up quickly. "I have to shit." Turning, she hurried toward the rear of the building.

"What is it with her?" David asked.

"What do you mean?"

"The way she's dressed, the way she's acting. What have you been giving her?"

"Nothing. Mary's not into that."

"What is she into? You?"

"I'm looking after her for Pomus, that's all. It's not something I want to do."

"Like hosing down the church?"

"What's wrong with that?"

"Nothing. But why are you doing it in the first place?"

Herb shook his head. "You're always judging me. You know nothing about my life. You still blame me for Billy and Rachel, when I had nothing to do with that."

David thought that was a left-field remark if ever there was one. He had never thought of Herb in connection with Billy and Rachel. Except Herb had been there the night Rachel had gotten her face burned. Herb had helped to carry them outside, and had assisted a neighbor in putting out the blaze. He had probably saved their lives.

David eyed him curiously. "Why do you say that?"

"I know what you think. I was just walking by when that fire started."

"By chance?"

"Yeah. A lot of things happen by chance in this town." Herb glanced in the direction Mary had vanished, added, "It doesn't pay to think too much about them."

"What does that mean?"

"Nothing."

David checked the time, stood, put a ten-dollar bill on the table. "Tell Mary I had to run," he said.

"You don't want to say good-bye to her yourself?"

"No. Gotta go."

Herb stared at the tabletop. "You might hurt her feelings."

"I'm sure she'll survive. Take care of yourself."

Herb glanced up, nodded. David patted him on the shoulder as he left.

Stanton met him at the station, exactly one hour after they had talked. The sheriff led him into an interview room with the ambiance of a box of plaster. David felt the walls, the lack of air circulation. Special Agent Krane waited for him with a notepad and a tape recorder.

The man was younger than David had expected, thirty-five, black as December. He was brutally handsome: his nose just a millimeter off; a tooth out of line; his black hair so thick he might have combed it with a pencil. He was writing with a pencil when David entered. Looking up, Krane did not smile or nod but fixed him with an unemotional stare. *Maybe breakfast had been a mistake,* David thought. There was a spark in Krane's eyes, a confidence in his muscular shoulders. Although younger than Stanton, it was clear the FBI agent was more experienced when it came to interviewing suspects. David knew he would have to be careful with every word. Unfortunately, he did not recall exactly what he had said the day before, and Krane had a transcript.

For a moment David wondered if he was underestimating the seriousness of the situation. This was a murder case—they clearly saw him as a potential suspect. Perhaps Stanton was right, and he should to speak to a lawyer.

Yet he did not know any lawyers, and he had done nothing wrong.

Stanton introduced them; they shook hands. David took a seat and Krane fed him the usual lines about telling the truth, making it clear that this was a legal statement. When asked if he understood, David said yes. Krane lit a cigarette and started the tape recorder. From the looks of his ashtray, the FBI agent had enough nicotine in his bloodstream to kill a cat. Stanton remained in the room, in the background.

"We will start where Sheriff Stanton did yesterday. In fact, we will go through that interview step by step. Is that okay?"

"May I have a copy of the interview?" David asked.

"Sure, I can have one typed up for you."

"I meant yesterday's interview."

"What do you want it for?"

"It gives you an unfair advantage."

"Do you intend to contradict yourself?"

"Anyone can accidentally contradict himself. Can I have the transcript or not?"

Krane met his eyes. They both knew what was going on—a jostling for position before they got down to business. Krane shoved over a dozen sheets. A small victory—it would not help. Krane would not give him time to cross-check his responses. The FBI agent glanced at his own notes.

"What were you doing out at Lompoc Beach yesterday?"

"Going for a walk," David said.

"Why did you choose that spot to walk?"

"It's nice."

"Where were you just prior to your walk?"

"In my car, driving up from Los Angeles."

"Why were you in Los Angeles?"

"I had just flown into LAX from JFK."

"You were in New York, then?"

"Yes."

"Why?"

"I was there on business."

"For how long were you there?"

"Two months."

"Was there any other reason you were in New York?"

"I enjoy the city. I did some sightseeing."

"Did you meet any friends in New York?"

"No."

"Anyone at all?"

"I had many appointments with art directors." David paused, added, "Do you want a list of them?"

"Maybe later." Krane made a note to himself. David shifted uncomfortably. They had just begun and already he could see Krane was trying to set him up. The next question was no surprise. Krane had done his research.

"Did you have any emotional reason for going to New York when you did?"

"I do not understand the question."

"Had anything upsetting in your personal life inspired you to go to New York?"

David spoke carefully. "I had just broken up with my girlfriend. It is hard to say how much that had to do with my going to New York."

"Had you planned the trip before you broke up with your girlfriend?"

"Yes."

"When did you buy your ticket to go to New York?"

Krane would be able to check when the ticket was purchased.

"I bought it the morning I left," David said.

"Why didn't you purchase it earlier?"

"No reason."

"Yesterday you stated that after your plane landed, you drove straight to Lompoc. Is that correct?"

"Yes."

"You drove straight to the beach?"

"Yes."

"You wanted to stretch your legs?"

"Yes."

"You like the beach?"

"Yes."

"At the beach you were met by Charles Beard?"

"Yes."

"Is he an old friend?"

"Yes. We've known each other all our lives."

"Does Charles Beard work at the beach as a guard?"

"He did up until yesterday."

Krane glanced at Stanton. The sheriff shrugged.

"We had to fire him," Stanton said.

Krane didn't care, went back to his notes. "At the beach, did Charles try to stop you from crossing a railroad bridge that leads onto Vandenberg Air Force Base property?"

"He advised me against crossing the bridge, yes."

"Why did you ignore his advice?"

"I grew up in this town. That portion of the beach is an old haunt for me."

"By 'old haunt' do you mean that you continue to go there regularly?"

"I go there occasionally."

"How often? Once a year? Once a month?"

"I would say once every two or three months."

"Did Charles explain the stiff fine you could get for walking on that portion of the beach?"

"Yes."

"He explained about the Western Snowy Plover quarantine?"

"Yes."

"And still you ignored his advice and crossed the bridge and headed north on the beach?"

"Yes."

"How far north of the bridge did you walk?"

"About a mile."

"Why did you stop after a mile?"

"I saw the woman's body."

"The body was half hidden behind a sand dune, in relationship to the water. How did you happen to see it?"

Stanton had not questioned him about this. "I just did."

"Did you start inland for any reason when you reached that spot?"

"No."

"So you saw the body from close to the water?"

David had to struggle to remember. He might have unconsciously come inland at that point. They could have a map of his foot tracks.

"I think so," he said.

"You are not sure?"

"I am not sure."

"Had you gone to that spot before?"

"Yes."

"When was the last time? Before yesterday afternoon?"

"Two months ago."

"Can you give me the exact date?"

He had checked his plane ticket in anticipation of the question. "June fifteenth, of this year."

"Was that the night before you left for New York?"

"Yes."

"What time of night were you there?"

"Around midnight."

"How long were you there for?"

"About two hours."

"Were you alone?"

"No. I was with my girlfriend, Sienna Madden."

"You stayed there together approximately two hours. What did you do?"

"We went for a swim, built a fire, ate hot dogs and chips. Made love."

"You had sexual intercourse on the beach?"

"Yes."

"How many times?"

"I don't know."

"More than once?"

"Yeah. Twice, maybe."

"Close to the fire?"

"Excuse me?"

"Did you have sexual intercourse close to the fire you built?"

"What kind of question is that?"

"A simple one. Answer it please."

"Yes."

"Did you make the fire out of nearby driftwood?"

"Yes."

"You said you broke up with your girlfriend before you left for New York. Did you break up with her that night?"

"She broke up with me."

"She was the one who ended the relationship?"

"Yes."

"Why?"

"I don't know why."

"Did she give you an explanation?"

"Not really."

"Tell me what she said, exactly."

"I can't, I don't remember."

"Did her decision to end the relationship catch you by surprise?"

"Yes."

"Had she shown any sign—at any time, that day or that month—that she wanted to end the relationship?"

"A week or so before that night, she got much quieter."

"Did you ask her what was troubling her?"

"Yes."

"What did she say?"

"Nothing."

"Did you two fight that night?"

"No."

"No?"

"I got upset, but I would not call it a fight."

"Did you try to talk her out of ending the relationship?"

"Yes."

"Did you plead with her?"

"Not exactly."

"What exactly did you do? Did you weep?"

"No. I . . . I asked her what was wrong. Why she was doing it."

"What did she say?"

"Nothing, it was weird. She just said she had to go."

"Was she upset when she said this?"

"Yes."

"Were you upset?"

"Sure."

"Were you angry?"

"No. Well, I was confused, more sad than angry."

"But you were angry?"

"It was a shock. I didn't know how to feel."

"Answer the question please."

"I was a bit angry."

"Did you grab her? Try to stop her from leaving?"

"No." Not exactly true, but fuck him.

"You didn't do anything to physically stop her from leaving?"

"No. We . . ."

"What?"

"Nothing."

"You were going to say something. Tell me what you were going to say."

"The second time we made love, it was after she gave me the bad news."

"How was that?"

"How was what?"

"The second time you had sexual intercourse with Sienna that night. How was it?"

David stared at the agent. "That is a strange question."

"Could you answer it please?"

"No. I don't think I can."

"Did you argue when you were making love the second time?"

"No."

"After you were done, did she leave the beach?"

David went to answer, stopped. He could not remember—really, it was like the question had opened a black hole in his head. "Yes," he said.

"You left the beach together?"

"No."

"You left separately?"

"Yes."

"Who left first?"

"She did."

"Where did she go?"

Again, he considered, the details were cloudy. "She hiked back in the direction of the parking lot."

"Did you follow her?"

"Not right away."

"What did you do?"

"I don't know. Cleaned up, I guess."

"You guess?"

"I really don't remember."

"Did you put out the fire?"

"I think so."

"Was she dressed when she left the beach?"

"Of course."

"Were you dressed?"

He hesitated. "Yes."

"Why do you hesitate?"

"I didn't hesitate."

"How long after she left the beach did you leave?"

"I don't know, ten minutes maybe."

"Do you remember?"

"Not really."

"You seem to have trouble remembering that part of the night."

"It was two months ago."

"But it was not an ordinary night. It was the night before you left. It was the night your girlfriend broke up with you. Tell me, when you came to the beach, did you come together?"

"Yes."

"Did you drive your car to the beach?"

"Yes."

"Then how did you leave the beach?"

"I told you, she left first."

"That is not what I am asking. You came in one car. Did you leave the parking lot at the beach together?"

David froze. "No. I left alone."

It was the question Krane must have been waiting all morning to ask. Certainly Stanton had not thought of it. "Then how did Sienna get home?"

David lowered his head. "I don't know."

"Was she at the parking lot when you got there?"

"No."

"Did she have a cell phone with her when she left you that night?"

"I don't know." He looked up, added, "Maybe."

"Could she have called a cab?"

"She must have. Yeah."

"Could someone else have picked her up?"

"No. She doesn't know anyone else in town." Except Mary and Herb, but there was no sense in bringing them into the equation.

David caught himself, thinking further. Was that true? Obviously there was no point in bringing up Mary—she was a kid, she couldn't even drive—but Herb was a known drug dealer. If Krane had another name it could broaden the field of the agent's investigation, probably take some heat off of David.

Yet he disliked throwing Herb at them just to make his situation more comfortable. Herb was not a close friend but he was not a bad guy either. On the other hand, David was curious what Krane might get out of the guy. Herb had been acting awfully strange that morning.

"Herb Domino," David blurted out. "She knows him."

Krane made a note. "How well does she know him?"

"Beats me. Ask him."

"I will." Krane paused. "Have you seen Sienna since that night?"

"No."

"Have you spoken to her?"

The question *he* had been waiting all morning to answer. Yet it did not bring him the satisfaction he had anticipated. "Yes," he said.

Krane stopped, looked at Stanton, who just shrugged. The FBI agent made a note then continued. "But yesterday afternoon you stated that you had not spoken to her in the last two months."

"That is correct. She called this morning."

"Where did she call from?"

"She was at JFK, in New York. She was about to board a plane for Los Angeles."

"How did she call? From a pay phone?"

"No. She said she was on her cell."

"Did she give you that number?"

"No." David paused. "I asked her for it."

"Why didn't she give it to you?"

"There was static on the line. We could hardly hear each other." He considered bringing up the number of her flight. It had sounded like she was about to take the same one he had taken. But if he gave them the information and they checked it out and it was wrong, it might make them more suspicious.

"Do you have any way to reach her?" Krane asked.

"No. But she said she would call me today from Orange County."

"What is she doing in Orange County?"

"I'm not sure."

"Does she plan to come to Lompoc to visit you?"

"Yes. She said she wanted to see me."

"When?"

"I'm not sure."

"Is there any way you can reach her right now?"

"You just asked that. No."

"Do you know the flight she was taking to Los Angeles?"

David paused. "No. But . . ."

"What?"

"She called yesterday afternoon and left a message. If you're worried if she's alive, you can listen to it."

"This message is still on your machine?"

"Yes. It should be. I didn't erase it."

David might have taken the wind out of Krane's sails. The FBI agent turned off the recorder, sat back. He appeared to be thinking.

"You better not be fucking with us," he said finally.

David smiled. "I wouldn't do that."

Krane gestured to the tape recorder. "Because without confirmation of Sienna's well-being, your story about that night is extremely vague."

David lost his smile. It troubled him as well, how hazy his memory of that night was. How did Sienna get home that night? He had not driven her home. Yet he did recall that her car had not been at his house when he had finally gotten home.

"Are you through taking my statement?" David asked.

Krane shrugged. "Sure."

"Then I have a question. Why are you guys fixed on the idea that the dead woman is Sienna? The sheriff met her for god's sake. She's a brunette, not a blonde."

"Hair can be dyed," Krane said. "Temp dyes, they wash out quick."

"I would have known if she dyed her hair. Your entire investigation is silly."

"What would you do differently?" Stanton asked.

"Stop focusing on me just because I found her."

"You didn't just find her," Krane said. "You've admitted to being at that spot two months ago, which is approximately when this woman died. Also, you've told us you built a fire there, and there is firewood right next to the body. It only stands to reason that we would investigate you first, try to clear you before we move on."

"Somehow I don't feel like you're trying to clear me."

"Somehow we don't feel like you're trying to help us," Krane said.

David was annoyed. "You don't know me. From the moment I found that body, you guys have been jumping all over me. Tell me—you took my samples—did you find any of my hair or skin on her?"

"We're still waiting on the medical examiner," Stanton said.

"But I want Sienna's samples," Krane said. "You told the sheriff she used to live in Santa Barbara. I want the two of you to go to her old place. Today."

"That house has probably been rented to someone else," David said. The thought of going to Sienna's house made him feel ill—the memories. He added, "It's a cute guest house, isolated. Those go quick in Santa Barbara."

"It doesn't matter," Krane said. "You say she lived there six months. The sheriff will be able to find a few stray hairs. You can help point them out for him."

"One brown hair looks like another brown hair to me. Let me just give you the address."

Krane stared at him. "Are you afraid to go?"

"No. I just don't see the point. Anyway, aren't you worried about me messing up the scene of the crime?"

"She died on the beach, in Lompoc. That house in Santa Barbara has nothing to do with the scene of the crime." Krane added, "Isn't that right?"

David felt flustered. "Sure. But forcing me to go there—it doesn't sound like something your normal policeman would want to do."

"I'm not a policeman, I'm an FBI agent. And as long as you don't touch anything, there is absolutely no reason you can't go there with the sheriff."

David was suspicious of the FBI agent's reasoning. The hair identification excuse was thin. It was probable Krane wanted him alone in the car with Stanton for some time so the sheriff could pump him for information.

"Let me think about it," David said.

"Think quickly." Krane leaned closer. "I have another question. This is off the record, but it's not something I want you to talk about outside this room. You hear me?"

"Sure."

"Have you ever heard of LESS?"

"Less?"

"L-E-S-S. Have you ever heard of it?"

"No. What is it?"

"Did Sienna ever mention it?"

"No. Tell me what it is."

"I can't, it's classified information."

"Does it have anything to do with the way this woman was killed?"

Krane glanced at Stanton. "We agreed not to talk about that," the FBI agent said, annoyed. The sheriff was not used to being scolded.

"David saw the body," Stanton said. "I didn't tell him anything he doesn't already know."

Krane turned to David. "Whenever there is a ritual killing, the media goes crazy. I would appreciate it if you didn't talk to anyone about the condition of her body."

"Fine. As long as there's a two-way street between us. I've told 'you what I know. Now you tell me what makes you think this might be the work of a satanic cult."

"This isn't a two-way street. Whatever gave you that idea?"

"Fine. You and the sheriff go to Sienna's house. I have better things to do with my time."

Krane sat back, gave him a hard look. "You're good, David. You act all open and innocent, but when it comes time to remember important details, you suddenly have mental problems. Right now, the sheriff's going to accompany you to your house. That message had better still be on your machine. For that matter, when Sienna comes to visit, I want to meet her."

"I am sure that can be arranged," David said.

EIGHT

Sienna's message was gone.

David took a moment to figure out what had happened. The answering machine's power plug had come out of the wall. He had probably accidentally pulled on it when he had replayed the message. The machine—it was digital—automatically erased when it lost power. He explained the situation to the sheriff, who stood beside him in the living room. Stanton shook his head.

"Krane's not going to like that," he said.

"I didn't erase it on purpose," David said. Indeed, at the back of his mind, he had thought about saving it for the sheriff—once again, to end all the questions about Sienna. He added, "I don't care what Krane likes."

"You're the one who offered the message. You know we're not asking for much. We just want to know she's okay."

"You guys need to chill. I'm the ex-boyfriend. I'm the one who's supposed to be obsessing on her."

"Why is she coming to visit? Does she want to get back together?"

"Who knows? She's a woman. She probably wants to cut open my chest and eat my heart." David knelt to plug in the machine. "She might have called while I was out."

"I thought you said she just got on a plane."

"Oh, yeah. You're right."

"I have to call Krane. May I use your phone?"

"Sure."

He stepped into the kitchen, four strides away, and watched as Stanton got on the phone. From reading the sheriff's expression, David knew Krane was not impressed with David Lennon's latest excuse. David didn't care, he still had his headache. Acting tough with Krane had been wearing. Krane had asked questions he had not asked himself.

"He says you had better come with me to Santa Barbara," Stanton said as he hung up the phone.

"That's ridiculous. There is no reason for me to go."

"You dated Sienna a long time. You probably know her landlord."

"I do. So what?"

"It might be worthwhile to talk to him."

"Her. Don't you need a warrant to go rummaging through the place?"

Stanton pulled out an official-looking paper. "The FBI gets what it wants when it wants," he said.

"Doesn't it piss you off that Krane has taken over your investigation?"

"No. He's smart, and he has the full resources of the Bureau. He gets things done quick. And between you and me, this ritual killing stuff gives me the creeps."

"Did he tell you what LESS means?" David asked.

"I heard about it the same time you did."

"But it must have something to do with satanic cults."

Stanton frowned. "I'm not sure. Krane would have told me if it was that simple. All I know is that LESS is important to him."

"How do you know?"

"Something in his eyes."

In the end David decided to go with Stanton, but not because of the body, or because of Krane's pressure. His recent talk with Herb continued to bother him, as well as Mary's dark-night-of-the-soul routine. The sheriff was always on the prowl, always had his eyes open. No one knew Lompoc better. David wanted to get his perspective on those two.

On the road, heading south, David explained his concerns. Stanton nodded a few times. It seemed the cop had been thinking along the same lines.

"What I want to know is why Pomus lets his daughter hang out with Herb," David said. "Why he has him working at the church."

"The second point is easy to understand. Pomus told me he's trying to rehabilitate him. Herb's reading the Bible—I know he goes to their prayer meetings on Wednesday nights."

"That's a joke. Herb is forever stoned. He will never give up drugs—his neurons can't fire without them. He'll never quit dealing—the money is too easy. Which brings up another question. Why haven't you ever busted the guy?"

"I never catch him carrying."

"That's bullshit, sheriff. Throw his jacket into an empty field and enough seeds will fall out of his pockets to grow a pot forest. Come on, tell me the truth."

Stanton glanced over. "This is off the record."

"My whole life is off the record. I'm going to die and St. Peter's going to meet me at the pearly gates and try to look me up in his book and he's not going to find me. He's going to assume I was never born."

"Are you always so morbid?"

"New York did it to me. Tell me about you and Herb. I swear I won't remember a word after I get out of this car. You can trust me, you know, I haven't killed anybody in the last two months."

"You might want to stop joking about that."

"Now you sound like a lawyer. Go on."

"All right. Say I follow Herb for a couple of months, catch him when he gets in a big load, put his ass away for five to ten. What happens then? The same people will want to buy the same dope. They will either go out of town to get it, or else, more likely, another two or three dealers will appear to take up the slack. But these guys—will they have the same attitude as Herb? What I am saying is there's a lot of dangerous shit out there. A kid buys a hit of Ecstasy to feel brave enough at a high school dance to ask a girl out on a date, and he ends up swallowing a megadose of acid and having nightmares for the rest of his life. You get my point? As far as I can tell, Herb has never lied to anyone about what he was selling."

"But he sells the hard stuff—coke and acid. Heroin, if someone wants it badly enough. He's messing up a lot of people's lives. I can't believe you let him run wild because he understands quality control."

"Believe it. Then go a step further, and look at the big picture. I know exactly who Herb sells heroin to—they're all long-term addicts—and I have his sworn promise that he will not expose anyone else in town to it that is not already addicted. As far as I know, Herb has never broken that promise. He knows if he does he will be moving to the northeast end of town."

"So you're saying he's poison, but he's a poison you know?"

"Exactly. I control what he does, within limits."

David did not buy the story—it sounded like the worst kind of rationalizing. Maybe the sheriff was not a knight in shining armor, after all. He could be getting a kickback. "I see," he said.

Stanton looked over. "There's nothing in it for me."

"I'm not saying anything." David added, "When I saw Herb this morning, he told me something weird. He said he knew I blamed him for what happened to Rachel and Billy. He was talking about the fire."

"Do you blame him?"

"No. Why should I?"

"Then what did he mean?"

"It was like a subconscious slip. Like he wanted to confess something." David paused. "Tell me what you know about that night."

"Aren't you getting a little off the topic? We just found a dead body on the beach. You're asking about something that happened ten years ago."

"I told you, he brought it up. It just got me thinking is all."

"Don't think about it, drop it. It's over and done with. Besides, Billy was your best friend. What could I tell you that you haven't heard before?"

"A lot. I never got your take on what happened, and you were on the inside of the investigation. I could never talk to Rachel about it—she would just break down and cry. I only got Billy's point of view, and he was the last person on earth you'd call objective."

"Because he blamed himself?"

"Yes. I'm sure that's why he killed himself."

Stanton sighed. "That was a terrible year, and it should have been the best. All you guys graduating, starting your lives."

"We're still starting. Just tell me what happened that night."

"You know the basic facts. Rachel's parents and sister went away for the weekend, and she wanted to have a romantic night with Billy. They got a little pot and wine and fell asleep on the couch with the TV on. But Rachel left a joint burning on the coffee table. It fell on the floor and the rug caught fire." Stanton shrugged. "They were out cold. By the time they woke up, the fire had spread and Rachel got her face burned. That's it."

"Billy always swore they didn't leave anything burning."

"So does everyone who falls asleep in bed with a lit cigarette. The fire did not start by itself. You have to remember Rachel's family tried to slap Billy's parents with a lawsuit. Billy said what he had to say to protect them."

"Billy wouldn't have lied to me. And Rachel backed up his story."

"They were stoned! It doesn't matter what they said."

"They were there, it does matter. Another thing, why did Rachel get burned and Billy didn't?"

"I was called out that night. The flames were raging. Billy was just lucky is all. If Herb hadn't happened by, and helped them, they both might have died."

"They both did die."

"You know that's not what I meant."

"I think Herb was the one who sold them the pot."

"Probably. So?"

David shook his head. "Nothing."

"There's no mystery about what happened that night. Or afterward."

"There is to me. Let me go on. Everyone accepted Rachel's suicide. Her face was ruined—she looked like she had on a Halloween mask. She was having operation after operation. Plus her own sister was Miss California. Everyone at school acted like committing suicide was the smart thing to do. But I knew Rachel as well as Billy. She was a tough girl, she would never have given up."

"So what are you saying? That Rachel and Billy were murdered?"

"You investigated both deaths. You tell me."

"They killed themselves."

"Just give me the facts. Start with Rachel."

"This is sick." Stanton put a wad of tobacco in his mouth, chewed, rolled down the window. It was like he wanted to let out the smoke. "All right, late one night I get a call from her sister, Teresa, to come out to her house. She's just found Rachel in the bathtub with her wrists slit open. I call nine-one-one, get an ambulance on the road, and head over there myself. I get there before the paramedics, find Teresa in the living room in shock—can't get anything out of her. The scene in the bathroom is nasty. Rachel's in the tub, fully dressed, the water a pink color. A bloody box cutter lies on the floor beside the tub." Stanton paused. "That's it—she killed herself. End of story."

"I forget, where were the parents?"

"They were out of town."

"What time of night was this?"

"I don't remember. Does it matter?"

"Indulge me."

"It was late."

"Why did Teresa call you first, instead of the ambulance?"

"She didn't know what she was doing. I was a friend of the family."

"Was the water running in the tub?"

"No."

"Was the water cold?"

"Yes."

"But Rachel must have left the water running when she slit her wrists. You said the water was pink, not dark red."

"I thought about that at the time. Teresa must have turned off the water when she found her sister."

"Did she say she did?"

"No. I got nothing out of her that night. I told you, she was in shock."

"But you must have questioned her after that night?"

"I did but I didn't ask that question."

"Why not?"

"It was not a murder investigation. There were no signs of foul play. Teresa did not kill her sister, and she was the only other person in the house."

"I still think the question is important. The water was cold, not hot or even warm. But nobody would get into a cold tub to kill themselves. So we have to assume Rachel was running warm water, at least letting it drip. That is the only way the water would change from red to pink."

"What's your point?"

"Rachel was dead a while before Teresa called you."

"That's possible. For all I know, Teresa was asleep when Rachel opened her wrists."

"You miss my point. Teresa must have turned off the water, and *then* waited to call you."

Stanton took a moment, then nodded. "You're right. I'm not sure I thought of that back then. Honestly, I can't remember. The idea might be in my report."

"Could you look at it for me?"

"If you insist. Anything else?"

"The obvious. Why was Rachel dressed?"

"She knew she would be found. She probably hated the idea of others seeing her naked."

"Sounds good in theory. But how many suicide victims who open their wrists in the bathtub wear their clothes?"

"I doubt there's been a study done on it."

"It doesn't matter, it's suspicious."

"Of what? Who would want to kill Rachel?"

"I don't know. The whole situation was weird. Especially when it came to Billy." David paused. "You were the first one on the scene that night."

"Yeah. Nobody called, I was on patrol. Back then, I always used to swing by the beach. His car was parked at the far end, facing the sea. I recognized it, figured he was sitting there with you. But when I drove up, I saw the blood. It was all over the place."

"Did he really put the gun in his mouth?"

"Yes. He used a three-fifty-seven magnum shell. Blew off the back of his head."

"I didn't need to know that."

"You're the one who keeps asking."

"Is there any way, any way at all, that someone forced that gun into his mouth?"

"I don't see how. Also, don't forget the suicide note. It was in Billy's handwriting. He was still depressed over Rachel."

"I read that note. His mom showed it to me. I said it at the time, it was in his handwriting but it didn't sound like him."

"Who did it sound like?"

"Don't ask that."

"Billy wrote it, his fingerprints were all over it. We found the pen and paper he used in his shirt pocket. The flash burn—from the shot—was on his hand and wrist. I turned the evidence upside down, trying to make it something other than suicide. But there was nothing." Stanton paused. "Except for one thing."

"What?"

"I don't want you talking about this. Don't run to his family with it. You have to promise me that. I'm sure it means nothing."

"Agreed. What is it?"

"When I was driving to the beach that night, I passed a car heading the other way."

"Was it coming from the beach?"

"Yes. I had already passed the last turnoff. But the car might have been from the south lot, the bigger one. Billy killed himself in the north lot."

"What time was this?"

"Three in the morning."

"Not many people out there at that time of the night."

"I know."

"How long was Billy dead when you found him?"

"He was still warm. He could have shot himself ten minutes before I showed up."

"Or just before that other car left?"

"Possibly."

"Why didn't you tell me this before?"

"Because all the evidence pointed toward suicide. I didn't want to mess up your mind."

"Believe me, it was already messed up. You didn't tell his family about the car?"

"No."

"What type of car was it?"

"You have to understand I saw it head-on, its lights in my eyes. But if I had to say, I would have said it was a Mercedes."

"Not many Mercedes in Lompoc. Wait a second! Didn't Rachel's sister, Teresa, drive one?"

"Yeah. She got it after she won her Miss California title. An E-class."

"Those have distinct headlights. Is that what you saw?"

Stanton hesitated. "I think so."

"Did you ask Teresa where she was that night?"

"Sure. She said she spent the night with her fiancé."

"Who was that?"

"I can't remember. He was out of town, I never spoke to him."

"How long after Billy died did you speak to Teresa?"

"I know what you're driving at. It was the next day."

"So this fiancé must have left town the next day?"

"You got it."

"That's convenient."

"It means nothing. Billy wrote that suicide note. He pulled that trigger. In the end, that's all that matters."

"Are you sure? Teresa might have been present when both suicides occurred. That's got to make you wonder." David added, "Rachel never could stand her older sister."

"I thought Rachel liked everyone."

"Rachel thought Teresa was a stuck-up bitch. Maybe it was inevitable—Teresa was such a fox. Do you know where she lives now?"

"No. She married that guy, whoever he was, and moved away."

"Her father will know."

"David. I don't want you stirring this thing up. You promised."

"I can talk to the dad without mentioning the suicides. I see him anyway, from time to time."

"How is he?"

"What can I say? He's a drunk. I have another question. Did you ever figure out where Billy got the gun? The family didn't own one."

"No."

"Did Teresa's dad own a gun?"

"I never asked."

"Could you check that for me?"

"No. I'm not going to bother them after all these years."

"You can look the information up on a computer."

"Why in heaven's name would Teresa kill Rachel and Billy?"

"I'm not saying that."

"Then what are you saying?"

"I'm just asking questions. I have been asked enough myself today." David paused. "When you searched Billy's car, did you find anything unusual?"

"No."

"What was his alcohol reading when he died?"

"Twice the legal limit. He had his courage up. But let me ask you a question. You sat next to him at graduation. Was he depressed?"

"He was distant." David added hastily, "That's not the same as being depressed."

"Did he go to the graduation party?"

"No. He said he had stuff to do."

"What kind of stuff?"

"The whole week before the ceremony, he was cleaning out his room."

"And you don't think he killed himself? His behavior was classic. He had it all planned."

"I'll never believe that. Not Billy—it just wasn't his style. Same with Rachel."

There was not a lot of room for discussion after such a pronouncement. Stanton concentrated on his driving and David stared out the window. The sheriff was taking the long way to Santa Barbara, staying on the coast. The wide blue of the ocean should have been calming, but David kept thinking of the secrets hidden beneath its waves, the world over. He could not be free of the feeling that he knew nothing.

Sienna had not lived in Santa Barbara proper, but in Goleta, a small city just north of the famous resort town. It was impossible to say where one city ended and the other began; however, Sienna had always told people she was from Santa Barbara.

Sienna had liked her privacy. The small guest house she had rented was several miles off the freeway, back in the hills, part of a large ranch owned by a rich widow named Mrs. Printkin. David had talked to her a number of times while he dated Sienna. The old woman could hardly walk but never missed her morning ride. He remembered vividly the smell of the horses as he had lain in Sienna's bed at night, their distant snorting in the dark. Sienna had thought the odor and sounds romantic, the stuff of other times.

David pointed out the guest house as they wound up the narrow road that led to the property—half hidden behind a bluff—but the sheriff made for the main house, a ranch-style mansion that had been built at the turn of the previous century. Sienna had told him how Mr. Printkin had only recently died, and David used to think how lonely Mrs. Printkin must have felt in such a huge place.

David opted to stay in the car as the sheriff got out.

"What's the matter?" Stanton asked.

"This is a police matter. I'm just along for the ride."

"Suit yourself."

Mrs. Printkin answered the door, spoke to the sheriff. David could not hear the discussion, but Stanton quickly took out the search warrant. Pulling down the sun visor, David tried to disappear into the seat. He didn't want to have to explain to the woman that he was a suspect in Sienna's murder investigation. Especially when he hoped to see Sienna sometime in the next few days.

Mrs. Printkin did not see him, and the sheriff was back in two minutes. He leaned in the passenger window. "The landlady says Sienna moved out June eighth," he said.

"She's sure?"

"She's old but she's sharp."

"That's a week before we broke up."

"Do you know where she was during that week?"

"No. I thought she was here."

"Did you talk during that week?"

"Sure. But it's possible . . ."

"What?"

"I don't remember calling her that week. I think she just called me."

Stanton straightened, glanced at the guest house. "Mrs. Printkin says the guest house is unlocked. I want you to come with me. I need you to identify any strands of hair lying around."

David got out reluctantly, the sun suddenly hot on top of his head. Three miles inland from the sea and the temperature had gone up ten degrees. Walking toward the guest house, David felt dizzy. The lemon tree outside her front door was too much of a reminder. The odor filled his brain with undigested bitterness. Her shampoo had smelled of lemon. But her lips had been sweet, he thought. Right then, he imagined he hated her to the exact same degree he loved her. Yet the balance was not a place of peace, only a no-man's-land where nothing could ever end.

"Are you all right?" Stanton asked.

"Just swell," David replied.

The house had questionable shade. Inside was warm but not stuffy. Mrs. Printkin had left all the windows open. The place was a studio with few corners to hide in, but it had a high ceiling and fine finishings: Corian for the kitchen counter, marble on the bathroom floor. Sienna had rented her furniture, kept it simple, but now the place was empty and sad. Staring down at the white carpet, David didn't see a single dark hair.

"Try not to touch anything," Stanton said, pulling out a Baggie and putting on plastic gloves.

"Like I am going to leave a print on her hair."

"Look around, you find any let me know."

David went into the bathroom, didn't know why. Perhaps it had something to do with those old heartstrings, making the puppet dance. The first time he had made love to Sienna, it had started in the shower. They had been dating a month and had barely kissed. She had called him down on a Saturday afternoon. She had wanted to go hiking in the hills behind her house. It was possible she had planned the shower to match his arrival. What a day, someone should have shot and stuffed him right then—his ear-to-ear grin preserved for the rest of time.

He had knocked on the door, heard the water.

"Come in!" she had called.

He hesitated—how deep did he dare go into the queen's palace? God, it took him ten minutes to reach the threshold of her bathroom. The shower curtain was translucent, flooded with smiling fish. California was always worried about a drought, ten minutes was a lot of water. Nevertheless she waited, probably hearing the torture in his breathing as they talked about the weather. Finally she popped her head out from behind the curtain and smiled at him.

"What the fuck is wrong with you?" she asked.

He was stunned, turned to leave. "Sorry."

"No! Join me!"

Now, in the bathroom, looking for dead hair he used to wash and help comb, he studied the same plastic fish and thought their smiles mocking. The lemon fragrance had returned, only now it was stronger. Was there another tree outside the bathroom? Funny, he did not remember one, could not see one out the window. Yet he suddenly felt as if he was drowning in squeezed juice. He breathed in but could not breathe out. Like during a kiss . . . yes, a kiss.

He thought of what it had been like to kiss her, to touch her, the water running over their heads, his hand on her breast, her tongue in his mouth. That afternoon, she had kept saying his name, over and over again, especially when he entered her and she began to moan. "*David, David*"—a mystic mantra to bind forever, never to liberate. He had fallen in love with her before that day, but after that, he was just falling.

"Sienna," he said as the dizziness swept over him and the room twisted into a four-wall epileptic fit. The water was on, he did not know how, and the tub was filling with lemon juice and blood. He was falling forward, going straight down, and even though he knew Stanton would find him, he doubted it would be in time. He would end up like Rachel Bronson, fully dressed but totally dead, a bright-eyed corpse floating in the cold, with no one left to explain what, or to understand why.

Just before he blacked out, he had the thought: nothing was as it seemed.

NINE

Getting dropped off at home, David was still feeling embarrassed. For his part Stanton had been a good sport about it, not saying much on the drive back to Lompoc, except to ask how he was feeling. David was not sure how to answer that question. He had never fainted before.

Stanton was satisfied with the trip. He had found five strands of Sienna's hair, and stored them in separate Baggies. David had verified the goods, without having to smell them. Like Karen, Sienna had worn her hair almost to her butt. But just seeing the evidence had caused his dizziness to flare back up. Really, he might explode if they met again.

"Are you sure you're feeling all right?" Stanton asked as David climbed out of the patrol car.

"Positive. I think it had something to do with getting drunk last night."

Stanton nodded. "I heard you went to Chubby's with Julie Stevens."

"I love how in this town a person can't have sex without local law enforcement knowing about it."

Stanton grinned. "You went to bed with her? I didn't know that."

"But you noticed her car parked out front all night, didn't you?"

"True. Julie—she's a good girl. Stick with her, forget that Sienna."

"That's what everybody keeps telling me. Hey, Sheriff, could you do me a favor?"

"I never saw you faint."

"Exactly. Do you remember the stuff I want you to check on?"

"Sure. But I'll get to it when I get to it. Krane is high maintenance."

"He should be happy with the hairs you found."

"I'm confident it will take the pressure off of you. But if she shows up tomorrow or the next day, bring her by the station."

"How long is Krane in town for?" David asked.

"He told me for as long as it takes."

Inside the house there was a message from Julie, his parents—whom he had never called back—and Sienna. Naturally he played the third message several times.

"David, it's me, you know who. It's about twelve o'clock. I'm in Orange County, at a friend's house, you can call back if you want. I would like that, I really want to see you on this trip. The number here is . . ."

Sienna left a 714 number, and told him she loved him before hanging up. David wrote down the number and immediately called back. Some guy answered; he sounded like he had just woken up. David asked if Sienna was there.

"Who is this?" the guy asked, none too polite.

"David Lennon. Who is this?"

The guy was amused. "I've heard about you. Where are you?"

"I am sitting on my couch in my living room. Is Sienna there?"

"No."

"Do you know when she'll be back in?"

"No."

"All right. Can you tell her I called?"

The guy chuckled. "Sure. I can tell her you called."

Putting down the phone, David felt annoyed and stupid at the same time. Yet if she was sleeping with the jerk, she would not have given him the guy's number. She had called him a friend, however, and said she was on the West Coast on business. What sort of business? The truth of the matter was he knew almost nothing about her life outside of their relationship. Even Herb knew things about her he did not know.

The phone rang. His heart thumping, David picked it up. But it was only Julie—Julie Stevens, whom he had had incredible sex with the night before. Hearing her voice made him feel guilty. He felt less suave than the day before. If Sienna did indeed come for a visit, he would tell Julie he was not a free man. No reason to mind-fuck her, he'd had enough of that to last a lifetime.

"You sleep like a dead man," she said with a laugh.

"Not usually. It was the alcohol."

"The alcohol! It was the sex! Admit it, I wore you out!"

"You were amazing. Ten shots of tequila last night and still my back hurts more than my head."

"You weren't too shabby yourself. I hope you didn't mind me sneaking off in the morning. I told you I had interviews to go to."

"No problem. Did you find anything interesting?"

"Maybe. You know Mauldin Construction? They do tons of remodeling around town. They desperately need an office manager, someone who can do everything. They seemed to like me, and the starting salary ain't bad. But I have no bookkeeping experience, and the last gal they had did. So I'm no shoo-in."

"I hope you get it."

"Really? I don't know. Sometimes I think I should just blow this town." She giggled. "I mean, sometimes I think I should just leave. When you were talking about New York last night, it really made me want to go. Do you have any plans to go back?"

"No immediate plans."

Julie hesitated. "Well, I'm just thinking out loud. I'm not as anxious to leave now that I've met you."

David had to smile, although his guilt was not getting any better. "You met me in high school, Julie."

"I didn't know you in high school. Seriously, David, I had a great time last night. It meant a lot to me, to be with a real man. I don't mean that as a cliché. Most of the guys in this town have nothing upstairs." She lowered her voice. "I could talk to you, you know?"

"I had a great time."

"Really?"

"Absolutely."

She seemed to brighten. "Cool. Do you want to get together later today?"

He hesitated. "What time?"

"I don't know, three hours?"

"What do you want to do?"

She giggled. "You mean, besides have sex? I don't care, go bowling."

"I haven't been bowling in ten years."

"I've never been. We can do anything, it doesn't matter. Should I call before coming?"

"Sure," David said.

They exchanged good-byes and David set down the phone and sat for a minute and wondered what the hell he was doing with his life.

Coming back from Santa Barbara, he had planned to finish reading the vampire book and continue with the painting. Now, with Sienna and Julie dancing in his head, he felt too restless. He decided to go for a long walk, burn off the stress.

His hometown. In the whole place there was no great place to walk, not unless you drove down to the beach. Since that area was now off-limits he hiked from his front porch, not really knowing where he was going. But fifteen minutes into his walk he found himself passing the old school: Lompoc High, Go Brave Indians. The gate to the track was open; he stepped onto the rusty cinders. Ten years and the place had not changed. The field could have been covered with the same grass, the bleachers inhabited with the same old pals. The only difference, for him, was that there were now ghosts in the stands.

How had he lost track of Billy graduation night? The ceremony had been in this very stadium and, like he had told Stanton, he had sat next to Billy while the diplomas were handed out. Then Billy had just said he had stuff to do, that he would catch up with him later. That was the last David saw of him.

Stanton had come to him first, before even talking to Billy's family. It must have been two in the morning. By then David was holed up with Karen and Charlie—the three of them watching movies in his bedroom, drinking wine and talking about what next, and wondering where the hell Billy was. The sheriff had knocked on his window instead of the front door, and David was never to forget Stanton's pale face peering through the glass—as if the man had just seen Billy's ghost and not his corpse.

"I need the three of you to come with me," Stanton said.

David was worried, but not enough. "Has something happened to Billy?"

Stanton spoke quietly. "Yes."

Karen knew. "He's dead."

David and Charlie both looked at her, not at Stanton. They were not there yet, she shouldn't have been there. Yet for some reason they looked to her for confirmation—only heard Stanton mouth the words.

"He's dead," the sheriff said.

Stanton took them to Billy's house, asked David to wake Billy's mother. That was as bad as it could get. The woman didn't break down into sobs, simply sagged into a chair and stared off into the distance, probably thinking what the years ahead would be like without her only child.

Still, they did not know how Billy had died. Stanton tried to explain. Again, none of it made sense. Suicide? Karen started shouting that it was not true, Charlie wept, and David argued. Billy's mother made no sound, however, only nodded her head. Perhaps she had seen it coming, who was to say? She never did.

Later, that night, along with Billy's mother, David had seen his best friend's body. The city morgue, not an easy place to enter, and an even harder place to forget. Someone had wrapped Billy's head in a white towel, closed his shattered mouth, his eyes—Christ, he looked like he was sleeping. Only now David had a few facts. His best friend had put a gun in his mouth before putting a bullet in his brain. When he looked closer, David saw that Billy's brain was still leaking; the towel was soaking up the blood. Billy's mom had lost it then, and he'd had to help her from the room.

Then there was the note. The sheriff let David read it after he'd seen the body.

Hello, Good-bye,
This is Billy, I am sorry, I can't take it anymore. Rachel's gone, I
have to follow. Please forgive us, I love you all . . .
                                                              —Billy

As he told the sheriff, it was Billy's handwriting but not his words. Please forgive *us?* Billy was supposed to have been alone when he died. Because of that one word, and because of the character of Billy's entire life, David never believed any of it. Sadly, he was alone in his lack of belief. Even Billy's mother, at the funeral, had allowed Reverend Pomus to use the S word. Two S words, actually, suicide and Satan, as if the two went hand in hand. Minutes before they lowered Billy into the ground, Pomus said that the Devil must have had a hand in what happened. Billy was too good to have fallen so early.

Billy's house was near the school. Leaving the track, David walked the two blocks over and knocked on the door. He had not spoken to Billy's

mother in over a year, and that had just been a quick hello at the mall. When Mrs. Baxter answered the door, he took a step back in surprise. Her grief had lingered like a slow-growing cancer. The woman was fifty but appeared seventy. Her once shiny brown hair looked as if it would crumble if touched.

But she smiled when she saw him, even though her hands shook as she opened the door. Coffee or Coke, she asked—he could have whatever he desired. Like at the high school track, he felt himself slip into a time warp as he entered the house. Photographs of Rachel and Billy on the walls did not help. There was even one of him, Billy and Charlie poised beside a cross-country trophy they had won their senior year. Sitting across from Mrs. Baxter, coffee in hand, David thought of Stanton's warnings about old wounds.

"How are you, David?" Billy mother asked.

"Great," he lied, quickly steering the conversation to her day-to-day schedule, not necessarily a safe turn of the wheel. There was not much going on in her life: work at the library; bingo on Thursday; church on Sunday—killing time in the hope it would not kill her. Yet David thought that another lie. Mrs. Baxter was not hoping for anything. In her mind the bullet that had gone through Billy's brain was still racing through the air, round and round the world, causing her to duck every time the sun rose. Staring into her face as she talked, he was struck by the flatness in her eyes, twin dial tones, no one left on the line to call home.

Still, it was she who brought up Billy, which made his task easier. He let her talk for twenty minutes about the time she had gone camping in Yosemite with Rachel and Billy. She might have been confused in her recollection; as far as he knew there was no ocean in the Sierras. Slowly, he steered the conversation toward the days before Billy's suicide. She was burnt out but she was not stupid. She saw what he was doing and, perhaps in payment, immediately hit him with a shocking revelation.

"All he was doing those last weeks of school was hanging out with his girlfriend," she said. Seeing him blink, she hastily added, "No, David, I'm not senile. Not Rachel, his new girlfriend."

"Who was that?"

"I didn't know her name, he never talked about her. But I knew he was seeing her. I think she spent a couple of nights here. Her blond hair was all over his sheets."

"That's amazing. I never knew. He didn't say a word about her to you?"

"No. And when I asked him, he got angry. It was as if he was ashamed of her. At the time, though, I figured he was feeling guilty about dating so soon after Rachel."

"How long do you think he was seeing her before . . ." Well, before he blew his brains out, but David couldn't say that. It didn't matter, Mrs. Baxter understood.

"At least two months. I know because it was right after Easter that he got real depressed."

"I'm sorry, but Rachel died in December. I remember Billy being bummed out from then on."

Mrs. Baxter shook her head. "This was different. When he started seeing that new girl, he got much worse."

"But if he cared about her it should have made him feel better."

"That's what I thought. That's why I didn't press him for information about her. Anything to help him forget Rachel, I said to myself. But whoever she was, she was not good for him. It was like he couldn't even sleep after he met her. I used to hear him get up in the middle of the night and go out."

"Did she live in town?"

"I think so. He was able to run over to her house at a moment's notice."

"Did you ever hear her voice on the phone?"

"Once."

"Did it sound like anyone you knew?"

Mrs. Baxter frowned. "I'm not sure."

"She sounded familiar?"

"Maybe."

"Why didn't you tell me about her before?"

"He asked me not to."

"*What?*"

"Before he died, Billy made me swear. He said, 'Don't tell David or Charlie I'm seeing someone new.'" She added, "He said, 'No matter what happens.'"

"But when he was dead, you should have told me. She might have had something to do with what happened. You should have at least told the sheriff."

Her eyes sad, she turned and looked out the window. The stadium was just visible through an outstretched branch. "What difference would it have made? He told me not to, he was my son. I felt like I should honor his last wish."

"Then why do you tell me now?" he asked gently.

She turned and studied him. Her mind appeared to make a strange leap. Was it because she was confused or insightful? He was never sure with her. She was like Billy in that way, difficult to anticipate.

"I heard about that body you found at the beach," she said.

"Why bring that up? It has nothing to do with this."

"I heard she was blond."

David felt annoyed at the twist their talk had taken. And here he had thought he was steering things. "She's not the girl Billy was seeing back then. She's almost certainly from out of town."

"But you found her near the spot where he died."

"No. Who told you that? I found her a mile up the beach."

Mrs. Baxter nodded to herself. "That's pretty close. It could be her."

"The world is full of blond women. I'm sorry, but what could she possibly have to do with Billy?"

"I could ask you the same question. Isn't she the reason you came here today?"

"No." He felt compelled to repeat himself. "No."

Mrs. Baxter looked at him with her sad eyes, and for a moment she reminded him of his own mother. "Just don't do anything stupid, David. Do you hear me?"

She was talking nonsense. Billy had probably never had a mysterious girlfriend. Nevertheless, he promised her he wouldn't do anything stupid. Like put a gun in his mouth and pull the trigger, he thought, that would never happen.

His walk was full of surprises. Four blocks over from Mrs. Baxter's house was Karen's new place of residence. He remembered that he had promised to give Karen a call, and told himself that was the reason he was knocking on her door in the middle of the day when Charlie was probably out trying to find a second job so he could support her and the two girls. Yet David's conscience was clear as he stood on the porch. He was not one to screw around with a buddy's girl.

Then again, there had been that one time in high school, before Karen had gotten together with Charlie, when they had made out for over an hour in his car. They had gone pretty far that afternoon, but maybe not far enough in Karen's mind. In a weird way he suspected she had latched onto

Charlie because he had rejected her, which was not precisely true. When they had made out, Charlie had not officially been Karen's boyfriend but they had gone out twice. David had felt guilty about the whole thing, yet he had not lost any sleep over it. Also, then and now, he cared about Karen, but he did not love her.

She answered the door, surprise! The girls were at her mom's. She was alone, getting ready for work. With a lingering hug, she invited him in, offering him more coffee and Coke. By now he had enough caffeine in his system to wire a fax machine, so he said no, he was fine. He sat on the couch, she sat beside him. He gestured to her uniform.

"Love the outfit," he said.

"Yeah. Don't know why Rite Aid likes us to look like we're about to milk a cow while we're filling prescriptions."

"When do you have to be there?"

"I have a few minutes. It was nice of you to stop by."

"Duane's not around?"

"No. He's not around that much. The girls have never met him. And in case you want to know, he didn't spend the night."

David shrugged. "None of my business."

"What about Julie?"

"What about her?"

"Did you sleep with her?"

"None of your business."

Karen gave him a hard shove. "That slut—she's just using you."

"For what?"

"I'm not going to say, you don't want to hear. What are you up to right now?"

Karen was one of the few people in town he could really talk to—maybe the only one outside of Reverend Pomus—and it humbled him to realize that he had stopped to see her because he was desperate to unload. Ever since he had awakened from that nightmare on the plane, he had felt like the world was a little bit skewed. He shook his head at her question.

"Can I tell you some stuff that I don't want you to ever repeat?" he asked.

"Of course," she said.

Where to begin? Not on the jet, surely, but when he found the body. Yeah, that made sense, he began to tell her about the last twenty-four hours, with the exception of his time with Julie. He was not surprised when she did not interrupt. Karen had always been a great listener. He finished by telling her about his inability to answer some of Krane's questions, and his fainting spell at Sienna's house.

Karen sat, thoughtful. "Since she keeps calling, at least you know you didn't kill her."

David forced a laugh. "I wasn't *that* angry at her!"

Karen stared him in the eye. "Yeah, you were. She broke you in two. You hated her. You probably still do. But let's set that aside. What bothers you most about what you've told me?"

"Fainting at her house. The dizziness came on like a tidal wave. But at least I can rationalize that. I drank a lot last night, and you know me, I seldom drink. I was back in the exact spot where I first got close to Sienna. And the lemon tree was there."

"The what?"

"There was a strong odor of lemons in the bathroom. I think there was a tree right outside the window. To me, Sienna always smelled like lemons."

Karen nodded. "Most psychologists say a person's smell is what sticks in your head, even when the other person is far away. At the same time, that doesn't explain your fainting."

"Maybe I just went into overload."

"You miss her. But she's not a physical addiction. Your passing out worries me. It might have nothing to do with her. You should see a doctor."

"He'll just tell me I'm stressed and give me drugs."

"He'll examine you. You could have something wrong with your brain."

"You're reassuring."

"I'm not here to reassure you, I'm here to help. Why do you think you're having trouble remembering what happened that night?"

"I'm not sure. I didn't know I had blacked out some of that stuff until the FBI agent put me on the spot. For example, for the life of me I can't figure out how Sienna got home. Sure, I told Krane that she had a cell, that she called a taxi. But I don't know if that's true."

"Do you think she had a friend waiting for her at the parking lot?"

"No. Who could it be?"

"You said Herb and Mary seem to know things about her you didn't."

"Herb couldn't have been waiting for her that night. He would have had to be there for hours."

"But it is clear Sienna planned ahead of time to break up with you that night."

"I'm not sure about that."

"Her landlady told you she had moved out the previous week. She wasn't planning to move in with you, that's for sure."

"What's your point?"

"That night, when exactly does your memory fail?"

"After we made love the second time. No, during it."

"But by then she had already told you she was leaving you?"

"Yeah. Call it a mercy fuck if you want."

"Let's not call it anything. Can you remember coming the second time?"

"What kind of question is that?"

"If everything else is a blur, that should stand out. Do you remember or not?"

David strained for a minute. "No," he said finally.

"What is the last thing you do remember?"

"Lying beside the fire, feeling like I was going to die. Her on top of me."

"Why did you feel like you were going to die?"

"Isn't it obvious? She was everything to me and she had just pulled that I've-got-to-go-David rabbit out of her hat."

"Did you feel physically sick?"

"Yeah."

"Bad?"

"I felt awful. It wasn't like we made love. It was like I was drowning."

"That sounds pretty physical."

"There's nothing wrong with my brain."

"What's the next thing you remember after that?"

"I'm not sure, driving home."

"You don't remember walking back to your car?"

"Not really. Hey, you know what post-traumatic stress disorder is, don't you?"

"Sure," Karen said.

"Soldiers often get it after being in battle. I never believed in it before, thought those guys should just get over it and stop complaining. But now I'm a born-again believer. Honestly, I think that's what my problem is, not my brain."

"It's possible. A psychologist would probably say it's likely. But I know you, David. You've always been strong. You're not the kind to go into over-load."

"I have to tell you something. I was not myself around Sienna."

"And you haven't been yourself since she left?"

"True. But it's been different, since that night."

"How so?"

David shook his head. "I can't explain it. But it's like something big did happen, between us, and I've just covered it up in my mind. Does that make sense?"

"Yes. Can I make a suggestion?"

"As long as it does not involve a brain tumor."

"Why don't you get yourself hypnotized?"

David paused. "I've never done that before. Have you?"

"Lots of times. It's very therapeutic, very relaxing. There's this man in town I see every couple of months. If I called him, I bet I could get you an appointment pretty quick. He's never that busy and he's not that expensive. But he knows what he's doing."

"But what would he do?"

"Put you in a hypnotic state and take you back to that night. You will be shocked what you remember. And everything is absolutely confidential."

"I don't know, let me think about it."

"Suit yourself. But let me say one thing I am sure of. Under no circum-stances should you see Sienna, not in this state of mind."

"But Sienna is the only person who can tell me what went on that night."

"She won't tell you," Karen said.

"What are you talking about?"

"You don't get it, do you? That girl is screwing with you. Everything she has said and done since she met you has been designed to mess up your mind. And now look at you—big slabs of your brain have been carved out and hung up to dry in God knows what wasteland. Sure, I know she is a fox and sure I know she says she loves you, but she is a witch. If she comes here, if you see her, I guarantee you are going to suffer."

"I am suffering now."

Karen put her hand on his shoulder. "I understand, really. But you forget how much more you were suffering two months ago. If you see her, the pain will start all over again. And she'll love it, girls like her always do."

"You barely met her."

"But I *knew* her, better than you knew her. She won't tell you anything about that night if she sees you can't remember. She won't give up the power it gives her over you."

"Gimme a break."

"You're the main suspect in a murder you didn't commit. Has it occurred to you that Sienna might have something to do with that?"

"Karen. You're being silly."

She glanced at her watch and stood. "Unfortunately time will tell. I have to get to work. If you want to see that guy, call me at the store and I will set it up for you."

"Thanks," David said.

Outside again, David walked, making good time but heading in no particular direction. His talk with Karen had left him feeling better, although he was getting tired of her bashing Sienna. Why couldn't she admit she was jealous and leave it at that? But the hypnotist was probably a wise suggestion, and it couldn't hurt to get a physical. Maybe he had a virus, there were lots of those going around. Like in the movie last night, he might have caught something from outer space. Anything was possible. The idea was more pleasant than the alternatives. On the other hand, he could not feel too badly about what was wrong with him when he was not sure if anything was wrong.

He ended up walking to the cemetery. Billy and Rachel had been buried beside each other—nondescript plots without views. He was surprised to find fresh flowers on both graves. The roses contained the only colors besides green in the whole place. Briefly, he wondered who had left them, while at the same time, he didn't care. Sitting on the grass between the two graves, he tried to imagine what it would be like to be dead. He had not been to the cemetery in years.

Then he saw Reverend Pomus and his daughter, Mary, hand in hand, walking the perimeter of the cemetery: he in his big brown suit, his dark tie flapping like a cloud of bad breath; she in a black miniskirt so short she may as well have been standing on her head. The cemetery was a square block—they walked each side. And in that whole time they did not so much as glance in his direction, although he was the only soul around. They did not seem to be talking. David had been worrying about her half the morning, and the sight of her spending quality time with her father should have been reassuring. But when they started on their second lap around the goddamn place, he began to wonder.

Still, they did not look at him, not until the end of the second lap. Then Reverend Pomus leaned over and kissed his daughter on the lips good-bye and left her standing in the south corner of the cemetery like a white statue dipped in black ink. Her gaze turned to him, and even over the distance, he could feel her eyes on him like a pair of cold hands. He remembered, seven years ago, pulling her from the sea, how icy her skin had been. He had been sure she was dead.

She walked toward him, slowly, her smile growing like the unfolding wings of a moth, so casual she could have been naked. If possible, she had on even more makeup than this morning. The gum she chewed was purple, the same color as her eyeliner, and she was popping bubbles as fast as she could make them. For some reason, he was sure she wanted him to stand at her approach, so he remained sitting.

"What ya doin'?" she asked, stopping less than three feet away, her pale legs roads to the moon. Fifteen going on twenty. But if she was trying to make him uncomfortable, she failed. He kept his eyes on her face.

"Catching up with old friends," he said.

She stopped smiling, nodded. "They were your best friends?"

"Yeah. You were five when they died. I don't suppose you remember them?"

"I remember Billy. He was cute. He killed himself?"

"Yeah."

"How did he do it?"

"A gun."

"How?"

"Mary. That's gross."

"Sorry." She touched his knee with the tip of her black boot. It was pointed—a kick in the balls could change a guy's life. "Are you feeling sad?" she asked.

"No." He paused. "I'm worried about you."

She smiled. "Don't be fooled by my personal appearance. I am a perfectly well-adjusted teenage girl. And I owe it all to you."

"You don't owe me anything."

"You saved my life. I must owe you something." She moved a step closer, and now he could not look up without looking up her skirt. Of course she had no underwear on. She added, "I would *love* to pay you back."

David shook his head, sighed and stood. "I am too old for you, Mary. You are too young for me. You are too young, period. Why do you go around dressed like that?"

"It reflects my inner mood."

"Then you must be in an awfully dark place."

She giggled. "I'm happier than you. Just look at you, sitting in a cemetery in the middle of the day. That's a pretty creepy thing to do."

"Well, you're in the same cemetery in the middle of the day."

"That's different, I came to see you." She nodded to the roses. "And the flowers Herb left."

David was stunned. "Herb left these? How do you know that?"

"He's always leaving flowers here. Didn't you know?"

"No. Why does he do it?"

"I never ask." She added, "He must feel guilty or something."

"Why do you hang out with him?"

"It's something to do. He's my father's pet. He needs attention."

"Do you like him?"

She patted him on the chest, flat palm, naughty grin. "I like you more."

"Drop the seduction routine, it bores me."

She laughed. "That's why I love you, David! You know, you're the only guy in town your age who doesn't want to fuck me."

"I doubt that."

"It's true." She popped her gum, offered her arm. "Will you walk me home?"

He hesitated. "Okay."

She did not lead him in the direction of Reverend Pomus's home, however. Rather, they headed back toward David's house. She explained that she had moved out, that she was living in one of Herb's rentals. Not with Herb, though—she was quick to point that out.

"I wouldn't sleep with him if he drugged me," she said, as they exited the cemetery and walked toward the same road he had taken to the beach yesterday afternoon.

"But how could your father let you move out?" he asked.

"He has a lot on his mind. As long as I am well-fed, he doesn't care."

"I find that hard to believe."

Mary was amused. "You've lived in this town all your life. You should be a true believer by now."

"I don't know what you're talking about."

"Sure you do. Has your girlfriend called back?"

"Yeah. Why do you ask?"

"Just making conversation."

"Did you and Herb really have breakfast with Sienna?"

"Lots of times."

"You've got to tell me what you talked about."

"When Herb was there, we hardly talked about anything. He was always hitting on her."

"How did she take it?"

"She ignored him. Then, when he wasn't there, we talked about you."

"Really?"

"Yeah. She was always trying to act like she cared about you. But I knew she was full of shit."

"And how did you know that?"

Mary stared at him. "It was obvious."

Again, David felt creeped out by her eyes. "She never mentioned you once."

"That doesn't surprise me."

Her house was only four blocks from his, a one-bedroom unit no bigger than his own. The place was clean enough, although the front lawn was completely dead. Indeed, it looked as if someone had poured gasoline over it. She tried to invite him in, but he told her he had to go.

"Got a date?" she asked.

"Yeah."

"Who?"

"None of your business."

"Julie Stevens?"

"Where did you hear that?"

"Daddy. Doing her?"

"No."

"Liar. She's a dyke, you know."

"Right. You're the one who's full of shit."

Mary's eyes were blue-black, the color of twilight, and now they sparkled with distant stars as she laughed again. It struck him then how carefree she sounded, how self-assured. Not the least bit like a troubled fifteen-year-old. She licked her lips, her tongue the same color as her purple gum.

"It's true. I know because I've done her," she said.

And with that she turned and went inside.

TEN

Home was the same as he had left it. Only two hours had passed and the red light on his answering machine was blinking. He wasted no time checking who had called.

"*Hi, David, it's Sienna again. You're a hard man to get ahold of. This is the fifth time I've called. I'm beginning to think you've got a new girlfriend. Anyway, don't bother calling back, I'm going out right now with my friend and we'll be out late. But I'll try to get you tomorrow. I haven't changed my mind, I really want to see you. I hope you haven't changed your mind, either. Love you, honey. . . .*"

Again, her message warmed his heart, and again, it annoyed him he could be so easily moved. He kept thinking what Karen had said, how Sienna was just playing with his head. But she sounded sincere enough on the message.

At the same time, he did not want to see Sienna before he had a clearer idea of what had happened that night. Karen was right about that—it gave Sienna too much power over him, even if the subject was never brought up. The hypnotist was sounding like a better idea all the time.

He made a point to save the message. The sheriff would hear this one.

Picking up the phone, David called the drugstore. Karen answered, and he asked if he could get an appointment for today.

"Feeling desperate?" she asked.

"No. You're the one who said he's not that busy."

"Let me call him and see. But you don't sound good."

"Quit telling me that. I sound fine. There is just a lot going on."

"Did she call again?"

He hesitated. "Yes."

"Did you talk to her?"

"No. But we're going to talk tomorrow."

She was silent a moment. "I'm not saying anything."

"Karen. You're always saying something."

"Only because I love you."

"I know. Seriously, I appreciate you talking to this guy for me. I think it could help."

"It will. But I need to warn you. The main reason people suppress memories is because they're traumatic. Going into this, you have to accept that something happened that night that was extremely upsetting."

"Duh. That was the night she dumped me."

"No, David, something else must have happened. I just want to warn you is all."

"I understand. Hey, can I ask you something off the wall?"

"Is it about my sex life?"

"It's about Julie Stevens. Have you ever heard that she is a lesbian?"

"Not in a long time."

"What does that mean?"

"In high school there was a rumor going around that she had gone down on Mrs. Miller."

"The psychology teacher? She was old."

"We were young. She was only forty at the time. That was the rumor, I don't know how true it was. Why do you ask?"

"Heard a rumor myself. Call me when you've talked to the hypnotist. I'll be here working."

"I'll call him the first chance I get. Bye!"

Working, sure. The manuscript seemed to stare at him as he set down the phone. He had promised himself he would avoid slipping into a dark mood by keeping himself busy and here he had done nothing useful all day. All he had to do was read right now, he could return to his drawing later. Why was he avoiding the book? It was almost as if the curse that was slipping over Cleo's life was affecting him.

David picked up the manuscript, made himself comfortable on the couch. Where had he left Cleo? Oh yeah, she was feeling more and more human and she was going to see Hector, an old friend who used to love her, or who still loved her. It depressed him to find that immortals suffered the same way humans did.

We decide to meet at a restaurant by the beach at twelve noon. It seems the bright sun is no longer a consideration, to either of us, and that tells me much. I arrive before he does—Hector has never been punctual. The view of the ocean is a delight, the sandy coast trailing north and south like a path without a goal. The waitress asks if I would like a drink and I order wine. Hector and his expensive taste in wines. For three hundred years he lived in Paris so he could order the perfect year. He knew them all, my old friend.

I find I am nervous, and the realization makes me more uncomfortable. Always around Hector I have held the eternal ace—he loves me and I do not love him. But this afternoon I feel he knows something I do not know. And I cannot disguise from myself how human I feel. The wine the waitress brings me tastes even better than blood.

Finally, he arrives, six feet tall, black as tar, handsome as an old memory, looking exactly as he did when we met twenty-five thousand years ago in Ash's laboratory. But he is not exactly the same as when we last met, thirty years ago. Even my weakened eyesight notices the changes. He is undergoing the same transformation as I am. He is no longer a vampire. That fact makes me relax. At the back of my mind I had feared he would kill me if he knew I was weak. His love for me has always been a volatile thing.

"Cleo," he says, and I stand for the hug and kiss. "I am so happy to see you again. You look as beautiful as ever."

"You are too kind," I reply. We sit and the waitress brings us more wine, which pleases Hector. He compliments me on my choice and has an extra glass, and we order food. He asks for steak, well-done, and I nod that I will have the same. We say little as we wait for our food, just enjoy the view, the flawless sky, the sun on the water, sparkling like a million stars that will never be found in the heavens. Hector sits with a serene smile, and out of politeness I match his demeanor. But inside all I can think about is what is happening to us. Already, though, I know he is happy with the change.

Our food comes, we eat and drink. Hector calls for another bottle. The flush in his face tells me he is now capable of getting drunk. The meat is good, the baked potato salty and creamy. I eat more than I should; it is almost as if my body demands the food. Hector notes my appetite.

"You will lose your girlish figure," he says.

I set down my fork. "Is that possible?" I ask.

He shrugs. "It should not be."

"Do you wish to talk here?"

"We can talk. What is there to talk about?"

"When did it start for you?"

"A month ago. You?"

"The same. Everything is changing?"

"It has changed. It is done, I think, at least for me. I am human again."

"How does that make you feel?"

"Do you need to ask? I can feel again."

"Is that a good thing?"

"You have to answer your own questions, Cleo. Why did you call me here?"

"To talk. To try to understand what is happening. Ash made us immortal. How can we become otherwise?"

"You ask if he gave me a warning of this change?"

"Yes."

Hector thinks. "He might have. Ash was fond of speaking in riddles. When I was with him, near the end, in his laboratory, he showed me how he spiraled the elixir he fed us around a magnetic field. He said that for each revolution the substance passed through, a year would be added to our lives." Hector pauses. "Of course I thought he was joking."

"How many revolutions did he put the elixir through?"

"I don't know. It doesn't matter."

"It does to me," I say.

Hector nods. "The point is he planned a limit to our immortality."

"How come you never told me this before?"

"I told you, I thought he was joking."

"Ash was never much for jokes. You didn't tell me because you thought it would upset me."

"You are upset."

"You use the word 'plan.' Do you think he knew we would change now?"

"I don't think he could predict the future."

"That is not what I am asking."

"But it is. You want to believe that Ash had a master plan for all of us. Even when he died, you wanted to believe that."

"You always said you thought he was still alive."

"I said a lot of things. None of it matters. We are alive, but now we can die. Is that a terrible thing? We have been given back the choice."

"One choice has been given to us, another has been taken away."

Hector reaches over and takes my hand. "Cleo. Long ago we realized we could do nothing to help the world, its people—that we could only do harm. Our lives have no meaning. Even our own pleasure cannot be told from pain. What is there left to do? I tell you; nothing. Let us enjoy our humanity, one last time, and then let us die."

I stare at his strong black hand and feel my lip tremble. "What about love?"

"What do we love?"

"I thought you still loved me."

"I do. But that is not enough reason to live. It is more a reason to die."

I have to smile; although he is right, it hurts. "Love does not give you hope?"

He studies me. Even though he is black, his eyes are a dark blue, deep water in a cold place. "What are you afraid of?" he asks.

I take back my hand. "I am not sure."

He reaches for his wine, drinks. "Do you want me to come home with you?"

I sigh. "You can if you want."

Later that night, naked in bed together, he asks me if I still love Ash.

"A man asked me that a few weeks ago," I say. "Just before I killed him. I told him that I still thought about Ash every day, and assumed that meant I loved him. But I don't know if that is true."

Staring at the ceiling, Hector nods. "I think about you every day."

I get on my knees, look down. "But not this last month?"

My insight surprises him, but he recovers quickly. "It is not like my love for you was merely a product of the elixir."

"How do you know? The compass might have gotten fixed in one direction."

"No. I loved you before Ash changed us."

"I did not know that. You gave no sign."

"How could I? Ash was there, he was powerful. We were just, you know, people. We knew nothing."

My stomach feels unsettled. "Do you still think about Ash?"

"Never."

"But you still think he's alive. Don't deny it, I know you do. And you must have a reason. Tell me."

Again, I surprise him. But not as much as he does me.

"I saw him once," he says.

I almost fall off the bed. "When?"

"Two thousand years ago, in Rome. I thought I saw him at the Coliseum. A face in the crowd."

"But you were not sure?"

"No. But it looked like him, and he was looking my way."

"Did you try to approach him?"

"No. I thought if he wanted to speak to me, he would find me. I was well known in the Senate then, everyone knew my name." He shrugs. "But I never heard from him."

I shake my head, stand, my stomach getting worse. "You never told me this before, either."

"I didn't want it to drive you crazy. Where are you going?"

"To the bathroom, I have to throw up."

The act of vomiting disturbs me more than it should. When I return to the bed, Hector wants to make love again but I push him away. For a long time he does not say anything, does not even move. Finally, though, he turns away.

"My love for you used to give me hope," he says.

"I am sorry," I say.

I hear him smile. "Cleo. My love."

He sleeps, and I begin to dream as well. Of Ash, a face in the crowd.

David set aside the book. Someone was knocking at his door. Getting up, he put the manuscript on the coffee table and covered it with a T-shirt from his suitcase, which he had yet to fully unpack. Again the story had sucked him in, thanks to the author's sparse style. He was not happy about being interrupted. He had a suspicion what was going to happen next in the story, and wanted to see if he was right.

"Hi, handsome!" Julie said when he opened the door. She was all blue jeans and blond hair, her smile so bright he needed sunglasses, the perfect contrast to Cleo's dark mood.

"Hey, what are you doing here?" he asked.

Her face fell. "That's no way to say hello. You told me to come over in a couple of hours and it has been a couple of hours. But I can go if you're busy."

He remembered now: he had said three hours and she had said she would call before coming. She was here, though, there was no reason to be rude. And she looked pretty damn good. Once more, he felt an unexpected wave of affection for her. Reaching out, he gave her a hug, which she was happy to reciprocate.

"I'm sorry, I was working and I forgot what we had talked about," he said. "Please, come in. You look great. Can I get you something to drink?"

"A Coke would be great."

"I have Cokes." As she came inside, he pointed to her Las Vegas T-shirt, the golden MGM lion set in a dark blue sky. He asked, "You interview in that?"

"Silly, I went home and changed. Have you been to Vegas?"

"Sure." He went into the kitchen, dug out two red cans.

Julie was looking around, sort of carefully. "When was the last time?"

"I don't know, four months ago." He had gone with Sienna. They had stayed at the Tropicana, across the street from the MGM. He handed Julie the Coke. "Do you want a glass?" he asked.

"No. This is fine. Did you have fun?" Julie asked.

"I'm not much of a gambler. After two days I'd had enough. When did you go?"

"Five months ago, with my ex. We played a lot of blackjack. I love it, I can get totally addicted. When we were there I won over a thousand bucks. Pretty neat, huh?"

David opened his drink. He was thirsty again; the walk had dehydrated him more than he'd realized. He was pretty sweaty; he hoped he didn't stink. "I lost two hundred," he said.

"Who'd you go with?"

"A friend."

She smiled. "A mystery friend?"

He shrugged. "It was not a big deal."

Julie stared at him a moment, her lower lip trembled slightly. She had on a tad of lipstick, cherry red—her mouth looked like dessert. All of a sudden he wanted to kiss her. She was asking about Sienna, though, she was giving him an opening.

"Julie," he began, but then the phone rang. God, what if that was Sienna? He answered quickly, Julie's eyes following him all the way across the room.

It was Karen.

"Got you an appointment in thirty minutes. Do you want it?" she asked.

"Karen, hi, yeah. That soon?"

Karen's voice was flat. "You're not alone. The bitch or the witch?"

"Julie's here, yeah. She says hi. Does it have to be in thirty minutes?"

"Don't lie. She didn't say hi. She didn't say shit. That's when he's available. I can call and cancel, but you sounded so worried—I went ahead and scheduled it. But don't feel pressured. If you want to do Julie instead I'll call him back and tell him you're fucked beyond hope. It's entirely up to you."

"Since you put it that way, I'll take the appointment. What's his name and address?" David picked up a pen.

"James Candle. He's on Score Road, number twelve-forty-five. He likes to be paid in cash. One hundred bucks. That's a deal, in case you're wondering."

"Do you pay him that?"

"No. But I'm an easy subject. I keep the assholes in my life to a bare minimum. Don't be late, David. He's a nice guy but he's got his quirks."

"I won't be late. Thanks, I'll let you know how it goes."

"Please do. Give Julie all my love."

David set down the phone. Julie was watching him.

"That was Karen," he said.

"You talk to her a lot?"

"Yeah. She's one of my best friends."

"You have an appointment you have to get to?"

"Yeah. I have this . . . this guy I need to see. I better take a shower, change. Can we get together later?"

"Sure." Her eyes lit up. "Want to take a shower together?"

The answer was yes, he did. But he shook his head. "I have to hurry," he said.

Julie held up her Coke can. "Mind if I finish my drink?"

He headed toward the bathroom. "Not at all. Have a seat. Sorry I have to run out. I hope I'm not being rude."

"You could never be rude, David."

He took a cold shower. The water felt like ice but his clammy skin appreciated it. He half expected Julie to barge in on him, but she left him alone. Drying with a towel that was as old as his first painting, he wondered how one dressed for a hypnotist. He decided he should be as comfortable as possible, pulled on a pair of pair of lightweight sweats and an oversized T-shirt.

When he returned to the front room, Julie told him a woman had called. He almost had a heart attack. "You answered my phone?" he asked.

"No. She left a message on your machine, and you have the volume on." Julie shrugged, still sitting, none too happy. "I wasn't trying to be nosy, I just thought you should know."

David could see the light on his machine. He tried to sound casual. "What did she say?" he asked.

"Nothing. Just that she was sorry she missed you, and she would try to get you later. Who is she?"

He hesitated. "Vegas."

"Ah." Julie sipped her drink. "Do you want to tell me about her?"

"Not now, you know, I have to run out."

Julie stood, threw her can in his garbage, forced a smile. "Are we still on for this evening?" she asked.

"Sure. Can I call you when I'm done?"

"I have some stuff I have to do. Can I call you? Do you have a cell?"

"Yeah, I have one. I'll take it with me. Let me give you the number."

He had to search for his cell. He did not normally carry it when he was in town. He gave the number to Julie and she memorized it on the spot. She did not write it down.

Walking her to the door, she suddenly turned and kissed him. It was not a bad kiss. Holding her was not bad either—she felt good in his arms. When they were done, she smiled again, and this time she was happy.

"I know we just got together," she said. "I can't expect you to have been living a monk's life. You don't have to hide anything from me. What I mean is, if you are seeing someone, I'm not worried about them. I know who I am and I know how I feel when I'm with you. Does that make sense?"

He forced a chuckle. "You're saying you can blow away the competition?"

She giggled. "Yeah. *Blow* it right away." She kissed him quickly, turned to leave. "Keep your phone on. I'll be calling soon."

"Okay," he said.

When she was gone, he checked the message.

"Hi, David, it's me. I'm still out but thought I would try one or more time. Sorry I missed you. Let me call you in the morning. Bye."

No I love yous. He was grateful for the bland message, but was surprised she had tried at all. After all, she had already said she was not going to call again until tomorrow.

ELEVEN

James Candle was much older than David had figured he would be. When the man answered the door of his modest home, David was sure he had the wrong place. The guy was white and wheezing, more wrinkled than a load of laundry. David could not imagine lying on a couch in a trance while listening to that sound. He'd worry the dude would die. Besides the heavy breathing and the finger-size liver spots all over his skull, Mr. Candle had the posture of a banana. When he took a deep breath, David imagined that large chunks of his flaky skin were about to peel off.

The strange thing was, when Mr. Candle was inside and seated in a comfortable chair, his breathing difficulty almost vanished and his posture greatly improved. His chair was like an extra skeleton for him. It was only when they were seated across from each other that David noticed how sharp the old man's eyes were. He studied him closely.

"Karen says you're having trouble remembering a traumatic instance," he said. "It might help if we talk about it before I hypnotize you. If that is all right with you?"

"That would be fine. As long as what we discuss in this room stays in this room."

Mr. Candle nodded. "Karen may not have told you this but I used to be a clinical psychologist. I'm still licensed in the state of California. Everything we talk about carries the doctor-patient privilege of privacy."

"Good." Yet even before he began to explain his memory lapse, David set very definite borders of where he would not go. He had no intention of bringing up the dead body on the beach and Krane's investigation into him. He liked Mr. Candle already but affection and trust were two separate things.

David talked in a general fashion about his last night with Sienna. He explained that they had sex on the beach, and Sienna surprised him by breaking up. But he did not go into the extent of his agony over the breakup. Perhaps it was unnecessary. Mr. Candle nodded as if he understood.

"And you are blank on what happened the rest of the night?" he asked.

"Sort of. I do remember returning home and going to bed. But that's it."

"Have you ever been hypnotized before?"

"No. But I have read about it. I think I understand it well enough."

"What do you understand?"

"That it involves suggestion, and it is relaxing. I know most people can be hypnotized."

"In this session, I will make some suggestions to you—at the start. But when we go back to that night, you are going to tell me what you see, not the other way around. My suggestions will cease at that point."

"Got it."

"Also, although most people can be hypnotized, the majority cannot reach a deep trance state. You may be one of those people, I cannot tell at this point."

"Do you think I will need a deep state to remember?"

"It's possible. Even under hypnosis, people can block traumatic events. I might even go so far as to say that unless you are completely sincere about wanting to remember that night, you will continue to block it."

"I want to know what happened."

Mr. Candle held his eye. "Are you sure?"

David shrugged. "I came here to remember."

"Very good. Do you feel ready to begin?"

David felt a flash of fear. "Why not?"

Mr. Candle stood and lowered the blinds; the room turned dark. He suggested David push back the chair he was sitting on. It was a big old comfortable thing; leaning back, David feared he might doze. He watched as Mr.

Candle turned a spotlight on a black-and-white spiral. A metronome was started and the spiral began to spin.

"Stare at the center of the spiral," Mr. Candle said. "Listen to the sound of the metronome. Relax, let go. I am going to count backward from ten. As I do so your eyes will begin to grow heavy and you will want to close them. Ten . . . nine . . . eight. . . ."

Staring at the spinning spiral was a novel experience. David was stunned at how quickly it cast its spell. He felt himself sinking, and before Mr. Candle got to five he had to close his eyes. The metronome continued to tick, although it sounded far away.

Yet at the same time he did not think he was hypnotized. He was too aware of the room, his body. He was more relaxed, true, but he did not feel in a trance. Mr. Candle finished counting and spoke to him some more, his voice very soft.

"Now imagine a stream of white light pouring into you from the ceiling. This light is warm and soothing. It fills you and surrounds you, and protects you from any outside influences. Imagine it and it becomes real."

David was not so sure about that. He had no problem imagining the white light pouring into his body, but for some reason it brought him no comfort. Indeed, it made him anxious. Yet he continued to feel as if he was sinking, and he supposed that was good. He realized the metronome had halted but could not say when it had stopped.

"I am going to count from one to twenty," Mr. Candle said. "As I count you are going to feel yourself rising up. Not out of your body, but into a higher and higher state of awareness. Rising up into a state of consciousness where you are fully able to contact your subconscious mind. One . . . two . . . three . . . you are rising up . . . four . . . five . . . six . . ."

Again, David was not sure he was having the expected results. The sinking sensation had graduated into a feeling of falling. It was not terrifying—he was not falling fast—but it was not pleasant either. The higher Mr. Candle counted, the deeper he fell. The gentleman sounded miles away. David noticed his breathing had slowed to a crawl. Despite all this, he was still not convinced he was hypnotized. He felt more sleepy than anything else.

"You are now in a deep state of hypnosis," Mr. Candle said. "You are relaxed and safe. Nothing can harm you. You now have access to your subconscious mind. You can see and remember everything that has happened to you in this life. Do you understand?"

"Yes," David whispered, amazed he could speak at all.

"How do you feel?"

"Okay."

"Do you feel ready to return to the night in question?"

David hesitated. "Maybe . . ."

"Are you afraid to remember that night?"

"Yes."

"Why are you afraid?"

"Don't know."

"The white light surrounds and protects you. Nothing can harm you."

"No."

"No what?"

"The light is . . . not there."

"Visualize the white light as a pillar. It pours into you from above, filling your head and heart. You are safe in the white light."

"No light . . . not there." David could hear himself speak, could sense the truth. The light was definitely not there, and his anxiety was growing. Mr. Candle took a moment to decide on a different approach.

"Is there a reason the light is not there?"

"Yes."

"What is the reason?"

"It is . . . obscene."

"Is it connected to the night in question?"

"Yes."

"Do you know the reason?"

"Yes." And he felt as if he did know, without knowing, and that the reason was much worse than he could have imagined. Yet he could not consciously remember what it was.

"Can you tell me the reason?"

"No."

"Why not?"

He did not know what to say so he said nothing.

"You know but you don't know?" Mr. Candle asked.

"Yes."

"Can we take you back to that night?"

"I am afraid."

"You don't have to be afraid. Nothing can harm you."

"No."

"No what?"

"You don't know." Again, David sensed the truth of his words. Mr. Candle was way out of his league on this one. At the same time, David didn't care what the man knew or didn't know. Even with the questions, he continued to sink, but slowly now. It was as if he floated in velvet darkness. Any question of light and protection was silly. What had happened that night had happened. It could not be changed now.

"Let us go back in time," Mr. Candle said from many light years away. "Feel yourself return to the beginning of summer. It is now two months ago and you are at the beach with Sienna. It is nighttime, you are beside the ocean. Can you see the ocean?"

"Yes." That was true, he could see the sea as if it were on TV inside his brain, the dark water churning in the warm night breeze like foam in a drunkard's final drink. But he could not see Sienna, he did not want to look into her face.

"Tell me what you see," Mr. Candle said.

"It is dark. There is a fire, I have made a fire. It is warm and I am cold. I have been swimming. I lie beside the fire. Someone is talking to me."

"Who is talking? Is it Sienna?"

"I am talking."

"But who is talking to you?"

"I am."

"You are talking to yourself?"

"Don't know."

"Look around, what do you see?"

"Skin. Naked skin."

"Is it Sienna?"

"Yes."

"What is she doing?"

"Talking."

"What does she say?"

"She says she has to go."

"She has to leave you?"

"No . . . yes."

"What do you say to her?"

"I am . . . scared."

"Why are you scared?"

"I am going to die."

"Why do you think you are going to die?"

"I am."

"But why?"

"It is . . . obscene."

"The reason you are going to die?"

"Yes."

"But how are you going to die?"

"With a knife."

"You think someone is going to kill you with a knife?"

"Yes."

"Who is going to kill you?"

He heard the question. He understood what was being asked. But all he could see was fire; her naked skin had momentarily vanished. The red flames seemed to grow taller in the darkness until it was the fire and not the white light that was standing like a pillar in his heart and brain. Drawing a breath into his body, he felt as if he were trying to animate a corpse. Yet a part of him desperately wanted to answer the question.

"Sienna is going to kill me," he said.

"She is going to kill you with a knife?"

"Yes. No . . ."

"Do you see the knife?"

"No."

"How do you know she has a knife?"

"I know."

"How?"

"I brought it."

"You brought a knife to the beach that night?"

"Yes."

"Why?"

"To kill me."

"I don't understand."

"It cannot be understood."

"Back up. You see the ocean. You see and feel the fire. You see Sienna. What is she doing besides talking?"

Sienna came back into view. Naked, so naked.

"She is crying," he replied.

"Why is she crying?"

"She is scared."

"Why is she scared?"

"She doesn't want to die."

"Why is she afraid she is going to die?"

"Because of the knife. She has to die."

"Do you plan to hurt her? Are you angry at her for breaking up with you?"

"I am angry."

"Are you angry enough to hurt her?"

"I am scared."

"Did you know she was going to break up with you? Is that why you brought the knife to the beach?"

"No."

"Why did you bring the knife to the beach?"

"To kill me."

"I don't understand. Explain."

"No." He could not explain. Sienna was talking. She was crying, he was arguing with her. Still wet, the dark strands of her hair clung to her face and shoulders like a lie broken in a thousand places. Her eyes burned with the light of the fire; she could have been a cat cursed to crawl over a mile of dying embers. She was telling him she had to go but she kept looking away, down the beach, at the dark sand dunes behind them. Even through the pain of her rejection he saw she was terrified. That she was waiting to die.

"What do you see?" Mr. Candle asked. "What is she saying?"

"She wants me to hold her. I want to be held."

"Where is the knife?"

"Near."

"Does she know about the knife?"

"Yes."

"Do you know about the knife?"

"No . . . Yes."

"Where is the knife?"

"In her bag, by the fire."

"She brought a bag with her to the beach?"

"Yes."

"I am confused."

"Yes."

"What happens next?"

"We hold each other. We kiss. We cry."

"You are crying as well?"

"Yes."

"Go on. Tell me what happens."

"I am afraid."

"You don't have to be afraid. You are safe here in this room. Nothing can harm you."

"You are wrong."

"Why am I wrong? What can harm you?"

His voice croaked. "Many things."

"I don't understand. Explain."

"No."

"Why don't you explain?"

"No."

"You are holding her, she is holding you. You are crying. You kiss. Tell me what happens next."

"We lie beside the fire. We touch each other. We get aroused."

"Do you want to make love?"

"Yes."

"Is the fear gone?"

"No. It is worse."

"Why?"

"Because I must die now."

"Why must you die?"

"I must. It was . . . agreed."

"You agreed to die?"

"Yes. It was . . . obscene."

"What is Sienna doing right now?"

"Looking down at me." And he was looking up at her, through her tangled web of hair. Into her wet and burning eyes, her head even. He saw her so clearly he saw himself, even felt his penis as it thrust deep inside her. He could have been plowing the moon. She was not wet and his dick was hurting her but it did not matter because the knife was near, so very near. . . .

"Tell me what happens next," Mr. Candle said.

"She stops."

"She stops what?"

"Making love to me."

"Why?"

"She wants me to roll over. She says she wants to rub my back. She wants me to lie close to the fire. She says it will make me feel better."

"Does it make you feel better?"

"No. She hurts me."

"How does she hurt you?"

She pinched him. He could see her nails, and something else. Red and silver.

He could see it all.

There was an explosion of sound. It was as if a meteorite had plunged through Mr. Candle's ceiling. David felt himself snapped from the deep well of his past and for several seconds he didn't even know who he was. His heart pounded and there was an excruciating ringing in his head.

"It's your cell phone," Mr. Candle said, sounding annoyed. "Don't answer it."

David opened his eyes, winced at the change in head pressure. The phone was on the table beside him. He had forgotten to turn it off because he never used it. Damn that Julie, she had made him bring it. Giving Mr. Candle what must have been a dazed look, he picked up the phone anyway.

"Hello?" he mumbled.

The voice was distant. "David?"

"Hey, it's you . . . God."

She paused. "Is something wrong? You sound awful."

"You caught me at a bad time. Can I call you back?"

"Sure." She hung up. Just like that.

"Christ," David whispered, setting down the phone and rubbing his aching head. He felt as if he had been blown by the jet stream. His eyes refused to focus, although he was able to see Mr. Candle stand and walk to the window. The light from the rising blinds did nothing to ease the pain between his ears. He shielded his eyes, gasped, "Please."

"Oh." Mr. Candle lowered the blinds halfway. "It's never a good idea to come out so quick."

David closed his eyes and took a couple of deep breaths. "I believe you."

Mr. Candle sat across from him. "Do you need more time?"

David opened his eyes, blinked. "It's going away."

"What's going away?"

"The disorientation."

"Do you still remember what happened that night? Usually, when I end a session, I give suggestions that you will retain everything you saw."

"Yeah, I remember. But it's not like I saw much."

"You spoke of a knife?"

David replied quickly. Like everyone else in town, the hypnotist must have heard about the body on the beach, and who had found it. "I don't know what that was about. I never saw any knife."

"But in the session you understood that it was there."

"I'm not sure. It was confusing."

Mr. Candle nodded. "I have to admit that was the strangest regression I have ever done. The subconscious often glimpses things it cannot explain but it seldom contradicts itself. You were all over the place. Did you see what happened after Sienna massaged you?"

"No. I assume we continued to have sex."

"Why assume that? You said several times how frightened she was."

"I did?"

"Don't you remember?"

"Well, yes, but I don't think she was behaving exactly the way you think she was."

"What do you mean?"

"Look, do we have to talk about this now? I don't feel so good."

"We need to do more than talk. You have to go back under, continue to explore that night. You were on the verge of a breakthrough."

"How do you know?"

"I have experience in the field. You had just reached the main point in the night that you are blocking."

David stood, although it required tremendous effort. The helium in his brain cells was leaking badly. He held onto his chair for support. "I don't want any more hypnosis today. I'll call Monday, set up another appointment." He reached for his wallet. "I owe you a hundred, right?"

Mr. Candle waved his hand. "Don't worry about the money. Stay, it's important. You came out suddenly. It's as if you've left a door half open in your subconscious. That is never a good idea. You need to go back and settle this thing once and for all."

"There's nothing to settle. Anyway, I think I saw all I am going to see."

"David, listen to yourself."

"What?"

"You are scared."

"I'm not scared. What is there to be scared of?"

"That is what we are trying to discover. You were scared in the session and you are scared now. Please, I don't think we need a lot of time. You are an excellent subject. You went very deep right away. You are here, you may as well face what you . . . face this thing."

David paused, spoke in a cold voice. "You were about to say I may as well face what I did."

Mr. Candle shook his head. "I'm not a judge. I'm only here to help you discover the truth."

"She just called."

"What?"

"Sienna. That was her on the phone. I didn't kill her that night."

"I never said you did."

"But you were thinking it." David stepped toward the front door. "Good-bye, Mr. Candle. Thank you for your time. But I think you have helped me all you can."

TWELVE

When David got home, he felt rough, on a couple of levels. The unexpected call had shocked his nervous system more than he had realized. After leaving Mr. Candle's, he'd had trouble keeping his car on the road. His heart kept fluttering in his chest and the pressure in his head returned with a vengeance, creating sparks at the edge of his field of view. It was almost as if he had slipped into deep-freeze hibernation during the hypnotic session, and Sienna's call had thawed him out by dropping him into a pot of boiling water. The second he got inside he popped four Tylenol and laid down on the couch and closed his eyes.

Why did she keep calling when she was out with that *guy?* He could not return the calls—like they had discussed—because she was on the move and he didn't know her cell number. Sitting up, briefly, he tried anyway, using the Orange County number, for all the good it did. He got the guy's machine: "Hi, this is David, please leave a message after the tone." So they shared the same name—wasn't that just great? Lucky Sienna, she didn't have to worry about whose name she called out when she climaxed.

Groaning, David laid back down and pleaded for the Tylenol to hurry up and dissolve in his bloodstream. He probably should have talked to her when he had her on the phone. She had called so many times and they'd yet to have a decent conversation.

The other reason he felt like hell was the memories the session had stirred, or rather, the *pseudo* memories. Much of what he had said aloud while hypnotized he had not actually seen. It was more like he had *sensed* a hazy truth of the events and narrated them spontaneously, without filtering them through his mind. Of course that was one of the purposes of hypnosis—to disengage an individual's critical faculties. That was one of the ways internal blocks were overcome. Yet, in his case, the lack of discrimination had produced questionable data. All that junk about obscene secrets and suicide agreements. What could any of that mean?

On the other hand certain images had been vivid. Sienna had brought a bag to the beach that night—a Louis Vuitton, no less. And there had been fear in her face—her eyes had been all over the beach, searching. Those were facts—he had no doubt about them. But why would she have brought a knife? Or rather, why would he have thought *he* brought it? His subconscious must have made up that part, to correlate with the shock of finding the body. He had not actually *seen* the knife in the session. From what he had read, just because a person was hypnotized did not mean their recall was 100 percent accurate. In fact, if that were the case, the average American had a fifty-fifty chance of being rectally probed by an alien sometime during their lifetime.

No, Mr. Candle was a friendly old man, but he was not the right person to help him stitch together the events of that night. In the end David figured he was just going to have to ask Sienna. She would tell him; why wouldn't she tell him? He had not seen any knife in her bag and the dead woman on the beach was a blonde, not a brunette.

"There, I am fine," he muttered. "Everything is fine."

Someone knocked on his front door.

"Shit." Louder, he did not want to get up, "Who is it?"

"Charlie!"

"What do you want?"

Charlie opened the door and David was treated to an upside-down view of his scraggly friend. The Tylenol had yet to kick in and the blue-sky glare around Charlie was as unpleasant as his obviously anxious expression. David needed one guess to figure out what was wrong.

"Can I come in?" Charlie asked.

"You are in." David sat up, felt dizzy. "What can I do for you?"

Charlie shut the door and sat across from him. A bundle of nerves, he looked everywhere in the room but at David. He nodded to the manuscript. "Is that the book you're doing the cover for?" he asked.

"Yeah."

"How's it going?"

"I've made a preliminary sketch. I'll show it to you when I've taken it further."

Charlie nodded, clasped his hands, unclasped them. "That's cool."

"What's wrong?"

Charlie finally looked at him, and his blue eyes looked like they had just inhaled liquid bleach. "Someone told me you went over to see Karen this afternoon," he said.

"Yeah. So?"

"Why did you go over?"

"What kind of question is that? She's my friend. I didn't go over to have sex with her, if that's what you're asking."

"I came here because I need to talk to you. I think Karen is seeing someone."

"Why do you say that?"

"Someone told me they saw her at the movies last night with a guy. They said they saw you there with Julie Stevens."

"Who are we talking about?" David asked.

"It doesn't matter. Are they right?"

"I went to the movies with Julie, yeah."

"Did you see Karen there?"

It was the next question that would be bad. "I saw her."

Charlie stared at him as if begging for mercy. "Was she alone?"

"Charlie. She's your ex-wife. You should talk to her."

"She's not my ex-wife! We're still legally married! Was she with someone or not?!"

David hesitated. He had been Charlie's friend first, and although gender loyalties might not be politically correct, they were real enough. "Yes," he said.

Charlie died; it was hard to watch. So many ways to die in this world and this had to be one of the worst. But he did not weep, he had class. So far at least.

"Who was she with?" he asked quietly.

"I forget his name." He added, "I don't think she was that into him."

"Why do you say that? Did she say that?"

"Really, Charlie, you need to talk to her about it."

"Do you think she's sleeping with him?"

"No. I don't."

"You're just telling me that to make me feel better. What does he look like?"

"I hardly saw him. He went to the bathroom."

"Does he look like he has money?"

David hesitated. "Yeah."

Charlie grimaced. "Fuck! That's what it always comes down to, doesn't it? She always wanted the better life."

"Karen's not that way. She married you, didn't she? Anyway, I know this is tough, and I'm sorry. I can imagine the pain you're feeling right now. God knows I've had enough of it myself. But I have to say something you're not going to want to hear, and I only say it because I care about you. Her dating Duane—it might not be a bad thing."

"So you do know his name."

"His name is not important. Your obsessing over her is. She moved out—what? Over six months ago? That's a long time, and she hasn't moved back in. Charlie, that's got to tell you something."

"Are you saying that I should just give up on my family? On my two little girls? It's different when you have kids. They need a dad. It's not like you and Sienna. You could just walk away from that. I can't do that."

"You can still be a father to the girls."

"Is this what Karen told you this afternoon? That she wants me to go away?"

David sighed. "We did not talk about you."

"What did you talk about?"

"Me. I'm losing my mind. Look, it's useless for me to get in between you two. All I can do is be there for you when you need me. And I am here, Charlie, you're my old friend. You can call me or come over any time you want to talk."

Charlie nodded sadly. "She told you that I should bug off. It's all right, you don't have to admit it." He added, "I wish I hadn't lost that job at the beach."

"It's not about money, Charlie."

"It's always about money. You were the one who used to say you didn't think you had enough bucks to keep Sienna."

"Let's not bring Sienna into this, all right?"

Charlie met his gaze firmly this time. "Whatever you want, David." He stood suddenly, stepped to the door, paused. "You went to see Billy's mom this afternoon."

"You been following me?"

"No. I stop in to see her every Saturday."

"How long has this been going on?"

"Years. Mrs. Baxter's a good woman, and she doesn't have a lot of friends. She told me you were over at her house, asking about Billy."

David shrugged. "The subject came up. I hope it didn't upset her."

"She's sensitive. What were you trying to find out?"

"Nothing in particular. I was just curious about a few things. Did you know Billy was seeing someone during the months leading up to his suicide?"

"Yes."

"How come you never told me?"

"I didn't know back then."

"Do you know who it was?"

"No. What difference does it make?"

"He was our best friend. I assume you would want to know as much as me."

Charlie looked away, out the window. "You have always idolized Billy in your mind. He was a nice guy and everything, but he was no saint."

"Where the hell does that come from?"

Charlie shook his head. "You tell me to get real with Karen, and okay, I have to think about that. Maybe I'm just all messed up in my mind. But you have to get real with your memories of Billy and Rachel. They died young, under weird circumstances. When people go like that other people turn them into something they're not. For example, Billy was a great long-distance runner. He won lots of races, set tons of school records. But who gives a damn? Who gives a damn now that we're ten years out of high school?"

"I didn't look up to Billy because he was fast."

"Sure you did. When we would go out running alone together you would always talk on and on about what Billy had done in his last race. That's just one thing. Off the track you looked up to him for all the wrong reasons. You thought he was cool, that he didn't get ruffled around other people, even around the teachers when they yelled at him for never doing his homework. But did it ever occur to you that he wasn't cool but cold?"

"Billy was always on our side. He was loyal."

"Really? If I remember right it was you who wanted to ask Rachel out at first. You talked about her for months. And then one day at lunch Billy strolled on over to her and the next thing we knew they were dating. Don't you remember how that made you feel?"

"You forget one thing. I never stood a chance with Rachel. I was a nobody in high school. Rachel and Billy were good together—they both had style."

"Did you think she had style when her face got all burned up?"

"That's not fair. I couldn't have been more supportive of her during that time."

"I'm not saying you weren't. You miss my point. You had Rachel up on a pedestal as well, and a lot of it was because she was pretty and she was a rebel. Billy was a rebel too, and when you're in high school rebels are like gods. But what made them rebels? It was just their attitude. They didn't do anything in particular. They didn't have a cause. They both got lousy grades. They just thought they were too good for the jock and the cheerleader crowd. They thought they were too good for everyone. Face it, you were infatuated with Rachel because she was pretty. And you were in awe of Billy because he had what you didn't have—lots of first-place medals and Rachel."

"You're just saying all this because you're upset about Karen."

"No. I've thought it for a long time. I just never told you is all."

"They suffered, those two. What gives you the right to judge them?"

Charlie shook his head. "Nothing. I'm sorry I brought it up. If you should bump into Karen later today, tell her to give me a call. I want to talk to her."

"What a stupid thing to say. I'm not going to see her again today."

Charlie opened the door. "That's me, stupid old Charlie Beard. Always the last one to know. You take care of yourself, David. You look worse than me, and I look like shit."

"You take care," David said. After Charlie left, he picked up the manuscript. The Tylenol was beginning to take effect. Notwithstanding Charlie's hard remarks—none of which were true—his head felt better. Since he had promised to see Julie later, he figured he had better get some work done. In his entire life, he had never taken so long to finish a book.

Where was he? Oh yeah, Cleo was sleeping with Hector. . . .

In the morning, Hector is dead.

I find him hanging by a rope from the kitchen ceiling. Naked, his powerful body the color of a troubled sky, his face drained of blood, his lips swollen into raw sausages, he looks like a ghost resurrected for silly games. I do not find a good-bye note and I am not surprised. Yet even in death there is a certain serenity to his features and a part of me envies his decision. For a moment I am tempted to follow his example. But a tear rolls over my cheek and the pain of his leaving makes me marvel at how much a human being can feel. It is foolish but I wish I had made love to him one last time. Not that I think the act would have changed his mind.

I cut him down and drag him into the living room, to the fireplace, pushing him inside with great effort. My fireplace is the size of a car, and I have a mountain of split logs. Without thinking, I begin to set the wood around him and under him, building up a pyre so large the Devil himself would have felt at home. Sprinkling the logs and Hector's skin with a half gallon of lighter fluid, I think of a remark he told me the previous night. He said, "You never understood Ash, Cleo. He made us into vampires because he knew how to do it. Love was not a factor."

"I think you are wrong," I say as I hold a burning match above his closed eyes, the smell of the fuel thick in my nostrils. "Love is always a factor." Dropping the match in his thick hair, I watch the flames spread over his head and peel back his eyelids. A last look into his blue eyes, and then I have to turn away. More tears come and I cannot stop them.

Yet I am required to stay close. A human body is not easy to cremate without a gas furnace. The pyre has to be constantly resupplied and it is not until well after lunch that my friend has been totally reduced to ash. Even then I still have to crush the remains of his bones. For a while I toy with the idea of renting a boat and dumping his ashes out at sea. But then I decide to use the ash to fertilize the orange trees in my backyard. I don't worry about him returning from the dead. Such stories are nonsense.

It is in the backyard, my task almost complete, that another wave of nausea sweeps over me. I do not make it to the bathroom, but vomit into my rosebushes. The attack is violent; it empties my already sensitive stomach. Catching my breath, standing out in the warm sun, a cold possibility enters my mind, and I decide to see a doctor.

His name is Dr. Tim Weiss. I find him in the yellow pages. He agrees to see me that same day and after I explain my concerns, he has his nurse collect from me a sample of my urine and asks me to sit in his waiting room. A young mother with a year-old child on her lap is beside me. She smiles and tries to make conversation but I ignore her. Only a month ago I might have killed her and her child for dinner.

Dr. Weiss finally calls me into his office. Fifty years old or worse, he has a rather undistinguished face, marked only by unkempt nostril hairs. He reminds me of a cereal box, and I do not study him closer, I do not care about his secret ingredients. I can only think of my urine, and what it reveals to his particular branch of modern science.

"You are pregnant," he says.

"Excuse me?" I really do not understand.

"You are going to have a baby. When was your last period?"

I take a moment to absorb the news. No, it cannot be absorbed, I will have to swallow it whole. "It has been some time," I say.

He glances at my form. "You are thirty years old?"

"Yes."

"If you knew when your last period was, we could estimate how far along you are. But if it has been at least a couple of months, we can use an ultrasound."

I remember being pregnant with Ash's child when he made me into a vampire. My body had expelled so much gross matter after that ordeal—from every orifice—that I had assumed I had miscarried. I try to imagine the condition of a twenty-five-thousand-year-old fetus and fail.

"Could the ultrasound harm the baby?" I ask.

Dr. Weiss smiles patiently. "It is a standard procedure. I can do it on you now if you would like."

I hesitate. "Please."

He leads me into another room and asks me to undress and put on a gown. His nurse returns with him a few minutes later and she rubs a clear gel on my belly while he turns on his instrument. It is strange but it is only then that I notice that I have already lost my girlish figure.

Dr. Weiss applies the ultrasound knob and directs my attention to a gray digital computer screen. The images mean nothing to me, and everything.

"You are three months along," he says.

"That makes sense."

"Are you married?"

"No."

"Do you wish to keep the child?"

"This is all so sudden. I need time to think. Can you tell the sex of the child?"

"Not at this point." He moves the device lower, sending a cold sensation into my spine. He taps a vague mass on the screen, split into four quadrants. He adds, "That is the heart. Everything looks good."

"He has a heart," I gasp.

The nurse giggles. "Didn't the father have a heart?"

I stare at her, speak in a cold voice. "I thought so."

The doctor wants to set another appointment for me but I leave without making a commitment. The reality of my condition strikes me as the most mysterious thing I have encountered in centuries. I am not sure I am happy about it. For the first time in my long life, I feel as if the sun might suddenly halt in the sky or else crash into the moon. Putting a hand over my belly, a shadow lengthens in my mind and despite all Hector said before he died I feel certain that Ash knew that this moment would one day come.

I wonder if he will finally let me find him.

David stopped reading. Nothing outside disturbed him this time; it was sheer inner excitement that had distracted him. And he had the author of the manuscript to thank for that. A twenty-five-thousand-year-old fetus? What a brilliant idea! It had to be used in the cover design, to hell with his original concept. Already he had an inkling of how it could be done. And the new cover could be much simpler, less busy, much cleaner.

A statue. What if Cleo was holding a small stone statue, cradling it as if it were her own child? The image would not be literally accurate but it could be painted to convey the antiquity of the infant. The more he thought about it the more excited he got. Even without finishing the book, he knew the infant was going to end up being the key. Surely it could not be a normal child.

David leafed through other photographs he had taken of Sienna that day in the graveyard. Upon further reflection, there was no reason to completely drop his first idea. A background of tombstones might be ideal, and Sienna was still a perfect model for Cleo. He seemed to remember one picture he had taken. . . . Ah, yes, here it was: Sienna holding a doll he had won at a town fair. The way she was looking at it captured perfectly what he had in mind. He merely had to replace the doll with the tiny statue. He could do all kinds of cool things to its face; maybe make its features so flat and emotionless that it could be mistaken for an alien. The publishers would probably like that angle. The novel could be seen as a cross between horror and science fiction.

David removed the old photograph from his camera lucida, put in the new one and locked in a fresh sheet of paper. Once again he called upon the magic of the device to make the projected image the size of his paper. He could see already that he would have to enhance the stone infant with his computer software—however he painted it. He might give it a radioactive glow, that could be cool. He was confident the author was going to endow it with supernatural powers.

He chuckled at his arrogance as he worked. He could be wrong about everything, the baby might not even be important. He decided he should try to talk to the author in the next week or so. The publisher had indicated she lived in New York. He made a note to call and ask for her phone number.

He worked for two solid hours, laying down the broad strokes of his new design. But his Lucy forced him to bend over while he drew; it was a crick in his back that finally forced him to stop. What he needed was another walk before his date with Julie. Turning off the camera lucida's high-intensity light, he covered his sketch and reached for his running shoes.

He drove to the beach to hike, and there was no good reason for him to go there other than the fact that he was pissed off that the place was off-limits. The rules about crossing the bridge and hiking north along the shore were still in effect, and he imagined the area where he had discovered the body would be roped off with tape.

Maybe it was curiosity that drove him as well. Yesterday, what with his gruesome discovery and the pressure of Stanton's questions, he had not had a chance to look around and search for his own evidence. But who knows? If he went to the spot, he might find something the police and the FBI had missed.

"Ain't likely," he said as he parked in the lot where Billy had blown his brains out. Evening was coming but the beach was still well lit, although deserted. He was surprised—he had thought the grisly murder would have brought out the natives in droves. Plus it was a beautiful evening—the long waves rolled toward the shore like smooth hands, and there wasn't a cloud in the sky.

It reminded him of that night, everything did. He had too many questions in his head. How had she managed to get home that night without a car? And where was she living anyway—that last week—after she had moved out of her house in Santa Barbara? None of it made any sense; it probably wouldn't until he spoke to her face-to-face.

David hiked north, at first along the track and then over the bridge, retracing his steps from the previous day. He was surprised Stanton had not hired someone to take Charlie's place. Nobody appeared to hassle him. He was left alone with his doubts—a blessing and a curse. He was anxious to return to the spot where Sienna had dumped him, and it was the last thing in the world he wanted to do. He wondered if he was doing it in defiance of what the hypnotist had said. It was like he wanted to call and shout at the old man that there was more than one path to the subconscious. Like how about absolute confrontation? If a nightmare had in fact started there, then perhaps he only had to return to the place to wake up.

Yet he never made it. Leaving the railroad track for the shore, he walked only far enough north on the beach to catch a glimpse of Mary and Herb having sex on the spot where he had discovered the body. The sun had swollen to an orange ball by then. There were shadows in the sand. But even from a distance he could see who it was. Mary had removed her clothes but not her makeup, and Herb was groaning as if parachuting through vaporized clouds of liquid drugs. If there had been a network of yellow tape securing the area, they had trampled it into the ground. David had never imagined two people could screw so hard and not hurt themselves.

Mary paused, however, and glanced in his direction. With her pale limbs and Herb's crusty tan, she looked like a spirit sitting atop an earthen tombstone. She was so white she could have been made of chalk. Herb did not notice her pause; he continued to plow the sky in the hope it would never stop raining fifteen-year-old fluids. Yet David did not think of the penalties for statutory rape right then, or even of the fact that Mary's father was the town's main minister. Her haunting gaze chased away such mundane concerns. She was smiling; she appeared on the verge of waving and inviting him to join them. At the same time she looked like a monster. Right then, if he'd had to choose one person in the whole town who would have had the nerve to slice up a young woman, it would have been Mary Pomus.

David tore his eyes away with effort, and quickly left the beach.

THIRTEEN

Julie picked him up at home; she insisted on driving. She had an old red Camaro, plenty of horses under the hood. She drove like a maniac.

"Where are we going?" he asked as they headed south.

"Santa Barbara."

Like he had not just been there—in a cop car no less—and fainted in his ex's bathroom. Yet he did not protest because she started talking in an excited tone about a play she had gotten tickets to. Something about identical twins that had gotten separated at birth, and how one of them needed a heart transplant, and how the other just happened to die, and how she had an organ donation card, and . . . whatever. The long day had worn him out. He leaned back in his seat and let her talk.

They arrived late and had to sit in the back row. The theater's acoustics were poor, and the actors were talented but obviously inexperienced. They had never taken classes on voice projection. David missed almost as many lines as he caught. Still, the play held his attention, and it was a shock at the end to discover that the main twin had actually murdered the other to get her heart. She even got away with it, and got to sleep with her surgeon, the moral of which—he supposed—was that shit happens.

Afterward, they walked the main street, and Julie held onto his arm the whole time. The night was so warm he could close his eyes and feel the sun on his face. They ended up at a bar in the marina, and the view of the docked boats in the light of the half moon was tranquilizing. Like the night before, he started with beer but Julie steered him toward tequila. The hard liquor tasted good with a bowl of nachos. Four shots each and plenty of cheese and salt and they were both giggling like idiots. But Julie threw him for a loop when she asked about his session with the hypnotist.

"How did you know I went to one?" he asked, not sure if he wanted to know.

She laughed, the blood fresh in her face. "Because I followed you!"

"Why did you follow me?"

"You were acting so mysterious about your *appointment*. I had to follow you. I thought you were going to see that bitch."

He wasn't as mad as he thought he should be. "Don't say that, Sienna wasn't a bitch." He added, thinking he was being funny, "She was a witch."

"Was it because of her you went to the hypnotist?"

He leveled a fresh drink near his mouth. Now all he had to do was pour. He was glad he wasn't driving. Of course Julie could get them both killed just the same, although he suspected she had more experience drinking and driving.

"Can't tell you that," he said.

"Why not?"

"It's confidential. Doctor-patient privilege."

"What are you talking about? I'm not a doctor or a patient."

She had a point; he thought she had a point. "I don't want to talk about her. I don't want you to get all jealous for no reason. I haven't seen her in months."

"How many months?"

"Two."

"And she's still calling?"

"She just started calling yesterday."

"You just got home yesterday! Why did you two break up?"

"I think it was because she dumped me."

Julie showed concern. "Why didn't you tell me?"

"I didn't want to be boring. Let's not talk about it. Let's talk about something else."

"Okay. How're Hector and Cleo doing?"

David shook his head sadly. "Hector's dead. He hung himself."

"Why?"

"Because he wanted to die and he finally got the chance." David downed his drink and burped. "And because Cleo didn't love him anymore."

"I thought you said Cleo never loved him?"

He stared at his empty glass. "True. She never did."

They drank and ate more, and by the time they stumbled out of the bar the moon was yellow and sinking into the sea and he was convinced he was going to have a worse hangover tomorrow than he'd had today. He was a lightweight next to Julie. He was not merely drunk, he felt as if he was walking a gangplank. She had to steer him away from the boats toward the parking lot.

In the car, driving north, she asked him more about Sienna and he said some stuff he probably shouldn't have. Like the very mention of her name was still driving him mad, and that she used to live in Santa Barbara. The former did not annoy Julie as much as he would have imagined, but she sure jumped on the latter. She pounded the steering wheel, excited.

"You need to take the acid cure!" she exclaimed.

He was flirting with a coma. "What's that?" he mumbled.

"You need to fuck another girl in the exact spot where you used to fuck her!"

"That constitutes a cure?"

"Yeah! It works every time! You go back to where your deepest impressions are of the other person and you have sex with someone else! It's super-profound. It breaks the cycle of cause and effect and liberates you from the karma of their genitals."

"You sound like a Buddhist who's just discovered masturbation," he whispered, not sure if he was being insightful or insulting, and not really caring either way.

"I'm not talking about masturbation! I'm talking about you having sex with me at Sienna's house!"

That woke him up some. "I don't want to do that."

"How do you know it won't work? Have you tried it?"

"I don't need to try it. It sounds totally insane."

"That's what's so cool about it."

"You're nuts. I mean, why the hell would you want to do something like that?"

"I'm trying to help you," she said.

"You're just trying to get laid."

"It's the same difference. Look, where did she live?"

"I'm not telling you that."

She grabbed his arm, shook him. "Come on, David, tell me! I've done this before! I promise you it will work."

"When did you do it?"

"When I broke up with Terry."

"Who did you have sex with after Terry?"

"None of your business. The point is it helped. Are you going to tell me where she lived or not?"

"Not."

Julie looked at him, smiled at him, with a face so red and devilish she could have been a hooker working the southeast corner of Dante Blvd. Her blond hair hung over the side of her face like a yellow whip; her blue eyes were magic mushrooms. Maybe it was the booze, maybe the late hour, but her gaze worked a strange alchemy on him. Like the previous night, he suddenly felt an overpowering love for her. He hardly knew her, he was still in love with someone else, but the emotion was as real as the moisture on her red lips. And following that, on its own breaking wave, he felt he had to make love to her right away.

"I'm not going to tell you," he said.

Her smile became a smirk. "You are."

Amazing, she got the directions out of him. Passing through Goleta, they exited the freeway and drove back into the dark hills. He stared out the window at the familiar scenery and thought that it was really tomorrow night and that he and Sienna were once more together. In a way the setting was perfect to try an acid cure, only he was with the wrong girl . . . Christ, what was he getting himself into?

They reached the big house on the hill, and the smaller one off to the side. Mrs. Printkin's mansion was as silent as a painting on a dusty wall. He knew from experience she traveled a lot—she could be away. It would not be a small matter if she wasn't and she called the cops and had them arrested. He tried to explain that to Julie but she leapt from the car and ran in the direction of Sienna's guest house, giggling like a nymph on a fertile field. Chasing her, pleading for her to keep her voice down, he did not catch her until she stood on the porch. Julie put her hand on the doorknob, and again he tried to stop her.

"I don't want to go inside there!" he hissed.

Gently, she pushed his hand away, laughing softly. "When we go in there, all your problems will vanish," she said. But as Julie opened the door and stepped into the black room, and he followed, he felt his problems were only beginning.

He smelled the lemons. The dark space was choked with the aroma. He assumed she smelled them as well, but they did nothing to calm her spirit. Her seduction was the equivalent of an assault. She got off his clothes, took off her own, and wrapped him with the full length of her body; and it was good, very good, and he was hard, very hard, and she was wet and moving and kissing and moaning and he thought, what the hell, this must be the reason why he had been born, and why couldn't his problems wait till another day?

She got him on the floor, on his back, and she licked down his belly until she was climbing a pole into the sky. He loved that, the way she sucked him, and he did not mind when she came up for air and asked if he would go down on her. Her lips were hot, her taste was salty, and the smell of the lemons in the air was sweet at last. It did not matter what the others said, if she was a lesbian or if she was using him. He wanted something from her that she alone was capable of giving to him. Something even Sienna could not have done for him.

He held her and loved her until he was exhausted.

Then, finally, he blacked out, and the dream began.

"Hey, sleepyhead! Get up, I don't want to miss our show," Julie said as she came out of the shower with only a towel on her head. David sat up in the dark, the light from the bathroom causing him to wince. He did not remember when he had gone to sleep but figured he had been napping for some time. Julie must have snuck back in the room while he was unconscious, taken a shower.

"What time does it start?" he asked, rubbing his eyes.

"Eight sharp. Do you want to walk over or take a cab?"

"Take a cab."

Julie paused, standing naked in front of him, her large breasts red from the hot water. "Are you feeling all right?" she asked, concerned.

He forced a smile, although there was an ache deep inside his guts that he knew meant trouble. "Great. I had a wonderful nap. How long was I out?"

"Three hours. I hiked down the Strip, had dinner at Caesars. Are you hungry?"

"No."

"You should eat something. I could order room service while you shower."

He climbed off the bed. "Get me a fruit plate, and coffee. Nothing else."

"You don't want some fish? Chicken? You need protein."

"No. I won't eat it."

He stepped into the bathroom—huge, a jet-setter's delight, with enough marble on the floor and walls to build a pyramid, and towels and mirrors everywhere. You could never have enough towels. Stepping into the shower, looking at his naked body over his shoulder, he thought he looked damn fine. Thin, true, but being rich was the only virtue that exceeded a tight ass.

The water came out like a volcanic waterfall, made him feel drowsy all over again, and perhaps he dozed, leaning against the hard wall. The next thing he knew he heard room service at the door, and imagined Julie signing the ticket, faking his signature. She was good at that, and other things.

He finished his shower, dried, and came out of the bathroom. Julie had put on a long black dress, cut low, and a string of pearls. Her powdered breasts looked like love; he thought how nice it would be to hold her all night. Picking up a piece of pineapple from the fruit plate, he pointed to their bag. "Are the tickets for the show in there?" he asked.

She shook her head, grabbed her miniature bag. "I've got them."

"And cash?"

Julie smiled. "You want to gamble after the show?"

"Of course, this is Vegas. We have to lose some money."

"How about win?"

"Nobody ever wins here. Nobody."

Julie continued to dress. "How's the fruit?"

"Delicious." The pineapple did taste fresh, but the strawberries were hard. He didn't eat much, although he drank more coffee than was good for him. They would be up late—it was Vegas, no one slept here either.

The Bellagio was not far, just across the Strip, down a quarter mile, but the taxis were so convenient. Besides, they were barely on time for the show, the famous O. Acrobats and water, music and movement. David felt himself drifting as he watched but he headed in the direction the creators of the show probably intended. When it was finished and they were walking out, he felt as if he had just emerged from a waking dream.

A voice spoke in his head: *The Agreement.*

Just those two words. They meant nothing and everything.

It was a question of perspective.

Julie took his hand, again looked worried. "Are you okay?"

He nodded, lied. "Super."

She gestured to the casino. "Want to play here?"

"Why not? We're high rollers."

They laughed together and headed for the blackjack tables. A handsome young couple dressed to kill, Armani and Maxine on the prowl. They sat at a table where the minimum bet was a hundred, the maximum fifty thousand. The dealer was a tall platinum blonde with eyes as dark as the high end of the spectrum and a mouth as sweet as Jell-O. Her attitude was cold, a silence borne of a stormy past. But with their appearance, a flicker of interest touched her pale features, although she quickly covered. Her name tag said: CLEO.

Nice name, David thought.

He gestured for Julie's bag and she pulled out a roll of Ben Franklins—twenty grand, enough to keep them amused. He bought hundred-dollar chips, black honeybees, took most of the stack. Julie liked to play but he *was* a Player. Another reason he had consented to The Agreement. . . .

But he could not think about that right then. Not wise.

They were alone at the table. Cleo dealt quickly, David getting twenty, wonderful, Julie twelve, Cleo showing five. Julie wanted to take a card, David stopped her. "She's going to bust," he said.

Julie nodded. "You go by the book."

But Cleo eyed him. "Do I look like the type of girl who busts?" Then she turned over her card, six. She drew, she had to draw. Ten—twenty-one, fuck. David was down a thousand, Julie a hundred. Bad beginning, but no need to get it back right away. He put out five hundred dollars, had Julie hold back.

"But I want to play," Julie complained.

"A minute," David said, his eyes on Cleo. "Let her bust first."

Cleo did not mind his stare. "Is that in the book?"

"Just deal," David said.

Cleo gave him another twenty. Unfortunately, she was showing an ace. She asked if he wanted insurance—cut his losses in half if she had blackjack. He shook his head, and she flipped her hole card over. A ten, blackjack, he had lost again.

Cleo was cool. "I told you, I never bust."

"Then we should go to another table?" David asked.

"No. Stay here. You can still win." There was warmth in her voice, the ice was melting. She wanted them to stay.

He did start to win, finally, after he had lost fifteen of his twenty grand. It was remarkable he stayed at Cleo's table that long. Because she never did bust, and for that reason, he didn't let Julie back in the game. Julie didn't care; she felt out of her league in front of a dealer with Cleo's luck. And she was looking Cleo over, no mistake, from tail to top, and David did not mind. Especially when Cleo dealt him eight consecutive winning hands. By then David had his money back, and was feeling inspired. He didn't care if the girl never bust, as long as she kept giving him tens, and was willing to have a drink with them when she got off. Julie had already asked about the drink, but had not gotten a definite answer. Cleo's shift ended at two in the morning, in two hours. He decided to play at least that long.

They kept the table to themselves. Cleo went on a break but was back in a blink. The cards gave and they took, neither side could make a move. But David knew Cleo was already on his side; to hell with the casino, it did not pay as much as a winner in a mood to tip. When she returned she gave him two blackjacks in a row. He had out heavy bets, it put him up twenty thousand. Now Cleo seemed to enjoy their company—he was tipping her honeybees—and David began to think of something more than money. Why not? Three ways was better than the freeway.

He continued to win, and still, she never bust. He figured the odds against that—over at least two hundred hands—must be millions to one. He told her as much and she nodded seriously.

"It happens to me a lot," she said.

"The casino must love you," Julie said.

Cleo gestured to the casino. "Do you see any love here?"

David put down five grand. "Here. We're serious about buying you that drink."

"Yeah. You've got to join us," Julie said.

"My man might not like it."

"You have a man?" Julie asked. "What's his name?"

"Hector."

"Love him?" Julie asked.

"No. He loves me. The love of my life is dead."

"How did he die?" David asked.

Cleo dealt him a twenty, a winner, and said, "He killed himself."

Near two in the morning David had over a hundred grand sitting in front of him, and a half dozen empty tequilas. Yet the liquor and the dough had been unable to halt the growing pain in his right side. His liver was squirting lava instead of bile. He had to wipe away the sweat on his brow when Julie was not looking. Breathing was a trick; he could inhale all right but exhaling brought stabbing cramps into his rib cage. It was as bad as it had ever been and it felt like it was just getting started. Even the Percocet back at the hotel room was not going to do the trick. He glanced at his watch.

"You on another five minutes?" he asked Cleo.

"Another two," she replied as she shuffled the deck. "I have to walk back to my locker."

"But you're going to meet us afterward?" Julie asked anxiously, and the pleading in her voice was a mistake. Cleo flashed a dismissive smile.

"Hector might worry," she said.

Julie had drunk too much. "But you said you don't even love him."

"I'll tell you what," David said to Cleo, pushing all his chips forward. "I win the next bet, you have a drink with us. I lose and we never talk again."

Cleo glanced down at the sum. "You can't bet that much at this table."

"Call your pit boss over."

Cleo turned and gestured and Manuel—an out-of-shape boxer in a bulging green suit and a neck-choking yellow tie—walked over. Cleo explained the bet, quietly, while Julie grabbed his arm and tried to pull him from the table.

"No way!" she hissed. "That's too much!"

David brushed her off, nodded toward Cleo. "Think what's at stake."

Manuel was agreeable to the bet, on the condition it be their last bet of the night. No whining that they wanted a marker, double or nothing, just walk away. David said that was fine with him.

"Because we are going to win and she—" he pointed at Cleo "—is going to bust."

Manuel was not impressed. He nodded for Cleo to finish shuffling and deal.

"I can't watch this," Julie said, getting up from the table. She had drunk more than he, she always did. Yet she did not turn away.

Cleo went to deal. David stopped her. "Do we have a deal?" he asked.

"Only if I bust," she said.

"Not if I win?" David asked.

"No."

"What is this about?" Manuel asked.

"Nothing. Deal," David said.

Cleo gave him twelve, bad hand. And she was showing ten. Julie looked like she was going to be sick. "You have to hit," Julie said.

David hesitated, stared into Cleo's eyes. They were not truly violet but blue—so deep and unblinking they could have been made of glass. She was tired, obviously burnt out on life, but he imagined in another twenty-five thousand years her eyes could be diamonds. For some reason he had faith that she could do him no wrong.

"I have to give her a chance to bust," he said.

"You don't want to hit?" Cleo asked, finally impressed.

"No," he said.

"Wait! You're sitting on shit!" Julie exclaimed.

"No," David said, still looking at Cleo. "I'm sitting pretty."

"Show your hole card," Manuel told Cleo.

Cleo turned over a two. They both had twelve. But Cleo had to draw, and he did not have to do anything. Manuel nodded for her to continue. Cleo reached for the shoe.

Queen of diamonds. Ten, twenty-two, bust. David had won. Everything. Julie let out a scream. "Yes!"

"I've got to go," Cleo said to David as she stepped back from the table. But she nodded faintly; she would find them if they remained in the casino. Manuel began to count his mass of chips.

"Want me to count you out?" he asked.

"Sure."

"Is a check fine?"

"No. Cash. All of it."

"You shouldn't walk around with that much," Manuel said.

"Let me worry about that," David muttered, and his pain belonged to a demon.

Cleo caught up with them twenty minutes later, near the front of the hotel. They went next door to the Monte Carlo for a drink. Julie was so drunk she would be swearing in her sleep. Cleo was quiet but friendly. She did not ask him what had possessed him to bet so much on one hand. It was like she had seen it all. Yet his wager had impressed her as gallant. She understood he had done it for her as much as for the money. For that reason, she would spend the night with them.

The three of them walked back to their hotel. But in the lobby David acted like he needed to get something out of his car. He asked Cleo if she would accompany him. Julie wanted to get upstairs and take a shower anyway. Sure, Cleo said. She was not afraid of him. She was the type who looked like nothing could scare.

In the parking lot he pulled out ten grand and handed it to her. "I need a strong narcotic and I need it now," he said. "Morphine, Heroin, Demerol— any of them will do. Just don't bring me any Vicodin or Percocet."

She didn't ask why he needed it, just took the cash. "Give me twenty minutes."

He nodded. "Hurry."

She was back in fifteen, brought him a bottle of Oxycontin—the new rage in pain control, powerful stuff. Fifty white tabs, eighty milligrams. He chewed down four pills and washed away the taste with a can of Coke in his car. He did not ask for his change and she did not offer it.

"You just took an overdose," she said.

He chuckled. "Don't worry, I can take anything."

Within minutes his pain began to ease. By the time they were back in the room with Julie, he was floating in a blue sky filled with diamond snowflakes. From the corner of the large bed, propped up like a mannequin without a dick, he watched as the two women began to kiss and touch and slowly undress each other. He did not participate, though. He was too stoned, and besides, he did not know if he had ever seen such a beautiful sight as Cleo's and Julie's bodies locked together. It was almost as if the drug had killed him, and he had gone to the other side and been met by two angels who had a yen for human sin. For the first time in a long time he was happy, and he did not think once about the horror that lay in the future, and the deal that he had made.

FOURTEEN

When David awoke, in his own bed, Julie was sitting at the table in his T-shirt, eating Special K. The T-shirt would have been large on him, and on her it was down to her knees. The angle of the light let him know she wasn't wearing anything under it, and that was a nice picture to wake up to. The only problem was he had never bought Special K in his life. And how had they gotten home?

"What are you eating?" he asked. He was naked, his head hurt, but otherwise all his parts appeared intact. She looked over at him and smiled with milk on her upper lip. She gestured to the box.

"What does it look like?" she asked.

"Where did you get that?"

"The closet. I had to open it, fresh box. I assumed you wouldn't mind."

He sat up, shook his head. The act was not helpful. "I always buy Corn Flakes."

"Well you must have picked up Special K by accident. Do you have anything else to say?"

"You look good in the morning."

"Not great?"

"You look awesome. How long have you been up?"

"Half an hour. I already took a shower."

"I'm surprised it didn't wake me."

"I tell you, you sleep like a corpse. Do you have a headache?"

"A little one. I didn't grow up drinking tequila. How about you?"

"I feel great. Last night was wonderful."

David put his feet on the floor and had to contemplate the next step of standing up. "What happened?" he asked.

She chuckled. "So I made that much of an impression?"

"I didn't mean it that way. I meant . . . how did we get home?"

"I drove, you slept. But I had to half drag you back to the car if that's what you're asking. You really zoned out at Sienna's house."

"Let's not talk about that place, okay?"

"The acid cure didn't work?"

He shook his head. "I had the strangest dream. I was in Vegas, with you, and we were gambling like big shots."

"What's strange about that? Let's do it someday."

"It was strange because I had pain in my body, deep in my guts, and the woman who is in the novel I am doing the cover for was a dealer at the Bellagio. Plus, it was so vivid, I felt like I was really there."

"It sounds nice."

"It was." A lie. The events in the dream had been pleasant enough, but the overall feeling had been oppressive. Even at the end, naked in bed with two beautiful women, he had felt as if he was smothering.

There was a knock at his door. Julie raised an eyebrow.

"Expecting company?" she asked.

He had a terrible fear it was Sienna, that she had driven up early. "No."

Julie stood. "Do you want me to get it?"

"Just a sec!" He swallowed a bitter taste, called out. "Who is it?"

"It's the sheriff!"

"What the hell?" David muttered. Then, "Sheriff! Could you come back later?"

"I'm afraid not, David. You have to open up."

David grabbed a pair of pants from the floor, pulled them on. Julie remained standing by the table, a spoonful of Special K in her hand, milk on her face. He tripped on his shoes on the way to the door. He realized that Julie had undressed him last night and put him to bed. She looked anxious.

"What does he want?" she asked.

"Beats me."

Opening the door, he was momentarily blinded by the morning sun. But he saw enough to know that there were two figures on his porch. "What is this about?" he asked.

"I'm sure you know," Krane said. He came into focus slowly: the crude handsome face, the thick black hair, the strong shoulders, the brutal confidence. Krane was smoking—he probably never stopped—and the smoke felt like a forest fire in David's brain. David forced himself to stand up straighter.

"I don't," he said. "And I don't appreciate getting dragged out of bed on a Sunday morning." He went to shut the door. "Call me tomorrow if you want to talk."

Stanton put his foot in the door, but the act was surprisingly gentle. His face was as miserable as his voice. In fact his expression reminded David of the night he had come to tell them Billy was dead. "You have to come with us," he said.

David paused. "Why?"

"Because we are placing you under arrest for the murder of Sally Wither," Krane said, pulling out a pair of handcuffs and reaching for David's arm. "You have the right to remain silent. You have the right . . ."

"Sheriff!" David snapped, stepping back. "What's going on? Who is Sally Wither?"

Stanton gestured for Krane to back off, then spoke to David. "The hairs we collected from Sienna's house yesterday—they match the hair of the woman on the beach."

"That's ridiculous! Sienna was a brunette. That woman was a blonde."

Krane spoke. "No. Sienna was a blonde. She had dyed her hair. Also, her name was not Sienna Madden, but Sally Wither. We have already identified her. She was from New York City, the only daughter of a prominent family. They have been looking for her for some time." Krane added, "You must have known."

David shook his head vigorously. "No! None of this is true. You have the wrong person. Sienna called me several times yesterday. I spoke to her. She can't be dead."

"David," Stanton began.

He spoke over his shoulder. "Julie? Julie heard her call. Julie, come out here and tell them about Sienna calling me yesterday afternoon."

Julie stepped forward, white as her shirt. David opened the door wider.

"Tell them," he repeated, putting a hand on her shoulder, as if that would steady the two of them. He might as well have been counting on the San Andreas Fault to prop them up. Julie glanced at the sheriff and Krane and then quickly lowered her eyes.

"I don't know what's going on," she mumbled.

"Julie!" David exclaimed, taking his hand back. "Tell them she called!"

Stanton raised a hand. "Calm down, David."

"Fuck that shit! You come here to arrest me for murdering my ex-girlfriend and you want me to calm down? What the fuck is wrong with you? Julie, tell them she called, goddamnit."

Stanton turned to Julie, spoke carefully. "Did you speak to Sienna yesterday?"

"Her name is Sally Wither," Krane quipped. He seemed to be enjoying himself.

"I did not speak to her, she left a message on David's machine that I heard," Julie said to Stanton.

"How did you know it was her? Had you spoken to her before?" Stanton asked.

"No. I didn't know who she was. I just heard the message is all."

"But she identified herself as Sienna?"

Julie shook her head. "No. But David said that was who it was."

"That's not true! She identified herself!" David said.

Julie was ready to join Stanton in the sad-eyed club. She looked at him as if he were made of glass. "She didn't actually say her name, David. The first time I heard it was when we were out last night."

"Why are you saying that?" he yelled.

Julie was close to crying. "Because it's true."

Krane jingled his handcuffs. "Let's cut to the chase, why don't we? You have the right to remain silent. You have the right to . . . ."

"Calm down, everyone," Stanton said, interrupting the FBI agent. "David, do you have any messages from Sienna still on your machine?"

David nodded like the Energizer Duck. "Yeah. I think I've got them. Come in, come in. I didn't erase them, that's for sure."

As the gang stepped into his place, David felt as if he were being cornered in a cave. His eyes and his brain were having a hard time adjusting. After the bright sun, his place looked as if it were trapped in yesterday's shadows. He almost knocked over the table his phone and answering machine sat on.

Maybe he did bump it; the machine hardly spoke when he pushed PLAY—just told him to leave a message. In his own voice no less.

"Gimme a second," David said.

"Take two," Krane said.

David knelt and studied the device. There was no red light blinking—there were no new messages—but the power was definitely on. Yet it was possible it had gone off for an instant when he had bumped the table, since there were no old messages to be found on the machine. Feeling a frustration that was close to despair, he leaned the top of his head against the wall and groaned.

"I must have accidentally erased them," he whispered.

That was good enough for Krane. While Julie wept like a little girl who had just lost a favorite toy, the FBI agent read him his rights, handcuffed him, and led him outside to the sheriff's car. It was early; no one on the block was out. It did not matter. David knew the entire city would know he had been arrested by lunch, and for the murder of a woman that was still alive. No, they would miss that last point. On a wave of gossip, he would be tried and convicted by dinner. Really, he wished he had never woken up. Las Vegas with Cleo and Julie and that nasty pain in his gut had been a mere preview. His life was the nightmare.

Massive Max booked him. The deputy could not have been happier to see him again. "I knew from the start it was you," he said while taking the mug shot. Krane and Stanton were not around. David was still without a shirt and a morning shower. The station's air-conditioning was stuck in the arctic. He could not stop shivering, which made his handcuffs jingle.

"That's because you're such an astute intellectual," David replied as he lined up in front of the camera. He felt no need to say cheese. Max paused and came around, his beady eyes the color and shape of raisins.

"You better watch how you talk in here. You're my prisoner now. Do you know what that means?"

"Why, Max, are you making a pass at me?"

Max grinned and pulled out his baton and tapped the side of David's head. "You guys all thought you were so hot in high school. You and Billy and Rachel and Charlie. Now look at you. Rachel went out looking like a monster and Billy hated her face so much that he had to blow his brains out. Then Charlie marries Karen and she dumps him, and now you're going to prison for life. The four of you—you're all dog meat now."

David kept his voice calm. "If you tap me with that baton again, I will rip it from your hands and stuff it twelve inches into your rectum. And if you insult any of my friends again, I am going to write an article for the local paper explaining how you tried to suck my cock while booking me. I might even draw a picture illustrating your feeble attempt. Do you understand what I am saying, Max?"

Max kept his grin in place but backed off a step and lowered the baton. "You're a con now, Lennon. You're not going to be drawing any more pictures."

David acted bored. "Let's get this over with so I don't have to look at you."

The rest of the booking was accomplished quickly, and Max put him in a cell at the rear of the station that had a high of fifty-five degrees. His handcuffs were removed, and he asked for a blanket or a shirt or something. Max just walked away whistling. He was not given a chance to make his one call, but Stanton had indicated when they had arrived at the station that he would be along soon to speak to him.

Soon was a relative term, and the time began to creep by. The cell was equipped with a bunk and a toilet, hospital-green tiles and concrete carpeting, but David could not even sit down, he was so cold and so wound up. He ended up pacing, trying to think how Krane could have made such a colossal mistake when it came to identifying the body. His thoughts tended toward the paranoid, and he began to wonder if Krane was setting him up to be a scapegoat, even though he knew he had not committed the crime. The FBI agent could have tampered with the hair evidence. It was possible. Since he had stepped off that plane in L.A. it seemed anything was possible.

Still, it made no sense. The moment Sienna arrived in town, the case against him would dissolve. Yet that could be a problem in itself. Sienna would not come to Lompoc unless she heard from him. If he didn't return her calls, she would assume he was blowing her off. She could fly all the way back to the East Coast without the slightest idea what had happened to him. Then how was he supposed to get ahold of her? Her real name was not Sally Wither—Krane had screwed up big-time there. Why, Sienna's pubic hair had been brown, not blond.

He had resisted getting a lawyer for too long. He needed one now, immediately. He had to get out of this place. That was all he could think about. It was strange, it was just a tiny room, and he had not been locked up long, but already he felt the subtle torture of incarceration. He could not resist grab-

bing the bars, feeling their strength. He worried what it would be like at nighttime.

Two hours later, Krane appeared, alone. He came in a cloud of smoke, with a fold-out gray chair and a carton of cigarettes, no tape recorder. He looked different than that morning, less cocky, more sympathetic. David was not in the mood for the good cop/bad cop routine, especially when it was played by the same guy. Yet Krane had also brought a blanket, and David accepted it hungrily.

"Why do you keep this place so cold? Using it for a morgue?" David asked.

"You will have to ask the sheriff about that." Krane unfolded his chair and sat outside the bars and studied David. He had done the same when they had met; it was as if he was looking for something specific. David sat in the corner of the bunk and huddled under the blanket. Before the FBI agent had arrived, he had been about to wrap himself in a roll of toilet paper.

"Where is the sheriff?" David asked.

Krane smoked. "You don't want to talk to me?"

"I want to talk to a lawyer."

"But you're innocent. Why wouldn't you want to talk?"

"Why do I have the feeling you have used that line before?"

Krane stopped to smile. "You are sharp, Lennon, I like that. I know you don't have to talk if you don't want to. But you can see I've come alone and unarmed. I don't even have a wire on me. What we talk about now, it can be strictly off the record."

"You won't even remember it after you leave the room?"

"If you want it that way."

"And you just complimented me on my intelligence. Give me one good reason why I should talk to you?"

"Because I can help you."

"How?"

Krane hesitated. "I might have seen cases like this before."

That got his attention. "Ritual murders?"

"Maybe."

"Tell me about them."

"I'm sorry but I can't discuss them."

David snorted. "You are going to have to do better than that."

Krane raised a hand. "I want to tell you more, you have to trust me on

that. But I am not as free to act as you might think. At the same time, if you can help me out, I might be able to throw a few interesting facts your way. It's even possible we might end up with that two-way street you mentioned before. What do you say?"

"You are so full of shit. Give me something and I will give you something."

"All right, I have seen two cases that remind me of this one. Both occurred in the last year."

"Where were they?"

"One was in Florida, the other in Southern California."

"How exactly did they relate to this case?"

"You guessed the main point. Each involved a ritual killing."

"Did you solve these cases?"

"No."

"Neither?"

"No."

"Did you work on them alone?"

"No one at the FBI works totally alone. I had a partner, Carol."

"Why isn't Carol here now?"

"She's dead."

"How did she die?"

"I don't want to discuss that at this time. I have told you two things I haven't even discussed with the sheriff. Now it is your turn to talk. That is fair."

"Nothing is fair right now. You are outside the bars, I am inside."

"That is not my fault."

"Is it mine? Tell me honestly, do you think I killed my girlfriend?"

"The evidence says you did. Yes, I think it is possible you killed your girlfriend."

David looked away. "Go find me the sheriff, I want a lawyer."

"I am sure you will get a lawyer, David. I recommend that you do. But I came here first, before the lawyers get involved, because I mean it when I say I might be able to help you. But you have to talk to me, and if you know in your heart you are innocent, you will talk to me. You are right, you are locked up. You can do nothing in here. But I'm all over this town, night and day. I'm not just trying to build a case against you, I'm here to find out the truth."

What he was saying did have a ring of truth to it. Krane was an asshole

but he had strength. "You think what happened here relates to your other cases?" David asked.

"Yes."

"But I have never heard of those cases. How can you think there is a relationship between them and still think I murdered Sienna?"

"The answer to that question is complex. In fact, I do not have a complete answer for you, even if I was in a position to tell you, which I am not."

"More double talk."

"No. I'm being honest. I'm an agent of the Federal Bureau of Investigation. I belong to a chain of command. I have people above me that I am responsible to. I cannot automatically spill my guts to you because your girlfriend ended up dead and you were the last person to be seen with her."

"Sienna is not dead! I spoke to her yesterday and the day before!"

Krane sat back, nodded. "Okay. Let's start there. Are you sure it was her?"

"Yes."

"How can you be so sure? People can sound like other people, especially on the phone. Did she tell you something that only she would know?"

"No. But Sienna has a distinct voice. It was her."

"Did you talk to her long?"

"No. We got interrupted each time."

"Why?"

"It just happened, lousy timing. But trust me, it was her."

"You mentioned yesterday that she said she was coming to see you. Is she still planning to come here?"

"Yes. But we never got a chance to set a firm date. And if she doesn't hear back from me, she might think I don't want to see her. I need my cell phone."

"You have a number where you can call her?"

"She left me a number in Orange County."

"Can you give me that number?"

"Yes. But it's at home, on a pad of paper beside my phone."

"Do I have your permission to enter your home and get that number?"

"Yes. As long as you bring me my cell."

"I will, I promise. How many times did you talk to Sienna over the last two days?"

"She called lots of times, but we only talked twice. She left lots of messages."

"Why did you erase them? You knew I wanted to hear them."

"I didn't erase them."

"Are you suggesting that someone else did?"

"No. But . . . it was weird, they kept getting erased because the power kept getting knocked off. I mean, the machine kept getting unplugged."

"But who kept unplugging it? You?"

David hesitated. "I don't know."

"Could Julie Stevens have unplugged your machine?"

"No."

"How well do you know her?"

"I have known her since high school, but we just started going out."

"Since when?"

"Since I got back from New York."

"Are you sleeping with her?"

"Yes."

"Do you trust her?"

"What kind of question is that? I trust her enough to sleep with her."

"That's a meaningless vote of confidence coming from a guy. Did you leave her alone in your house at any time when she could have erased the messages?"

"Not really." He thought of his shower yesterday, his sleeping deep that morning and the morning before. He added, "Maybe."

"So you don't really know her?"

"What do you have against Julie?"

"I'm just entertaining the idea of other suspects. That is what you want me to do, isn't it? Besides, I had a tail on you yesterday. You went to a hypnotist in the afternoon and Julie followed you there and sat outside while you were inside."

David was astounded. "You had me followed? Isn't that illegal?"

"No. Anyway, everything we say right now is off the record, remember?"

"Who followed me?"

"Max."

"Max? That guy is an asshole."

"Agreed. But I was busy and he wasn't. He said Julie followed you to the hypnotist. That raises two questions: what were you doing there, and why was she following you?"

"Julie already told me that she followed me. Her motive was simple—she was afraid I was off trying to see Sienna."

"So she is jealous of Sienna?"

"Not exactly. Look, Julie has nothing to do with any of this."

"Then answer my second question. Why did you feel the need to see a hypnotist a few hours after being grilled by an FBI agent about a murder? Was it because you were still having trouble remembering what happened that night with Sienna?"

Again, Krane's insight caught him off guard. It was almost as if the guy had seen this script before. But to confide in the agent—when he might be the very person who could get him convicted—would be insane. "I went for a personal matter. It had nothing to do with this," David replied.

Krane nodded. "You're lying but that's okay. I know that's why you went."

"You spoke to Mr. Candle?"

"No."

"Other people—in your other cases—had trouble with their memories?"

"Yes."

"Could you elaborate?"

"No. When you saw Mr. Candle, did you get any more insight into that night?"

"No. It's my turn to ask. Are you certain Sienna Madden is Sally Wither?"

"Yes. There is no doubt about it."

David snickered. "Then who have I been talking to the last two days?"

"I don't know. Maybe no one."

"So I have just been imagining these calls?"

"It is a possibility. You have to admit how odd it is that she has left several messages and no one has heard them except you."

"Except me and Julie. Don't forget Julie."

"Who has never spoken to Sienna in her life. Who says she never even knew Sienna's name at the time of the call. Her opinion is worthless. No, Sienna and Sally are the same person. The hair is a perfect match. Also, I spoke to her mother in New York. Sally fits Sienna's description perfectly. In fact, the sheriff had her mother fax a picture of Sally to this station and he was able to identify her as the young woman he saw you with several months ago. Except for the different hair color, of course."

"No. That is not possible. I spoke to her and she is alive. I am not nuts."

"If it is any consolation, I believe you think you spoke to her."

"Thanks a lot. I have a mental illness and you want to be my shrink. Why are you talking to me at all if you are convinced Sienna is dead?"

A note of sympathy entered Krane's voice. "There never was a Sienna, David. For whatever reason, she made up that entire identity. You have to accept that as a fact before we can get anywhere."

He shook his head. "I do not accept that."

"You will in time, I think. But let me answer your other question. I'm talking to you now because—even with the discovery of the Sienna/Sally connection—the mystery is far from cleared up."

"You are referring to the ritual killing?"

"Yes."

"Great. You think I'm evil enough to kill her but you draw the line at me being a satanist."

Krane considered. "What if you killed her and it wasn't your fault?"

David had to laugh. "Are you saying she made me do it?"

"It's a possibility. Look at you, you can't even remember what you did that night. Maybe she placed you under some kind of compulsion."

David stopped laughing. "You saw that before in your other cases?"

"I saw suspects who should never have been considered suspects. In a lot of ways they reminded me of you."

"Are any of them still in jail?"

"No. They all got off."

"But they all had trouble with their memories?"

"Yes."

"How did your partner die?"

"I can't talk about that." There was pain in Krane's voice.

"You were close to her?"

"Yes."

"I'm sorry."

Krane stood. "I know you are. I'm sorry you are in this mess. I will honor my word and not use anything you just told me against you in court. But I have to be frank with you. You are still my main suspect in the murder of Sally Wither. So far you are my only suspect, and unless another one shows up you will be convicted of murder in the first degree."

David stared. "It will never happen. I did not kill Sienna because she is still alive."

"And because you still love her?"

"Love is not a factor."

Krane shook his head. "I think you're wrong."

With that, the FBI agent turned and left.

FIFTEEN

David was given an hour to digest Krane's words, before Stanton arrived. During that time the temperature in the cell rose steadily. David figured Krane had ordered Max to stop with the torture.

An odd thing happened during that spell. David started to cry and he could not stop. He did not believe Sienna was dead—he knew that was impossible. Yet an overwhelming sense of loss gripped him, thick as four walls, and it would not leave no matter how much he reasoned with it. His face buried in the cot, the blanket over his head, he tried to stifle the sobs but they only slowed when he stopped resisting them. And afterward, he felt oddly empty, drugged, a Styrofoam ball set to drift on a flat sea. He wondered if he needed to eat. Since his arrest, he had not even been offered a glass of water.

Stanton arrived soon after with food and clothes. It seemed Julie had brought the latter to the station, hoping to see him. The sheriff explained as much as he sat in the cell beside him, on the cot, watching as David downed the ham sandwich and Coke he had brought.

"I didn't think you wanted to see her anyway," Stanton said. "Not in here."

David nodded. The food and drink helped; at least he felt in control of his emotions once more. "I don't know what I would say to her," he agreed.

"She's pretty shaken up by the whole thing."

"She's a good girl. I shouldn't have yelled at her this morning."

"She doesn't blame you. She told me to tell you, whatever you need, she would get it for you."

"I need a lawyer."

Stanton was grim. "Talk to one before you talk to Krane again."

"You heard about that?"

"Sure. I'm not happy about it. He snuck in here when I was out. He had no right. This is my town, not his."

"I didn't mind talking to him."

"David, he's a professional. He knows how to get information out of people. Nothing you tell him can help you . . ." Stanton's voice trailed off.

He had said enough. The sheriff thought he was guilty. David put down what was left of his sandwich. "She's not dead," he said flatly.

"You have to stop saying that. I spoke to her mother."

"Sally's mother, not Sienna's."

"They are one and the same."

"How did you locate Sally's mother so quickly?" he asked.

"Once we determined that the hairs matched, we sent out a photograph of her to every FBI office in the country. New York still had her photo on their active board. They called us within minutes."

"Wait a second, where did you get a picture of Sienna?"

"Herb gave us one."

"Herb? How did he have one?"

"He said he took it one morning when they were having breakfast."

"That's insane. How did he know you wanted one?"

"Krane asked him for one. Yeah, that guy's been all over town asking questions. God knows what he knows, he doesn't share it with me. That's why I tell you not to trust him."

"Sheriff, stop it. You can't be on my side. Not if you think I did it."

Stanton looked pained. He reached over and gripped David's arm. "You know I cannot look at you without thinking of my own son. Steve and you guys—you were all born the same year. I take out pictures of him in first grade, and see you and Billy there. How can I not be on your side?"

"That woman was sliced and diced! You have to hate whoever did that to her!"

Stanton shook his head. "I have been a cop a long time. There's a vast difference between premeditated acts of violence and impulsive acts. Any cop who has been around will tell you that. You take anyone and put them in the wrong situation at the wrong time, and they can crack. For example, I had a deputy fifteen years ago—I won't mention his name. The oldest trick in the book happened to him. He came home early one afternoon and found his wife in bed with another guy. This cop, he was as straight as paper. Went to church every Sunday, worked as a coach for a Little League team, wouldn't drink a beer unless it was a special occasion. But when he saw his wife naked in the arms of another man, he just lost it. He whipped out his baton and began to beat the guy on his back. He hit him so hard, so many times, he paralyzed the poor sap for life. Then he went to work on his wife . . ."

"Did he kill her?" David asked when Stanton did not continue.

"No. But he rearranged the bones in her face so radically that she never looked the same. The weird thing is, when he was done, and they were unconscious, a profound calm came over him, and he sat down and called me."

"What did you do?"

"What could I do? I arrested him, and he was convicted of assault and sentenced to ten years. But I didn't hate him for what he had done. He was a good man, he was not naturally cruel. That's the point I'm trying to make. We all have ugliness inside us which can be brought out under the wrong circumstances. That's not to excuse the majority of the violent crime in society. Most people who lash out violently deserve to be locked up. But there is always that small percentage who are pushed into a mistake. Those people, I don't think, should be destroyed for life."

"At least I know what category you think I fall into."

"David . . ."

"That type of rationalization is so weak. It reminds me of your explanation of why you don't arrest Herb. If I cut her up, I should be punished . . ." He had not meant to put it exactly that way.

"I'm not saying you should get off scot-free. I did not let the deputy I spoke of go free. At the same time, I don't want to see you put away forever because of this. That is why I want you to get the best lawyer you can, and stay away from Krane. Look, someone else came by to see you this afternoon. I'm sure you can guess who it was."

David felt a stab of pain. All the people who would be hurt by this: his parents, Charlie, and perhaps most of all . . . "Karen," he said.

"Yes. I had a talk with her about your relationship with Sienna. She explained how that woman messed with your mind. Now I don't know what happened that night. You don't even know, I know you're not lying about that. But whatever did happen, we can be certain Sienna had a big part in pushing you over the edge. Did she deserve to die because of it? Of course not. But was she partially responsible for what happened? Yes, I think she was, and so does Karen."

"God, thanks. I feel a whole lot better about myself. I'm sure I'll be able to sleep like a baby tonight. Except for the small fact that you are both telling me that you think I killed my girlfriend."

"The physical evidence—in combination with your testimony yesterday morning—makes you guilty. Plus no one can find Sienna to speak to her."

"You're all going to look pretty stupid when she drives into town tomorrow."

"I would enjoy that feeling." Stanton paused. "But she's not going to be driving into town, tomorrow or the next day. You're going to have to start accepting that."

"Krane said the same thing."

"Then his visit wasn't in vain."

"Did Krane get that guy's number in Orange County? The guy Sienna said she is staying with?"

"Krane told me about it. I went to your house. There was one seven-one-four number on the pad by your phone. I called it from your house. The guy who answered said he had never heard of any Sienna."

"That's impossible."

"That is what happened."

"Did you get the guy's name?"

"Yes. David Smart."

"You have to pull his phone records. She called from his house yesterday."

"I can pull them . . ."

"Don't say it that way, like it will show nothing. Just do it."

"I said I would. But you need to get a lawyer."

"I'm going to do that. I have to make some calls. Did you bring my cell phone? Krane promised I could have it."

"I did not. He was wrong to promise that. You are under arrest for murder. The law does not allow me to give you a cell phone to make all the calls you want. But I can bring you a phone in a few minutes to call a couple of people."

"Sheriff, please. I need it in case Sienna calls. She knows the number. If she doesn't get me at home—before flying home to New York—she'll try my cell."

"No. I can't do it. You are being naive to ask for it."

David wondered if the sheriff had taken possession of the phone himself, to see who was calling him these days. He lashed out. "Damnit! And you say you sympathize with my predicament?"

"She's not going to call you. Get over it, David. She's dead."

Such a simple word, only four letters, with such deep power. Dead.

David put a hand to his head. It did not merely ache—his skull felt as if it had an alien embryo deposited inside, deep down inside where the brain stem automatically made the day-to-day decisions of life: eat, sleep, shit, fuck, die. So much easier to be a hunter in a primitive age, he thought. To kill out of hunger, to love out of lust, to live and die at the hands of natural forces. This nightmare that he had fallen into—it had all the resonance of a bad acid trip taken in the company of a winged demon. When he stopped and thought about it, nothing about the last few days had felt natural.

"I don't know who to call," he said quietly.

"How about your parents?"

"It would kill them to hear about this." Since he had returned home, he realized, he had not called them. Just kept forgetting . . .

"They're going to hear about it sooner or later."

"Later then. I can't call them."

"What about Reverend Pomus? He knows what's happened. He called, said he wants to talk to you. He knows lots of people. I'm sure he could help you find a lawyer." Stanton added, "And you might want to talk to him anyway."

"So we can pray together and I can ask God for forgiveness?"

"Prayer is not a bad thing."

David considered. "If Pomus wants to see me, let him see me."

"I'll have him come immediately. He cares about you. He sounded pretty shook up when he called." Stanton stood. "Is there anything else I can do for you?"

"Yes. Did you check who owned that gun Billy had in his mouth when he died?"

"Jesus! How can you think about that at a time like this?"

"I'm in prison. There isn't much to do in here except think. Did you check on the gun or not?"

Stanton hesitated. "I did. It was owned by Teresa and Rachel's father."

David snorted. "So Teresa was there when her sister committed suicide, and she was there when Billy died from a wound inflicted by a weapon owned by her father. Do you still think I am inventing coincidences?"

"We don't know if Teresa was at the beach that night. I told you, I wasn't sure about that car that was heading back to town."

"Sure you were. You just blanked on it for some reason."

"I don't know if I like what you are implying."

David shrugged. "I'm not saying anything. And you're right, it has nothing to do with what is happening right now. But I can tell you one thing. The second I get out of here, I'm going to talk to Teresa's father."

"Let it go, David. It will only stir up old wounds."

"Who cares about old ones? It's the new ones that bleed." David stopped and closed his eyes. The pain in his head was a constant. He added, "Thank you, Sheriff, for everything. I mean that—perhaps one day I can repay you. But if you do talk to Pomus, ask him to give me an hour before coming. I need to take a nap. I don't feel so good."

He rested but did not sleep. He kept thinking of Billy and Rachel. One day in particular, the state cross-country meet, their senior year, the three of them alone together in Sacramento for the weekend. Even Coach Sander and Charlie had not been present. The coach's wife had been about to have a baby, and Charlie had been sick with the flu. He and Rachel were Billy's only support, and there was a good chance their man would win.

David had not qualified for the event, nor had their team as a whole. Back then the race had been two miles long, not the present-day five kilometers, and Billy had one of the best times in the country that year with 8:58. But he was up against six other guys who had run under nine minutes, and one of them was from Sacramento, Kirk Tucker, and he was used to running in the heat. That day the temperature was in the nineties—although it was November—and the humidity level felt like 100 percent.

David and Rachel were in the stands, top row. Standing up and turning around, they would have a great view of the entire course after the herd left the stadium. The place was half full, all hard-core running fans from all over the state. The race was to start in minutes, and Billy was already down on the track, stretching. Rachel was dressed for the heat, wearing cutoff blue jeans and a white halter top. Her long chestnut hair was all over the place, her face free of makeup, but as always her thick lips still looked like she had lipstick on. She was chain-smoking, sharing a Coke and hot dog with him. She didn't give a damn if Billy won or not, she said, but his races always made her nervous.

"How can they run in this heat?" she asked, wiping her hair out of her eyes.

"It won't help Billy, that's for sure. It's been cool back home, this last month."

"That's not fair."

"Sports are seldom fair. At least Billy is in better shape than I've ever seen him."

"You think he'll win?"

"He stands a good chance," David said.

Rachel looked exasperated. "Show some confidence! Lie to me!"

"He will definitely win."

"Better." Rachel pointed to a group of men down on the track, looking over the runners like they were cattle waiting for the block. "Why do those guys have badges on?"

"They're visiting college coaches. A few are from out of state. A lot of scholarships are going to be decided on this race alone."

Rachel shrugged, smoked. "Billy doesn't care. He said he would never run in college. I don't even think he's going to go."

"That's a mistake."

"How can you say that? Just because he has talent?"

"Sure. That talent can open doors for him. He can go to a school neither of us can afford. UCLA and USC are both looking at him."

"But that would mean he would have to move away."

"L.A. is not that far."

Rachel studied him. "You think I'm selfish. You think I just want to keep him for myself."

"I didn't say that."

"I can read your mind. You're easy, David. And it's true, I do want him for myself, forever. He can't go to college unless I go with him."

"You can. Your grades are not bad."

"Compared to whom? I'm a B-minus student. That will get me into general ed classes at a junior college. Billy's not doing any better. If he gets a scholarship to a UC school, he'll just flunk out."

"They never let their star athletes flunk out."

"He won't even be a star runner in college. You said it yourself, there are a half dozen guys in this race who could win. You're the one who has to go to college. You're the only one of us with a brain."

"All I can do is draw."

"But you're incredible at it, and you could learn to paint." She smiled suddenly, adding a leer. "You can always paint me, *all* you want."

He knew what she was referring to. To save money, they were all staying in the same motel room. That morning, Billy had gotten up early and gone off to have breakfast by himself. He wanted to give the food plenty of time to digest before the race. David had slept late, and had only awakened when Rachel had opened the bathroom door and strode across the room naked from her shower. At the time, she had acted like he was still asleep, and he had done his best to pretend, but they had both known what was going on. A man couldn't sleep with one eye open.

Rachel's smile widened as she stared at him, and she gave him a shove in the chest. "That should inspire you to become a painter," she said.

He laughed. "It does. As long as Billy doesn't discover my motivation."

"Don't worry, David. I love him but I don't tell everything."

That remark was to haunt him later.

The race started and they screamed Billy's name as the herd rounded the track and left the stadium. They climbed up onto the top bench and looked out across the junior college's back fields. The course was entirely flat, boring, designed for fast times and nothing else. The school had been built on the outskirts of the city; there was plenty of room to roam. Except for the track, the runners did not have to repeat a single portion of the course. The grass fields were wide and marked with a line of white chalk. No way to get lost on this course, David thought.

They had brought binoculars—they could see Billy easily. True to his habit in important races, he settled behind the front pack, staying in contact with the leaders but not sweating a few yards' difference. Billy usually ran his second mile faster than the first, and his finishing kick was powerful. But in David's mind Billy looked like he was already straining. The heat was devastating. Even standing still, a cold drink in his hand, David felt slightly dizzy. He hoped Billy was able to adjust as the race continued.

"How does he look?" Rachel asked as he peered through the binoculars.
"It's still early."

"Bullshit. You always know how he's doing right away, even when you're
in the same race as him. Is he in a groove or not?"

David put down the binoculars. Billy was in twentieth place, if he was
lucky. "I think the heat is bothering him," he said.

"Fucking Sacramento," Rachel muttered.

By the first mile, Billy had moved up to tenth, but to David he still looked
like he was straining. He was swinging his arms a lot, his head bobbing from
side to side, his stride wobbling slightly, which meant his legs were probably
heavy. The time for the first mile was slow—4:45. No surprise, the conditions made a sub-nine two-mile an impossibility.

At the mile-and-a-half mark the pack turned back toward the stadium,
running straight across an open grass field, the white line no longer a factor,
the gateway to the track the only beacon the runners needed. Finally, Billy
had drawn even with the front five, and for the first time since the start of the
race David had hope that Billy would win. Beside him, screaming like one of
those cheerleaders she detested, Rachel grabbed his arm.

"Can any of them outkick him?" she asked.

"Tucker can." And Tucker was leading the final charge by five yards.

"Don't tell me that!"

"No one can outkick him!"

"Yea!!! Billy!!! Run!!!"

Maybe Billy heard her—the love of his life, it was possible—and the cheer
might have distracted him. For at that moment he did something David had
never seen him do before in an important race. He stormed into the lead,
pushing the others to run faster to keep up. David was shocked. Billy's ace in
the hole was always his finish. Straight up, he could run a quarter mile in less
than fifty seconds, and he had been known to break fifty-six seconds at the
end of a hard two miles. His strategy against strong runners was always to
hang back until the final two hundred yards and then lay it all on the line.
The two of them had not needed to talk strategy before the race—it was a
given that he would rely on his kick.

"Billy!!!" Rachel screamed louder.

David cheered as well, but inside he was worried. It was possible Billy had
taken the lead because he was feeling strong. Yet he did not look strong. If
anything he looked like a man desperate to complete the last few yards of a

race. His stride was labored, he was clawing at the sky with his arms. And even after they entered the stadium—which would be in a few seconds—they still had a quarter mile to run before they reached the chute. David did not see why it was so important to Billy to enter the stadium first. His frantic burst had given him the lead but he had five guys within ten yards of his heels. And they were drafting off him, physically and psychologically. It was always harder to lead a tight race near the end.

For a few seconds they disappeared beneath the shadow of the stadium as they ran into the tunnel under the stands. David and Rachel turned an about-face, and the roar that went up in the crowd was deafening. Only people who were obsessed with running—or who had a kid in the race—would have been there in the first place. But the noise quickly fell to a shocked silence as Billy came storming out of the tunnel.

Billy came out too fast, too tight on the right side of the tunnel. He had to turn right to complete the final lap, but he came out within inches of the wall and ran smack into a red-coated race official. The collision was brutal—Billy was in full kick, and the official was an old guy with the body of a bird. They didn't merely fall down, they went flying, round and round on top of each other, only coming to a halt as the rest of the runners sped by.

Rachel squealed in horror. The rest of the crowd stayed quiet. Billy got up quickly—even tried to help the official up—but he was obviously dazed and his leg was bleeding. Of course none of that really mattered. The clock was all that counted. He had already lost ten seconds to the front runners and there was no way he was going to make that up in one lap.

He finished the race, though. Limping on his bloody leg, he jogged around the track and finished in the top thirty. The crowd gave him a bigger cheer than the winner, which was the local guy, Tucker. Billy was cheered even as he walked away from the track and into the shade under the stadium. David and Rachel wasted no time in catching up with him.

"That fucking official!" Rachel said as she embraced her sweaty boyfriend, not caring that she got all slimed. "You would have won!"

Billy was still trying to catch his breath, but he shook his head philosophically. "I know, I had it in the palm of my hand. But what can you do? Shit happens."

"You have to lodge a complaint," David said. "That guy should not have been standing there."

Billy shrugged. "He's an old guy, why get him in trouble?"

Rachel was furious. "Don't be such a good sport! You deserve that first-place medal, not that Tucker dude!"

Billy shook his head. "They all know I would have won. Tucker knows. What difference does a medal make?"

David hugged his friend. He had never been so proud of anyone in his life as he was of Billy right then. In a way, what Billy said and did that day meant more to him than if Billy had won the state title.

In the present, however, locked in a claustrophobic jail cell and staring at a possible life sentence, David saw things differently, and it amazed him that he had never looked at that day from an objective perspective. David knew running, he knew Billy's running, and he knew that Tucker would have won that race no matter what. But what struck him was that Billy had also known that. Ironically, Billy had already given up when he had burst into the lead. He had only taken the lead because he realized he had nothing left. He had spent his last strength to fool the crowd into thinking he was going to win.

His veering hard to the right out of the tunnel had been insane.

Billy had run into the official on purpose.

Afterward, he had acted detached so as to look cool. But inside he must have known he had sought out the collision for fear of being humiliated in front of his girlfriend and his best friend. Running out of energy the way he was—which was clearly the case—it was doubtful he would have finished in the top ten. Once again, David was amazed he had not seen the truth before, and wondered if Charlie's words about Billy yesterday had cleared his mind somehow.

Why had Billy felt the need to do it?

David wondered if he had known Billy at all.

SIXTEEN

When Pomus arrived, with Max, he insisted on being allowed into the cell. He then dismissed Max with a wave of the hand. Max tried to protest but the minister gave him a hard glance, and make no mistake, Pomus could look scary when he wished. Max went running.

Pomus sat on the cot beside David, his bulk a trial for the springs, and put an arm around him. Pomus had on his usual brown suit, green tie, and was sweating from the hot day. But for a long time he said little, just held him, told him he was there to help. There was genuine feeling in his voice, and David was swept away by it, and began telling him that he was innocent. Pomus nodded as if he understood.

"I have been asking questions, hearing weird stuff," he said. "I think it's possible someone set you up."

David sat back. "Really? Who have you been talking to?"

"I can't tell you, I don't want to get my sources in trouble. And it doesn't matter, I'm sure you can guess who they are. Just accept that I know most of the facts of the case and I'm anything but convinced you are guilty."

"That's good to hear. You're the first person to say that today."

"You know how most people's minds work—you're guilty until proven innocent. Forgive them and move on. But I'm disappointed that few people are focusing on the fact that Sienna lied to you. From what I understand, she made up a whole new identity before she met you. That's got to tell you something. She couldn't have been up to any good. I'm not surprised she was knocked off."

David's hope at being understood took a big step back. "But Sienna's not dead. The woman they're talking about is not her."

"What do you mean? Didn't they match the hair?"

"I've spoken to Sienna in the last two days."

"I did not know that. You have told them that?"

"Yes. They don't believe me. But Julie Stevens heard Sienna when she called and left a message on my machine."

"Play them the message."

"I can't, I accidentally erased it."

"That is too bad. Who is this other woman?"

"I know nothing about her."

"But she was from New York, like Sienna?"

"Yes."

"Why did you lie to the sheriff? Why didn't you tell them at the start Sienna was from New York?"

"I don't know. I didn't know her address, and I didn't go there to see her."

"Still, that looks bad, particularly when this new girl is from there."

"I have never in my life heard of Sally Wither."

"But the authorities have matched the dead woman with Sienna's picture, via the family. That woman is definitely Sally. I heard they got a copy of her dental records, and they match."

David had not heard about any dental records. "What matches?"

"The corpse and Sally."

"All right! But Sally is not Sienna!"

Pomus shook his head. "This is confusing."

David sighed. "Tell me about it."

Yet the remark about matching dental records shook David. Could she be dead? He did not see how that was possible . . . Yet everyone, except him, was positive she was.

Pomus continued. "I think you need a fresh perspective on this. Sienna lied to you, and to everyone else she met in town. She obviously had something to hide. Then there is this problem with your blurry memory, not to mention that she was killed in a ritualistic fashion. If you ask me, I think you were drugged and set up by a satanic cult. And I think Sienna belonged to that cult."

David might have considered the bizarre idea, except Sienna was alive and at the moment he was not drugged. He told Pomus as much; the minister shook his head.

"You have to look at the facts, David. That FBI agent has put you in jail and he intends to keep you here. Stop talking to him, he is not your friend. The only real friends you have now are Jesus and your soon-to-be-lawyer, and we have to get you that lawyer by tomorrow."

"You can't get Jesus to bail me out?"

"I'm talking to him all the time. But there's a lawyer I know in L.A., Simpson, who is simply brilliant. We go back a long ways. He owes me a favor. I have already spoken to him and he said he would be happy to drive up tomorrow to talk to you. Now I don't want to pressure you, but the sooner you make a decision on representation, the better. They want to arraign you this week, before a judge, to see if there is enough evidence to send this thing to trial."

"Bail would be set at the arraignment?"

"Yes. But Simpson is a magician. I told him about the case, what I knew, and he said he thought he could get the charges dropped."

"How?"

"Lack of evidence. I think that FBI agent jumped the gun when he arrested you."

"I don't know, Krane is shrewd."

"Talk to Simpson."

"I can't afford a guy like that."

"It's not a problem. Like I said, we go way back. He will represent you for free for now."

"But what if it does go to trial?"

"Let us worry about that after the arraignment. Can I tell Simpson to come?"

"Yes. But I will have to speak to him before I decide to let him represent me."

"Sure. I'm just trying to help out. But he will tell you what I am telling you now. Keep your mouth shut. Everything you say can and will be used against you."

"But I have done nothing wrong!"

Pomus squeezed his shoulder. "I understand, David. This pretty woman shows up in town and lies to you and tells you she loves you and wraps your heart around her finger and soon you don't know whether you're coming or going. And now you're in jail and all confused and you don't know where to turn."

David felt cold inside. Pomus was humoring him, it was obvious. Like Stanton, he believed he was guilty. The minister was only suggesting the alternative possibilities to show that he was on his side. He just wanted him to beat the rap. A friend would do that, of course, but it struck David as obscene that a man of God should not be more concerned about the truth.

"I may not be able to remember everything that happened that night, but I know who I am," David replied. "Even if I was drugged, even if I was somehow brainwashed, I know in my heart I could never hurt Sienna."

"Can I tell you something? Something very few people know about me?"

"Sure."

"I need you to keep it private. It's a deeply personal matter."

"I won't tell a soul," David promised.

Pomus looked away, through the bars, at the far wall—rectangular bricks painted pale green. There was no window in the cell, no view of the back parking lot. And the fluorescent light overhead, it was like a tube filled with uranium gas. The harsh white glow stripped the life out of the air. Beneath it the flesh on Pomus's face appeared loose and gray. When he spoke next, it was as if he were in a confession booth that had no exit.

"I was not young when I got married. I had been a preacher for twenty years. But when I met Jane, I fell in love in an instant. She was the prettiest little thing. I wanted to marry her after our first date, but it took several months and constant badgering on my part to get her to consider it. But she finally consented to be with me, even though she knew what I was, which was a fire and brimstone soul winner, a bitter man who only saw black and white, who had not an ounce of empathy for those who deviated from what he considered the Lord's path. I was a piece of work then, David. You might think I'm not much different now but believe me I am. That man was cold as ice, and he made Jane's life miserable. There was nothing she could do that I didn't find fault with. Even when it came to my morning coffee. I would literally throw it back at her if it was too cold or hot, or too weak or too strong." Pomus stopped and shook his head. "Was it any wonder that she finally asked me for a divorce?"

David did not quite know what to say, so he said nothing. Pomus continued.

"I remember that day well. I was watching a baseball game on TV and she walked into the living room and told me she was leaving me. No warning, no explanation, no chance for us to try to work it out. God knows she had the right, after all I had put her through. But I did not see it that way, no sir. I immediately accused her of cheating on me, and that was only the beginning of my abuse. We fought for the next week, without resting, and I would not let her out of the house. In the end I hurt her, I physically hurt my wife, and then, when she was lying there on the bed crying, something deep inside me snapped, and I knew that everything I was, everything I stood for, had nothing to do with Jesus Christ. It was only then that I truly became a Christian. Because it was only then that I learned the meaning of forgiveness."

Another pause. David felt he had to say something.

"But had she cheated on you? Was there anything to forgive?"

"Jane had done nothing wrong, and even if she had, that is not the point. I was a walking judge and jury. My mind was obsessed with trivia. There was no room inside me for compromise. I didn't understand the core of Christ's teaching, which is: no matter how sinful we are, no matter who we harm, He will forgive us. It's such a simple insight, something I had said a hundred times to my own parishioners, but I could not see it until right then. That day, it was not that I had to forgive Jane. I had to forgive myself." He added, "That was the only way I was able to let her go."

"Jane is Mary's mother?"

"Yes. Didn't I mention that?"

"No. Where is she now?"

"I have no idea. I let her go completely. That's what I had to do. From that day on I was a changed man. God was with me. I could meet the worst sinner and not judge them. Jesus is all that matters, and Jesus forgives."

"But what about justice?"

"Justice does not exist in this world! Could I give Jane justice for what I had put her through? If I punished myself would it make her feel any better? Of course not. You know we have had this argument before. The Eastern law of karma is not valid because it does not allow for the intervention of grace.

It does not matter how the Buddhists and the Hindus try to frame it. Karma is cause and effect. Who could ever get free with such a system? Sin has to be forgiven, it has to be wiped clean. No evil act can overshadow the power of God's grace. That is exactly what allowed me to change. I'm here because of that grace, here to help you."

David had not seen Pomus so worked up in a long time. "I wouldn't want God to forgive me if I sliced up a young woman," he said. "Especially if it was someone I loved."

Pomus stared at him, shook his head, sighed. "You have to get out of this jail. You have no idea what a lifetime behind bars means. You can try to imagine it but the reality will be a thousand times worse."

"I am innocent."

"That is what I am saying. We are all innocent in the eyes of God."

"No. I am innocent in the eyes of man."

"Then talk to Simpson, let him deal with the men who have put you in here. I am not opposed to common sense. That's what I have been telling you since I walked in here. Play this human drama out, play it to win. But know that there is a greater power behind all that is happening to you."

"That I can well believe."

"Good. Then we are in agreement." Pomus stood slowly and pulled out his red handkerchief, dabbing his forehead, towering over him like an over-dressed snowman in a crowded sauna. His little sermon had gotten his breath up; he wheezed noticeably. Again he patted David on the back, and added, "I talk too much. It's a bad habit. I love to preach. But I mean well. It breaks my heart to see you stuck in here."

David squeezed his hand. "I know you mean well. And I know I can never thank you enough for the help you are giving me now."

"If the situation was reversed, you would do the same for me."

"I would . . ." David had to stop; the thought of Mary and Herb naked on the beach put a lump in his throat. "Reverend?" he said.

"Yes?"

"I need to tell you something. It's not easy for me."

"Just tell me. I will understand."

"No. It's not about me. It's about Mary and Herb. I saw them . . . I mean, I have seen them together, and I don't think he's a good influence on her."

"What are you trying to say?"

"Herb is the town pusher, and Mary's young and impressionable. It doesn't matter that he goes to your prayer meetings every week. People don't change overnight. I mean, maybe you did but most of us don't." He shook his head. "If I had a daughter, he would be the last person I would want hanging out with her."

"Are you sure you don't judge him too harshly? I know he sells drugs but he is honestly trying to change. He's not a coward. You do know it was Herb who saved your two friends from that fire when you were all in high school?"

"I haven't forgotten."

"I can talk to her if you are concerned. See what is going on inside her head."

"Thanks. It's none of my business, but it worries me that she's not living with you. She's only fifteen."

Pomus waved his hand. "She's just down the block. I see her every day. Frankly, between you and me, she's not that easy to live with. She's strong-willed. She's a lot like her mother that way."

David nodded, not sure why he was afraid to tell Pomus the whole truth. Perhaps he feared the man would not believe him. Pomus did not believe him when he said he had not murdered Sienna. On that front, according to Pomus, Jesus and a high-priced lawyer were the only things that could save him from a life of hell.

"I can imagine," David said.

Pomus turned to leave but then stopped. David watched him closely, and noticed the sudden change in him. It was as if at the last moment the minister had finally let his real feelings show on his face. Yet it was not an expression David could easily decipher. Before he spoke next, Pomus appeared both worried and distant—a peculiar mix. He looked down at David, just stared, then he shook slightly as if chilled.

"There is something I didn't tell you about that difficult time with my wife," he said finally. "Something that might relate to what is going on here."

"What?"

"I saw a demon."

David smiled. "Did it have leathery wings?"

Pomus shook his head. "I'm being serious. It was after we'd been arguing for several days. I left Jane to get something to eat. McDonald's, a hamburger, something quick. When I walked back into our house, I noticed a dark area around the couch. It was at the far end, where I usually sat to watch TV. At first I thought it was from eyestrain. The two of us had not been sleeping much. But when I blinked and rubbed my eyes, it did not go away. It did the opposite, actually—it started to coalesce, take on shape. I saw two legs, two arms, a head. It was larger than a man and it was black, although I thought I saw a red glow around its head."

"Why do you say it was a demon?"

"I don't know what else to call it. It never got completely clear. It was like a cloud made of soot. But as I stared at it, the eyes became visible and they were strange. They were neither dark nor red, they were more like holes. Holes into nothing. When I stared at them, I found it impossible to look away." Pomus added, "I don't know how long I stood there like that. It could have been for hours."

"Hours?"

Pomus nodded gravely. "It had me hypnotized."

"What did you do? Did you pray for it to leave?"

"No. To be frank, I forgot who I was for a while."

"Then what happened?"

"What do you mean?"

"Did it go away?"

Pomus shrugged. "It faded from view. I couldn't see it anymore."

"You imagined it. This sort of thing—domestic abuse—you had to be feeling tons of guilt. And you're a minister—it's no surprise you would imagine a devil coming to punish you for fighting with your wife. You hadn't slept in days. Your stress level must have been off the scale. What you saw— it doesn't surprise me at all."

"Don't fool yourself, David. What I saw was real. It was a demon."

"I don't believe such things exist."

"If you'd seen it, you would have believed it."

"Why are you telling me this? How could it possibly relate to my situation?"

Pomus sighed. "This murder was a satanic killing. No one is focusing on what that really means because we don't want to. I'm no better. I came here today to talk to you about lawyers and legal strategy and getting you out of this place. I'm a minister, like you said, and I don't even want to talk about what's really going on here."

"Which is?"

"Do you have to ask? We've had these arguments before. You know my point of view on the time we live in. These are the last days, all manner of forces are gathering—demons and angels. This is the most crucial period in humanity's history. Jesus Christ, the Antichrist—they are only waiting to appear. This type of killing—it is a sign."

"No. It is just the twisted act of a demented individual. The police and the FBI have searched in vain for the last fifty years for any large-scale satanic movement."

"They have looked in the wrong places. I can't tell you how I know this, not now, but I am sure of it. Trust me, David. Also, this is not an isolated ritual killing. There have been others. That guy, Krane, he knows about them."

"How do you know what he knows?"

Pomus waved the question away. "I told you, I can't reveal my sources. And it doesn't matter, it is true, it is a fact. I tell you, there is more here than meets the eye. We are just pawns in a larger game. God only knows how it is going to turn out in the end."

"But what does your demon have to do with me?"

Pomus stared him in the eye. "Maybe it didn't really go away. Just because we can't see it, that doesn't mean it's not right here, working in this very town. You have to admit, Lompoc has seen more than its fair share of tragedy." He added quietly, "When we buried Billy, I talked about this. But no one wanted to hear it."

"I remember," David replied, not sure what else to say. He was not interested in demons, and Sienna had certainly not been interested in the Devil. The few times he had tried to talk to her about religion, she had brushed him off as if he were wasting her time.

SEVENTEEN

When Pomus left, David went through the bag Julie had brought to the station. There were pants and sweats inside, two fresh T-shirts, his toilet kit and ten chocolate bars. He did not remember telling Julie that he was a chocolate freak; nevertheless, he was grateful for the candy. He ate a bar after Pomus left.

Two hours after David saw the minister, Stanton came by with fried chicken and mashed potatoes. He brought milk and Coke—David drank both, although what he really wanted was a bottle of Evian. Stanton said he would see what he could do. The sheriff seemed happy that he had agreed to meet with Pomus's attorney.

"His name is Simpson, from L.A. Have you heard of him?" David asked as he ate. The chicken tasted great, all things considered, and the potatoes were still warm. He had read somewhere that all cons thought about was food and sex. Thank God he had Max to help him with the latter.

"Vaguely. I know his firm—Hadfield and Green. They have a good reputation. He would have to be smart to be their lead criminal attorney."

"Pomus didn't tell me that."

Stanton nodded. "I understand they save him for their heavy hitters."

"No relation to OJ?"

Stanton smiled. "No."

"Pomus thinks Simpson is going to get me out of here."

"I couldn't comment on that."

"I understand." David added, "You didn't tell me about the matching dental records."

"You didn't ask. But I warned you, Krane is busy building his case."

"Don't put it all on Krane."

"In the end, on this case, he's the boss."

"But everything you discover must be disclosed to me and my lawyer."

"At the appropriate time, David. That's why you need a lawyer. He will know what to ask for, and when."

"Right now I'd like to ask a question about the condition of the body, if you don't mind. It was all left vague to me. She had been killed in a ritualistic manner. What exactly does that mean?"

"She was opened with a knife and disemboweled."

"I got that part. What was done with her organs?"

"I should not discuss that right now. Have your lawyer request the information."

"Has the coroner completed his report?"

"Not a final report. It takes time to do DNA and tox screen tests. Those guys hate to make mistakes. But he has filed a preliminary report that your attorney can see."

"I'm sure it will make for interesting reading. Can I use the phone?"

"Who do you want to call?"

"Does it matter? You said earlier that I could use it."

Stanton stood. "Let me see if I can find a cord that reaches back here."

The sheriff returned in five minutes, phone in hand. He went to excuse himself but David bid him stay. "I'm going to call my house, check my messages," he said.

"To see if Sienna called?"

"Do you have a problem with that?"

"You can call whoever you want."

David dialed the number, punched in the secret code, listened. No voice message but at least ten hang ups. He let Stanton listen to them. The sheriff was unimpressed.

"It could be anybody," he said.

"Everyone in town knows I'm in jail. They wouldn't call me at home."

"It could be your parents calling. They might have heard something."

"They would have left a message."

"Why didn't she?"

"I'm sure she feels frustrated that she's unable to catch me."

"You're reaching."

"You are. You have been from the start." David handed back the phone. "Tell me, did you think of me as a suspect when we drove down to Santa Barbara yesterday?"

"No."

"But today you're convinced I'm guilty. All because of a few hairs. Think about it, Sheriff, you've known me all my life. Can you see me with a long knife, cutting open a woman I love, and walking away with her heart and liver?"

"No. But you buried yourself with your statement."

"There could have been someone else on the beach that night."

"Who?"

"No idea. But when I went to the hypnotist—I know you've heard about it—I did remember one thing I had forgotten. Sienna was scared that night. She kept looking up and down the beach. It was like she was expecting a visitor."

"Then you blacked out?"

"I never said I blacked out."

"Whatever. Amnesia is the oldest card in the deck."

David had no answer for that. His excuse felt cliché to himself.

Stanton left, and he did not come back. David did not have a watch. He did not know what time it was, whether it was dark or light outside. He could hear nothing from the front of the station. With the cessation of visitors, time began to weigh heavily on his mind. Pomus had been right about one thing. He could not imagine a lifetime of this.

His cell had two walls of bricks, two of bars. The bars on his right led into another cell. Fortunately it was empty. He didn't need a drunk pissing on him. The cot was in the corner against the walls, the mattress as thick as one of those romance novels he used to paint covers for and just as irritating. Next came the sink and the toilet. The latter were clean and white, ads for Lysol. The odor filled the cell like an antiseptic for the sinful. Maybe if he stopped and prayed Jesus would bring him a box of Ajax. He thought Pomus had lost it for a few minutes there with his talk about that demon.

He decided he had to do something about the fluorescent light. The sterile white glow was rotting his imagination. Moving the cot into the center of the cell, he folded the mattress over twice and climbed up and reached out and unscrewed the tube. He might have been in too much of a hurry. The tube came out and flew past his nose and cracked on the concrete floor. Wiping up the mess, he cut his finger; the injury bled like crazy. He didn't call for help, though. He was afraid he might get Max, and the guy would spread the rumor all over town that he had tried to commit suicide. He ended up bandaging it with toilet paper.

But he didn't get the dark he craved. There was another fluorescent light down the hall, off to his left. He wished he had a rock to throw at it. He wished he had a book to read, the manuscript he was supposed to be working on. Of course now he wouldn't be able to read without the light. He didn't know what the hell he was doing.

He laid down, tried to sleep, failed, tried to concentrate on his case. The People versus David Lennon in the matter of Sally Wither. Who the hell was she? Sienna could never have had such a boring name. Yet it did not escape him that both names began with S. He had never asked Sienna if she had a middle name. For that matter, he had never seen her driver's license, never seen her use a credit card. He had paid for everything.

"I suppose I'm still paying," he told the walls.

The big fact that was keeping him sane was Simpson's comment to Pomus—that the attorney said he could get him out right away. But the remark did not stand up under scrutiny. Simpson only knew of the case through Pomus, and the minister did not have all the facts. Also, David found it impossible to believe Krane would have arrested him unless he was confident he could keep him in jail. David sensed power in Krane, Stanton saw it as well. Krane was on his third case of this type. He had not solved the others but he was determined to solve this one. Maybe he thought this one held the key to the others. He might even be operating out of revenge. His voice had faltered when he had spoken about his dead partner, Carol. David did not think that had been an act.

But common sense told him that Krane was his enemy. The FBI agent had admitted as much. If he could not find another suspect, he was going to focus on him and get the conviction. David wondered if Krane had interviewed Mary or Herb. He would have liked to talk to them. Why did they have to have sex on that spot?

And they had known Sienna. Herb had even taken pictures of her.

The thought was distasteful. But it did send his mind off on another tangent. The time the two of them had taken a road trip up north, along the coast. That had been only three months ago, hard to imagine.

They had not planned the trip. On a whim, waking up together one morning in Lompoc, they decided to drive north to Morro Bay for lunch, home of the big rock and thick fog.

"I know a place on the water, close to the rock. They have the best fish and chips," David told her as they drove up Route 101. The day was sunny; he had not brought a jacket. Just his usual casual pants and a long-sleeved white shirt; a sweatshirt was stowed in the trunk if he needed it. Sienna had on her favorite long black leather coat, a red blouse and gray slacks. She was always cold.

"I haven't eaten fish and chips since I was in England," she said.

"When were you there last?" It was rare that she talked about her past.

"Two years ago, in the summer. It was lovely."

"Were you there on business?"

"I wasn't there with a guy. Is that what you want to know?"

"It might surprise you to learn that I do not live my life in a constant state of jealousy."

She punched his right shoulder lightly, a habit of hers. "That's not something I want. You have no reason to be jealous."

"They all say that."

"Who is *they?* The female species?"

"Exactly. Are you ever jealous of my past?"

"No."

"Why not?"

Sienna looked over at him and smiled in that way only she could. It had been wonderful to wake up beside her an hour ago and know that he was going to spend the whole day with her.

"You have no past. You only started to live when you met me," she said.

"Sometimes I feel that way."

"Not all the time?"

"No. I remember a past life that did not include you."

"You were probably a frog."

"Thanks!"

"How young?"

"I was two."

"You don't remember when you were two."

She shook her head. "I remember this place. Keep going."

The road entered a maze, winding up and down along the rocky cliffs. The back and forth motion seemed to make Sienna drowsy. She lay her head back and put her feet up and passed out. He must have looked over at her a hundred times.

Two hours later they were in Big Sur, and they were lucky to find a two-hundred-dollar room in a tiny hotel entrenched deep in the redwoods. The place was booked but late that night they had the hot tub to themselves. Sienna was in a bold mood. Taking off her suit—he had purchased it at a nearby shop, along with toothbrushes—she sat on his lap and kissed him forever. For him, it was a magical moment: there were fairies in the trees; the elves stopped to sing. Rain began to fall but the steam rose up and kept them warm. Afterward, they were both satisfied and tired, yet Sienna did not want to leave the tub when he got out.

"I'll come soon," she said. "You rest."

"I can't leave you out here alone."

"You can, I won't melt." She glanced up at him, still naked, her brown hair wet and tangled like a mermaid's mane, her green eyes drowsy but restless as well. "I need to be alone for a few minutes."

He had never gone on a trip with her before, had never spent an entire day with her for that matter. He did not know what she meant, but in that moment, he did not want to know. He just wanted to love her. He nodded and walked away. He was half asleep by the time she came in, and he felt her snuggle up to his side; a feeling of absolute comfort.

The next day they crossed the Golden Gate Bridge, and still they felt no urge to stop. Sienna continued to doze in the car. She told him he must be boring her. In the evening, close to the Oregon border, they halted in a place called Eon, a small town wrapped by tall trees and a lonely harbor, stumbling upon a traveling carnival that looked too big for the city and too strange for America. The fair was made up of European Gypsies, African dwarves and Middle-Eastern strongmen; and the white-faced clowns who walked the aisles looked like figures cut from a tale, laughing and sneering, daring them to join in the fun.

"Of course that makes you a prince now." She leaned over and kissed h
on the cheek. "My prince. You saved me."

"How did I save you?"

Sienna just laughed and looked out the window.

They arrived early for lunch at Ed's Wharf, and took a booth in the cor
ner by the windows. They had a clear view of the giant rock; it looked like
something that had crash-landed on earth at slow speed. Outside, in the cold
water, two seals played games with a pile of seaweed. Sienna seemed
enchanted by the creatures.

"That's what we should be in our next life. Imagine—no responsibilities,
no worries. We could swim anywhere we wanted whenever we wanted,"
she said.

"What about great whites? They patrol these waters, feeding on seals."

"Thanks. Ruin my fantasy why don't ya?" She added, "Do the sharks
come in this close?"

"Not in large numbers. But surfers and fishermen see them often
enough."

She pointed at the seals, delighted; they were doing a water dance. "We
should give them names," she said.

"David and Sienna?"

"Romeo and Juliet. And if a shark gets them, he'll take them both in the
same gulp. They don't look like they can live without each other." She
turned back to him, took his hands. "Like us," she said.

They ended up splitting an order of fish and chips. Sienna ate little,
focused on her coffee. She could drink ten cups a day and never act wired.
She called it her drug, like everyone needed a fix of something.

After lunch, they kept going north, not discussing the matter, just driving,
enjoying the coastal scenery and each other's company. True to the area, a
low-lying bank of fog crept in from over the water. It shadowed them,
though, rather than grabbed them whole, turning the sunshine into a flirt.

They came to Hearst Castle. For travelers, it was almost a religious obligation to stop and gawk at the billionaire's palace, high on the hill, with
wide views of the ocean that could no longer be had on either coast. Sienna
thought the mansion gaudy, however; she wanted to keep driving.

"Have you ever taken a tour?" David asked.

"When I was young. My parents brought me here."

Sienna giggled and held onto his arm as they moved from one booth to another. Most offered the usual fun: throw the dart and pop the balloons or dunk the fat man with the ball. David tried his hand at the latter and won a pink doll with a face like an angel. It pleased him, the way Sienna cuddled it, as if it offered her some sort of protection. But when he asked her to try to dunk the fat man, she declined, saying her wrists hurt.

"I have carpal tunnel," she said.

"I didn't know that. Do you take anything for it?"

"Pills. When it is bad."

"You never told me that."

"Why should I? Pain is boring."

"Like me?"

"Yes. But at least you are a fun bore."

"I am so grateful," he said.

They found a fortune-teller. What was a traveling carnival without an old witch who could read the future? Yet this woman was not that old, maybe fifty, and she looked more Persian than Gypsy. Her was hair long and gray, adorned with oversized jewels that could not possibly have been real. She did not have a crystal ball, although the sign said she was a master at reading palms. Five dollars a hand, which made him assume that he would have to shell out twenty bucks to get both their fortunes told.

Sienna thought it too expensive, but David was intrigued by the way the woman caught his eye. Her face was austere, her nose narrow, the lines around her eyes fine but deeply etched, as if past tragedies had come upon her from above.

"I want to talk to her," he whispered to Sienna.

"Why? I can always rub your hands." She touched his ear with her lips. "I'll rub whatever you want."

He stared at the woman, who appeared to be waiting for them, dressed in her black robe. "I want to ask her if you really love me," he said.

Sienna glanced at the woman, did not seem to approve. "If you have to," she said. "But leave me out, save the five bucks."

"I think it'll be ten each."

"More the reason."

They sat at the table, and the woman just nodded and took his hands; she was not much of a conversationalist. She had a soothing touch; however, her fingers were hot and moist, like warm towels, and she took her job seriously, studying his hands for several minutes before uttering a word. Sienna yawned and looked bored.

"You are a good man," she said finally, a bit of a rasp in her voice. "You have a sensitive heart. You see things and you want to hold onto them. Are you an artist?"

David smiled. "Yes. How did you know?"

"You have oil paint under your nails," Sienna muttered.

The woman ignored her, traced a line on David's left palm. "This is your intellect line. See how clear it is? How close it runs to your heart? You were born to create things of beauty." But when she looked to his right hand she frowned.

"What is it?" he asked.

She hesitated. "The left hand represents what you came into this world with. The right hand tells your future as well, but from the point of view of the present moment. Do you understand?"

"Yes. Are they very different? Did I mess up my destiny?"

The woman returned to his left palm, traced a thick line that ran from above his thumb down the center of his hand to his wrist. "This is your life line. See how long and strong it is?"

"Yes. That's good, isn't it?"

"Yes." She turned to his right palm, traced the same line, which did not come anywhere close to his wrist. "But here your life line is cut off. It just stops."

"That's bad?"

"I have never seen one stop so suddenly."

David smiled nervously. "Even in people who ended up dying young?"

The woman shook her head. "No. Usually with an early death there is some sign of it in the left palm as well."

"I believe that," Sienna said sarcastically.

The woman stared at her. "I know what I know. I have read thousands of palms."

Sienna was annoyed. "Then you should know better than to try to upset people by telling them they are going to die young."

"I did not say your young man was going to die young. The difference between the lines—it is a mystery to me as well." She frowned as she looked at Sienna. Then she beckoned impatiently. "Let me see your hands."

Sienna drew back. "No. I'll pass."

"I'll not charge you. Let me see your hands."

"No."

"If she wants to do it for free, let her," David said, not happy with his reading. Reluctantly, Sienna allowed her hands to be taken. The woman shivered.

"You are cold," she said.

"I am skinny. Skinny people get cold easily," Sienna replied.

"I don't," the woman said, bending over, perhaps finding the lines on Sienna's palms harder to read. They were not as distinct as the ones on his hands. The woman seemed to strain the whole time she searched.

"What do you see?" David asked finally.

The woman spoke to Sienna, tracing a line that started below her left little finger. "This is your heart line. You see it is straight and unbroken. That means that you were born to love deeply. Also, this line that intersects it—it does so when you are close to thirty. How old are you now, child?"

"I'm not a child. I'm twenty-eight."

"It's at this age you'll meet the one true love of your life."

Sienna nodded, glanced at him. "That sounds good."

"Does it say his name?" David joked. But the woman was already shaking her head, focused on Sienna's right palm, the present-day one that had messed up his future. She traced Sienna's other heart line.

"But you see this path is cracked and broken. The line is seldom in one piece."

"What does it mean?" David asked. Sienna was not going to ask. She was staring at the woman with ill-disguised contempt. Again, the woman spoke directly to Sienna, not intimidated.

"It means you have not given the love you were born to give."

"To whom?" Sienna asked.

"It doesn't matter to whom. It only matters that you give it, and soon."

Sienna had heard enough. "You don't know me!" she snapped, taking back her hands and grabbing her doll and fleeing from the table. David rose clumsily, reaching for his wallet, knocking over his chair.

"I think you upset her," he said, pulling out a twenty. The woman waved away the cash.

"Go with her, if you love her." She thought he was a fool to do so.

David shook his head. "She's not a bad person. You scared her is all."

The woman lowered her head, did not reply, just looked depressed.

Later, lying in bed beside Sienna in a cheap motel on the other side of town from the circus, the pink doll wedged between them, David heard her weep, a soft childlike whimper. It went on for twenty minutes, but he was not sure if she was truly awake so he said nothing. Better to let her rest, he thought. And in the end she was silent.

EIGHTEEN

Jack Simpson was short and bald, his head so smooth it could have been used to shine pennies. He had a sober expression, a detached professionalism; his pale blue eyes blinked but the absence of eyelids made the motion largely invisible. He had asked how David had felt after spending a night in jail, but David could have said that he had wanted to open his veins with his teeth and Mr. Simpson would have just nodded. The lawyer's complexion was ruddy, the color of wine mixed with tap water. Maybe he had an allergy to the cologne he wore. His pores labored in the station heat. The air-conditioning was not a problem anymore, it was broken.

Simpson spoke in a quick precise tone, sounding smart. David listened closely.

"I have been reviewing the evidence against you. I think we stand a good chance of having the case dismissed, at least for the time being. The district attorney wants the arraignment to take place tomorrow. That's quick—I think the FBI agent who arrested you is pressuring him. It should work to our advantage. In an arraignment the burden of proof is on the DA. He has to present the judge with enough evidence to convince him that this thing should go to trial. However, the burden of proof is not as stringent as a trial. The DA doesn't have to meet the criteria of reasonable doubt. But he must show that he has a reasonable chance of convicting you in front of a jury. In other words, his facts must be physical facts."

"They have the hair from Sienna's guest house. It matches the dead woman."

"That is their key evidence. Yet it is not as strong as it appears on the surface. In fact, if they did not have your own statement—which connects you to the location of the body—they would not have bothered to arrest you."

David frowned. "Are you sure about that?"

"Yes. Let's look for a minute at what they don't have. This woman was carved up with a knife. Do they have the knife? No. Have they found a knife at your house that matches the type of blade that was used to kill this woman? No."

"They are checking out knives at my house?"

"Yes. You didn't know?"

"No."

"The FBI agent says you gave him permission to search your house." Simpson held up a hand as David went to protest. "Don't worry, I'm sure he got a judge to give him permission. The search is not a bad thing. I would not have challenged it had I been here earlier—assuming there is no murder weapon at your house. In court they will have to admit they searched your house and found nothing that ties you to the murder."

Simpson let the remark hang. David spoke quickly, "They can search all they want, they won't find anything."

"Good. Let me continue. They think they have a motive for this murder. Your girlfriend was dumping you and you got upset. But that is weak. I assume you have had other girlfriends, and they have broken up with you, and you didn't kill any of them?"

"Not that I know of."

"Good. You have no criminal record, and there's nothing in your past that suggests you are a violent person. The town sheriff has told me as much, and he has known you since you were a boy. Their problem gets worse. This woman was not simply murdered. She was killed in a ritualistic fashion. Let me ask you a question. Are you a satanist?"

"No."

"Can a single person in town testify that you are a satanist?"

"No."

"Yet this was a satanic killing. You see their difficulty. They are talking about an extremely twisted act. Their motive does not hold up."

"Could they have other evidence we do not know about?"

"It's possible. But they do not want to show all their cards at this point. It will weaken them if this ends up going to trial. They merely want to tell the judge enough to keep you locked up. But even on that point they are not worried. You grew up in this town. Your roots are here. It would be better if you had a wife and kids, but still, you're not a flight risk. They're not hell-bent on keeping you behind bars, not if it means exposing their full case against you. They'll let you go, if they have to. They can always arrest you later."

"I'm confused. You're not trying for bail?"

"Why should I? You didn't do anything wrong. Look, they don't have a single witness who says they saw you kill that woman. They don't have a single piece of your clothes with her blood on it. For all we know she came back to the beach the day after you broke up and a drifter killed her. She could have come back two weeks later—when you were in New York. They're far from certain when she died. The judge will consider all that."

David started to feel better. It had been a long night, without a clock, a window, a phone. He had slept at most two hours, and even when he had been unconscious, he had dreamed of comparing palms with Sienna.

"You've spoken with Reverend Pomus," David said. "He tells me that you're old friends. He must have told you that I don't think that dead woman is my ex-girlfriend. I mean, I spoke to her not two days ago."

"I'm not going to bring that up at the arraignment."

"Why not?"

"The FBI has proof that the woman you were dating is the dead woman."

"They are mistaken."

"Fine. Leave it till later, if this goes to trial. Prove it then."

"But I want this point cleared up now."

"It is their job to clear things up, not yours. Your job is to stop talking to them."

"I felt free to talk to them because I'm innocent."

"Innocence is overrated in a murder investigation. What can be proven in court is all that matters. There are many people in the jails of this nation who are innocent. There are still more guilty people walking the streets.

This is not a moral dilemma that you must confront. This is a legal fight you must win."

David was not sure but he thought his lawyer had just told him that he believed he was guilty, but that it was irrelevant. David tried not to take it personally. He was getting used to the attitude.

"Why would the FBI arrest me if the evidence against me could be pushed aside so easily?" David asked.

"They might have wanted to shake you up to get information out of you. I hate to say it, but they might have already succeeded with their plan."

"What Krane and I discussed—he said it was off the record."

"Somehow I find that hard to believe."

"Would he just lie?"

"Everybody lies."

"Let's get down to the nitty gritty. I like what you have to say. It makes sense to me. I want you to represent me. But I don't have the money to pay you right now."

"It is not a problem. I owe Pomus a favor, this is my way of repaying it."

"But what if this thing does go to trial?"

"Let's just get you out of jail first. Agreed?"

David nodded. "That sounds good to me."

Simpson had come early, eight o'clock. David did not shower or eat break-fast until after the lawyer had left. David had not known the station even had a shower until Stanton led him to a large bathroom in the far corner of the building. The sheriff gave him a fresh towel, did not bother handcuffing him. The hot water made him feel human again. Afterward, back in the cell, the two of them shared bear claws and coffee—Starbucks no less. David offered to pay for the food but Stanton waved his hand.

"We have petty cash for that," he said.

"Such a deal. Free room and board. If I get convicted and go to the peni-tentiary will you still bring me my cappuccino?"

"I don't think they would allow that." Stanton paused. "Like your lawyer?"

"Yeah. He's no bullshitter. He says you're the enemy."

"It's probably true."

Charlie and Karen showed up around lunch—Stanton let them in. They had not come together; their timing was a coincidence. There was moment of tension between them as they sat on the folding chairs outside the bars, but it did not last. Their focus was on him. Karen had brought him more stuff from home: clothes, his boom box, CDs, a few magazines, a bag of cookies, a six-pack of Coke, his watch—smart girl. Still no Evian in sight, but she had remembered the manuscript as well, and his drawing pad.

"I figured you might get some work done," she said.

"If you're really bored, you can always masturbate," Charlie said, handing him the latest *Playboy*. David laughed as he took the magazine.

"Thanks. You're helping to keep me heterosexual."

"Has Massive Max tried to kiss you yet?" Charlie asked.

"I think he's afraid I might bite him."

"I wouldn't be surprised if Max was the one who killed that woman," Karen said. "That guy has always given me the creeps."

"I heard you thought I was guilty," David said.

"Who said that? The sheriff? I didn't tell him that. I just said how Sienna fucked with your head is all."

The remark warmed David's heart. It had shaken him yesterday to think his friends believed he was capable of murder. He asked what the local gossip was and got a pleasant surprise. He had misjudged his fellow Lompocians. They were full of conspiracy theories—some comical.

"Lots of people think Sienna was a member of a cult, and that they sacrificed her because she pissed them off," Charlie said. "Look at the facts. She shows up in town out of nowhere, says almost nothing about her past, makes up a phony name, and then tries to leave for no reason."

"How does everyone know so much about her?" David asked.

"Hey. People talk," Charlie said.

"You mean, you talk," Karen said.

"Like you're not telling everyone who comes into the drugstore what a freak she was," Charlie said.

"She was a freak," Karen said. "I knew that the day I met her. Don't try to defend her, David. That chick had skeletons in her closet, no pun intended."

"It's no surprise someone knocked her off," Charlie added.

David glanced at Karen, back to Charlie. "Charlie, she's not dead. This whole thing is a misunderstanding. I talked to her yesterday afternoon."

Charlie was hip to the idea. "I heard that. That's another theory. People are saying she faked her death. Personally, I think she had a twin sister, and knocked her off for inheritance reasons."

"That is so cliché," Karen said.

"That doesn't make it any less likely," Charlie said. "I heard that FBI agent went back to her place looking for more skin and hair samples. But he couldn't find anything. The carpet had been shampooed and vacuumed with one of those high-powered machines. The walls had been painted, and the bathroom had been practically soaked in Lysol—the one chemical that wrecks any kind of DNA test. Think about that—that's suspicious."

"How do you know all this?" David asked.

"He must have given Max a back massage," Karen teased.

Charlie chuckled. "Max talks to whoever talks to him. He told me he went with Krane to Sienna's place. Can you imagine that guy at a potential crime scene? He's going to compromise the evidence so much that your case will probably just get tossed out. Someone told me that he's trying to get a book deal in New York—the inside scoop on the satanic murder. Can you imagine? Max can't even read."

"Stanton had no trouble finding hairs two days ago," David said.

"That's just it. Now those hairs look like they were planted," Charlie said.

"Interesting," David muttered. It was, very.

"People in town know you," Karen said. "They know you're not into the Devil."

"But Rachel and Billy are back on people's minds," Charlie said. "Suicides and ritual killings often go together. Lots of people are saying you were set up for this crime because you know who killed them."

David shook his head. "I don't want that kind of talk going around."

"You're not going to stop it," Karen said. "People are talking about Herb and Mary—they're huge suspects. They're always together, and that Mary—the way she's made up—she looks like Lucy Lucifer. I heard they were down at the beach yesterday."

"Who told you that?" David asked.

"I don't remember."

Charlie snorted. "I'm the one who told you, Karen. What is it with your memory lately? I'm the pothead."

"I thought you said you quit."

"I started again when you dumped me."

"I didn't dump you."

"You packed my bags. It's the same difference."

David held up his hand. "Please. I'm in jail for murder here. What's the media coverage like? Are they talking about it on the radio? Are there reporters outside?"

Charlie answered. "It is all they are talking about on the radio, and there's been a dozen reporters outside—continually. You didn't know?"

David shook his head. He'd had no idea.

"You're big news all over the state," Karen said. "But that's not necessarily a bad thing because the more attention that is focused on this, the more the police and the FBI have to look for other suspects."

David did not believe that but he let it pass.

"Plus we know Mary and Herb knew Sienna," Charlie added.

"Sally Wither," David said. "She's the dead woman, remember?"

"Whatever," Charlie said. "The more time that goes by, the better you look."

"Has anyone questioned Herb?" David asked.

"If he hasn't been questioned, that FBI agent's going to get to him," Charlie said. "He's been around to see me twice."

"What did he ask?" David asked.

"He drilled me for hours. He knows our entire history by now."

"Did he ask about Billy and Rachel?"

"He asked about everything. But I kept telling him you were an okay guy, that he had the wrong guy. I think he listened."

"If he listened David wouldn't be in here," Karen said.

"That's not true. If you ask me, I think it was Stanton who was behind David getting arrested," Charlie said.

"Why do you say that?" David asked.

"The sheriff's always protected Herb. I think he knows he's guilty."

"That idea is just idiotic enough to be true," Karen said.

"You said the same thing when I asked you to marry me."

"I did not. I just said *maybe*."

Charlie was touched, God bless him. "No, you forget. You said that marrying me might be just idiotic enough to be a good idea."

Karen was impressed. "How can you remember what I said eight years ago?"

"I remember everything you say. Even when it's not nice."

"I'm always nice to you," Karen said.

"Except when you're not," Charlie said.

David interrupted. "Stop. Let me clear up a point. Are you saying that

Sienna's guest house had been painted and cleaned in the last twenty-four hours?"

Charlie answered. "Yeah. Max said the FBI agent gave the landlady hell for it, but the woman just shrugged and said no one had told her to leave the place alone. But it's odd, don't you think, that after leaving the place alone for a couple of months, she suddenly has it worked on?"

"It's very odd," David agreed.

After Karen and Charlie left, David read the *Playboy* and looked at the pictures. The Playmate of the Month was an amazon redhead, with breasts so big they looked like they could feed a herd of baby zebras. Her turn-ons were autumn breezes and candlelight dinners, and her turn-offs were nosy people and handguns. The magazine said she had an IQ of 150 but David was unconvinced.

He wondered why he had not heard from Julie today.

Stanton said she had not come by the station.

To amuse himself, he sketched a picture of Max at McDonald's with a bunch of kids, putting the deputy in spotted leotards and showing him eating a dozen Big Macs. He gave the drawing to Max when the guy wandered into the back to verbally abuse him, and Max tore it up immediately. David did not feel like the effort had been wasted. The look on Max's face had made it worthwhile.

Finally, feeling a strange reluctance, he picked up the manuscript and started to read. Cleo was pregnant and looking for Ash, her ancient lover. But she did not know where to look so she went searching for Yril instead— Ash's sister, another old one. Cleo's search took her to Europe, Australia, and finally back to North America, where she found Yril in a retreat high in the Vancouver mountains. The novel continued to captivate. David felt Cleo's tension as she drove up the long dusty road that led to Yril's abode. The search had been long and tiring. Cleo was now eight months pregnant.

Yril answers the large door, she does not look surprised to see me. Shorter than myself by a head, she has dark eyes and rich chocolate skin, although Ash possessed neither quality. Yril's mouth is her prize, lips ripe as fruit, thick and sensual in a crude way. When we were human, twenty-five-thousand years ago, she'd had no interest in learning, in art or music, in anything deep and inspiring. She only cared about men and food, silly gossip and violent contests. As vampires, I didn't know what she liked, and I went out of my way to avoid her.

All those centuries we were evenly matched in strength, but she could take me now. Her back and arms are heavily muscled, and her long gray robe does not hide the fact that she stands with her squat legs slightly apart, ready for battle. For all I know she has a personal trainer. And of course I am pregnant, she sees that in an instant.

"Why are you here?" she asks.

I gesture to my stomach. I am excited about my child-to-be, but I do not enjoy being pregnant. It is like wearing a space suit I am never allowed to take off.

"It belongs to your brother. You are going to be an aunt," I say.

Yril sucks in a breath. "You are human too!"

"Yes. You have no reason to fear me."

Yril points to my unborn child. "But this child—how can it be alive?"

"I am not sure. But it is very much alive." Reaching out, I take her hand to put it on my abdomen. "Do you want to feel it kick?"

She withdraws, mutters under her breath. "Ash was only a half brother."

"Does that mean you are not going to invite me in?"

"Tell me why you are here."

"I am looking for Ash."

"Ash is dead. You know that."

"I saw Hector six months ago. He said Ash was alive, that he had survived the cataclysm."

"Hector is always saying things."

"He said it just before he killed himself."

Yril mocks. "After all this time you would not make love to him?"

"I never loved Hector, any more than you ever loved me."

She is curt. "If you feel that way, you have no reason to stay."

"Don't you want to see your niece? Your nephew?"

"You want to stay here until the child is born?"

I gesture to the forest that surrounds us. "This is such a lovely place. I would like to stay." I add, "If that is all right with you."

Yril considers. She is not brilliant but she is shrewd. It is not possible to live for so long and not develop the latter ability. She does not believe what I say any more than I believe her. We play a game, two washed-out vampires, and all that matters is who wins.

Yet a flicker of hunger crosses her face as her eyes stray momentarily downward, toward my baby. She nods and opens the door wide. "You may stay as long as you like," she says.

I smile as I step inside. "You are too kind."

Later, after I have rested and we have eaten, we walk in the woods together. Yril has three female servants and four male guards—all German, blond and blue-eyed, fit and young. I consider the number seven carefully, what it will take to overcome. Yet we are alone now, Yril must still be thinking.

The evening sun is warm and orange, casting the tall trees in a devilish light, but a peaceful one as well. The strong odor of pine is like a shampoo in my hair. Stooping to pick up a pinecone, I put it to my nose.

"How did you end up here?" I ask, drawing in a whiff.

"I am here only part of the year. The summers are pleasant. How did you find me?"

"The Internet."

"Same old Cleo. Never likes to answer a straight question."

"You are no different. If it is any consolation it took me a long time to find you."

We walk for a while in silence. Finally she says, "I have known where you were living for some time."

"Why didn't you visit?"

She ignores the question. "It doesn't bother you that I knew?"

"No. You must remember, I don't frighten easily."

Yril stops, touches my arm. The evening is pleasant but her hands are cold. As are her eyes, small and black like circles drawn in a cave. What makes the package even worse is her sudden smile. Her lips could be attached to wire, her mind to a wasp.

"You didn't as a vampire. But how do you feel now, as a human?"

I glance down at her hand, back at her eyes. "Your point?"

"You are pregnant, about to give birth. That must frighten you. I mean, if what you say is true, this fetus has been in you all this time. You must wonder what it will be like."

"The way you say it—it's like you're talking about an ancient ruin."

"Is that not possible?"

"What?"

"That it might be something ancient?" She loses her smile, lowers her voice, adds, "Something evil?"

"Yril. We are too old and have committed too much real evil to believe in fairy tales."

She takes away her hand, shakes her head. "I am just saying we don't know what kind of baby it will be. It could be . . . different."

"Are you suggesting I kill it?"

"No! What a horrible thought! How can you say that?"

"I can say anything, it doesn't matter. It only matters what I do. Please tell me, what are you driving at?"

"Did Ash know you were pregnant when he changed you?"

"I never told him. I never told anyone."

"Why not?"

"I didn't want to distract him."

"That is not an answer. Ash did not force you into the change. You must have been concerned what it would do to the child."

"I was in love with your brother. I trusted him in all ways."

She gets annoyed. "That is still not an answer."

"When I found out I was pregnant, it was wonderful. When Ash described what he could do for us, I was filled with the same wonder. The two feelings felt as one to me. I had faith everything would be all right. I was not afraid."

Yril continues to walk, impatient. "I don't understand you, Cleo. I never have."

I follow. "That much is obvious."

There is no reason for me to be surprised the next morning when Yril enters my bedroom with her four male bodyguards. They carry drawn guns, wear expressionless faces—more thralls than employees. She must pay them well, and provide them with other types of distractions. Illegal drugs? Perverted sex? Yril was always the queen of hedonism. There is a glazed look to their eyes, a frightening emptiness. Yet they are alert as well, ready to kill if necessary.

Yril is chipper. She acts like her armed entrance is entirely natural. And here I am still in bed in my pajamas.

"I have been thinking," she says before I can rise. "That this child might require special care. For that reason I want to control the remainder of your pregnancy. I want you to stay in this room. You have a nice view, a large bathroom. We will bring you whatever food you like. When the time comes, I will call the finest doctor. The baby can be born in this very house."

I sit up, put my feet on the wooden floor. "I do not like this plan."

Yril smiles. "You are being careless, Cleo. It is a good plan. This fetus cannot be natural. We have to take precautions." She adds, "You must cooperate."

I glance at her guards, back at her. "I want bacon and eggs for breakfast, toast and orange juice. Make the eggs scrambled, and I prefer the juice freshly squeezed."

Yril loses her smile. "Is that all you have to say?"

"Yes."

She hardens her tone. "Try to escape and you will be shot."

Standing, I wobble toward the bathroom. My urge to pee is worse than my urge to drink blood used to be. "I won't cause any trouble," I say.

Later, sitting in the bathtub and eating my breakfast, I contemplate my situation. I have come to Yril for one reason only: to find Ash. And now I am certain he has recently been in contact with his sister. Because Yril does not plan to kill the child. Her talk is all talk. She wants the baby, and she wants me out of the way. The second the baby is born, I am to be killed.

To take me hostage, her desire for the baby must be strong. She knows I am a formidable opponent. She risks much by keeping me in this room, even with her guards. Ash must have told her something about the baby—a unique quality it possesses. It is the only reason she would expose herself to such a risk.

"He told her it would be immortal," I say to myself. Clearly Yril is not happy being human again. Her recent condition devastates her. As she walks around the house, she looks in every mirror. No doubt the idea of saggy breasts and gray hair keeps her up at night. Her mind is easy to read: she sees the baby as a chance to regain her immortality. Ash must have spoken to her at length about the child. For all her surprise when I showed up, she wasn't really surprised at all.

It is possible she will try to drink the baby's blood.

Ash must have confided in Yril because he did not know where I was. Call me if you see her. That sort of thing. Why else would he have talked to her? He always knew what she was.

I cannot sit around and hope for Ash to rescue me.

But I have a plan, and it calls on me to wait, to be patient. Not my strong suit.

The days go by, I let them. I move from eight months pregnant to nine. Yril never visits. But her guards come, with the maid, when the food is delivered. Always two nice German young men, with the other two below my window. They sleep, sure, but they do not sleep much. All four are always around when I am fed. Yril set the condition. She has installed bars. I can open my windows but I cannot climb out of them. The rules of the game have been established, and everyone knows them. It is only when the food is brought that I have a chance to escape.

These guards, though, these maids, they are cold but they are still human. Yril has told them I am dangerous, but she has not told them what we once were. That is easy to read. The awe is missing and, besides, Yril would not have been foolish enough to confide in a human.

The guards are wary in my company; they are not wary enough. They believe what they see: a weak pregnant woman. They keep their guns drawn in my presence, but they do not keep a finger on the trigger. When the food is brought, I smile and ask how they are doing. Occasionally they smile back. One maid, Rita, likes me. Often she asks how I am feeling, if she can get me anything special. So slowly their guards drop, even as my belly grows larger.

It is a Sunday afternoon when I make my move. Every other day, it seems, Yril jumps in her red Porsche and rides off to town. I can see her drive off from my window, and she is definitely not in the house when Rita and the guards, Karl and Dieter, bring me my lunch. I sit on the bed as they unlock the door. My, how their trust has grown. Karl does not even have his gun out, and Rita is all smiles.

"I have brought you Indian food today," she says, holding the silver tray high. Rita is tall and thin but remarkably agile. Yet she is homely, like all the maids in the house, and I wonder if Yril hates the competition. She continues, "We have biryani chicken, basmati rice and vegetable samosas. Does that sound nice?"

"Wonderful. Could you put it there? Thank you so much." I nod to the stand beside my bed, where I have been taking my meals for the last week. Also, I groan as I move, painfully, the weak pregnant woman, hardly able to get around the room. The act has its desired effect. Dieter looks out the window as Rita crosses the room with the food, admiring the scenery, and Karl is just bored.

The tray will not come with a sharp knife, I know, but Yril is not above allowing me a butter knife and a fork—plain instruments, both stainless steel. On the surface those two items would not appear as much against a house full of SS. At the same time, Yril should know better. I am no longer a monster. My supernatural strength has faded and my blinding reflexes are gone. But I am twenty-five centuries old, and I have practiced every form of martial arts known to modern man, and many versions that have long since been forgotten. It does not matter my condition, I am still Cleo.

Such a fool, that Yril, I think, *she deserves to die.*

Rita puts the tray down and lifts the lid off the food. She must be hungry—she gazes at it with desire, as the steam wafts through the air with a dozen spices. "Just call when you are through," she says.

"I will," I reply, as I grab the butter knife and squeeze it tight in my fist and bury the tip in the side of Rita's neck. The blade is dull but my thrust is concentrated. Blood spurts from her pale skin, red and dark, wine poured for a captive's cup. I have cut the jugular; she is not given a chance to cry out. She can only stare at me, with amazement. Then she is falling for the floor.

Pulling out the knife, I stand and turn toward Karl. I have caught him by surprise but he is well trained. As I cock my arm, he reaches for his gun. He is not afraid and he moves quickly. My throw is perfect, however. The knife catches him in the left eye. There is blood on the tip, his and Rita's, venom in my speed. He shouts in pain and forgets about his gun for a moment.

Then I have the tray in my hand, and am facing Dieter. He has already turned, already brought up his gun. But he blinks as he tries to understand the sudden change in the room, and in that moment I launch the Indian lunch at his face, simultaneously diving to the right side and onto the floor. Dieter gets off a shot that hits my bed. Before he can clean the rice out of his face, however, I have swept his feet out from under him and we are on the floor together beside the chest of drawers. Luck favors me in that instant. The fork lands beside my hand and, raising it eagerly, I put it in his trachea— three quick stabs.

The gun comes out of his hand, into mine. Karl is no slouch. His eyeball red and swelling, he is already taking aim at my head. Indeed, to my surprise, he gets off a shot; the bullet whizzes past my hair. But I do not let him take a second shot, burying a bullet in his wide open mouth. The recoil is brutal, magnum shells. Karl's brains light up the far wall.

Rushing to the window, I see the other two guards have already entered the house. There is no advantage in my remaining in the room. I rush to the door. Outside, in the hallway, I know where I am going. The one day I was a free guest, I memorized the layout of the house. There is a tiny closet adjacent to my bedroom, which is at the end of a long hall. I hide in it before the other two guards make it to the second floor.

Then I hear them. No, just the one, I correct myself, creeping toward the bedroom door, which I have shut. The other must be cunning, holding back, or else he is a coward. It does not matter, I think, he cannot be far. As soon as the first guard walks past the closet, I kick open the door and shoot him in the back of the head. Then I roll on the hallway floor, like a heroine in the movies, leap up and shoot the fourth guard, who stands at the top of the staircase with a smile on his face. I wonder what the hell he was thinking.

I find the other two maids downstairs, hiding in a closet.

They plead for me not to kill them, in German, but I kill them anyway.

Then I sit down and wait for Yril to come home. I have lunch; there is plenty of extra biryani chicken and samosas in the kitchen. My mood is optimistic and my hunger huge.

Yril does not come home until two in the morning. Walks in casually, her cheeks flushed, alcohol on her breath, sex in her strong stride. Looks attractive—wears a tight-fitting tan jacket, a short pleated skirt. Her dark hair is mussed and her lipstick smeared but she is ready for more action. Her face could be all of twenty-five, the same age she was when Ash performed his alchemy on us all. But her eyes grow old and bitter when she sees me and my gun.

"Come, into the living room. I want to talk," I say.

Scared, she acts insolent. "What do you want to talk about?"

I wave the weapon. "Come, Yril."

When we are comfortable, I make a fire—with one hand—and let the flames grow. The heat fills the room, while outside the trees stand like a thousand gray soldiers. Yril is not as fascinated by the crackling incandescence as I am. She keeps wringing her hands, glancing around.

"There is no one else here," I say.

She tries to stare me down. "You're not sure about that."

"But I am. I could always tell when you were bluffing."

"What do you want?"

"Information about Ash."

"How do you know I have any?"

"You do." I come closer, sit beside her, keep the gun ready. I have already searched her, disarmed her. "Tell me what you know."

She thinks. "Will you let me go if I do?"

"I might."

Yril stares at me, shakes her head. "You won't."

I raise the gun, tap the side of her head. "You of all people should know there are many ways to die. It is better you talk."

She finally looks at the fire. So many nights and this will probably be her last. Her breathing is strained, her voice painful. "He called recently, when I started to become human again. I didn't even know he was still alive. He was looking for you."

"Did you tell him where I was?"

"No."

"You said you knew. Why not?"

"Because he would not tell me why I was changing."

"You asked?"

"Of course."

"So you told him you didn't know where I was?"

"Correct."

"But he gave you a number where he could be reached?"

"Yes."

"Where is it?"

She hesitates. Her only leverage. "Upstairs, my desk drawer. It's on a piece of paper. It says ASH on it."

"Where is he?"

"New York, I think. Not sure."

"What did he tell you about my child?"

"Nothing."

Cocking the hammer, I put the gun to her temple. "Please, Yril."

She weeps, it is not pleasant to watch. But at least she is quiet about it.

"He told me that you were probably pregnant, and that the baby would be a god."

My heart skips in my chest. "He said that? 'A god'?"

"Yes."

"What did he mean?"

"I have no idea." She looks at me sadly. "Cleo?"

"Yes."

"I will go away, vanish. It can be like it has always been between us."

Sitting back, I shake my head. "No. I am going to be a mother now. I have to think of the welfare of my child."

She turns very white. Goes to speak.

I shoot her in the heart.

NINETEEN

The judge, Keri Smith, was sixty and black. She had serious lines on her face, a grave demeanor. She'd obviously seen plenty of hard times during her years in the chair. She appeared intelligent, not given to rash decisions, academic even, and her gray hair, set in a bundle of small curls atop her head, reminded David of a silver crown. Of course her black robe was nowhere near royalty, and in a certain sense of the word she could end up being his executioner. No reason to relax yet, he thought, not with her.

The district attorney, Mack Deacon, appeared soft by comparison. David had seen him around before, at the beach and the mall, and had known who he was. Mack was fifty and fat, sagging ungracefully in a green suit that might have been bought online, and a yellow tie so thick it could have been a banner for the seventies. He was bald and trying to pretend he wasn't. The rust-colored strands he had combed over didn't even cover the equator.

But for all of that David could see the DA was no pushover. Sitting beside Krane—who wore a white shirt, gray sports coat, no tie—he appeared organized. He'd already opened his briefcase, taken out a file of papers so thick it could have been published, and he was conferring with Krane in a steady whisper that reminded David of the drip of the faucet back in his cell. Deacon did not look tough but he acted confident, and David figured that was probably worse.

Sheriff Stanton was in the rear, in uniform. There was a lively crowd behind him, only they were forty feet back and outside. Stanton had the key to the door and wasn't playing any favorites, even with the press. He could not have been worried about the next election. The only *civilian* present was Reverend Pomus, and he was in the far corner, a powerful presence in a black suit and serious hair gel. David's attorney, Jack Simpson, had said the minister might be allowed to put in a few good words about him. David was happy to see him. Pomus had hugged him when he had come in, patted him on the back and told him not to worry.

Still, David did worry, although his lawyer appeared the picture of cool. Jack Simpson was wearing a warm yellow suit, a gold watch, and was eating cashews only seconds before the judge entered. Breakfast, he explained, wiping his hands on a large white napkin. Apparently he had slept late at the local Holiday Inn and had had to hurry to the courtroom, not overly stressed about his lack of retainer or his client's life.

The arraignment started quickly and picked up speed. David was surprised at the lack of formalities. Five minutes after Judge Smith entered the court the DA was listing the reasons why he, David Lennon, should be tried for murder one for the killing of Sally Wither.

Whoever that was, David thought.

The DA stood as he spoke, but stayed behind his desk, near the FBI agent. His voice was loud and unrefined but he compensated by taking frequent pauses and glancing at his notes. His points were direct and familiar.

David Lennon had been involved with Sally Wither for six months.

He had been dumped by her two months ago on Lompoc Beach.

On the same beach where her body was found.

Indeed, he was the one who had found her body, only minutes after returning to town after having been gone two months.

Two months in New York—the victim's hometown.

The body appeared to have been decomposing for two months.

Mr. Lennon had admitted to being on the same beach two months ago.

In fact, he had admitted building a fire the last night he had been with Ms. Wither, and the remains of that fire could still be found where her body had been found.

Mr. Lennon was vague in his remembrance of that night.

In his statement, he had contradicted himself about the facts of that night.

The DA finished by handing the judge a copy of David Lennon's sworn testimony. He gave a copy to Simpson as well, who ignored it. David sure looked. Mack Deacon had highlighted a ton of lines with a yellow marking pen.

Judge Smith asked Simpson to speak. David's lawyer stood and stepped to the center of the room, dividing the DA and Krane from the judge. He spoke quickly and with intensity, yet he appeared strangely detached from the proceedings. The overall effect was impressive. He said the district attorney had no case because:

The police had no murder weapon.

They had searched the defendant's house and found no murder weapon.

The search had not produced even a similar knife.

Mr. Lennon had no motive to kill the victim.

The victim had been killed in a ritualistic fashion.

Mr. Lennon did not belong to a cult.

Mr. Lennon had never belonged to a cult.

Indeed, he had never been arrested in his life.

Mr. Lennon was well known around town as an upstanding young man.

But the victim was a newcomer to town.

She had lied about her name to Mr. Lennon.

She had lied to everyone she had met in town.

She could have died anytime—from one month ago to two months.

There were no witnesses to the crime.

There was not one piece of physical evidence that tied Mr. Lennon to the crime.

Anyone could have killed Sally Wither.

Simpson returned to his seat beside David. They both stared at the judge. She was scanning the paper the DA had handed her, the stuff he had told Krane during his initial interview. She frowned as she read, and David felt a cool liquid in his intestines that he had not consumed with his mouth. Yet she turned toward the DA first.

"Has the coroner found any skin under her nails?" she asked. "Signs of struggle?"

Mack Deacon got up. "No, Your Honor. But it appears she was first stabbed from behind, then mutilated." He reached for a paper on his desk, held it up. "I have a copy of the coroner's preliminary report here."

David had not known she had first been stabbed from behind.

Judge Smith stuck out her hand. "Let me see it, please. When will the final report be issued?"

The DA came around his desk. "Dr. Lindst has requested another month."

Judge Smith scowled. "So long?"

The DA gave her the papers. "It is a high-profile case."

The DA returned to his chair, but he did not sit down. The judge read for five minutes. Simpson snuck a cashew into his mouth. David tried to keep his breathing even and deep. Again, finally, the judge addressed the DA.

"There are no signs of the defendant's hair or skin on the victim?" she asked.

Deacon glanced down at Krane, cleared his throat, looked back at the judge. "No, Your Honor. But the body was in a volatile environment for two months. Any strands of hair surely would have blown away. Also, if I may add, there are no signs that there has been another fire in the area. Only the one fire beside where the body was found, the one fire the defendant says he lit when he was alone with the victim."

Judge Smith studied the coroner's report further, then spoke to the DA. "Was the coroner able to specify the type of knife that was used in the murder? For example, did it have a jagged edge? Was it a switchblade? How large was it?"

"It appears to have been a medium-size knife with a jagged edge."

"Any other specifics?"

"Not so far."

"The defendant didn't have a knife in his place that fit into that broad a category?" she asked.

"No, Your Honor. That in itself is suspicious."

"How so, Mr. Deacon?"

The DA spread his hands. "How did he cut anything? It is our belief he removed all the sharp knives from his house that same night, before he left town. All he had in his place were butter knives."

The judge got annoyed. "You'll have to offer some proof if you're going to make such statements."

Simpson spoke before Deacon could respond. "Your Honor, like most single guys his age, Mr. Lennon eats out a lot. He has no need for a full set of knives."

Deacon did not reply. Judge Smith continued to study the papers the DA had given her. David could already see a pattern in the proceedings. It appeared to favor him. The judge was not interested in psychological or behavioral factors. His state of mind when he last saw Sienna . . . Sally. Her lying to him in their relationship. The fact that he'd gone off to New York City. Even his inability to remember exactly what had happened that night. No doubt such details would become important if the case went to trial. But for now the judge wanted physical facts, like Simpson had said, and therein was the DA's problem. He had none.

David assumed. But life was full of surprises, especially when it came to death.

Judge Smith was shaking her head. She looked seconds away from dismissing the whole thing. The DA hastily leaned over, whispered to Krane, who shook his head firmly. But for once the DA looked defiant. He reached for his briefcase. Krane went so far as to try to stop him, but Deacon shook him off. The DA drew a sealed Baggie from the case, a handful of photographs. Clearing his throat, he spoke to the judge.

"Your Honor, there is another piece of evidence the state would like to introduce."

Judge Smith was annoyed. "Evidence that was not worth mentioning before?"

"The evidence in question relates to a blood sample, which is currently being subjected to DNA testing. I'm sure Your Honor can understand why the state would be reluctant to introduce preliminary DNA tests at an arraignment. Such evidence is not a hundred percent accurate—it can be challenged." The DA paused. "But I feel Your Honor should know about it now."

Meaning he knew Mr. Lennon was about to be set free.

"You may proceed," Judge Smith said.

David glanced at Simpson, wondered why he did not object.

The DA held up the Baggie. "What I have here are clippings from Mr. Lennon's carpet. When his house was searched, a special spray I am sure Your Honor is familiar with—luminol—was used on the carpet. It revealed a trail of bloodstains leading from the front door to the bathroom. The stains had already been largely washed away. We suspect they had been shampooed. If not for the luminol, they wouldn't have been visible. It is these bloodstains that have been subjected to DNA analysis. And they prove that the blood does indeed belong to Sally Wither."

Simpson finally spoke. "Objection. The district attorney has already stated that the DNA evidence is preliminary and therefore not conclusive. He cannot use the word 'prove.'"

"I agree," Judge Smith said.

"The analysis is preliminary but the odds that the blood belongs to Sally Wither are ten thousand to one," the DA responded.

"Objection. Are those odds scientifically accurate or are they merely a colorful phrase?"

"Do you know the precise odds?" Judge Smith asked Mr. Deacon.

"No. But the odds are overwhelming that the blood does belong to Sally Wither."

Judge Smith nodded. "Make your point."

"The point is obvious. This blood was trailed from the front door—on someone's foot—and into the bathroom, where it was presumably washed off."

"Did you find evidence of blood outside?"

"No."

"Did the blood leave distinct prints?"

"Your Honor, the blood clearly belongs to footprints." Again, Deacon held up his pictures. "I have copies."

Judge Smith nodded. The DA gave Simpson copies before approaching the bench. These his lawyer was interested in. Yet to David they just looked like ill-defined marks on his floor. Bigfoot could have made them. Simpson leaned over and spoke in his ear.

"What is this shit?" he asked.

David shook his head. "I have no idea."

"Did Sienna ever cut her foot in your house?"

"Not that I remember."

Simpson gave him a look, like he had better improve his memory fast. Then he turned his attention back to Judge Smith and got to his feet, holding the photos in hand.

"Your Honor, these pictures are meaningless. They don't show clear footprints. They show blobs of nothingness. I mean, if the district attorney has actual prints that can be identified as belonging to my client's feet, we would be interested to see them."

"Your response, Mr. Deacon?"

"Your Honor, this 'nothingness' counsel refers to is dried blood. True, because of the nature of the carpet, we were unable to get clear prints. Nevertheless, the evidence is overwhelming that someone—covered with Sally Wither's blood—entered Mr. Lennon's house and walked into the bathroom."

"Do we have evidence who that someone was?" Simpson asked. "Were traces of my client's blood mixed in with this blood?"

Mack Deacon acted annoyed. "We're not saying that the defendant was bleeding when he returned from the scene of the murder."

Simpson finally showed ire. "But you are saying that he was at one time covered in the victim's blood. Is that correct?"

Judge Smith used her hammer. "Gentlemen, these proceedings are to proceed through me. Mr. Deacon, you do not strengthen your case by exaggerating. Based on this evidence, we do not know if anyone was 'covered' with blood. To me, these marks do resemble footprints, but they are far from clear. Let me ask a question. Can we be sure these footprints belong to a man?"

Deacon feigned innocence. "I am not sure how that could be done."

"Measure the prints. How big are they? Big enough to belong to a woman or a man?"

Things were not going as the DA had hoped. "It is unclear at this time."

"Time, Mr. Deacon, will not change the size of the prints," Judge Smith said.

The DA shrugged. "Her blood is all over his house. He was the last one to see her alive. He was the one who found her body. He had opportunity and motive. How many reasons does the state need to take this to trial?"

"None of this evidence ties my client to the murder," Simpson spoke before the judge could respond. "If this goes to trial, there isn't a jury in the land that would convict Mr. Lennon. Why take it that far? Why keep my client locked away? Why this rush to decide on a killer? Mr. Lennon lives here—he has all his life. He isn't going anywhere. Let the police continue their investigation. If fresh evidence appears that implicates my client, so be it. But for now, in the interests of justice, he must be set free."

"Mr. Deacon?" Judge Smith asked.

"Your Honor, Mr. Lennon is young and single. Three hours after leaving this courtroom, he could be in Mexico. Or else on a plane to Europe. What's to stop him? At the very least, if he is to be let go, ample bail must be posted."

"We are not asking for bail, but for the dismissal of all charges," Simpson said.

Judge Smith held the Baggie close to her face, focused on his pieces of carpet. If they were stained, none could tell from this distance. "Any other remarks?" she asked.

There were none. They all stood, briefly, as the judge retired to her chambers to think. She had indicated the break would be short, however. The DA and Krane got up and strolled out into the hall. David remained seated. Simpson had gone back to his nuts.

"How did it go?" David asked his lawyer.

"Great. Except for the blood on your carpet."

The judge returned twenty minutes later and stated that the district attorney had failed to provide enough evidence to send the matter to trial. David Lennon was free to go.

TWENTY

The sheriff took him out the back of the court, to avoid the crowd, and drove him to the station so that he could collect his stuff. Fortunately Max was not around. Stanton had sent him out to write speeding tickets. Stanton said Karen had called, wanted to have a party for him at her house. That sounded like fun to David. He told the sheriff to take him there instead of home.

Parking outside Karen's house, Stanton offered his hand. "I'm happy you got off," he said.

David shook the man's hand. "Krane did not look upset either."

"You noticed that?"

"Sure. He didn't want the DA bringing up that last piece of evidence. What was that all about?"

The sheriff caught his eye. "You're the one who should know."

They were talking about two different things, but David did not feel like arguing. "Sienna never bled on my carpet," he said.

"We're talking about Sally Wither."

David shook his head. "Never met her."

Yet he no longer said it with the confidence he had at first. He had just come from an arraignment where everyone in the court had been convinced Sienna was Sally. Slowly, he was beginning to accept that it was possible—

unlikely, but possible—that Sienna was indeed dead. The very idea shook him to the core.

Stanton turned away, shrugged. "This case could not get more weird."

"I can't argue with you." David opened the door, went to get out, but then paused, and added, "Krane only arrested me to shake me up."

"Don't bet on it. He was the one who found the blood on your carpet. And he didn't have to give it to the DA, not yet, but he did. What does that tell you?"

"That he works both sides of the fence."

"Now you're catching on." Stanton nodded. "Enjoy your freedom."

"But don't leave town?" David asked.

"You got it."

The party was small: Karen, Charlie, Julie and Herb—plus a ton of food and beer, which made up for plenty of missing guests. Karen tried to explain the lack of attendance.

"I don't think anyone thought you would get off so quick." Happy, relieved—she had kissed him hard when he had come through the door, held onto him a long time.

"I sure as hell didn't," Herb said, smoking a fat one in the corner, and sharing it with Charlie. Karen had already complained about the odor but since the girls were not around, no one listened to her. David found it interesting that Charlie would get stoned in front of Karen. Maybe he had given up hope of getting her back, or maybe it was just great pot. David had almost taken a hit himself, but he had, after all, just gotten out of jail.

"I'm not surprised," David muttered. "You're probably one of the people who put me in jail."

Herb was hurt. "I didn't tell that FBI agent nothing."

Charlie laughed. "You told him David was crazy about Sienna."

Herb was slurring. "What's wrong with that?"

" 'Crazy' is not a word you want to hand the FBI when they're looking for a murder suspect," Karen explained, before turning back to David. "Tell us everything that went on at the arraignment."

He gave them a quick summary, but left off the rabbit the DA had pulled out of his hat at the end. David didn't want them worrying about it and, besides, he couldn't explain it. Of course they would probably hear about the bloody carpet from Max.

Charlie and Karen were intrigued by David's belief that Krane and the DA were not on the same page in the courtroom. They saw conspiracies everywhere.

"How do we know the base police did not dump the body there?" Charlie asked. "Who the hell really knows what goes on out at Vandenberg? They are always shooting shit out into space and the public knows nothing about it. This chick might have worked there for all we know, and discovered something that they didn't want her talking about. The whole satanic angle might just be a cover."

"I agree," Karen said. "In all of this almost nothing has been said about the base. Why don't we see any comments in the paper about what the base has to say about the murder? The military could have something to do with the confusion over the identity of the body. It might have planted the confusion. God, for all we know, Sienna was in the Air Force."

"I don't think that's true," David said.

"Why not?" Karen asked.

"She was too frail."

"Yeah. That girl had no strength," Herb added.

David gave him a look but Herb was already too far gone to notice.

Julie barely spoke the whole time. Perhaps she felt she was not among friends, or else she was worried about how she had behaved when the police had shown up at David's door. But it was Julie who insisted on giving him a ride home, and when they were in the car she tried to address that morning.

"I hope you're not mad that I couldn't identify her voice," she said. "I probably shouldn't have put it the way I did. I was nervous, and I was just trying to tell the truth, and trying to protect you at the same time."

She said it like they might have been contradictory goals.

"I'm not mad. I'm just happy to be out of jail."

Julie lowered her voice, put on a serious face. "What was it like in there?"

He wanted to laugh and say it was a novel experience. Yet there was something wrong with the picture. Julie had on tight jeans and a tank top. She could have been on her way to the beach. Her tan breasts were pushed up and smiling, either aching for the sun or sex. Her sober expression was rehearsed.

Then there were his feelings for her. He felt as if he couldn't stand to talk to her, although he was anxious to fuck her. The incongruity confused him but did not cause him guilt. He felt she deserved his animosity because she was lying to him about something.

Something big. Just a feeling . . . he wanted to test.

He ignored her question, and asked, "How's it going with the job search?"

"Lompoc's a tough town to find anything that pays decent. But I have a few leads."

"Really? Where?"

"Here and there. Let me see what develops and I'll tell you about it."

"Did Lanson Construction call you back? You said they wanted you for an office manager, but that they were worried about your lack of bookkeeping experience."

"Yeah. They're one of my better leads. I hope they pan out."

It had been Mauldin Construction she had spoken about.

He smiled. "That's great," he said.

At his house, he politely rebuffed her efforts to come inside. Despite her recent lie, turning her down took tremendous will. He did not understand how he could be obsessed with the idea of one girl and the body of another.

Inside, there were another half dozen hang ups on his phone. No messages.

His house was remarkably tidy for a place that had been searched by the police.

David laid down to take a nap, set the alarm for one hour hence. As he dozed he realized he had barely thanked Simpson for his help. After Judge Smith's dismissal, the lawyer had patted him on the back and told him to call him the next time he got arrested.

He told himself he went to Mauldin Construction because it was better to know than to not know, although he no longer believed that was true. Since his return, it seemed the more he found out the more miserable he was. He was still riding the high of being out of jail but it pained him to think that Julie had been lying to him from the word go.

His excuse for stopping by the company was lame. He told the secretary at the front desk that the firm's personnel manager had called him about recommending someone for a job. The secretary was so startled to see him—he was, after all, the cult guy with the knife—that he was ushered into the PM's office quickly. The personnel manager, Ted Jar, must not have read the newspaper. He had no idea who he was—or Julie Stevens for that matter.

"She never applied for a job here," he said.

David thanked him for his time and drove to Lanson Construction. They didn't know about Julie Stevens's terminal case of unemployment either, although the woman at the front desk did ask for an autograph. As he signed her business card, she giggled and confided that she had always been a fan of the "dark arts." No one had ever asked him for an autograph before. He suspected his new association with Satan would make it easier for him to get dates.

He was on a roll, even if he was not sure if there was a bottom to the hill he was on. He went to Macy's next, woman's wear, where Julie was supposed to have slaved her ass off. Finally he met people who knew her. Yes, they said, she had worked at the store for five years, but had quit two months earlier, not giving a reason. She had definitely not been fired. He was unable to pin down the exact date of her leaving, but it sounded very close to when he had left for New York.

"Why am I not surprised?" David said to himself when he was back in his car, sitting in the mall parking lot and staring across the street at the Baker's Square where Julie had picked him up. And make no mistake, last Friday, she had latched onto him like a leech on a vampiric pilgrimage. She had entered the restaurant for that purpose.

Still, it made no sense, her lies. She was not stupid. She must have known that he would eventually find out about her fabrications. He seriously doubted that there had ever been a Terry Haven, her ex, or even that her father had Alzheimer's. She had insisted on picking him up, every time. She had been afraid for him to come over to her house.

At the very least, she was desperate to hide what she had been doing the last two months. It was possible the desperation had made her sloppy. Throw out a bunch of lies, she thought, I'm a fox and David's a lonely loser. The dude will believe anything.

On the other hand, it was possible there was a darker side to her approach. Was it conceivable that she had not been worried about her lies because she figured he would not be around long enough to find out about them?

"Stop it, she didn't sleep with you to kill you," he said aloud.

Talking to himself did not help. Julie had been in his house the two times

Sienna's messages had disappeared. He knew he had not accidentally erased them, he wasn't that big of a klutz. Krane had been very suspicious of Julie. It had been the FBI agent who had told him that Julie had followed him to the hypnotist. What kind of chick trailed a guy she had just met? The jealousy excuse didn't cut it, especially since she had told him a few days ago that the competition didn't bother her.

David sighed, spoke to his windshield. "Yeah, she did it, she's the one. Cut out Sienna's organs, and now she's going to cut out my heart."

A working theory. He was making progress.

Only Sienna was still alive. And what did anyone want with his heart?

He was nowhere, man.

Yet he had places to go, things to do.

"Did you check who owned that gun Billy had in his mouth when he died?"

"I did. It was owned by Teresa and Rachel's father."

"So Teresa was there when her sister committed suicide, and she was there when Billy died from a wound inflicted by a weapon owned by her father. Do you still think I am inventing coincidences?"

"Let it go, David. It will only stir up old wounds."

"Who cares about old ones? It's the new ones that bleed."

Ten years ago. Another time, another cast of characters.

Impossible that it could have anything to do with Sally Wither.

Sure. It was impossible that Sienna was alive and she was still calling him.

"Let it bleed," he said.

He started his car and drove toward the Bronsons' residence.

Gerald Bronson, father of Miss California Teresa and Dead and Forgotten Rachel, was a handsome alcoholic. Only fifty—he'd had the girls young—he showed no outward signs of liver damage. He had a small skull and tight skin, angular features; his bright blue eyes jumped out of his tan face like headlights. He'd been in the navy, still wore his blond hair short, and had so many tattoos he could have slept on a printing press. He had Rachel's wide sensual mouth, and he knew how to use it. His smile was extraordinarily disarming. Word had it that Mrs. Bronson had not left in grief after Rachel's suicide, or even because of her husband's drinking. She had split because of Mr. Bronson's wild ways.

The latter was not a rumor Rachel had confirmed while she was alive. She had never talked about her dad, which indirectly gave credibility to an uglier rumor that continued to circulate around town: that Gerald Bronson had sexually abused his girls. Billy had said as much, once, and he had never been one to gossip.

Mr. Bronson grinned when he saw who it was at his door, invited David in, offered him a Bud Lite. There was baseball on the TV, pizza on the floor. Life was good, or else forgotten. Mr. Bronson wanted to know all about the arraignment. God, the guy had already heard about the bloodstains on the carpet. David suspected Max had started a Web page.

David wanted to make a deal with Mr. Bronson. I tell you about the trial and you explain how that gun of yours got into Billy's mouth. While you're at it, tell me everything you remember about Rachel's suicide.

"The water was cold, not hot or even warm. But nobody would get into a cold tub to kill themselves. So we have to assume Rachel was running warm water, at least letting it drip. That is the only way the water would change from red to pink."

"What's your point?"

"Rachel was dead a while before Teresa called you."

"That's possible. For all I know, Teresa was asleep when Rachel opened her wrists."

"You miss my point. Teresa must have turned off the water, and then waited to call you."

Somehow, though, David could not figure out how to explain his deal. So he just answered all of Mr. Bronson's questions about the arraignment, tried to get him into an open and trusting mood. That worked about as well as if he had thrown mud in the guy's face. The instant he tried to bring up Rachel, Mr. Bronson scowled and reached for another beer.

"I told you a long time ago I don't talk about Rach," he said. "It's not something I want to even think about. You feel the need to be morbid, David, you buy her a dozen red roses and go sit in the cemetery and cry on her tombstone."

"She doesn't have a tombstone."

Mr. Bronson caught his eye. "Why are you pushing me?"

"I have my reasons. Don't you want to hear them?"

Mr. Bronson put down his beer, stood. "I think you'd better go."

David stood slowly. "You knew her. You were her father. You loved her.

You had to love her at least as much as I did. It doesn't matter what happened to her face, you know she wouldn't have killed herself."

That stopped Mr. Bronson. He clenched his fist; if he'd still had a beer bottle in his hand, it would have shattered. But then the tension went out of him, and he sat back down in his chair. David thought he saw a tear in his eye, but he could have been wrong. The man stayed tough, although when he spoke next his voice was weary.

"Of course she killed herself," he said quietly. "Teresa was here that night, you know. There was no one else here."

David returned to his seat. "But Teresa could have lied."

The man did not snap at him as David expected, and that told David a lot. Mr. Bronson had considered the possibility. Yet he shook his head. "Teresa would never have hurt Rach," he said.

"Are you sure? They weren't that close."

Mr. Bronson shrugged. "If there was a problem between those two, it was on Rach's side. She was jealous of Teresa's beauty, especially after Teresa won that Miss California crown. It was stupid, you know—Rach was plenty good looking."

Glad you found her attractive, David thought.

"I never heard Rachel bad-mouth Teresa," David lied.

Mr. Bronson grabbed another beer. There were empty bottles in the corner, demons in the closets. If he peeked down the hall, at the open bathroom door, David could just see the tub where Rachel had opened her wrists. Fully clothed, no less.

"You didn't live with them," Mr. Bronson said.

"Is Teresa still married to that same guy?"

"Jim? Yeah, they're still married. Much to my surprise. You know he's twenty years older than her?"

"I didn't know that. What does he do?"

"He's a doctor. A big shot transplant surgeon. They live in Miami."

For an instant David could not speak. He was a rock, ice. He feared he could crack. "What's his name?" he heard himself ask.

"Doctor James Rean. You thinking of calling her? I wouldn't bother. Teresa's changed since she got married. She's gotten hard. She doesn't take my calls anymore."

David sat there for a moment, staring at nothing in particular. Then he reached in his pocket, took out his wallet, and removed the card the doctor on the plane had given him. There it was, right there, Dr. James Rean. But what was even more surprising was the name of the clinic where he worked. Life Extension Service Systems.

"Have you ever heard of LESS?"

"Less?"

"L-E-S-S. Have you ever heard of it?"

"No. What is it?"

"Did Sienna ever mention it?"

"No. Tell me what it is."

"I can't, it's classified information."

On the top left corner of the card, the clinic's initials were printed in bold letters.

LESS.

TWENTY-ONE

David got out of the house. He was not even sure what he had said.

He sat in his car and thought: who was Teresa Bronson? He had not known her well, but Rachel had spoken about how shallow she was. A self-absorbed beauty. She was only twenty-one when she had won the Miss California crown, and then she had met the rich doctor and split. She had not even fulfilled the crown's requirements to help open malls and get photographed with sick kids. She had worked all her life to win the title and once she had met Dr. Transplant she had not given a damn about it.

There was no point in wondering if it had been a coincidence that Dr. James Rean had been sitting beside him on the plane. The odds against that were billions to one.

So what did it all mean?

David did not have a clue.

He needed to see Krane, talk to him, but knew the FBI agent might not tell him shit. Not without major leverage. Then again, knowledge was power, and Krane could not know about the Teresa/Rean/Rachel/Billy connection. It did not matter how many questions the agent asked around town, David was from Lompoc. He knew its history. If he played his cards right, he might get the FBI agent to talk. Krane had been afraid to keep him in prison, had been afraid to let him go. The man had to be feeling as desperate as himself.

From a remark Stanton had made, David knew Krane was staying at the Motel 6 off the main drag. David had been surprised to hear that. He had assumed the FBI could at least spring for the brand new Holiday Inn.

David drove to the motel, parked and walked up to the front desk. He was not in the mood to spy. He just asked for Krane and the clerk called his room and two minutes later David was sitting in a chair across from the FBI agent. Krane sat propped up on the bed, his shirt off, smoking a carton of Marlboros. There were enough butts in his ashtray to assassinate the surgeon general, and the smoke in the room looked like a den of ghosts on acid. What was weird was that Krane did not appear surprised to see him.

"How was your party?" Krane asked.

"You heard about that?"

"I told you, I hear about everything. Your lawyer was pretty smooth this morning. I was impressed. He destroyed Deacon."

"I think you were the one who destroyed him. How many other pieces of evidence did you force him to hold back?"

"A few."

"Such as?"

"That woman had a high dose of narcotics in her blood when she was killed."

"What does that mean?" David asked.

"Beats me. Maybe she was a junkie."

"Why didn't Deacon bring it up?"

"Because he didn't know what it meant. It didn't support the case he was trying to make."

"Deacon looked like he pissed you off in court."

Krane shrugged. "What can I say? He doesn't like being a team player. That happens. DAs and law enforcement are natural enemies."

"Stop the bullshit, would ya? You wanted me out and I want to know why."

"You can't always get what you want." Krane added, "You know, it's probably against some law for us to talk right now."

"I know about LESS. It means Life Extension Service Systems."

That caught Krane's interest. "How did you find that out?"

"Tell me why you wanted me back out."

Krane smiled, lit another cigarette, nodded. "You're smart, David. Did I ever tell you that?"

"Yeah. You tell me every time you're about to treat me like an idiot."

Krane blew smoke. "Have you heard the phrase 'lightning rod'?"

"Yes. Did you let me go so that you could see what came my way?"

"In a sense. I arrested you for the same reason."

"I don't understand."

Krane hardened suddenly. "How did you find out about LESS?"

David's turn to smile. "Not so fast. You only get crumbs first. You have been suspicious of Julie. I thought you were way off-base. But I found out in the last two hours that most of what she has been telling me about her recent life has been lies. I'm pretty sure now that she was the one who erased Sienna's messages."

"Why?"

"I don't know why. But I think she's a lesbian. I know, I know, that sounds like something out of left field. But I think she and Sienna might be somehow tied together. She quit her job in town around the same time Sienna disappeared."

"You mean died?"

"I don't mean that," David said flatly.

"Was Sienna bisexual?"

"She never gave any sign but I suppose it's possible."

Krane considered. "Interesting. Yet it doesn't tell me much."

David sat silently for a moment, let the tension between them increase. Krane was a master manipulator. He had to be stunned to show his hand. The FBI agent just stared at him as he slowly coated both their lungs with tar.

"Dr. James Rean. Transplants. Florida. LESS," David said.

Krane dropped his cigarette, almost fell out of the bed. "Fuck!" he said as he tried to smother the burning butt with a pillow. He ended up grabbing a towel, making a mess of the situation. David sat impassively. Let the man come to him, he thought.

"How the hell do you know about Dr. Rean?" Krane demanded.

David sat back in his chair, relaxed. "I'm glad to see you know him. Let me give you one more crumb, no, two, before you start talking. I can take you back ten years with Rean, to when it all began. And I can bring you totally up to date with him as well."

"How?"

"I talked to him last week."

"When? Where?"

David shook his head. "Tell me about those two ritual murder cases you worked on. The ones that got your partner killed."

"I told you, they're classified."

"I won't tell anyone about them. I have no reason to. And you know I didn't kill Sally Wither."

"Really? That was her blood on your carpet. No one planted that."

"Fuck you. You know I didn't kill her."

The lines were drawn. Only a question now of who blinked. Krane got off the bed, went into the bathroom, dug into what sounded like an ice chest and returned with two cold beers. Handing one to David, he sat in a chair across from him. For a moment it seemed he would light another cigarette but then he sighed and pushed away his carton. Looking around the bland room, he muttered, "I hate this fucking town."

David had a sudden insight. "Does the FBI even know you're here?" he asked.

The question made Krane laugh. "God, you are a piece of work. Your mind is so messed up that you can't remember whether you killed your girl-friend or not. But you are somehow able to read my mind." He held up his hand as David went to speak. "But hey, you're only half right. The FBI knows I'm here, but a lot of people in the Bureau are not happy about it."

"Why?"

"Beats me."

"I thought we had decided to drop the bullshit."

Krane drank his beer. "I'm being serious."

"As you are fond of saying, you will have to do better than that."

Krane stretched out in his chair. "Okay, you've got me. I need a break when it comes to Dr. Rean. Maybe you're the one to give it to me. But let me warn you, David Lennon. If you repeat a word of what is said in this room, I will plant evidence to put you back in jail. And that evidence will be such that you will definitely be convicted of murder one. Don't think for an instant this is a bluff. No one fucks with me and gets away with it. Understood?"

David thought he was bluffing. "I understand."

Krane took another sip of his beer and began.

"This tale does not begin with me. I only got involved last year. It was six years ago when a rich businessman named Henry Gold and a young reporter named Dana Sandoval crossed paths. Dana worked for the *New York Times*, a third-year apprentice with more brains than experience. Gold was a Manhattan big shot—plenty of old money. He owned a hunting magazine, a swank hotel on the Upper East Side, a thirty-percent stake in a small but powerful pharmaceutical company. Take note, he had ties to the medical community. He regularly drank with the best doctors in town, but he probably drank too much. At sixty years of age he had severe cirrhosis of the liver. People said he looked okay and seemed to get by, but in truth he was dying. He needed a transplant, and he was placed on the lists. Do you know anything about them?"

"Only what Dr. Rean told me last week."

"Jesus Christ! Really?"

"Yes. Continue with your story."

Krane held his eye a moment before going on.

"We're talking about nationwide donor lists. People get ranked—many factors are involved. The severity of the illness; the age of the patient; his or her lifestyle. Gold didn't fare so well on that last point. His doctors told him to stop drinking but he was an alcoholic. He wasn't going to stop until he died. Plus he had another shot against him. He didn't have a single blood relative who could act as a donor. That fact surprised me when I heard about it. I didn't know anyone could donate a liver and live. But I guess you only need a part of your liver to get by.

"Anyway, things were looking pretty grim for Mr. Gold. Even with his money, he couldn't buy himself a liver. This is what brought Dana into the picture—originally. You might have read articles about the controversy surrounding rich people getting bumped up on donor lists. It's not supposed to happen. There are groups out there that watch those lists closely. Like everything else when it comes to health and money, there are a lot of politics involved. But the system is supposed to be pretty clean. A guy like Gold was never going to get a liver. It didn't matter what cause he donated to.

"Enter Jack Sandoval, Dana's father. He went to the same health club as Gold and knew about his situation. They were acquaintances more than friends. Don't ask me why Gold was still going to the gym when he was about to die. Maybe he went to take a sauna. It was while they were both in the sauna together that Dana's father noticed Gold had had his operation. The scar was visible from across the room. Mr. Sandoval asked him about it and Gold just grunted and said he was feeling better.

"That could have been the end of it right there. But Mr. Sandoval happened to tell his daughter about Gold's scar that same night. Right away, like any enthusiastic reporter, she smelled a story. Her father was able to give her just enough detail. Gold had been all over the country looking for help. His situation was hopeless. And now all of a sudden he has a brand new liver. Of course Dana thought he had bought it somewhere.

"Like I said, she was inexperienced. Her version of digging into the mystery was to head straight to the club and confront Gold. 'Hey, where did you get that liver and how much did it cost you?' You can imagine how that went over. He yelled at her to mind her own business, threatened to have her thrown out of the club. He made a mistake, though. He showed how much her questions scared him. It would have been better to just tell her he'd had the surgery overseas and leave it at that.

"Dana thought she was onto something. She went to her boss, told him about Gold and his new liver. He suggested she check into who had been on the donor lists for the last few years. Told her to look for people who were unlikely candidates but who nevertheless were still alive today. Follow me closely, this guy was shrewd. He was not necessarily telling her to search for people who had received organs who weren't supposed to. You understand?"

David nodded. "Sure. He wanted her to explore the possibility that they had received them from someplace other than the national program."

"Exactly. That would be a huge story. That the organs were out there, that they could be bought if you had the money and the connections. The editor also told Dana to check into whether Gold had recently left the country or not.

"The *New York Times* has incredible resources. They find out stuff the FBI misses all the time. It pisses us off but it's a fact. At the same time they have to be more careful than us, the way they operate. Dana was given enough rope to go digging, but not enough to hang them all. Let me clarify that remark. As she studied the donor lists, she found four people who had desperately needed heart transplants. Four people who should have died sometime in the last three years, but people who were still alive and doing well. Four rich New Yorkers who had not been given hearts by the regular national program. Make no mistake, 'rich' is the operative word here. These people were in Gold's category. They probably all knew each other. When Dana found out about them, she went running back to the paper with what she thought was the story of the year. Right away she ran into a wall. They wouldn't publish it. You can probably guess why."

"These were influential people. They could sue the paper."

"Yes. She had not found the smoking gun. She knew they had received organs but she did not know from where. Plus none of them seemed to have left the country in the last three years. That puzzled her. Her paper's reaction to her investigation frustrated her. Out of frustration she repeated the same mistake she had made at the beginning. She contacted the four people in question directly. Naturally, they refused to talk to her. Private medical matters, why should they talk to a reporter about that?"

"Did they threaten to sue the paper?" David asked.

"No. They were smart."

"The suits would have drawn attention to the matter?"

"Sure. They didn't want that. They had something to hide."

David was intrigued. "What happened next?"

"Dana made another bold move. Without consulting her paper, she went to the FBI and laid all the evidence on the table. This was at the New York office—they were intrigued. An agent with thirty years experience was assigned to her, Trent. He started to work with Dana, and from his case notes it appears he worked with her full-time for six months. Then the case was closed."

"Why?" David asked.

"Dana was raped and strangled in Central Park. No connection could be made between the murder and her investigation. Her death was seen as a random act of street violence. At least that was what Trent said when he closed the case."

"He didn't pursue it?"

"Hardly. He moved to Phoenix and took an early retirement."

David frowned. "No one else in the Bureau looked into it?"

"No. When Trent filed his final report on the mysterious transplants, he gave the impression that the whole matter had been much ado about nothing."

"And he was believed?"

Krane shrugged. "He was FBI. Why shouldn't the Bureau believe him?"

"He might have been bought off. For all we know, he might have killed Dana."

"That is a leap, to put it mildly. But I don't blame you for making it."

Krane paused. "Let's jump ahead five years, to last year. I'm working out of the Miami FBI office and we get word of a ritual killing out in the Everglades. The body's a mess—it's been rotting in the swamp for a month. Fortunately there's a wallet in the pants pocket, a driver's license. Max Sharp—thirty years old, handsome, male. He came from a wealthy family with extensive political connections. His dad had gone to college with the governor. They were best buddies. There was a lot of heat on the FBI to solve the case. Max had been cut up bad. His intestines had been laid out in a pentagram. His internal organs had been removed. There were satanic symbols left in the area: a rock with six-six-six carved in it; a black candle; some kind of weird incense. At first, my partner, Carol, and I thought it was going to be a tough one.

"But we found a suspect right away. His girlfriend, Bonnie, a twenty-five-year-old college student. In fact, she was the one who found his body, and she was forthcoming in explaining that she had last seen Max out in the Everglades, close to where his body had been found. But forthcoming might not be the best word to describe Bonnie. She told us a lot but she also couldn't remember a lot about the last time she had seen Max."

"Fascinating," David whispered.

"I knew that would be your reaction. But at first Carol and I did not worry about her mental lapses too much. Unlike the case here in Lompoc, there was plenty of her hair and traces of skin on Max's body. It seemed clear that she had been the last one to see him alive. And there was no explaining how she knew where his body had been dumped unless she was the one who killed him. The case looked open and shut.

"The only problem was Bonnie herself. The more I talked to her, the more I realized what a sweetheart she was, and how devoted she had been to Max. She had never done anything wrong in her life. She was a straight-A student in college. She certainly had never been involved in a satanic cult. Yet all the evidence pointed toward her carving up her boyfriend."

"Had Max hid his true identity from her?" David asked.

"No. That would have been hard to do. He was well known in the state. But he had not been dating Bonnie long when he was murdered—three months. Another point: Max's family was insistent that Bonnie could not have murdered Max. They knew her, they adored her. They were not going to let us prosecute her. They insisted we look for other suspects. The governor even called our office to tell us to keep digging.

"We fed the names of all the parties involved in the case into our computers. The FBI has software that sorts relationships. It's not complicated—it simply looks for names from other cases. It is a blind form of investigative work but sometimes it produces good results.

"We got a hit on Max Sharp. He was the nephew of one of the original four heart-transplant people listed in Dana and Trent's four-year-old case. That man's name had been Ted Sharp, and he had been dying of congestive heart failure before he had miraculously shown up in Manhattan with a fresh ticker in his chest. I guess it goes without saying that he was very rich as well.

"The connection sparked our interest. Here we had a case that had been closed under mysterious circumstances that had dealt with internal organs, and here Max was missing most of his organs. What got us even more curious was how brief Trent's notes were. Once again, this was a guy who had worked with Dana for six months, and yet his file was only ten pages thick. Ordinarily, even if he was making lousy progress, he should have had reams of paper. FBI agents are required to document everything they do. From what Carol and I could tell, Trent had done nothing. He had hardly looked into Dana's murder. He had not even requested a copy of the police report on the investigation into Dana's death for his file.

"Carol was anxious to interview Trent. His last known address was in Phoenix, but she was unable to track him down. It seemed he had moved and told no one where he was going. Another point: Trent had retired two years short of qualifying for his full pension. It made no sense unless . . ."

"He had been involved and bought off," David interrupted.

Krane nodded. "Something did not look right. But our own case was a mess. We could not find Trent, we were unable to discover anything else about Dana's death, and we had a suspect that looked for all the world guilty as sin but whom we were hesitant to prosecute. But we went ahead anyway, arresting Bonnie, against all kinds of political pressure, and here we ran into another wall. Her lawyer was good. He hammered the motive issue and her squeaky clean past. You had to see Bonnie in court that day, dressed in a long white dress, a ribbon in her yellow hair. She had the face of an angel. The judge could not imagine her carving up Max. We couldn't imagine it. The case did not go to trial. Like you, Bonnie was released." Krane added, "And like you she was represented by a lawyer from the firm of Hadfield and Green."

David gasped. "Don't tell me Simpson represented her?"

"No, another man, Davis. Just as clever. Look, I don't know if it means anything. Hadfield and Green is a huge firm. They have offices in eight major cities. It could be a coincidence."

"Does their name show up in the next case you and Carol worked on?"

"No."

David frowned. "One of the reasons you threw me in jail was to see who would show up to represent me."

"You are perceptive."

"How is Bonnie now?"

"She seems fine. She's back in school."

"Has she remembered anything new?"

"Not that I know of. Let me continue. We did not close the case on Max, but we had nowhere to go with it. Then, six months later, we heard about a similar type of ritual killing out in California, in Riverside. You know the area? Thirty miles east of Orange County?"

"Yeah. I hate Riverside. It's always hot and smoggy."

"That's an accurate assessment. We heard about the case through the L.A. office. They called us, they were open to whatever help we could lend. This time the victim was a woman, twenty-five, pretty . . ."

"Rich?" David interrupted.

"Oh yeah. Cindy Parker's family had enough money to buy a Vegas casino. She was found much the same way as Max: most of her internal organs removed, her intestines arranged in a pentagram. She was also discovered in an isolated spot, but she had only been dead a week at most. Also, it was a stranger who stumbled across her body. He was just a hiker out for some exercise in the hills behind Riverside. He had no connection to Cindy. For a while we were all stumped. Cindy's family insisted she was not seeing anyone special. She certainly had no cult affiliations. There were no signs that she had put up a struggle with her assailant. We could find no unusual hair or skin on her body.

"But talking to her best friend, we found another side of Cindy her parents knew nothing about. This woman said Cindy had been seeing a mystery boyfriend for close to six months, and that this guy had been madly in love with her. But she knew him only as Mike—the friend had no last name. She had no idea where he lived, what he did for a living. Only that he had been older than Cindy by ten years. Get this, even though her parents had never heard of Mike, Cindy had been living at home when she was killed."

"Do you think the parents were lying to you?"

"It was a possibility we had to consider. Cindy's best friend believed that Mike had been over to their house several times. But she could not prove it—she was not on good terms with them. Here is another point to chew on. The friend said that Cindy was very ill when she died, but her parents flat-out denied that. They said Cindy had been the picture of health. In fact, they tried to get us to investigate the best friend as a possible suspect. But we were able to clear her right away. She had been on the other side of the country when Cindy died."

"Was the coroner able to find signs of illness?"

"Yes. Cindy had a brain tumor the size of a golf ball."

"God. The parents must have known."

"They swore they didn't. And a doctor we consulted said it was possible she had shown no signs of being sick. Brain tumors can be tricky that way. You and I might have one this very second and not know it."

"A cheery thought." David considered. "Wait a second—had Max been ill?"

"Not that we know of. His parents said he had been fine. Still, we wanted to go back and examine him. The coroner had approached his body with the understanding that Max had suffered a violent attack. It was possible Max could have had something seriously wrong with him that the coroner had missed. But Max's body had been cremated, so that turned out to be another dead end." Krane added, "It was not the only one."

"You could not find this Mike?"

"No. And we looked everywhere. Carol and I even went back to our computers and fed in everyone's name who was even remotely connected to the case, hoping to get a hit like we had on the Max case. But we came up with nothing.

"That didn't stop Carol. She was full of fire, you would have loved her. She kept insisting there had to be a connection between Max's and Cindy's murders, and what Dana had been investigating. She dragged me back to New York to try to find out more about Dana. Of course we had flown up to New York when we had been working the Max case, but Dana's father had had nothing to tell us. But since then he had stumbled across a box of her papers, and when we came knocking on his door again, he was only too happy to let us go through them.

"By studying the credit card information of the original transplant group she had identified, Dana had discovered that each of the organ recipients had made a trip down to Miami, and taken a Caribbean tour aboard a ship called *Lazarus*. Don't laugh, that was really its name. You must think that whoever was behind the tours was trying to wave a flag. 'Hey, look what we're up to. We're making vibrant people out of corpses.' But I think it was indicative of the arrogance of those performing the transplants."

"So you are saying these people had their operations out at sea?"

"Yes. What better way to insure privacy? It would be physically impossible to raid them in the middle of an operation. Dana had gone so far as to obtain a list of port calls the *Lazarus* had made. That ship would leave Miami and cruise around the sea for two weeks at a time. There was no record of it docking anywhere except Miami. Dana wrote a question in capital letters in her file: WHAT KIND OF TOUR SHIP DOESN'T VISIT ANY ISLAND? Good question."

"You said she had studied the credit cards of these people. How much did they pay for these tours?" David asked.

"Two or three thousand. That means nothing. These people were rich—they could hire the best financial experts. They could have transferred hundreds of thousands and we wouldn't have known about it. Not without major auditing."

"Which you were afraid to do?"

Krane shrugged. "We come back to these people's position in society. It was difficult to run to a New York judge and say they had obtained their organs illegally. It was impossible to go to the same judge and say they were involved in the murders of Max and Cindy. We had connections—Dana had found connections—but that is not the same as proof. Worse, we were not even sure what we were trying to prove. You see our problem?"

David nodded. "On the surface it appears these murders were performed to collect organs for transplantation. But that is crazy when you tie the families of those getting the organs to those who are getting killed."

"You got it. Plus who would perform ritual murders to get organs if they were trying to keep their activities quiet? Nothing made any sense."

"How did you come across Dr. James Rean and LESS?" David asked.

"That was easy. Carol and I staked out the harbor where the *Lazarus* docked and saw him board every time the ship set sail. He was the only constant in the four tours we observed. But don't get the impression we sat at the harbor for days on end. The *Lazarus* had to notify the harbor when she was going to set sail. We merely showed up on those days. Once we had his name it was easy to discover the name of his business. Officially, it is LESS that sponsors these tours."

"Is he the president of LESS?"

"We are not sure who the president is."

"Did you get a warrant to board the ship?"

Krane hesitated. "Carol and I were about to do that. We were going to get a warrant to search Rean's office."

"What happened?"

"We had a breakthrough on Agent Trent, an anonymous tip. He was supposed to be living in El Paso. The tip provided us with an address. But because I had to fly back to Riverside to continue the search for Cindy's mystery Mike, I didn't accompany Carol to Texas." Krane stopped.

"What happened?"

"I don't know. I never heard from her again."

"*What?* She vanished?"

The memory obviously pained Krane, but he kept most of it inside. "She called minutes before she reached Trent's house. She said she would call back the minute the interview was finished." A weary shrug. "I never heard from her."

"You flew down to Texas?"

"Of course. But before that, I contacted the El Paso FBI when I did not hear back from her. They got to Trent's in minutes. His house was deserted. There was absolutely nothing inside. Not even a hair on the floor. Trent would not have had a chance to move out and clean up." Krane sighed. "I doubt he ever lived there. I suspect the anonymous tip was a setup to lure us both to El Paso."

"She could still be alive."

Krane just shook his head.

"I'm sorry for your loss. Really."

Krane slowly drank his beer. "She has two daughters, ten and eight, both bright as the sun. Her husband is a professor of literature at Miami State, great guy. I had to go to them and explain that Carol was gone, and that I didn't know the slightest reason why."

"Her disappearance must have spurred on the investigation."

"It spurred on *an* investigation. Specifically into Trent and his whereabouts. But I got nowhere trying to link her disappearance to the murders of Dana, Max and Cindy."

"Why not?"

"That is a question that does not have a simple answer. I think many factors came into play, and I might be partly to blame when it comes to the FBI's attitude about the matter. I did not react well when Carol vanished. Immediately I started raving about the transplant conspiracy and satanic cults. I came off as unstable and paranoid. Even my immediate boss—who has tremendous faith in my abilities—tried to pressure me to take a vacation. But I think I was only a part of the problem. There was, once again, no proof that all these things were related. If you study the MO on Max's and Cindy's deaths, there are similarities but also significant differences. When it comes to Dana's murder, the MO is totally different."

"But it was what Dana was investigating that matters."

"You are preaching to the choir. I'm just trying to explain the FBI's point of view. Dana was clearly related to Trent—they had worked together. And because of that the FBI was interested in what she had been doing before she was killed. But they took it no further. Satanic killings were irrelevant. They wanted Trent. They considered him the key to Carol's disappearance."

"Did they find him?"

"Not yet. They haven't given up looking."

"Are there other factors that might be holding the FBI back?" David asked.

"I know what you're thinking. Have higher-ups in the Bureau been pressured to sweep this whole thing under the rug? Ordinarily, I would say such things don't happen in the real world. But there's no arguing with the fact that the FBI is reluctant to look into Dr. James Rean."

"You never got your warrants to search the *Lazarus* and his office?"

"No. But I suspect the searches would have uncovered nothing."

"Why? You think Rean knows you're onto him?"

"Oh yeah, he knows. I pulled a Dana—just walked up to him one evening at the harbor, minutes before the *Lazarus* set sail. The confrontation did not shake him one bit. He turned out to be quite charming. But he told me nothing, except that the cruises were private and that he was not obligated to talk to me about what happened on them."

"But you must know something about the guy?"

"Only that he trained as a transplant surgeon at Harvard Medical Center. He went into private practice for a while—very successfully, I might add— and then founded LESS ten years ago."

"Ten years ago," David whispered.

"Yes. Is that important?"

"It might be. Let me ask another question. When I spoke to Rean on the plane, he said he performed all types of transplants. Isn't that unusual?"

"Yes. Apparently he has the training. He is unique that way."

"Unique people are often targeted."

"An interesting way of putting it."

"Did you have trouble getting assigned to this case?" David asked.

"Yes. My boss had to pull strings to get me out here, even though I was the most qualified one to come."

"Someone tried to block you? Is that why you're staying at the Motel Six? Are you picking up the tab on this little investigation?"

"All those things are possibilities." Krane paused, studied him. "I have told you a great deal. My payback had better be good."

"You told me much more than I thought you would. Why?"

Krane continued to stare at him. "Let's just say I have my reasons."

"But the names you used—they were all made up?"

"I changed none of the names."

"Trust is not a quality I associate with you."

"It's your turn to talk, David. We have a deal. Tell me about your meeting with Rean. You met him on the plane ride back from New York?"

"Yes. He was sitting beside me."

Krane's eyes widened. "Tell me everything."

David discovered his memory of his talk with the doctor to be fairly complete. He finished his explanation by showing Krane Dr. Rean's business card. Krane studied it a moment before handing it back.

"In your statement you said you had never heard of LESS," he said.

"Rean never used that name around me. And I never looked at his card until this afternoon."

"Is that what brought you here?"

"A lot of things brought me here."

David's turn to talk, and talk he did, although he did not sound as coherent as Krane had. He did not have a clear chronology in his mind. He started with his visit with Teresa's father—how Teresa was married to Rean—and quickly segued into Billy's and Rachel's suicides. Krane let him ramble: that was good and bad. David was not sure if the FBI agent thought him unstable and paranoid. On the other hand, the more he talked, the closer he felt to Dana and Carol, even to Krane himself. They were all trapped in an invisible web. People had died, evil men were walking the earth. At one point—while he was trying to explain how the water in Rachel's suicide bath had been both cold and clear—he felt as if the truth must be very simple. That there was a single key that could explain everything, only they were looking at the facts backward. He felt, for a short time, as if he were sitting before a mirror. Only his reflection stood behind him.

Then he didn't know what to say. He brought up his suspicions about Herb and Mary—and their torrid sex on the sacred spot—and drove what was left of his logic into a black cul-de-sac. A silence fell between them. Krane's gaze was far-off and thoughtful. David could hear his heart beating, but felt almost no need to breathe. Had a part of him died when he had found that dead woman on the beach?

Was she Sienna?

Finally Krane lit a cigarette, took another drink of his beer. "I have to think about what you've told me," he said.

David had wanted some sort of confirmation, anything. It was obvious Krane had not known Dr. James Rean had a direct connection to Lompoc. "We can't talk about it now?" David asked.

"No."

"Why not?"

Krane stood, stepped to the window, searched outside as if to see if they were being watched. It could have been a trick of the light but he suddenly looked very pale—a pale black man, not a common occurrence.

"This town is not what it appears," he replied.

David was reminded of what Pomus had said. The minister thought there were invisible monsters walking the streets of Lompoc, pulling their strings. He did not imagine Krane believed in such nonsense, but there was no denying the FBI agent appeared haunted.

In the jail cell, Pomus had been about to leave, when he had finally told him what he wanted to say all along—his tale about his vision of the demon. David sensed it was the same with Krane. The agent had not truly explained what was gnawing at him. David felt it had something to do with Carol. Krane had cut his story short there.

David suspected the two had been lovers.

"You must miss her a lot," he said gently.

Krane continued to stare out the window. "Yeah."

"Did it all just end there in Texas?"

Krane looked over sharply. "What do you mean?"

"There is something else. Something else about her."

Krane searched for a place to put out his cigarette. He had just lit it but suddenly he was acting like it was burning his fingers. But there was no ashtray beside him, and in the end he stared at the burning tip of the cigarette, and went very still.

"Yes," he said softly.

The room felt heavy, the ceiling could have lowered. "Did you hear from her after El Paso?" David asked.

Krane sighed. "I don't know."

It was the last answer David expected. It was a yes or no question. "Did she leave you some kind of secret message at the house where she was supposed to meet Trent?" he asked.

"It wasn't that way. It wasn't that . . ." He did not finish.

"Simple?" David said.

"Yes." Krane added quickly, "She called, after she disappeared, and left a message on my home machine. But I don't know if it was her."

"But you must have recognized her voice?"

Krane was clearly distressed. "It sounded like her but it wasn't her. It couldn't have been her. I mean, the stuff she was saying, the way she was saying it—it couldn't have been Carol."

"What did she say? How did she say it?"

Krane came back to the bed, sat down, finally put out his cigarette. Putting his palms tightly together, as if he were praying to a hectic God, he stared down at the floor. When he spoke next, he was no longer the tough FBI agent. He was more like David—confused, scared. Finally, at last, they were equals.

"She left the message in the middle of the night, in a completely flat tone. All the years I worked with Carol, I never heard her speak that way. Her voice was soft and monotone, it sounded drained of life. At the same time she was sad. The sorrow in her voice was heartbreaking. She could have been a child lost in a vast empty place." Krane sucked in a ragged breath, added, "And I wasn't even sure if it was her."

"But it must have been her."

Krane snapped. "It couldn't have been her! What she said—Jesus Christ—she didn't know anything about it. But it was all she talked about."

"What did she say?"

Krane calmed himself, with effort. "The message was about Bobbie. That was my girlfriend in high school. What she said was, 'Why did you leave Bobbie? She could see you, she was calling to you. Why did you leave her?' Then she would start over in that same spooky voice, again and again, a dozen times. 'Why did you leave Bobbie? She could see you, she was calling to you. Why did you leave her?'" Krane shook his head, wiped the sweat off his brow. He added, "I never told Carol about Bobbie. I never told anyone the full story."

David let some time pass. "If you tell me, I swear, I will keep it private."

Krane looked at him as if they were both crazy. "Do you know why I smoke so much?"

"Why?"

"So I won't drink all the time. Did you know that is true of a lot of smokers?"

"I didn't know that. When did you start smoking?"

"In high school. You're not surprised, are you? You really are smart, David. Or else you're some kind of sorcerer. You walk in here and get me to talk about all kinds of things I don't want to talk about. How do you do that?"

David shrugged. "We're both looking for answers."

"No. We're both looking for peace of mind. We're just hoping the answers will give us that. But I've been at this longer than you. Some mornings I wake up and feel like I've been investigating these ritual killings all my life. And I'm beginning to think the more I find out, the more fucked up I'll feel. What do you think of that?"

"Then why do you keep going?"

"Because I have nowhere else to go."

"Because of Bobbie?"

Krane laid down on the bed, against the pillows, as if he were tired. "Bobbie was a long time ago. She was my first love, the first girl I ever had sex with. It was crazy but I thought of marrying her even back then. But Bobbie would have made a lousy wife. She was wild, she liked to do dangerous things. Our senior year in high school—it was only a month before we were supposed to graduate—she talked me into hijacking a small motorboat docked off the beach and taking it out a few miles. This was in Craton— that's a tiny town on the northeast coast of Florida. You understand, we were going to bring the boat back when we were done with it. But that night, it couldn't have been any darker. There were plenty of stars, but no moon, and the lights from the shore were as useful as my glowing watch. And of course we were both drunk as hell. We had a quart of Jack Daniels and we finished half of it before swiping the boat, and the other half out on the water. I wasn't too worried, though. As long as I knew which way the shore was, I figured we'd be fine. We motored out a few miles and it was nice.

"Then Bobbie fell overboard. That doesn't sound like a big deal and it shouldn't have been a big deal. But several factors came together to conspire against us. First, I was sitting at the front of the boat and she was at the rear. She was handling the motor. So I wasn't even looking when she went overboard. All I heard was a splash, but I was so drunk I didn't turn around right away. I waited ten seconds or so. I know that doesn't sound like a lot, but in those few seconds the motor pushed me out of sight of Bobbie. Also, I think she fell overboard because she passed out. I don't think she woke up until she was in the water. She sure as hell didn't cry out when she went overboard. It was only when I turned around and saw that she was gone that I heard her calling for help. All of this sounds slightly unbelievable but it happens all the time to people when they mix the ocean and alcohol.

"The sea was not rough, but it was no lake either. There was a two-foot chop and a brisk south breeze. Like I said, I could hear Bobbie calling but I was hearing her over the sound of the ocean. By the time I finally got the boat turned around, she must have been a hundred yards behind me. Still, I thought, it's no big deal. Bobbie can swim and I can hear her and I'll just go fish her out of the water. I called to her to relax, that I was on my way. But I was a little worried. I couldn't see her. The water was like an ocean of black ink. I'm not exaggerating, I couldn't see ten feet in front of my face.

"I missed her as I swung around. I don't know by how much. Once again, I was so drunk, I didn't think to tell her to keep shouting. In the dark I couldn't gauge how far back I'd gone. I might have missed her by less than twenty feet but I think that first time around I overshot her by more than a hundred yards. When she called to me again she sounded farther away, and it was just then the breeze picked up a bit. The noise of the sea got worse. I called to her to keep shouting, that I was coming, but I don't think she heard me. She continued to shout but she took long breaks in-between. When I swung around I missed her again.

"Then I got even more confused. I could still hear her, faintly, but I could not tell from which direction her voice was coming from. That might be hard to believe as well, but again, it happens all the time when you're out on the sea at night. The way sound carries over the water changes all the time. I could have sworn she was off to my right, but when I steered in that direction, her voice grew even more faint. I quickly reversed my course, but then I think I angled away from her and went too far. Because the next time I called out to her, she didn't respond at all.

"It was a nightmare, I started to panic. I didn't know if she had stopped calling to me because she had gone under or if I was just too far away to hear her. I didn't know what to do. I tried killing the motor and standing up and screaming her name, but all I heard back was the fuzzy echo of my own voice. Just as bad, the chop began to turn my boat around, and I lost all sense of direction, if I had any to begin with. When I restarted the motor, and continued to search, I had no idea if I was heading away from her. All this time I could see the shore, but I had not orientated myself to it the instant Bobbie fell overboard. I don't know if that would have helped—it might have. Let's be frank. Back in those days I thought I was pretty hot, but I acted just like any other punk kid caught up in a crisis. I got scared, I fucked up."

Krane fell silent, staring off in the distance. David let a minute go by.

"You never found her?" he asked finally.

"No. I searched for another half hour, but then I got worried that I was going to run out of gas. I wasn't scared for myself, getting trapped out at sea, but I decided the best thing to do would be to go back to shore and get help. Yet in my heart I knew it was too late, that Bobbie had already drowned." Krane added, "That's why Carol's message shook me up so much."

"What was the fallout?"

"It was bad. The first thing I did was lie to the police. What a coward, I know, but I didn't think telling them that we had been drunk would help the search for Bobbie. They didn't check my blood-alcohol level until the next morning, and by then my system was clean." Krane shrugged. "We searched all that night and most of the next day, the Coast Guard helping out, but we never found her body."

"Did people blame you?"

"Sure. My family had no money but Bobbie's parents sued us anyway. My mom and dad ended up losing their house. But I still kept lying about us being drunk, I don't know why. I guess it's that way with lies, once you start them, they gain a life of their own."

David considered. "You say you didn't tell anyone exactly what happened that night. But half the town must have figured out the basic scenario. They would have known how you kept missing her in the dark. They would have known about your doubts afterward. That call must have been a prank call, someone from your hometown trying to mess with your mind."

Krane sighed. "No. It was Carol."

"You just said it couldn't be Carol."

"I know. It couldn't have been her."

"I don't understand what you're saying."

Krane looked at him. "Don't you see, none of it makes sense! I don't have an answer for that call any more than you have an answer for what happened your last night with Sienna."

"Did you keep a copy of the call? Have the voice analyzed?"

"No. I couldn't take a message like that into the FBI. After Carol disappeared, I told you, they all thought I was losing it. A tape like that would have just confirmed their suspicions."

"But it could have been proof that she was still alive."

"It's doubtful. We had no copy of Carol's voice on tape to compare it to. Her husband didn't even have a home video with her talking on it. Besides, the person who made that call *knew* I would not dare to bring it into the FBI. They knew how much what happened with Bobbie upset me, and how much it has haunted me since."

"Who are *they?*" David asked.

Krane forced a crooked smile. "*What* are they," he muttered.

"Something else happened?"

"Sure. It gets better, or worse—it depends on your point of view. But what I'm going to tell you next, it's complete bullshit. If you told me the same thing, I would say you were nuts. All I can say is these things seemed to have happened to me."

"*Seemed* to?"

"Yes. I don't know if they actually happened."

"Go on," David said. He knew now why Krane was talking—to a suspect in a murder case, no less. The answer was simple: he was just trying to get it all off his chest. David could see the pain in his face when he spoke next.

"I told you, when Carol flew down to El Paso I was still working on the Cindy Parker murder in Riverside. I was trying to find her mysterious boyfriend, Mike. When Carol disappeared, I returned to the case. What else was I supposed to do? I was in California when I got that weird message from Carol, and I was so upset that I bought a bottle of tequila and hiked back into the hills behind Riverside, to the spot where Cindy's mutilated body had been found. Don't ask me why, it was a morbid thing to do. But a part of me felt that if I sat on that spot, stayed there all night maybe, I'd get a sense of what was really behind these killings. So I sat in the dark in the center of that barren gully and drank my booze and tried to imagine that Cindy was alive to talk to me and explain what the last hour of her life had been like. And all the time I heard Carol's voice in my head, telling me I had left my girlfriend to drown.

"Cindy's remains had been removed, of course. There wasn't any yellow tape to mark off the area. There was just me and my bottle and a black sky overhead. The gully was made up of rocks and sand and a few weeds. The surrounding hills were worn and tired. There was a chill in the air but I didn't care. The alcohol in my belly was warm.

"I'm not sure how long I sat there before I dozed off. The bottle was mostly gone—I must have been incredibly drunk. But when I woke up, I did not feel drunk. I did not have my watch. I did not know what time it was. The chill had crept into my bones while I had been unconscious, and some type of overcast had blown in. The stars were all gone. The sky looked like an old gray blanket. It was not as dark as it had been out on the boat with Bobbie, but it was pretty dark. I tried my flashlight but for some reason it wouldn't work, and I had put new batteries in it before I had left my hotel.

"I was thinking about leaving when I noticed a dark shape surrounding me. It was in the form of a pentagram. When we had found Cindy, her intestines had been arranged around her body in that shape. It blew my mind. When I had passed out, the pentagram had definitely not been there. But now, examining it, I saw that it was made of someone's intestines. It appeared no different than the pentagram the police had found on the first day, only now I was the one in the center, and it was soaked in fresh blood.

"I had my cell phone, I tried to call the local sheriff. The surrounding hills seemed to be blocking my reception, so I climbed up the hill immediately behind the murder scene but I still couldn't get through. In the distance I could see the lights of Riverside, but they looked much farther away than they should have been. Also, they looked darker."

"Do you mean dimmer?" David asked.

"No. They looked darker, as if a black veil had been placed between me and them. But that didn't bother me as much as what I saw when I looked back down into the gully. I saw something—this is hard to believe. The pentagram was glowing with a faint red light. The guts glistened as if the blood that coated them had been drawn from a radioactive mutant."

"Could it have been some type of reflection?"

"No. The gully was shielded from outside light sources."

"Shit."

"You believe me? You don't have to believe me. I wouldn't believe you."

"I don't know what to believe. Go on."

"Should I? I don't know why I am telling you this. What good does it do me?"

"Confession is good for the soul."

Krane shook his head sadly. "I think that message from Carol was accurate. I think I overreacted that night and left Bobbie to die. Talking about it can't help her."

"Did you hike back down to the pentagram?"

"Yes. It was odd, though, when I got close the glow faded. Then, when I stood inside the pentagram, I couldn't see it at all. Only the outline of the intestines. I didn't know what to think. I was about to leave the area when I saw a figure approaching. It was a young woman, a girl, dressed entirely in black. Her hair was black, straight and short, and her face was so pale it looked like a mirror. For a minute I thought I was staring at a ghost, that Bobbie had returned from the dead to haunt me. She was coming from the other end of the gully, walking slowly, in no hurry to reach me. I really noticed her walk—it was like she had all the time in the world.

"But when she got closer I saw it wasn't Bobbie. This girl was younger, and she was very thin and stood with a kind of self confidence you don't see in teenagers. She stopped only a few feet away, right in front of me, and it was as if her whole body mocked me. Maybe she had the right to treat me like a fool, I don't know. I was scared of her, that's for sure, I couldn't even speak. She appeared to know that, though. That I was a law enforcement officer, that I carried a gun, but that her simple act of standing before me had me completely unnerved. She just stared at me, smiled—her lips were as dark as her clothes. She could have been clad in black leather. Her jacket and pants were tight as skin. She looked like a bag of bones.

"Then she raised her right hand, very slowly, and there was something large and gross in it. In the dark I couldn't tell what it was, but she brought it closer, near my chest, and I finally saw what she was holding. It was a human heart, freshly cut out of someone's chest. At that instant I was sure that I was looking at Cindy's heart. The police never had found it. I could smell it, the stench of raw meat. In that moment, I imagined I could feel the pain it must have caused when it had been cut out of its owner's chest. I felt nothing but pain right then, as if that was all there was to life.

"I wanted to scream but I couldn't. It was the way she kept staring at me. I couldn't see her eyes but I could feel them on me and they were like razors slowly tracing different parts of my brain, cutting out my past, my future. If I could have drawn my gun, I would have. I would have shot her in the head and let her brains splatter the ground. I was sure she was the one who had killed Cindy.

"But she seemed to read my mind and it made her smile widen, and she brought the heart closer. She touched me with it—I felt its sticky warmth through my shirt. I felt the blood on my chest, felt it drip down toward my belly. Then, going up on her tiptoes, she leaned over and spoke in my ear. I felt her breath on the side of my face, and there was something familiar about it—the scent. It reminded me of peppermints, it was not a foul smell, but it was still a cold breath. And when she spoke I felt ice in my veins. She said very softly, 'You are going to die.' "

Krane fell silent. Again, he was not looking at David, but staring at a wall. Trying to think, trying to remember. He was not shaking, though. He appeared calm, like a man who had been told the bad news and finally accepted it. Of course they were all going to die, David thought. It was just a question of when and how horrible it was going to be.

"What happened next?" David asked.

"I woke up, it was morning, the sun was in my eyes. I was lying on my side with my face in my bottle. It was empty. Everything else was as it was supposed to be. There was no pentagram, no disembodied heart, no scary-eyed chick. There weren't any bloodstains on my shirt. The only thing that was real, that I could verify with my five senses, was that I had a terrible hangover." Krane paused, shrugged. "So I imagined it all."

"Do you believe that?"

"Sure. It's the only explanation. Excess tequila often causes hallucinations."

"You don't believe that."

"I do believe it. What else do you want me to believe?"

"If you don't believe it, then why did you tell me about it?"

"Fuck you, you asked. I told you because I'm bored and I want to fuck with your mind." With that Krane grabbed his beer, took a hit. He probably wished it was tequila or else Jack Daniels—something stronger. He acted annoyed but he was frightened as well. David realized there was still another reason the FBI agent had told him so many secrets.

Krane believed his vision, what he had been told.

He thought he was a dead man.

TWENTY-TWO

Leaving Krane, David found himself in his car and staring at a bloody sunset. He decided to drive down to the beach to get the most out of it. Like his first day home from his trip, he decided without actually exercising his own will. He was a puppet, he thought, his strings were silver wire, so sharp they were capable of severing his very reason. And what was worse was that no one was pulling his strings. It was only the most random of all universal forces that was in control. Fear.

Like Krane, he was afraid. That was why he drove to the beach. He wanted to walk on the shore and find another dead body and know that it was not Sienna and let his fear blow away like the sand on the wind.

There was no wind when he reached the beach, however. No people, only shallow gray waves and desolate bird sounds. The sun had already set; the black-blue pot of the sea had dissolved it. The sky was orange and purple; a single round cloud burned with a yellow lining. Getting out of his car, the shadows lengthening, he headed north, along the railroad track, toward ground zero.

A train caught him in the middle of the bridge, though. It came out of nowhere, a skyscraper on wheels, so fast, like it had caught him and Billy so many years ago. Like that day, he was afraid to try to outrun it, to escape the shaking bridge and the crushing noise. As it tore by, he hugged the rusty side girders and closed his eyes and counted the seconds. The train was gone before he got to sixty but he didn't stop or open his eyes until he reached a hundred.

Charlie was wrong, they were the cowards. Billy had been the brave one. David knew that like he had never known anything before in his life. In his last moments, before pulling the trigger, Billy must have somehow spit in the face of death. His friend wouldn't have ended it any other way.

The near brush with the train took something out of him. David felt too weary to continue, turned around and headed back toward his car. To his surprise he found Herb parked not far from him in the lot. Herb had left the space open between them, the spot Billy's car had occupied when he had died. An old habit the gang shared—none of them dared to park there. Herb waved, indicated he should climb in beside him. David did so, and got the shock of his life.

Herb was drinking a quart of Bacardi Rum straight from the well of life and holding onto a pillowcase stuffed with cash.

Hundreds. Thousands of hundreds.

"What the hell?" David gasped.

Herb looked at him with a face made of papier mâché. He was tired and scared, and maybe more sober than he had been since before his first communion, although his breath smelled like an alternative energy source.

"I'm leaving town, man, I'm splitting for good." He gestured with his pillowcase and bottle. "This is all I'm taking with me."

"Why are you leaving?"

Herb shook his head, reached in his stash, pulled out more money than could be counted in a car. The hundreds were tied with red rubber bands, fat packs of wealth. He tried to give them to David. "I want you to take this," he said. "Keep some for yourself. Give most of it to Charlie and Karen."

"Why to them? Herb, I can't take this money. This is over a hundred thousand you're giving me!"

"Take it, fuck it. You guys all got to get out of town for good. Tell Charlie and Karen that. Tell them to take the girls. That's what the money's for."

David tried to push it away. "Herb, no. It's not our money."

Herb looked at him with sad eyes. "You think it's drug money?"

"Of course it's drug money, you idiot. Answer me, why are you leaving town?"

Herb shook his head, drank from his big bottle, stared at nothing. "I'm just leaving is all," he said.

David heard fear; these days, in Lompoc, it grew on trees. But there were no trees at the beach, just darkness and dead things. "Is it because of Mary?" he asked.

Herb sighed, asked, "How come you're so smart, David?"

"Because I've refrained from killing several million brain cells a day. Look, I know you're involved with her, you can't deny it. What I want to know is why? I mean, she's only a girl."

"My friend, you have no idea what Mary Pomus is."

David felt cold. "Did she kill that woman?"

Herb shrugged, as if that was no biggie. "I don't know, she might have. That chick is into weird shit. All I know is I've got to get away from her."

"What kind of weird shit is she into?"

"I don't know if I want to talk about that. You don't want to ever fuck her, that's for sure. You know, there is strange and there is sick and then there is Mary Pomus. No, don't even go there, David. There isn't a shower in the world hot enough to wash off them cooties."

"You can't be leaving town because of her cooties?"

Herb gave him a straight look. "That is exactly why I am leaving."

David fumed. "You're not making any sense."

Herb took out more wads of cash, forced them into his hands. "If you don't want the money, Charlie and Karen will. You have no right to decide for them."

"Why don't you give it to them yourself?"

"Because I'm in a hurry." He added quietly, "Don't tell anyone I've left."

"Because you want to get a head start?"

"Don't tell Stanton. He'll tell Pomus and then he'll tell Mary."

"Should I give Stanton some money? His usual cut?"

Herb was unimpressed. "What I gave him, he just spent on keeping his kid alive."

"Steve? What's wrong with Steve? I thought he was doing great."

"That's what the sheriff tells people. Steve was in a motorcycle accident five years ago, cracked his skull so wide open you can shine a light from one ear to the other. He's in a permanent coma, a vegetable. The guy had no insurance when he went down. The cut I gave Stanton every month, he only took it for his son's sake. What's wrong with that?"

For some reason the money Herb had forced on him suddenly felt dirtier. "I didn't know," David said.

Herb nodded, stared into the depths of his bottle. "That fire, the one that burned Rachel's face, I didn't start it. You know me, David, I wouldn't have done something like that. I'm a fucking waste but I'm not evil."

David felt his heart pound, he strove to stay calm. There were secrets here in this car, in the half-life of Herb's decayed brain. He knew they could wash up on the shore, or—if he was not careful—just drift out to sea and be lost forever.

"You got there immediately," he said calmly. "You helped save them. Everyone saw you as a big hero. But it was too much of a coincidence that you happened to be walking by at that exact moment."

"Someone told me what was going to happen."

David almost choked. *"Who?"*

"I can't tell you, man."

"Herb!"

Herb grabbed his arm, stared at him hard. The alcohol vanished from his breath. His eyes were suddenly as clear as the Mercedes headlights Stanton had seen the night Billy had shot himself six feet from where they sat. Plus his grip was strong; the power of true dread.

"You joke, but I do need that head start," he said. "If I tell you what I know about that night—I kid you not—I won't be alive tomorrow morning. My throat will be slit. It will be my guts that will be lying all over the sand. Do you hear me?"

David felt as if he stood only two inches away from enlightenment, and one foot from despair. Yet he did hear him, knew instinctively that he could push Herb no further. "What about Sienna? What do you know about her?" he asked.

Herb let go of him, screwed the cap on his bottle and began to put his money bag away. "Nothing. Except every time I saw your girlfriend, I saw someone who was just waiting around to die," he said.

"Die? How?"

"I don't know that, man, but she had the look. And if you stay here, you'll have that look too." Herb stashed his pillowcase behind his seat and glanced at him one last time, adding, "If you don't have it already."

David drove home; he felt lousy. He was so tired he did not even bother to lift Herb's money off the passenger seat, just left it lying there and went inside. He didn't care that it was still early; it was dark and he was going to bed. He looked forward to that, sleeping in his own bed again. Undressing in the living room, he did not bother to brush his teeth. He simply padded into the bedroom and crawled under the blankets and closed his eyes.

His right hand brushed against a naked female back.

He spoke impatiently. "Julie. You didn't tell me you were coming over."

The female turned over and faced him in the dark.

"It's not Julie, silly boy. It's Sienna."

Then she was kissing him, her naked body pressing against him, her tongue deep.

David almost flew out of the bed to the light switch. The shock of the bright light was more than matched by the shock of who was in his bed.

"Mary! What the hell?" he gasped.

She giggled, Ms. Goth Queen, she was happy. Her naked limbs were the color of pearls, her dark eyes were frozen lava. And her lips, her tongue—that had seconds ago been connected to his lips and tongue—were scary. She plopped onto her knees so that there was nothing to see but how naked she was. He was naked as well; the draft down around his balls felt like an army of marching bacteria. He couldn't get Herb's insane remarks out of his head.

"Surprise!" she shouted.

He reached for a sweatshirt to cover himself. "Mary, this is crazy. How did you get in here? You shouldn't be here. Get dressed and go home. Now."

Mary smiled mischievously. "Okay. I will do whatever you want."

With that she stood from the bed, left the bedroom, and walked out the front door, shutting the door behind her. *What the hell,* David thought. Turning on another light, he didn't see any of her clothes around, and, peeking out the window, he couldn't even find her outside. Of course the street was dark. It was possible she could walk naked all the way home without attracting attention. He hoped so—he didn't want her explaining to the police where she had just been.

He wondered how she had gotten into his house.

He *always* locked the door when he left.

"This town is not what it appears," he mumbled as he turned off the lights and climbed back into bed. God forbid it was any worse than he imagined.

He did not sleep, though, not right away. He kept thinking of the different females that had been in his bed: Sienna, Julie and Mary—from now on she would have to be part of the list. And his mind went back to that morning in that motel room in Sacramento, ten years ago, when Rachel had walked naked across the floor in front of him, while Billy had been out, looking for breakfast, getting ready for his race. Like all spurious sexual moves, that peekaboo had returned to haunt them later in the week.

Blame it on seventeen-year-old hormones. He had tried to do that back then. It was better than examining his loyalty to his best friend.

They had been at his house, he and Rachel, and they had both known Billy would be over soon to pick her up. She had only stopped by to borrow a CD. That had been her excuse. But when they were alone together, in his bedroom, she had started to tease him about her exhibitionist spurt. Before she even began, though, his head had been replaying her Sacramento line. *"Don't worry, David. I love him but I don't tell everything."* The mutual telepathy—it only made her teasing worse.

"So you want to paint me sometime?" she asked, seemingly out of the blue. "I can hold a pose a long time, I don't mind. I can stare off into nothing and think of nothing. I heard artists like that."

"Like what exactly?" he asked.

"A blank expression. Then you can paint what you think you see, or what you want to see." She giggled. "You can paint me any way you want."

He felt bold, he felt guilty. "Like Sacramento?"

She nodded. "Sure, David."

That was enough, right there. They talked for another few minutes but it did not really matter. The sexual fuse had been lit—something had to blow. Ten minutes later they were making out, and it was good, kissing Rachel, she tasted like dreams of desire. And it was bad, touching her, because she was only a dream, and the moment couldn't last.

Then they both heard the knock at the door, and got up quickly, and straightened their clothes and tried to hide the blush. Billy, when he came in, was as casual as ever, and Rachel leaned over and hugged him the same way she always did, and life went on.

Until that Saturday night, three days later, when Rachel lost half her face in the fire. That fire that hadn't even touched Billy. David never kissed Rachel again after that, never even thought about it.

He awoke to the sounds and color of fire, of wailing sirens and a flickering red glow. Dazed, he staggered out of bed and peered out the window. In the distance he could see flames. They had to be three stories high, or else they were much closer than they appeared. For a second he wondered if he was dreaming. He was so tired he almost went back to bed.

A part of him, though, worried about the direction of the fire. Getting dressed, he climbed in his car and drove toward the flames. Why wasn't he surprised to discover that it was the Motel 6 that was burning down? No, it was only a portion of the building that was in ruins, the north end, where Krane had been staying. Room 18—the roof had already caved in, the support beams glowed like hungry coals across a queen-sized bed that gave the sick appearance of a funeral pyre.

He got out of his car, moved as close as he could, till the heat was practically burning the skin off his face. There was something lying there, in the middle of the hellish soot, that looked like it had once been human. From the way they had contained the flames, it looked as if the firemen would probably be able to save the remainder of the structure, but David doubted anyone could save the FBI agent.

He backed away from the inferno, his skin tingling, and walked around. It was four in the morning, and a quarter of the town was present. The air was full of smoke, hot from the flames. Eventually he ran into Charlie and Karen, both in bathrobes, holding hands, as if they had been roused from the same bed. Charlie told him what he already knew. Krane was dead, the only apparent casualty.

"Do you guys know how the fire started?" David asked.

"I spoke to Stanton," Charlie said. "Krane was a chain-smoker. He says he figures the guy just passed out with a lit cigarette between his fingers."

David snorted. "He's a sheriff and he says something that stupid?"

Karen looked worried. "You can talk to him yourself. He's looking for you."

Charlie was also concerned. "Yeah. The word is that you went to see Krane this evening. Is that true?"

"I went to talk to him. I didn't go to light him on fire. Where is Stanton now?"

"He drove over to your house to find you," Charlie said.

David nodded. He could see it all now, happening all over again. The last one to see the victim alive, very suspicious. This time he wouldn't be surprised to find witnesses coming out of the woodwork to testify that he had been arguing with Krane in the motel room. Julie would probably be one of them. He could be back in jail by sunrise.

David underwent a transformation right then. Since he had returned from New York, crap had been hitting him from every direction. It was like he was nailed to the walls of a boxcar that was careening down a railroad that had accidentally taken the Cesspool Exit. He had been the victim, he thought, when everyone else was saying he was the cause.

He decided it was time to reverse the order of things.

"I better get back and check on the girls," Karen said. She went up on her tiptoes to kiss Charlie on the lips. Then she hugged David, patted him on the back. "Take care of yourself. Stay out of trouble," she said.

He promised her he would, and then she was gone, walking home.

"Things better between you two?" he asked.

Charlie nodded, watching her go. "Much better."

The reply warmed his heart. Something decent in a sea of muck. "Let me ask you a weird question, Charlie. If you had a hundred-thousand dollars right now, in cash, do you think you could talk Karen into grabbing the girls and leaving town with you?"

"Funny you should say that. Tonight we were talking about that. Karen is sick of this place—she would leave in a heartbeat. I'm the same, this town has begun to give me the creeps." He added, "But neither of us has any money."

David had parked down the street, away from the chaos. He bid Charlie to follow, and a minute later they were sitting in the front seat of his car and his friend was counting fat packets of hundreds.

"Where the fuck did you get this?" he gasped.

"Herb. It's part of his profits from a decade of dealing. Just give me ten grand. You and Karen can have the rest."

"There's over a hundred grand here! I can't take that much. We have to at least split it, David."

"No. You need it more than I do. Take it, and the four of you start fresh far from here. My only condition is that you get out of town immediately."

"What's the rush?"

"Bad shit is about to come down around here. Herb knew it was coming—that's why he split. Yeah, trust me, he's gone for good. But he doesn't want anyone to know it, not yet. Respect his wishes, he was pretty scared when he left."

Charlie was dazed. "You're making no sense. What's going to happen?"

He nodded in the direction of the fire. "Krane shows up in town to investigate a ritual killing and a week later he is dead. This place is at the heart of an evil scheme that's spread nationwide. Krane told me about it this afternoon, what he knew, and that was the reason he was murdered."

"Is this related to that dead woman on the beach?"

"Yes. The same people who killed Krane killed her. Isn't that reason enough to get away? And if it isn't, then just trust an old friend. You don't want Karen or the girls anywhere near Lompoc."

"But what about you? How are you connected to this scheme?"

"I'm not sure, but I have my suspicions. That's why I have to leave as well. I have to continue Krane's investigation."

"But you need to talk to the sheriff, tell him what you know."

"He might be a part of it. He's not the knight in shining armor we thought. Herb told me he has been paying off Stanton for years to let him operate his drug business. For that reason alone, you cannot tell the sheriff what I'm doing or where you're going. Just leave, it is that simple. And tell no one about the money except Karen."

Charlie smiled as he stared down at the cash, his face caught in the red glow of the dying flames. Already the crowd had begun to disperse, drifting away in the smoky night like a swarm of moths that had lost interest in a worn-out campfire. They had seen enough. There would be plenty of material for fresh gossip in the morning, and surely his personal appearance on the scene would be hotly debated.

Charlie sounded like a little kid when he spoke next.

"Karen will freak out when she sees it. We've never had a cent to our name. This is the sort of thing you always dream about."

What David was saying was not real to Charlie. David supposed it did not matter. The money was real, Karen and the girls. His old friend would leave.

"It is like a dream," David agreed, for the first time letting himself feel the grief of Krane's death. A manipulative and scheming man, but also a brave and resourceful soul. The FBI agent had only been trying to do his job. Now he was gone, and who was there left alive in his Bureau that would try to understand his death?

"Then, going up on her tiptoes, she leaned over and spoke in my ear. . . . She said very softly, 'You are going to die.' "

David said good-bye to Charlie and drove away. He had his shoes on his feet and his wallet in his pocket, not to mention plenty of cash on the seat beside him. He felt no need to go home, no desire to talk to Stanton. He just kept driving, south, through Santa Barbara and down to Los Angeles and LAX. There he parked his car in lot C, like before, and when the sun rose, he was sitting on the first flight heading to New York.

TWENTY-THREE

The view out the window was not the classic New York skyline. The art director's office was only a fifth-floor medium-sized box, and the building across the street was taller than most clouds. The art director, Miss Winston, had a midget in her genetic tree, and wore glasses so thick and star-struck they looked like they had been lifted from a spy satellite. He doubted she could even see out the window.

The office was jammed with art portfolios, books and manuscripts. It could have been described as messy but since Miss Winston appeared to be a highly organized woman—and loved his work—he preferred to think of it as creatively uninhibited. She was a smart person, although young to be in her position. He had just finished telling her about his new concept for the cover of *Vampire of My Heart*, and she had gotten it immediately. She liked his idea of making Cleo's child a statue, to convey its antiquity.

"Are you going to do effects on the child?" she asked.

"I was thinking of keeping it dark but giving it a radioactive glow," he said.

"Is she lifting it out of the grave to give to her partner?"

"Not exactly. I want to give the impression she gave birth to it in the open grave."

"How are you going to do that?"

"Don't worry, there won't be any blood on her clothes. I'll send you a sketch as soon as I get back home. I made one already but left in sort of a hurry. I didn't know I would be seeing you." In reality he had to show her a sketch. They would not let him start painting without seeing the basic design.

Miss Winston clapped her hands together, excited. "It sounds innovative. I'm sure the author will love it. What did you think of the end of the book? It was shocking, wasn't it?"

He had not read the end. "She's an amazing writer. But you know, I left home without the manuscript. Do you have a copy lying around here I could take? I'd like to study it some more while I'm traveling."

"Sure. I'll have a copy made up before you leave."

"I wanted to ask a favor. Please tell me if it is inappropriate. I was wondering if I could meet with the author. You told me once that she lived here in the city."

Miss Winston brightened. "I'm sure that would be fine. The last time she was in, she said she would like to meet with whoever was doing the cover. I know she would be delighted to hear your idea." She added, "Unfortunately, I don't have her phone number, just her address and her e-mail."

"Thanks. That isn't a problem, I can always e-mail her."

Ten minutes later David left the publisher with Marcy Goldberg's *Vampire of My Heart* in hand, and the author's personal information. He planned to walk back to his room at the Plaza. It tickled him to think that he was staying at such an expensive hotel, and that all the potheads back in Lompoc had made it possible. Yet, once outside in the sun, the thought of going back inside felt ridiculous. The sounds and sights of Manhattan, which had often grated on his nerves the last time, were somehow soothing now. Staring straight up, at the skyscrapers, he felt as if his soul could take flight and touch the clouds. For the first time in a long time, he was at peace. Getting out of Lompoc had done him a world of good.

Yet his subconscious did not let him enjoy the peace.

He walked where his legs took him, seemingly all over town.

He ended up at the address on the slip of paper Miss Winston had given him.

Was it by accident? Standing outside the residence, he reflected on many things; days of introspection compressed in a few moments. He thought of a mysterious young woman who loved mysteries. Of her serious carpal tunnel, a common typing injury. Most of all he thought of the doom in her voice, a virtual copy of Cleo's doomed narrative.

Marcy Goldberg's house looked like old money, as Krane had been fond of saying. A fence made of moss-laden redbrick, a gate topped with polished brass. The driveway was long, lined with lonely trees with heavy hearts. The branches hung to the ground, mingled with flowers and dead leaves. He was still in the center of the city but as he stared in the direction of the half-hidden house he felt as if he had just awakened in Sleepy Hollow.

All dreams end, he thought, not knowing what his head was trying to tell his heart. He did not want to push the small gold button atop the large black mailbox. It must have been because of the nameplate there, the two words stamped in raised silver:

THE WITHERS.

The art director had given him the address of the dead woman on the beach.

It was no accident. He had come to New York to come here.

His hand betrayed him, it moved. The bell buzzed. A voice spoke over an invisible speaker. Young, male, a deep voice. "Who is it?" he asked.

"David Lennon. I'm here to see Mrs. Wither."

A long pause. "Does she know you're coming?"

"Just tell her I'm here." He added, "I knew her daughter."

Knew, not know. He was not ready to admit to himself that Sienna was dead, however. He could not; he had spoken to her, and nothing could alter that fact.

There was another pause, then the lock on the gate hummed softly and popped open. Walking up the long driveway, David felt he could be killed in the next minute and it would not surprise him.

A young black man met him at the door. He was extraordinarily handsome, with a face both refined and utterly intimidating. David was reminded of an African shaman, and at the same time he thought of the Deep South and a long tradition of gentle manners. The conflicting impressions did not help to clear his mind. The guy had on a white suit, a black shirt, and the heavy gold chain around his neck was as pale as the summer sun on a water-parched plain. The man could not have been more that twenty-five and yet he projected remarkable authority.

Despite all that, David felt as if the man was exerting immense effort to keep his emotions in check. David did not sense danger, though, that the guy wanted to hurt him. Quite the reverse, David felt very welcome as the man nodded and gestured for him to come inside.

"I've told Mrs. Wither you're here. She will be down in a few minutes," he said.

David crossed the threshold, felt the air-conditioning on his sweaty face. The house was spacious, smelled of lemons, Sienna. "Does she know who I am?" he asked.

"Yes. You're Sienna's boyfriend." He offered his hand. "I'm Rudy Turbel, an old friend of the family."

David shook his hand. Had Rudy just confirmed that Sienna was dead? He shook his head to keep the room from spinning. "I'm sorry, Rudy, I'm confused. How does Sienna relate to Sally Wither?"

"Sienna was Sally's nickname. We called her that as a kid."

He was in no danger of falling over. He was suddenly too stiff, too heavy—he felt as if he had been built from the ground up. Yet his creator had left out an important part. The wizard had forgotten to give him his heart, and his brain was filled with straw. All he could do was mumble. "So Sienna's dead," he said.

Rudy did not act surprised; rather, he stared at him with great compassion. "Yes, she's dead. But you just came from Lompoc, didn't you? You must know."

David nodded, then stopped. "I wasn't sure," he said.

Rudy took his arm and led him deep into the house, to a lovely library with books that ran to the ceiling, and low-lit lamps that guarded every corner. David was brought a drink with ice, and sat on a couch beside a fireplace large enough to cremate a vampire's remains. Rudy patted him on the back and left him alone to stare at the photographs of Sienna, on the walls and on the tables. Sometimes a blonde, occasionally a brunette, many times a child, always beautiful. His Sienna—he wished she had told him her real name was Sally. It would have made his life so much simpler.

The mother entered the library. She was younger than David had anticipated, fifty, with short gray hair. Her eyes were a different color than her daughter's, brown, and she wore extra weight. But the small nose was the same, the oval face, and she moved as Sienna did, with grace and mystery. She smiled when she saw him, happy rather than sad, and there was not a trace of accusation in the room.

David must have stood. A moment later they were hugging and almost crying in each other's arms. When he held her he felt strange relief, and she was saying that it was all right, and patting him on the back, and none of it made any sense whatsoever. But it was obvious she knew how much he had loved her daughter.

Eventually, they settled on the couch. Rudy brought her a drink, then disappeared again. Sienna's pictures looked more alive, he thought, when he sat beside her mother. It was as if the walls had eyes. There were things he had to ask if he was ever to have any peace of mind. There was no gentle way to broach the subject.

"They're accusing me of killing her. You must know that?" he said.

Mrs. Wither sighed. She wore a cream-colored turtleneck sweater, white slacks. Her makeup was heavy but effective; she did not need jewelry to appear elegant. Her accent was closer to Boston than New York.

"I know, I spoke to Sheriff Stanton and that FBI agent, Krane," she said. "They said you were their main suspect and I told them they were crazy. I hope to God they finally listened to me."

"I appreciate that, I really do. But how can you be so sure about me? I mean, how do you know who I am? It was my understanding that you had lost contact with Sienna."

"I see the truth has suffered in the translation. We did lose touch with Sally the last two months. That's why we got worried. That's why we reported her missing to the FBI. But before then she called regularly. She told me all about you. She told me how happy you made her." Mrs. Wither added in a pleasant voice, "She was very much in love with you, David."

The words should have warmed his heart.

"Did you tell the sheriff that Sienna and Sally were the same person?"

Mrs. Wither frowned. "I don't know if the topic came up. We spoke of her as Sally on the phone. That's her name. I have never called her Sienna."

David felt that was a lie. That would have been one of the first questions out of Stanton's mouth. Yet he did not want to accuse the woman of being a liar. Maybe she honestly did not remember.

"When she was in Lompoc she called herself Sienna Madden," he said.

"I know, she told me. She said you and her landlady knew her by that name. You have to understand that Sally went to the West Coast to get away from everything. I think it appealed to her to be incognito. The excitement of being a stranger in a strange land. I'm sure she meant no harm by it."

"I'm sorry, I don't understand. What was she trying to get away from?"

Mrs. Wither tensed, tried to hide it, looked down at her hands. They were older than Sienna's, but they were the same hands. Yet he did not feel as if he spoke to a ghost. The spirit was inside him; he was the one that felt haunted. Already he could see that Mrs. Wither had accepted her daughter's death.

"That is a story," she said quietly.

"Mrs. Wither, I'm not sure Sienna . . . Sally told you everything about us. It's true we were very close. I loved her more than anyone I had ever met before. She seemed to love me the same. But the last time I saw her, at the beach, she broke up with me. It was very sudden. She never explained why she did it." David paused, asked gently, "Do you know why?"

"Yes."

"Could you tell me please?"

The woman looked at him sadly. "When Sally went out to the West Coast, eight months ago, she was very sick. She had leukemia. She had done massive amounts of chemotherapy, and had several experimental treatments, but nothing was working. She was dying, to put it bluntly, and she wanted to have an adventure before she died. Of course I tried to keep her here, to take care of her, but Sally was always strong-willed. She got on a plane and flew away, didn't even say where she was going. But then, when she met you, she called and told me how happy she was, and I quit pestering her to come home. Don't you see, David? It was you who kept her alive those six months. It was your love, and it was only because you meant so much to her that she kept the truth from you. She didn't want you to pity her. It was out of love that she left suddenly. Her time had finally run out, she knew it. She called and told me she was slipping away. She didn't want you to have to watch her die. I argued with her to tell you, that it was better that way. But she refused, and in the end it was her decision to make. I respected that." Mrs. Wither added, "But she never did come home."

David could only absorb so much, and he had passed his limit when he had found Dr. James Rean's business card in his wallet. All he could hear was that Sienna had been sick the whole time she had been with him. His head slumped, his eyes strayed to the floor. The same carpet Sienna had once walked on.

"She should have told me," he muttered.

Mrs. Wither touched his arm. "Don't be angry at her. Her motives were pure, even if they caused you so much confusion. In her mind she thought she was making a great sacrifice by not telling you. Please, just pass it off to the dramatist inside her, and forgive her."

He raised his head, forced himself to speak. "When did you last talk to her? What was the date?"

"Sheriff Stanton asked me the same thing. I don't know the exact date. She must have called me. I can't find the call on my phone bill. I think it was a day or two before she broke up with you."

"You're not sure?"

"No, and I am sorry. The last time we talked it was brief. It could have been after she broke up with you."

"Forgive me, you know I found her body at the beach on the same spot where we broke up?"

"Yes. The sheriff explained that to me."

"The last time you two spoke, did she mention the beach?"

"No."

"What did you talk about?"

"Her coming home. Remember, she was in a lot of pain when she called." Krane's words whispered in his brain.

"That woman had a high dose of narcotics in her blood when she was killed."

For the sake of his sanity, he had to force himself to remember Sienna's words.

". . . I don't know how to say this, I miss you. Yeah, I miss you a lot. Is that a bad thing? You probably think it is, that I don't have the right . . . just hearing your voice on the machine made me tremble, but made me happy too. Real happy, David. I'm in the middle of a big transition right now, so I don't have a permanent number. But I promise to call tomorrow . . . Miss you, honey. Love you."

Mrs. Wither stared at him, waiting for his questions. The woman had already come to terms with her loss. How could he explain that her daughter *might* not be dead? For now, the charade would have to continue. It was more illuminating, anyway, than the last week of his life had been.

"Was she going to go into the hospital?" he asked.

"She didn't want to do that. She wanted to die at home."

"Do you have any idea who killed her?"

"No. From everything I've heard, it must have been a very sick person.

But to tell you the truth, I don't really care who killed her. Don't look so surprised. Think about it a minute. The last time Sally called she was in pain. What did she have to look forward to? Another month of agony? Two months? In a way her killer did her a favor."

"I'm sorry, I can't see it that way."

"I have to see it that way. I can read your mind. I know what you're thinking. She's her mother and she should be dying to know who murdered her daughter. You're even thinking that I'm not that upset over her death. But you have to understand that I have lived with her impending end for over two years. It's a terrible thing to say, but I'm happy it's over and done with, for Sally's sake. I'm grateful that she was allowed to go from your loving arms to her grave so quickly."

The woman's choice of words disturbed David.

"She was killed by a satanist," he said.

Mrs. Wither briefly closed her eyes. "It doesn't matter. All I care about is that she's not suffering anymore."

"Did Sally ever speak to you about a woman named Julie Stevens?"

"No."

"Mary Pomus? Herb Domino?"

"No. Who are these people?"

"Suspects. When Sally disappeared, how come you didn't call me?"

"I didn't know your number or your last name. Sally always just called you David. I didn't know you lived in Lompoc. I thought you lived closer to her, in Santa Barbara."

"How come you didn't call the police?"

"I did call the Santa Barbara police. They knew nothing. Then I went to the FBI. They did what they could but they had no leads. For a long time, it seemed as if Sally had vanished from the face of the earth. It wasn't until that Agent Krane called that we knew anything definite."

"He's dead."

"What?"

"Agent Krane. He died in a fire last night in Lompoc."

For once Mrs. Wither showed distress. "What happened?"

"His motel room caught fire and he died. No one knows how it started."

"That's terrible! Does it have anything to do with Sally's murder?"

"I don't know, that's what I'm trying to find out."

An uneasy silence settled between them, during which David was plagued by guilt. This was Sienna's mother he was talking to, he thought, he should not pound her like she were a material lead. Yet there were so many gaps in his knowledge, utter impossibilities, that he did not know what else to do.

He noticed a picture on the wall. Sienna, her mother, and an elderly man—that could have been her father—eating at the same deli he used to go to the last time he was in New York. The deli that made the giant turkey sandwiches. Thanksgiving every day of the year.

David gestured to the fat manila envelope he had set on the coffee table.

"That's a copy of Marcy Goldberg's *Vampire of My Heart,*" he said. "An hour ago I told the art director at the house that's publishing the book that I wanted to speak to the author. I'm doing the cover for the novel, you see. That woman—her name is Miss Winston—gave me your address." He added, "The whole time I knew Sally, she never gave me your address."

Mrs. Wither nodded. "I know."

"Sally wrote this book, didn't she?"

"Yes."

"She set it up so that I would be given the cover job, right?"

"Yes." She added, "But Miss Winston didn't know that. She was simply told by her boss to give you the job, and not to make a fuss about it."

"Meaning she was ordered to let me think I had earned the cover on my own merits?"

"That's not fair. Sally put her heart and soul into that book. She was working on it up until the last week of her life. It's a miracle she finished it. She did not choose you to do the cover just because she wanted to throw a job your way. She wanted you because she felt you had the vision to create an incredible work of art. Something that would grab the public's eye, make them buy her book, cause her work to live on after she was gone. Who knows? Had she lived she might have told you she was the author. It surely would have come out. Like with her illness, I urged her to be more open with you. But at heart she was a creator of fiction, and I think she kept her identity a mystery to add to her ability to write mystery. Whatever, I cannot say exactly what went on in her mind. But she paid you the highest compliment by arranging for you to do the cover. I honestly believe that, David."

"But I got the job by chance. I only submitted my portfolio to that publisher after I came here, two months ago."

"No. They didn't call you because you put in your portfolio. Sally had already shown it to them months before that. They called you because she had told them to call you."

"Do they know she's dead?"

"No. They don't even know her real name."

"You have to tell them."

"Why? Many writers have remained anonymous their whole lives. A pseudonym gives that privilege. Sally can remain anonymous in death. It was her wish."

"Have you read the book?"

"Yes, of course. The end was stunning, wasn't it?"

"The whole book impressed me. The dark mood was overwhelming." He added, "I guess it's not hard to figure out what inspired it."

Mrs. Wither hesitated. "True. It wouldn't take a genius to figure that one out."

David pointed to the picture on the wall, the family deli. "Is that Sally's father?"

"Yes. Cory Wither." She added, "He passed away last year."

"I am so sorry. I didn't know."

"How could you know?" Mrs. Wither stared at the picture, her expression more distant than grievous. That had been her manner throughout their conversation. She was sympathetic without being truly warm, a quality he had identified in Sienna from day one. Mrs. Wither added, "We were together thirty years. In all that time I don't think we ever spent more than a week apart."

"This last year must have been terrible for you."

"Most of the time it doesn't feel real to me," she said.

She insisted he stay for dinner. The least she could do, she said, after all he had been through. He probably should have protested. She was a friendly woman but there were holes in her story large enough to give a coma patient a nervous breakdown. When he reflected on her explanations for Sienna's behavior, he felt like he must have been nuts to have been involved with the girl. Because Sienna had lied about virtually everything she had ever told him, and Mrs. Wither somehow made it seem like a virtue.

He was hungry though; he was tired of being awake and having to think. He had barely slept on the plane the previous night. When she said she had fresh salmon cooking for dinner, and salad and rice, it sounded good.

Besides, he didn't want to be rude. She had recently lost a husband, a daughter—it did not matter that the daughter might be fooling them all. Mrs. Wither thought she was dead.

Good food, no extra company. David did not know where Rudy had gotten to. An old Hispanic woman in a long gray dress served them. Her name was Maria and if she ever smiled every mirror in the house would probably crack. She appeared to dislike her job and then some. She was a great cook, however, and Mrs. Wither could be charming company. They talked mostly about books—novels that Sally had loved. David was not surprised to learn that she had been obsessed with horror. The old stuff, the classics, *The Exorcist* and *Carrie*. David explained the cover he had planned for Sally's book and Mrs. Wither beamed with pleasure and asked if he wanted dessert. He ate what she offered. For someone he didn't trust, he felt strangely comfortable with her.

They talked for hours and it grew dark outside.

The house itself intrigued him. When Mrs. Wither asked if he wanted to spend the night he nodded without hesitation. They'd had several glasses of wine with dinner. The Plaza seemed far away. She took him on a tour of the house and he bumped into a vase of roses but she caught it before it could hit the floor. She laughed at his clumsiness, and he laughed as well.

The house was old but had wonderful sweeping curves. Each room seemed to lead into another. There was more space than there were walls. He had never been in a mansion before, and this one filled his head with wonder. The abstract art, the red cedar wood—two sets of winding stairs that went up faster than he could climb. Yet he never felt overwhelmed, never felt anything less than comfortable as he moved through the four floors. And the more time he spent with Mrs. Wither, the more he felt he had misjudged her. Sienna's love had initially seemed cold, but deep inside her passion was alive. He wondered if the same was true for her mother.

He supposed he was a little drunk.

He learned that Sienna had grown up in the house. Just the three of them. He asked how she had taken the death of her father and Mrs. Wither shook her head. They had been close, she said.

At the rear of the house was a small greenhouse. Mrs. Wither received a call as they stepped inside, and for a time he was alone with the flowers and plants. There was even a lemon tree, in full bloom. Drinking in the bittersweet odor, he tried to stare through the greenhouse's opaque ceiling and imagined he saw the Milky Way. He must have been hallucinating. He was in the town that never slept. The galaxy couldn't be seen from the top of the Empire State Building.

Mrs. Wither returned and led him to a room. Another shock that did not surprise him. Sienna's bedroom, Sally's room—she insisted he sleep there. He should have been intimidated. Her smell was everywhere, on the low-set bed, the Spartan desk, but he did not mind. He was not a ghoul, he thought, this was not her coffin. She had lived here and grown from a cute baby into a brilliant writer. He stepped to her closet and discovered a hundred outfits he had never seen her wear. They were hers, though, the style. Black leather, gray wool, expensive silks. But there were no photographs of her on the walls, nothing that revealed her deepest opinions. There was very little decoration, period.

Mrs. Wither left and he undressed and lay down to sleep. He was more than a little drunk. His thoughts floated like postage stamps attached to astral letters. The feel of the bed was delightful: a silk comforter; soft sheets; and her long hair, he felt as if it was draped across his pillow. He was sure he would be asleep in minutes.

Pain interrupted him, physical pain, deep in his guts. It was nothing dramatic, but it seemed to flow into him steadily and without reason. The food had been good, the wine delicious. Dinner should not have made him ill. Anyway, this pain was not a digestive complaint. It seemed to seep into his organs from beneath the mattress. How many nights had she lain here feeling sick? He wondered if he was picking up old impressions of her pain, but the explanation sounded too far-out to him. He was an old boyfriend, not a psychic. Really, he did not know how to explain it, but it sure felt real.

He had never felt her pain when he had slept with her.

The sensation lessened and he dozed. Yet it did not completely stop. It moved upward, across his face and became hotter, cooking oil splashed on pale flesh. Yet the discomfort grew ever more distant, to where he did not feel it was really his pain at all. Or Sienna's for that matter. If she was not dead, he reasoned, she could not have been seriously ill. The pain must belong to another, he thought, or else it was just all in his head.

He thought of Rachel, going to see her at the hospital two days after the fire.

Intensive care. Because of the life support equipment and the monitors, the room had not been entirely closed but it had felt like a coffin. The worst thing was the smell: rubbing alcohol mixed with burnt flesh. No, the worst was her face: white bandages dripping dark red. What hair the fire had left behind, they had shaved off. And she had only one eye to stare at him with; the other was covered with green gauze. One eye and one mirror was more than enough, he thought at the time. He was only a teenager, he didn't know shit, but she looked like someone who would have been better off dead.

He tried to hide his tears but she saw them.

"I look like a monster," she whispered.

He shook his head. "You're going to be fine. Give yourself time to heal."

She just turned away. "I can't be a monster."

He awoke in the night with no idea what time it was. But there was no delay in his cognition of where he was. Sienna's house, her bedroom. He came to with the absolute conviction that she was still alive and just waiting to appear.

He heard sounds, realized they had disturbed his sleep. A woman softly moaning; it sounded more like pain than pleasure. He told himself as much as he got out of bed and stepped into the hallway. He was not a pervert but he was curious.

The house was dark but he remembered every detail of his tour. At the end of the hall on the left was the master bedroom. The noise was coming from there. He could see that; the door was cracked slightly. He suspected he would see a lot more if he opened it all the way.

"What the hell are you doing?" he asked himself.

He needed answers, he told himself.

Going up on his tiptoes, he opened the door further and peered inside.

Mrs. Wither was in bed with Rudy Turbel. They were naked, they were having sex, and it was none of his goddamn business. She only sounded as if she was being hurt because she was enjoying herself so much. It was obviously a tender moment between two people who cared deeply for each other. Indeed, she was making the same sounds Sienna used to make when she was in his bed. He had no right to judge either of them.

Yet the sight of the two of them together made him sick to his stomach.

David returned to Sienna's bedroom, got dressed, picked up the manuscript, and quietly left the house. He walked a few blocks, not sure where he was headed, and then hailed a cab. He was back at the Plaza in ten minutes, and then, without having slept in his thousand-dollar-a-night bed, he collected the cash Herb had given him, checked out of his room and took a different taxi to the airport, reaching JFK at five in the morning. Delta's big board said there was a six o'clock nonstop to Miami. He bought himself a first-class ticket.

TWENTY-FOUR

What was in a name? Krane had believed they called the ship *Lazarus* out of arrogance. To openly flaunt the fact that they were transplanting organs illegally. But the FBI agent had not thought through the name. Christ had not helped Lazarus over a bad liver or a failing heart. He had plucked the dude right out of the grave. That was what it said in the Bible, and, as Pomus might have said, if that was not true then they were all screwed.

David stood at the marina where the big cruise ships docked. He had taken a taxi straight from the airport. It had taken him an hour to find the *Lazarus*—and it took that long only because the harbor was literally the size of his hometown. No one was trying to hide Dr. James Rean's floating operating room. It was lined up beside all the other boats.

The morning sun was soft and soothing, the blue water flat as a field. He had enjoyed walking around the marina. The giant cruise ships were impressive, havens for the earthbound. They seemed to call to a part of him that wished to escape from reality. Yet he had come to Miami for answers, for truth. Now all he needed was a plan of action.

The *Lazarus* was half the length of the largest of the ships, two football fields long. The hull was a flawless white; it gleamed in the morning light like a preacher's stairway to heaven. And it looked new, expensive, a toy for those who had wearied of all other playthings.

The marina was busy but not hectic. Numerous ships were being loaded with supplies, worked on by maintenance crews. There was security but it appeared lax. For example, the *Lazarus* itself had only one uniformed guard overseeing its main plank. David watched him from a distance for twenty minutes and did not see him stop a single person and ask for ID. Krane and his partner Carol had sweated getting a warrant to search the ship, but being a nobody could have its advantages. He suspected, with the barest margin of disguise, he could simply board the ship.

That margin, though, would be a requirement. He didn't want to get turned away the first time. He would not be able to come back later. Fortunately, nearby, there was a large stack of Coke crates sitting unattended on the dock. The man in charge of them was trying to restock three ships all by himself. He attacked each ship plank, jogging the angles, disappearing for five minutes at a time. His dolly was getting a serious workout. Perhaps that was why he kept a spare one by his crates.

David walked over and borrowed that extra dolly. He took a stack of crates for good measure. He was glad to see the Coke was in glass bottles. Plastic containers and aluminum cans didn't do it for him. He was a purist when it came to soft drinks.

He strode toward the *Lazarus*. The guard nodded as he passed, said nothing. He kept moving, got another ten steps. "Excuse me," the guard said at his back.

David turned, tried to sound bored. "What is it?"

The guard smiled pleasantly, a big boy with a hearty thirst. "Could I have one of those Cokes?" he asked.

David gave him two bottles. The guy popped off the tops with his bare hands.

He went up the plank, onto the ship. The deck was an idyllic blue, the doughnut-shaped life preservers wore happy faces, and the steel railing looked as if it was capable of encircling paradise. A crew of four swabbed the deck, two electricians worked on lights, and men and women of all colors and shapes were coming and going with food. But he did not follow them, did not inquire the direction of the kitchen. His plan was to wander around and act lost.

He was not a spy, what did he expect to find? The simplest answer would have been operating rooms that were used for organ transplants. At the airport he had bought a small but expensive camera to photograph such rooms.

He had fantasies of running to the FBI with his proof. Like they would trust him when they would not listen to Krane. The truth was, he didn't know what he was doing.

Yet that did not mean he did not believe he would discover something of interest. He *sensed* something about the ship—he had from the moment he had seen it. A cold premonition that seemed to reverberate out of an icy past. The ship felt familiar to him. So pretty, so perfect, but it stunk. Yes, it smelled of evil, he was sure of it deep inside.

Moving with his dolly and drinks, he walked into a different door than the others, and immediately found himself free of traffic, in a long hallway that had been designed for those with narrow vision and long legs. There were a hundred doors on both sides. Not a single brass knob was locked. Luxurious suites, all—he only had to glance in a few to see the occupants were used to five stars. He could not believe that the usual guests only paid working-class fares to enjoy such opulence.

He searched a large percentage of the main floor and bumped into nothing more threatening than a couple of cleaning ladies. He ran across a miniature casino, empty, and wondered what kinds of bets people who stole organs made. Did they put their souls on the table, roll the dice and hope nobody was watching?

He searched another hour, four more decks, and just found more luscious rooms for all the rich sick people. He felt like giving up.

Then he found an elevator, rode it down as far as it would go and emerged into a fresh hallway that was neither long nor well lit. *Déjà vu* touched him again. The nerves at the back of his skull grew colder still, and he felt his heartbeat in his hands. Here the floor was a sober gray, the walls paneled with insulating wood. He knew if he spoke his voice would die in the air. Leaving the dolly beside the elevator, he reached for a door at the end of the hall.

Not locked, again, how lucky. Holding his breath, quietly he stepped inside. The room was rectangular, sixty feet long, divided into cubicles. Green curtains flowed from the ceiling, sheltering nothing more dramatic than a series of beds. Were they set up for recovering patients? He could not be sure. There was equipment above each mattress, wires and monitors, and unusual eyeglasses and headphones, but the place did not smell like a hospital. No rubbing alcohol or dried blood. To him it continued to stink of bad people and wicked ideas. How could he explain that rationally? He only knew that the way Dr. James Rean had smiled at him on the plane had made him feel the same way this room did.

"Creepy," he whispered.

He studied the strange eyeglasses, the headphones, realized he had seen the setup before, in New Age magazines. They were part of light/sound machines that strobed the eyes with color and pulsed each ear with various frequencies, all of which was supposed to bring the different hemispheres of the brain into coherence and dramatically alter the state of consciousness. No, he thought, this was not a hospital room, it was a high-tech sweat lodge. Looking around, he spotted an isolation tank in the corner. Warm water, Epsom salts, utter darkness—those were the boxes people floated in to escape all sensory input. Supposedly one hour in them was equivalent to five hours of sleep. David had read about them but had never fancied the idea. Maybe he was claustrophobic, but they looked like coffins to him.

He noticed a glass cabinet in the opposite corner.

He walked over, saw several rows of bottles and stacks of wrapped syringes. The liquid inside the bottles was clear as Evian but the cabinet was locked. Going down on his knees, he tried to read one of the labels.

O3-KETAMINE.

He had heard of ketamine before, but could not place it.

He stepped to the isolation tank, lifted the lid and peered inside.

Naked, lying on her back and looking every bit as beautiful as the day she had won the Miss California contest, Teresa Bronson—now Mrs. Teresa Rean—opened her eyes and smiled at him.

"Hello, David. Nice of you to join us," she said.

They sat at a table in her private suite and ate breakfast. The view was seaward, the windows floor to ceiling, wide open. They were high above the waterline but the salty breeze coming through the windows felt as if it had been scraped from the ocean surface. He thought the suite gaudy. Who needed a chandelier when you were taking a cruise on the wide open sea? He imagined a nasty storm, rough waves, the chandelier falling, the many-faceted crystals shattering. Even a medium-sized swell would make it sway. Then the chandelier would spin and the light would dance and somebody would have an epileptic fit—probably him. Seeing Teresa again, without a stitch of clothes in that plastic sarcophagus, bathing in a black pond of salted water, had taken the wind out of his sails.

Still, he could not take his eyes off of her.

She had on only a white bathrobe. She had let him watch her put it on.

Teresa had in fact aged but the years had only improved a very refined design. By unspoken law Miss California was required to have tan skin and wholesome features and Teresa still possessed those qualities in abundance, but the last decade and the loss of ten pounds had hollowed her bones and sharpened her gaze to the point where she was more an enigma than a queen. She still smiled at every turn and her teeth were white as a tube of tooth-paste. But she had joined the same club as her surgeon husband. Her smile was a reflex, her warmth lacked spontaneity. As he sat before her, eating the bacon and eggs she had ordered for him, and her own bowl of milk-drenched Special K—the same cereal that Julie Stevens had enjoyed so much at his breakfast table—he suspected the mind behind the beauty bore only a faint resemblance to the girl he had grown up with in Lompoc.

Yet he knew her, she was an old friend. And very sexy.

She spoke to him as if they were pals. She asked all the standard questions. How was Lompoc? What did the new mall look like? Were Charlie and Karen still together? Had Herb gotten busted yet? Was Pomus still lecturing about sin and grace? He answered each of her questions as if the answers mattered to both of them. He ate his bacon and eggs—they were excellent. There was toast and coffee as well. She refilled his cup often. He had not eaten on the plane, he was very hungry.

But he did not ask her any questions. He waited.

She was having trouble with the top of her robe. Pesky thing, it kept falling open, peekaboo. He chose not to look, not every time.

Finally, the inevitable moment came, she stopped talking and just stared at him. Her eyes were so blue they could have been bought. Strange eyes, he thought. They seemed to see things that were not there, even when they were focused on him.

"You were expecting me?" he said finally.

No hesitation. "Yes."

"That was how I got on the boat so easily?"

"Yes. James and I have both been waiting for you to arrive."

"Why?"

"You met him on the plane. He gave you his card."

"I did not know he was your husband when I met him. He didn't tell me."

She shrugged. "You're here now."

me about that. She tried once, I know, but you guys got interrupted. Don't look so surprised, she told me a lot of things."

He flushed. "Really? I didn't think you two were close."

Her tone became bitter. "We were not close at all. No love lost there. But we were still sisters. Sisters talk, especially late at night when they're bored. There was another thing she told me that you never knew. That afternoon when the two of you were fooling around? Billy saw you, he saw you through the window as he walked up to your house. You had your hand on her breast and she had her hand on your crotch and your best friend saw you. How do you think that made him feel?"

David shook his head. "I don't believe it."

"You don't want to believe it."

"No. He would have told me. Anyway, we were young and stupid and we would have stopped even if he hadn't come over right then."

Teresa snorted. "You had a chance to fuck Rachel and you would have stopped? Excuse me, I don't think so. You were obsessed with her. I saw the way you followed her with your eyes. When she would bend over to pick up a newspaper or something, you would get a hard-on. You would have had no qualms about destroying your relationship with your best friend if it meant you could have her."

"That's not true. I'm not like that. Not now, not then. I'm not like . . ." He didn't finish.

"Like me? Is that what you were going to say? You are a lot like me. You are exactly like my husband. You just haven't accepted it is all. Here you are, flying around the country, acting the big shot, trying to solve these mysterious deaths. Why, if you could trade the truth—even trade the lives of those two FBI agents you mentioned—just to be with Sienna again, you would do it in a heartbeat."

She was hurting him, he wanted to hurt her back. He wanted to grab her by her long blond hair and throw her into the sea. But he could not because some of what she said was true. And much was false, he was not enough like her to be intentionally cruel.

"You speak of Sienna like you knew her," he said.

Teresa sat back in her chair. "Yeah, I knew her."

"How?"

"Does it matter? I knew her." Teresa added, "She was nothing."

"Did her mother call you and tell you I was in New York?"

"Yes."

He drew in a shuddering breath. "And this is not a conspiracy?"

Teresa unexpectedly reached over and took his hand, stroked his palm. Her blue eyes were back on his face. If she had bought them she had paid top dollar. She appeared full of fire and energy and yet it was mostly smoke and hot air. She was beautiful, she was seductive, but she was nothing. He didn't want her, like she imagined, he didn't even like her.

"What do you want, David? Just ask me that—just ask yourself that—and you'll finally get somewhere with what is troubling you."

He took back his hand. "I did not come here to ask you for therapy."

She nodded, turned and stared out to sea. She spoke in an offhand tone. "Rachel did not know Billy had seen what you two were up to until after she got burned."

"That makes no difference."

Teresa smiled to herself, her gaze still distant. "I suppose it makes no difference that the guy later killed himself?"

"He did not kill himself because I touched his girlfriend's breast," he snapped.

She did not answer, not directly, just continued to smile at the horizon. Studying her face, her cockiness, he suddenly remembered something Billy's mother had told him.

"All he was doing those last weeks of school was hanging out with his girlfriend . . . Not Rachel, his new girlfriend . . . I think she spent a couple of nights here—her blond hair was all over his sheets . . . It was as if he was ashamed of her. At the time, though, I figured he was feeling guilty about dating so soon after Rachel . . . When he started seeing that new girl, he got much worse . . . But whoever she was, she was not good for him. It was like he couldn't even sleep after he met her. I used to hear him get up in the middle of the night and go out . . . He was able to run over to her house at a moment's notice . . . Before he died, Billy made me swear. He said, 'Don't tell David or Charlie I'm seeing someone new.'"

"It was you!" he gasped.

She glanced over, intrigued. "A major revelation?"

"You dated Billy after Rachel died! You slept with him even though you were engaged to someone else!"

Teresa acted bored. "You don't know that."

"Billy's mother saw you."

She suddenly snapped. "She never saw me! No one saw us!" Then her smile returned, she mocked him. "You'll never be able to prove it. And besides, who cares? Just a bunch of old gossip."

"I care, and I think his mother would care. She told me how depressed you made him feel. How he couldn't sleep after you got your hands on him." He shook his head in disgust. "Then you try to insinuate that I was responsible for his suicide." He added, "If it even was a suicide."

"Once again, you overstep your bounds as a polite guest."

"I spoke to Stanton. It was your dad's gun that killed Billy. And the sheriff saw your car out there that night."

"Funny, he didn't mention my car in his report."

"Were you there? Please, just tell me the truth. I have to know."

She turned on him, vicious. It was almost as if she were two people. One a witch, the other a butcher. "Why do you have to know? All right, yes, I was in the car with him, I helped him write that note. Even better, my fiancé was there with us. He didn't want to miss a thing. But he got sprayed with so much blood, he couldn't get the stains out of his sports coat. That's why he was in such a hurry to get out of town the next day. Does hearing that make you happy? Can you sleep better at night knowing that I had to help Billy put the gun in his mouth? That at the very end he got scared when he thought of his brains splattered all over the ceiling of the car. Does any of this really help you, David?"

"Is it true?" he asked.

"None of it matters! Everything you ask is unimportant! You're an artist! You know about paintings! But this picture—the way you hold it in your hands—you have it upside down! You will never understand it that way! Talking the way you do—thinking the way you are—you will never know why either of them killed themselves!"

"Then tell me what to do! Tell me so that I can understand!"

Teresa relaxed in her chair, went back to the view, gestured casually. "Your cell phone is ringing. You had better answer it," she said.

He took the phone from his pocket. The caller ID listed his home phone number.

"Hello?" he said.

"Hi. It's me. Where are you?" Sienna asked.

"Florida. Where are you?"

"Your house. I used my old key. Can you get back here by midnight?"

"Yes. Sienna, are you all right?" He spoke casually, even though he had finally begun to accept that she was dead.

There was a long pause. "Yes. I'm fine. I'll see you tonight. Don't be late."

She hung up. He did not consider calling back. He knew she would not answer. The picture was not upside down. It had been reversed, transposed inside a mirror. The only way to truly understand what was going on was to break the glass. Teresa stared at him with what might have been her version of compassion. She had heard him refer to the caller as Sienna, and it had not fazed her one bit.

"You going back to Lompoc?" she asked.

"Yes."

"I think that's best. Everything will get cleared up once you're home."

TWENTY-FIVE

On the plane, another first-class seat, on his way back home. Miami to Dallas to Los Angeles. But he did not have to go straight home from Texas. It was still early, and Sienna had said he had until midnight. He was picking up three hours flying east to west. He had checked the airline's flight schedule. He had time for a detour, if he had the nerve to take it.

Plenty of free time. He spent it finishing Sienna's novel.

Cleo called Ash in New York, got him on the first try, and he agreed to fly out and see her at her home in California. But he did not arrive for a week, and Sienna spent many pages describing Cleo's state of mind as she waited. Cleo's emotions ran the gamut from excitement to despair, love to hate. Why had Ash avoided her all these years? She could not think up a good excuse, and in the end she decided she would not ask for his reasons.

Because Cleo was so close to having her baby, Ash took a taxi from the airport to her house. It struck David that Sienna did not specify the name of the town where Cleo resided. Only that it was north of Los Angeles. It could have been Santa Barbara or Lompoc.

What hit him harder was Sienna's description of Ash. When the alchemist arrived at Cleo's front door, David discovered that Ash looked just like him. Tall, thin, and muscular, with wavy brown hair and a strong jaw. But Sienna had given Ash green eyes instead of brown. Eyes like her own, deep and mysterious, with long dark lashes. He wondered at the significance. It was an important question. Who did she see herself as in the book?

Their reunion was warm and sweet, and also, strangely flat. Cleo was delighted to see Ash and he acted loving toward her, but they were both guarded. It was impossible to catch up on twenty-five centuries so they didn't even try. Sitting in her living room, beside the fireplace where she cremated Hector, they spoke about politics and the weather.

David saw the brilliance of the scene. Neither was real to the other. They had remembered each other for so many centuries that they had become like shadows in each other's minds. They could hold hands but they could not touch.

Ash was like Cleo, no longer a vampire.

That evening he took her for a ride down to the beach in her car. They walked along the shore. They were alone, late at night, a clear night with a thousand stars in the sky. Ash stopped and pointed to the North Star. David knew the time of revelation was at hand. There were not many pages left in the book.

"You see that star," Ash says. "It is the North Star, sometimes called the Pole Star. It was in that exact position in the sky when I changed us twenty-five thousand years ago. That length of time is significant. It is called the Precession of the Equinoxes or the Platonic Year. Because the Earth slowly wobbles on its axis, it describes a circle in the sky, and the Pole Star does not remain the same. Did you look up at the night sky ten thousand years ago? If you did you would have seen Vega was the Pole Star."

"I did look," I say. "I have always loved the sky."

Ash nods. "I remember. You must also remember that I also loved the study of astronomy and astrology. Alchemy cannot be separated from either discipline, and there is a basic principle of alchemy that states: 'As above, so below.' Meaning that what happens in the cosmos also goes on inside us. We are not separate from the galaxy. We are inside it but it is also inside us. The soul does not merely inhabit the body. The universe inhabits the soul."

I am taken by the tone in his voice. He is not just trying to explain a hidden truth, he is trying to apologize. But I do not know if it is for something he has already done, or for something he is about to do. I feel the beginning of contractions, it cannot be long.

"Do you believe in the soul?" I ask.

"Of course. Don't you?"

"I am not sure. All this time, I have never seen one proof of God."

"Belief in the soul and belief in God are not the same things. I do not believe in God."

I have to smile, the concept seems absurd. Yet Ash is so wise, he has obviously lost none of his intelligence. "Then what do our souls do without God? Wander around lost for eternity, with nowhere to go?" I ask.

"What does any human do except wander? Alive or dead, it makes no difference, it is up to us to determine our fate."

"What does this have to do with the alchemy you performed on us?"

He turns his back on the North Star, looks at the sea. His face is dark, but there is a gleam in his eyes. The waves are calm, his voice as soothing as always. We have not bonded, him and I, for whatever reason, and that troubles me. But worse, I feel cut off from the environment. The night is beautiful, with many shapes and shadows, and yet it is merely a black-and-white painting to me, or else I am only a frame. I hold what I see in my mind and yet I am consumed by a certainty that I will be unable to alter what is about to happen next.

Or else it is Ash himself who distorts my reality. I want to listen to his gentle voice but I am certain he is going to tell me things I do not want to hear. He speaks, and I have to follow every word.

"The north and south poles of the Earth have magnetic fields. Each twenty-four hours we pass through a complete cycle and we age one day. Back then, in those days, when I took your blood and mixed it in my solution, I spiraled it around a magnetic field. I spiraled it in the opposite direction of the spinning of the Earth. The effect erased the aging process. With each turn in my lab, your solution gained a day of life. And I left all of our solutions running at high speed for a long time. Do you understand?"

"Yes. Then when you injected the solution back into our veins, we were made immune to the aging effects of the rotating Earth." The simplicity of his secret stuns me, but I have to ask, "Can you make the solution once more? And give us more years?"

"No. A Platonic Year is the longest any of us can live in one body. I knew it even back then. Like I said, there is a significance to the length of time. The old religions used to say that twenty-five thousand years was all a man or woman needed to evolve from an animal to a god."

"But we have not become gods. We are simply mortal again."

"Yes. We have had so much time but it has not been enough time. But perhaps we would have become gods had we allowed ourselves to take different bodies these last two hundred and fifty centuries."

"Do you mean like in reincarnation?"

He hesitates. "Not necessarily."

"I don't understand."

"When I erased the effect of aging in us, I fear I erased something else."

"What?"

"That which made us human." He pauses. "You have not asked why I avoided you all these years?"

"Was it because you saw me as something less than human?"

"Yes. And it hurts me to say that to you. But look at you, look at Hector, at Yril and myself. During all this time, can you honestly say you have truly loved someone?"

"Yes. I have loved you."

"No. You remember loving me, it is not the same thing. I remember loving you. But do you love me now? Do I love you? I tell you, we are incapable of it."

I shake my head. "It is not true. And even if it is true, we are mortal now. We can love again. We can love each other."

"Can we? We have cheated the system for so long. We have caused so much pain to so many. What gives us the right to know love, Cleo?"

"Because we are human now. Humans are born with that right. Okay, so we can never be immortal again. We are about to have a child, *our* child. How can we help but love it?" There is pain in my heart and in my abdomen, and I do not know which is worse. "Isn't that why you have come back now? So the three of us can be together?"

"No," he says.

The word is small, and so huge. It fills the galaxy and threatens to smother the very life out of me. The pain in my gut grows worse. I am a balloon about to pop, a leaf about to fall. "Then why have you come?" I ask bitterly.

"Because after all this time, I don't want to die," he says.

"I don't understand."

"I think you do."

"No. I don't know what you are talking about." A *squirt* sounds between my legs, and warm fluid fills my underwear. I gasp, "I think my water has broken."

Ash takes my arm. "Let's get back to the house."

"No. I need to go to the hospital."

"Let's go to the house first. You need your things. Don't worry, there is time."

Neither the ocean nor the stars calm me. I am scared as we walk toward the car.

At the house, though, I feel slightly better. Quickly I shower, and then stuff a few things in an overnight bag. My contractions are long and intense. They remind me of war and defeat, and I wish I was alone.

I have already made arrangements at a nearby hospital. I pick up the phone to call to tell them I am on my way, but Ash is on the phone, talking to a man. They hang up the second they realize I am on the line. I am wary as I come back down the stairs. But I do not bring a gun. I tell myself that he is wrong, that he does still love me. He is in the kitchen, making himself a roast beef sandwich.

"Who were you taking to?" I ask.

"A friend."

"Who?"

"You don't know him. His name is Mike. I wanted to alert him that the baby is on the way. He is going to help us take care of it."

"I don't want anyone taking care of my baby except me."

He puts the sandwich in his mouth, chews. "What about me?" he asks.

"You just said you don't want a family."

"I did not say that exactly."

"Don't play games with me, Ash. You implied it." I turn toward the door. "I'm going to the hospital now. I don't want you to come with me."

He is on me in a second, at my back, with the knife he used to cut the roast beef. I feel the blade press into my throat as he whispers in my ear. "I don't want you to leave. I already told Mike you would be having the baby here."

I keep my voice calm. "Perhaps you should call him back."

"No. I don't want to do that."

"Do you want to kill me? Is that what you want?"

"No. That is not necessary. You remember long ago how I could occasionally predict the future? That I had been born with the sight?"

"Yes. I remember."

"Well, back then I saw that you were pregnant, and that when you had the baby you would hemorrhage and die. I knew that as I worked on my alchemistic experiments. It was one of the reasons I worked so hard. I didn't want you to die, I wanted to protect you. I worked night and day to save you."

"Are you saying I will hemorrhage now?"

"Yes. It is inevitable. But at a modern hospital, they will be able to operate and stop the bleeding and you will live."

"Then why don't you be a nice man and take that knife away from my throat so I can get to the hospital?"

"Cleo, you are not going anywhere. I told you, Mike is coming here."

"Who the fuck is Mike?"

"He is going to be my father," he says.

Ash drags me upstairs and ties me to my bed. The position is not flattering. Using rope, he secures each limb to a separate bedpost, and leaves my legs spread wide open. I feel more helpless than I did in Yril's house. I can push and moan in pain, that is about all. And my pain has returned like a demon, my contractions are getting harder, with less time between each one.

"Would you like a glass of water?" he asks.

"Please."

He returns a moment later, offers me a sip, sits on the chair beside the bed. "Are you comfortable?" he asks.

"Gimme a break."

"Do not be angry with me. I have to do this."

"I've read a lot of books about couples having babies and nowhere—not once—did it say that the man has to tie the woman up."

"I need this baby," he says.

The room is warm, I am suddenly cold. There is ice in my abdomen as well as fire, and the ice cracks and cuts, and the fire cannot be put out. A furious contraction makes me gasp for breath.

"You want this child so you can continue to live," I say.

"Yes."

I am sick of life, sick of the lack of love in my life. But I know I love my child, and I cannot bear the thought of this monster getting his hands on him. And I know it is going to be a male child, I have seen the latest ultrasound.

"Are you going to drink his blood?" I ask.

"No. I am not going to harm him physically. He is to be turned over to Mike, and Mike will take good care of him."

"But you can't do that! He is mine!"

"I told you, you are going to hemorrhage while giving birth and die. You will not be alive to take care of the child, and besides, it is better that you don't."

So much pain. "Why is it better?"

"Because you would want to destroy the child."

"You are insane!"

He shakes his head. "I told you, I knew about your pregnancy twenty-five thousand years ago. I went ahead with my experiment on you anyway. One reason was to save you. The other was a matter of insurance. Like I said, I knew even then that we could live no longer than a Platonic Year. The heavens turn and nothing can stop them. I knew the day would come when we would become mortal again. We would start to age, we would start to die." He added, "But I also knew that the laws governing the cycles could be over-ridden by switching bodies."

"Switching bodies?"

"Yes. Don't look surprised. You had training as an alchemist. You should have figured it out by now. The soul enters the body at the first breath. A person's astrological influences are set at that instant. Just before your son is born, I am going to kill myself. My soul will float out of my body. At the same time another soul will enter this room. It will be your child's soul. Naturally, he will try to enter the body. But he will not be able to enter. I will be there, I will stop him."

"You are going to possess my baby?"

"You can put it that way. But I prefer to say I am going to borrow his body. To tell you the truth, I do not know if his body will last another twenty-five thousand years or if it will die as quickly as any other human being. In either case I will continue to live, and then, if necessary, I will transfer to another body when I am old."

"That is the sickest thing I have ever heard!"

"Sick is irrelevant. It will work."

"But why must you use my child? Go to any maternity ward at any hospital. Go blow your goddamn brains out there and jump out of your body and steal someone else's baby."

"I just explained. It is possible our child can live another twenty-five millenia. It has survived that long in your womb. It is likely that it has unusual physical qualities. It is best I use it and not another."

I whine like every other mortal does when faced with issues of life and death, and I hate myself for it. But not as much as I hate him. "Best for whom? Ash, you are going to try to rob your own child of his very life! Doesn't that disturb you? You must love him a little."

"Love is not a factor with us."

"It is with me! Please, for my sake, don't do this!"

He speaks with patience, nothing more. "Cleo, I have told you, when I erased the aging process, I erased something deep inside us. Maybe it was inevitable, as the myths say, that to live like a vampire means you must become a vampire. I don't know. But I do know that I mean to carry out my plan. You can plead all you want, it will not change my mind. My body will die, and you will die, and Mike will come, and the baby will be taken care of until it is old enough to take care of itself."

"And he will be you?"

"Yes. He will be me."

I turn away. "Get out of here."

He stands. "I can leave for now, if you wish, but I will be back later."

Ash leaves. My contractions come and go; they are extremely painful. For a first-time mother, I am having the baby quickly. I hear the doorbell, Mike has arrived. The two talk downstairs but I cannot hear what they say. Ash must have agreed to pay the guy millions, and tied the money to the welfare of the child. Ash would be careful.

Ash—I do not know him. When he first arrived, when we kissed, I felt everything would be all right. The years were mere numbers, I thought. He looked as I remembered him. But now I understand what he said to Yril. He sees himself as the new god who is destined to be born again and again. The years have not been kind to him. They have driven him insane.

Still, there are things he said that are probably true. What right do I have to love when I have murdered thousands to stay alive? Yet I find it ironic that I still feel love for him. Even when he is willing to destroy our child, and let me die, so that he can go on living. My love must be genuine, I think, for it is as insane as he is.

I do not doubt that he is capable of possessing the baby.

Downstairs they laugh, and I curse them in my mind.

Then I remember an old friend. The knife I have kept under my pillow for many years. Ash could not know about it. It surprises me that I had forgotten about it. Must be getting old.

Twisting my head to the side, I bite the top blanket and slowly pull it back. I work on the sheet next, and it is not long before I have the butt of the knife in my mouth. The blade, I know, could be used as a razor. There is only one problem. The rope that binds my wrists is twenty inches away and my knife is only six inches long. It does not matter how hard I strain to reach the rope, my neck cannot grow in length. Ash is smarter than any Boy Scout. He has not made a mistake with his knots. I cannot cut myself free.

But I can cut myself. An interesting idea.

He was counting on me dying after him, I think.

It could be a contest of wills. A test of love versus ego.

My blouse is short-sleeved, my arms are bare. Maneuvering the knife with my teeth and head, I place its tip against the soft spot inside my right elbow. Then I lean forward suddenly, jerking my face toward my arm. The blade slides through my veins and blood spurts onto the bed. I stab a few more times for good measure. Soon the bed is as wet and red as an operating table. The sight of the blood, of my own dismal end, does not frighten me. I am content to die to preserve the integrity of my child's soul, and perhaps my sacrifice will mean something to God—if there is one. Yet I doubt he will forgive me for the life I have led. I would not if I were in his position.

I cut the other arm as well. My anger at Ash gives me strength—I practically saw off my elbow. My blood is a fountain, my torn flesh a nightmare. Rotating the knife in my mouth and cocking my head at a difficult angle, I stab my sternum. But then I feel sick to my stomach, and sad. Twenty-five thousand years of fighting to stay alive and here I am dying by my own hand. It does not seem fair.

Yet I do nothing, do not shout out for help, not yet. Let the blood drain further, I say to myself, let the end become inevitable. Long ago, I realize, Ash did indeed see how I would end. In a sense, I am hemorrhaging to death.

The room begins to blur, my contractions halt. As my skin grows cold and I shiver, it gets harder to breathe. Still, I do not cry out. The timing must be perfect. I must move within an inch of death.

Time, blood, life and love—it all flows by me.

Finally, I begin to choke, gasping on air that has nothing left to nourish. "Ash!" I shout. "Ash!"

For a moment I fear he does not hear me, that I have waited too long. But then he is at the door, at my side, and he is grabbing my arms and trying to stop the flow of blood. It is a trickle now, it is too late.

"Cleo! What have you done?" he cries.

Mike steps to the bedroom door. He is tall and black, dressed in white, wears a stethoscope around his neck. He is a doctor—I had expected as much. Ash would have taken every precaution. But I am not worried, it is a good thing actually. It will be easy for him to save the baby. There is no chance he will be able to save me. With the last of my strength, I look up at Ash and smile.

"Now my soul will be there to meet yours," I say. "I will fight you for the right of my baby's soul. You won't get inside his body."

Ash sits back, shakes his head. "I will let the baby die inside you."

"No. It is a special baby. You will not let it die." My smile grows as I nod to my bloody blade. "Better take the knife and cut your throat. Or else I will beat you to the other side."

He sees the danger, picks up the knife, turns to Mike. "Cut the child out of her in exactly two minutes," he orders.

Mike nods. Looks like nothing can surprise him.

Ash turns back to me, surprises me by kissing my forehead. "You're brave, Cleo. You would have made a good mother."

"We'll never know, will we?" I say.

Then my eyes close and I am falling, into an ancient well made of transparent walls and a million memories. Far away I hear Ash slit his throat, but I cannot see his blood. All I am left with is the sound of my baby's heart. It grows in strength as my own heart slowly fades. A light surrounds the thought of my child. A white light filled with all the qualities Ash thought he had destroyed in me. I die but I am still Cleo, I still have power. When we meet on the other side, it will be no contest.

David finished the novel and collected the four-hundred-plus pages and put them back inside the manila envelope. The ending had shocked him deeply, in ways he could not explain to himself. At the same time it had filled him with the certainty that he would never create the cover for the book. In a sense, he felt the story had all been for naught, that Sienna had wasted her time writing it.

Yet he could not stop thinking about Cleo.

"Cleo," he said aloud, and he thought, *nice name*.

The same thought he'd had in his dream of Las Vegas.

He decided right then to take that detour.

TWENTY-SIX

City of Sin, the famous Strip, all the lights and colors. No need to drop acid in this town, just go outside and walk around the block. Peering through his taxi window, David felt as if Sienna sat beside him. The last time he had been in Las Vegas she had been at his side. Even though he knew she was on the West Coast and waiting for him, he felt he was closing in on her big dark secret. And it wasn't that she was dead.

His taxi dropped him off at the Bellagio and he went inside, to the blackjack tables, and asked if Cleo was around. He smiled as he asked, and explained he had won a lot of money off her the last time he was in Vegas. The pit boss just grunted, he probably got the question all the time.

"She'll be on in an hour," he said.

David could have fainted right then. He had never been in the Bellagio before. He had no way of knowing that Cleo was a real person. And here she was, only an hour away from starting her shift.

He thanked the pit boss and went over to the lounge area, where he could keep an eye on the blackjack tables, and ordered himself a Coke. He had a pencil and paper in his pocket, a picture of Sienna in his wallet, but not one of Julie. Taking out his tools of the trade and using a folded newspaper as a desktop, he began to draw Julie. He was as accomplished at sketches as he was at painting. He could have drawn the Devil.

Cleo came on at exactly seven. He recognized her immediately.

Naturally my beauty intimidates. He sees a tall thirty-year-old blue-eyed blonde with bronze skin and lips so red they hint at many hungers. He wants to touch me, but he is a gentleman. There is a gun in his coat—I smell the gunpowder—but he carries it as if it were a wallet. A police officer, I think, not the best type to kill. Yet I like him, want to touch him as well, so a police officer it will be.

David stood and walked to her table. He did not carry a gun but he had finished his sketch. Cleo was setting up, flushing her eight-deck shoe. There were no players at her table yet. She looked up as he approached, nodded but did not smile. He sat in the chair directly in front of her, kept his sketch folded. He almost felt sorry for her, when the emotions should have been reversed. It had only been three hours since he had read about her bloody end. Her name tag read: CLEO.

"Hi," he said. "I'm not here to play blackjack. I've been waiting for you to come on. My name is David Lennon and I'm from Lompoc, California. Recently a good friend of mine has gone missing and I'd heard—through the grapevine—that you might know her." He paused. "Do you mind if I ask about her?"

Cleo was wary. "Who's your friend?"

He took out his photograph of Sienna, a black-and-white of her from the graveyard in Northern California, placed it on the green table. "Do you know her?" he asked.

Cleo leaned closer, hesitated. "That's Sally."

"Yeah. Sally Wither." He continued in a casual tone of voice, although his heart was a hurricane in his head. "Sally and a girlfriend of hers were here a few months back. They said they met up with you, had some fun." He unfolded his sketch of Julie, set it on the table beside the photograph. "You know Julie, don't you?" he asked.

Cleo took a step back. "What sort of friend are you?"

"I'm Sally's boyfriend. Trust me, I'm only trying to find her. I'm working with the Lompoc police on this. You can call them if you like, ask for Sheriff Stanton."

Cleo did not relax. "I can't call anybody right now, I'm working."

"That's fine, you don't have to call. I just need to know when you saw them last."

She hesitated. "I don't remember, maybe four months ago. I only hung out with them the one night."

David grinned. "I heard you girls had a great time together. That you went back to their hotel with them, joined in some real reindeer games."

"I don't know what you're talking about. We had coffee is all, gambled a little."

"Come on Cleo, Sally won a bunch of money off your table, and then you three went back to their hotel. It was the MGM, wasn't it? But you went on an errand first, before you went up to the room, didn't you? Sally told me all about it. You picked her up some Oxycontin? It's okay, I'm not a cop, I know Sally liked her drugs."

"I don't know what you're talking about. I don't do drugs."

David stood up from the table. "I understand, I didn't mean to put you on the spot. But I was just wondering—really, you can tell me the truth, I won't be jealous—did you enjoy doing her?"

Cleo answered. Perhaps she thought he was only the jealous ex and wanted to get back at him for all the questions. Brushing aside her blond hair, catching his eye the way the vampire Cleo might have, she nodded. "At first Sally wasn't feeling well, but later in the night she got going. Then there was no stopping her. She was great, really, the best I ever had."

He nodded. "Same here."

TWENTY-SEVEN

He stood outside his house, stared at the door, at the note pinned above his mail slot. MEET ME AT THE BEACH. YOU KNOW WHERE. The note had been printed, he could not tell if it was her handwriting. Inside, the lights were off, it was dark. The street was silent and deserted, twenty-five minutes to midnight.

He was tired from his travels, sick of her games. He did not want to get back in his car and drive down to the beach. But did he have a choice? He would not be able to sleep knowing she was waiting for him. Better to confront her, he thought, finally get his questions answered. Then he could sleep for days.

David drove to the beach, where he was hit by another mystery. There were no cars around, either in the main south lot, or in the smaller north lot. Had she taken a taxi to the beach? Had her pals Herb and Mary dropped her off? Feeling like there was more to his conspiracy theories than paranoia, he parked in the north lot and got out of his car. It was only while he was walking toward the train track that he realized he had parked in the spot where Billy had committed suicide. Superstitions died hard. So did best friends. He almost went back and moved his car.

The moon was big, high in the sky, white as living snow, and the sea was flat as a sheltered lagoon. He had never seen the ocean so free of waves; it was as if it had spent its last drops of energy and was now waiting for time to end. There was a strange sense of anticipation in the air, absolutely no wind. Leaving the parking lot and stepping onto the gravel that cupped the train track, he felt a layer of sweat form between his skin and his shirt. He was not frightened, nor hot from exercise. He was just confused, and his heart refused to stop pounding.

He stumbled twice as he crossed the bridge. The bright moon provided plenty of light but created even more shadows. Leaving the bridge and the track, now officially on base property, he veered to the left, onto the sand, and plowed through the weed-choked dunes till he reached the water. In the far distance, up on a hill, he could see the ghostly silhouette of an empty missile scaffold. Closer, less than half that distance, he could see a flickering orange glow. A campfire, probably Sienna. The strength went out of his legs but somehow he kept walking. North to where he had rescued Mary from certain death. To where the love of his life had dumped him. To where he had found the rotting body.

It seemed to take forever to reach the spot.

Julie Stevens waited for him beside the campfire.

She wore a loose white gown. Without the red belt, a few ironed frills, it could have been a toga. Her nipples were visible through the fine material, no underwear. Her blond hair was combed long down her back and she wore no makeup. Her face, her entire manner, was relaxed but watchful. He felt like spitting in her face.

"Hello," she said.

"Where is Sienna?" he demanded.

Julie had a bag beside the fire, Louis Vuitton, exactly like the one Sienna had brought to the beach that last night. Julie reached over and removed a CD player from the bag, one that came equipped with an attached speaker the size and shape of a paperback novel. She pushed a button and Sienna spoke.

"Hi, David. I feel stupid leaving this message. I'm sure you don't want to talk, not after what I did. I can't tell you how sorry I am about that. But I was thinking about you, and I heard through the grapevine that you were back home. I mean, I don't know how to say this, I miss you. Yeah, I miss you a lot. Is that a bad thing?"

Julie made another adjustment. He could hear planes in the background.

"It's me. But before you say anything, I can hardly hear you. I'm on my *cell, at the airport, JFK. Are you there? . . . I'm coming out to California. My plane leaves in a few minutes. I should be on board but I wanted to call you. I need to ask you something."*

Julie fast-forwarded through the CD menu. The plane sounds stopped.

"Hi, David, it's Sienna again. You're a hard man to get ahold of. This is the fifth time I've called. I'm beginning to think you've got a new girlfriend. Anyway, don't bother calling back, I'm going out right now with my friend and we'll be out late. But I'll try to get you tomorrow. I haven't changed my mind, I really want to see you. I hope you haven't changed your mind, either. Love you, honey . . ."

"Enough," David said. "When did you two burn that CD?"

"That afternoon," Julie said, no need to explain what *that* meant.

"How many selections did you record?"

"Almost a hundred. But I could make up a thousand combinations, depending on the need."

"With slight pauses in between?"

"Yes. We didn't think you would notice those."

"I noticed but didn't know what they meant."

Julie stared at him, her blue eyes dark. "Now you do."

"So where is she now?"

"You're the one who found her body."

His own body shuddered. So she was dead, after all.

"Did you kill her?" he asked.

"No. She's not dead."

"More mind games? You just said I was the one who found her body."

"True. You found her body, but you also read her book. That story was about her. In a sense, like Cleo, Sienna was an alchemist. You don't mind me calling her that, do you? She used that name with me as well, when we were alone."

"I don't give a damn what you call her. Is she dead or not?"

"I just told you, she's not dead. I know, you want me to explain. But it doesn't work that way. I cannot explain anything to you, that won't help. You have to realize the truth for yourself." She added, "Isn't that what Teresa told you?"

"You know where I've been?"

"I know you flew to New York and to Miami. I don't know if you flew straight back from Florida."

"I stopped in Las Vegas."

"Ah. Cleo. You spoke to her?"

"Yes."

"How was that?"

"How was what? I'm not a lesbian, she didn't do anything for me."

"Sienna is not technically a lesbian, she is bisexual. You should have figured that out by now. I'm the same, I love everybody."

His patience was exhausted, his nerves were shot. He felt like he had when he had awakened on the plane beside Dr. James Rean, lost between the cracks. Standing on the beach, between the moon and the fire, a wave of dizziness swept over him and he had to reach out an arm to steady himself. It was if the two colored lights fought for his soul, the red light of the flames and the white light of the heavens. The heat of the fire played over his sweaty face, while the dark water lapped quietly at his back. His heart continued to pound in his head, a rhythmic echo arising from a lost and lonely place. He just wanted to go home and go to bed.

Yet he felt as if something bad would happen if he left too quickly.

Julie was studying him closely. "You know," she said.

"What do I know?" he asked bitterly.

"The truth. In a way, you have always known it."

"Right, I got it. You and Sienna are messed-up bitches who just love to fuck with people's heads."

Julie ignored him, gestured to their surroundings. "What happened that night? Do you remember? You went to that hypnotist so that you could remember. He tried to help you but I interrupted him. That was the reason I called when I did, played you that Sienna message. But now it is safe for you to remember. This trip has been good for you. It has opened you up. Now all you have to do is stop fighting with yourself. Stop the questions. Stop looking outside yourself for answers. Let yourself go back in time two months. Let yourself see what happened. Is that too much to ask?"

He shook his head. "I'm not going to play your game anymore."

She came closer, put a finger on his arm, her touch having a powerful effect on his mind. The outline of her nipples were poems in the dark. Despite his fear, he felt strongly aroused. He did not get an erection, however; the stimulation went deeper. He could feel her breath on his cheek, he could smell it, as if she were momentarily breathing for him. His hatred for her did not leave but his desire for her could not be ignored.

"How do you feel?" she asked.

He shook his head. "Stop."

"Tell me how you feel. Tell me what you remember."

She was asking two separate questions, trying to make them sound as one. Like his breath, his will felt suddenly connected to her. He wanted to shake off her hand and storm away, but a part of him felt an obligation to answer. As if earlier, two months ago, he had agreed to cooperate with her. Like they had a deal of some kind.

He lowered his head, tried not to breathe the same air she did, but it did not help.

"I remember her telling me she had to leave," he muttered.

"What else do you remember?"

He looked up. "Why are you doing this?"

"I'm trying to help you."

"Gimme a break. You've been lying to me since I met you."

Julie came closer, put a hand on his shoulder, spoke close to his ear. "That doesn't matter. The lies were only to help you. You needed to hear them. Tell me what else you remember about that night."

He frowned, feeling pain in his chest. Was it loss? When Sienna had told him she was leaving, the sense of loss had been devastating. Yet this pain had a different character—fear more than sorrow. He could not be remembering clearly. Why would he be afraid of Sienna? Yet he did recall how her eyes had searched the beach, terrified at what they might find. He had seen the same thing under hypnosis.

"I'm afraid," he whispered.

"What are you afraid of?"

David had to close his eyes. He was not back in the hypnotist's chair. He was sinking deeper, seeing a variety of images from that last night. There had been the fire, of course, her naked body sitting on top of him. She had already told him the news and they were both upset, desperately trying to make love despite the anguish. Yet once again he felt her pain was unlike his own. She was definitely scared; she could not stop looking around. And the knife in her bag was not a pleasant thought.

He remembered the knife clearly.

His eyes flew open, he stepped away from Julie. He pointed to the Louis Vuitton bag beside the fire. "Let me see what's in there!" he demanded.

Julie did not question his order. Leaning over, she picked up the bag and held it wide open for him. Empty, the CD player had been the only thing inside. Then again, he thought, there could be hidden pockets on the sides. He took the bag and threw it into the night. She did not seem to mind.

"I don't want to stay here," he said.

"You're upset."

"I don't want to play these games."

She came close once more, put her arms around his waist, pressed her crotch to his. The odor of her breath was rich with lemons, or else lemon drops—it did not matter. At least he thought it did not matter. Until he recalled that he had bought lemon drops in Las Vegas, had chewed on them all the way home. The memory threw him off. He did not know for sure whose breath he was smelling, his or Julie's, and the uncertainty had a devastating effect on him. He trembled in her arms, she felt it.

"Stay here, let me make you feel better," she said gently.

"How can you make me feel better?" A bitter question, but he was asking for help. It was good to hold her, her body felt like home, so familiar.

"I can massage you. Remember how Sienna massaged you? What could it hurt?"

He shook his head. "I don't know, it's late."

She took a step back, reached for the top of her gown, let it fall beside the fire. God, it was true, she had nothing on underneath. The sight of her body filled him with a profound longing. Still, he did not get an erection, not even when she reached down and began to undo his pants. Nor when she took him out and touched him. He wanted her but he was too uneasy.

She did not seem to mind his lack of physical response. Helping him out of his shirt, slowly stripping off the rest of his clothes, she held his hand and muttered sweet things as she got him to lay beside the fire, facedown so she could massage his back. The way Sienna had massaged him, she said. He did not know why he cooperated.

She climbed on top and he felt her silky pubic hair brush against his butt.

Yet lying facedown, his uneasiness lessened. It was not as if it went away, but it seemed to recede into the distance. Or else he did—he felt strangely disassociated.

His will was not his own, he decided to accept the fact for a few minutes. It made it easier to accept what was really in his head. In a sense what Julie was trying to tell him rang true, even if she was a liar. Since Sienna had left, he had felt as if he was at war with a portion of his mind. A portion he had been holding at a distance, trying to deny. But he saw that this portion had been so abstract that it had been almost impossible to pierce his denial, to even recognize that it existed.

As Julie massaged his shoulders and down his spine, his naked body seemed to sink deeper into the sand, while his mind felt like floating away. He remembered he'd had the same floating sensation with Sienna, that last night, right after she had pinched his butt. Julie was working down that way.

His sense of disassociation increased. His concern over Sienna, dead or alive, became more distant. Julie's hands were all over him. Like she had advised, he felt the urge to drop his many thoughts. All that counted was the present moment, the pleasures of the flesh, Julie's hands and the warmth of the flames. His mind was just another mind, the world was filled with them. They were all nuisances, he thought, not a single one of them came equipped with an OFF switch.

He felt drunk. And he had not been drinking, not then, not now.

Julie continued to massage him, deeper and harder, but not so hard his muscles tensed. She was a manipulative person but she sure had the touch. While she worked on him she spoke about Sienna, how she understood why he had loved her so much, and how Sienna had loved him as well. She talked about Sienna's book, and how hard Sienna had worked to perfect the narrative tone. She had wanted Cleo's thoughts to replicate her own, so that when a person read the book they experienced what it was like to be in her mind. Finally, Julie explained how difficult that night had been for Sienna. How she had not wanted to hurt him, not at all, but how circumstances had forced her to take drastic action.

Julie did not explain the nature of the circumstances.

She did not tell him what the drastic action had been.

She kept massaging him, his butt finally. She even pinched him there.

The pinch on the butt, the sharp sting, it was important. His drunk feeling fled and he experienced a sudden shift—to a place that was not the least bit warm or comfortable. He was suddenly back with Mr. Candle, the hypnotist, listening to himself babble about an unknowable blasphemy.

"Tell me what happens next."

"She stops."

"She stops what?"

"Making love to me."

"Why?"

"She wants me to roll over. She says she wants to rub my back. She wants me to lie close to the fire. She says it will make me feel better."

"Does it make you feel better?"

"No. She hurts me."

"How does she hurt you?"

David's head was a melon cleaved by an ax. He experienced an even larger shift, and this time the red and gray of his brain matter threatened to rupture. He was suddenly with Sienna, that night, and he was with Ash. *He was not with Cleo.* Julie was wrong on that point. Ash was the alchemist. He had not entered the story until the end but he had haunted it from the beginning. Ash and Sienna were the twins, the ones with the identical minds.

He saw Sienna massaging him, sitting on top of him. Only she was not pinching him as Julie was, she was doing something else. He saw her reach into her bag, draw out a syringe and a vial of liquid, watched as she inserted the needle into the vial. He could read the label on the bottle: O3-KETAMINE. He saw the quick flash of her red nails, the sparkle of the long silver needle, and he watched as she stabbed the syringe deep into his buttocks.

He saw the whole thing through her eyes.

He leapt up, he could not bear to lie down. Julie fell to the side, in the direction of the fire, and the flames briefly touched her legs. She did not cry out in pain, however, not when she saw his face. A look of infinite satisfaction filled her expression. She looked at him as a lover, she looked at him as if he had just arrived. And worst of all, she stared at him as if he was not really there.

"Hello, Sienna," she said.

He tried to run, tried to hide, but everything turned black.

TWENTY-EIGHT

When he came to he felt naked and sore. He could tell he was on his back on the floor on a thin rubber mat. It was warm; he smelled lemons. He moved and heard the ring of metal. When he opened his eyes, he saw Sienna's bathroom ceiling, and two sets of handcuffs and chains that circled his wrists and ankles.

A face swam into view, peered down at him. Dr. James Rean.

"How do you feel?" he asked.

David had to swallow to speak. "Dizzy."

"You've had a major shock. Do you know where you are?"

"Sienna's guest house."

"Yes. Do you know why you are here?"

"So you can harvest my organs?"

Dr. Rean smiled, the well-educated mouth with the teeth one size too small. "No. You don't have to worry about that. Do you feel well enough to sit up?"

"I think so."

Dr. Rean helped him into a sitting position, filled a paper cup on the sink with water. David remembered that Sienna had been a freak when it came to water. All the water in her guest house had been put through a reverse osmosis filter. The water tasted good; he drank two cups. He felt stupid thanking the doctor for it.

David was *almost* naked, he had on a green hospital gown. His chains, attached to the cuffs, circled the wall heater and the plumbing beneath the sink. The arrangement was thorough—he wasn't going anywhere. The bathroom window had been closed over with a half dozen hammered boards, although warm yellow light came from the direction of the living room. It was obviously daytime.

He had his back to the tub. Dr. Rean sat across from him and rested against the wall. The good doctor had on blue jeans, a green T-shirt, a great tan, and he looked happy and relaxed. He gestured to David's hospital gown.

"Sorry about that. It's the best we can do given the circumstances."

"Which are?"

He nodded. "You want answers, that's fine. I'm here to give them to you. The time for secrecy has passed. Last night you had what we call 'Initial Breakthrough.' It will not be long before you have 'Total Breakthrough.' After that you will have no need to ask questions. But until then, to make you more comfortable, I'm here to tell you what is going on."

"You could make me more comfortable by removing these chains."

"They are only there for your protection, trust me."

"I do not trust you."

Dr. Rean smiled. "A poor choice of words, given the situation. But let us not argue over whether you should trust me. Let me tell you my story, and your own story for that matter. You see, what I am about to say, you have heard it before. You just don't remember."

David coughed, his head hurt. "I'm all ears."

"Let's go back in time, say ten years. I was a very successful surgeon on the East Coast. As I told you on the plane, I do mostly transplants, and I was doing the same back then. But I had a serious problem of supply and demand. So many people needed organs—hearts, livers, kidneys, lungs—and there were only so many to go around. The way the national donor lists are set up, it didn't matter how important the patient might be. I could only give out what was given to me. The situation was frustrating, unacceptable actually. With some friends of mine, people of like minds, I began to look around for a solution.

"You have spoken to Krane, and I have talked to him as well. He figured out a portion of the truth. You know some of what I am going to say next. With my partners, I traveled to several Third World countries, mostly in Africa. But we visited many villages in India as well. Do you know what a year's salary is in one of those villages? You give them a hundred bucks and they feel like a king. Give them a thousand and they think they've died and gone to Krishna's abode."

"You started to buy organs from the Third World," David said.

"Yes. It was not difficult—there are millions of people anxious to sell them. And it was a simple business at first, although extremely profitable. We did not have to bring the organs into the country. We were able to transplant them on the *Lazarus*. We flew the organs straight to the boat, via a helicopter we kept stationed on a certain Caribbean island. And no one got hurt. You only need one kidney to live, a part of a liver. The first year we did over two hundred transplants and took in a million dollars apiece. You have to understand, in a place like India or the Sudan, we were able to blood- and tissue-type thousands and no one asked questions. We just had to hand out twenty-dollar bills and people came running to be typed. We only transplanted organs that were close matches. Our success rate was very high, better than most American hospitals.

"But we still had a serious problem of supply and demand. The number one killer in the world is heart disease. It doesn't matter what we discover about the relationship of diet and blocked arteries. In the end it is usually the heart that kills you. It will probably always be that way. But after we were in business a year or so, we began to entertain the idea of taking healthy young hearts and putting them in some of our sickest patients. Now before you get on your moral high horse and accuse me and my partners of being killers, let me explain a few pieces of reality to you.

"The greatest wealth we have as a species is our genes. Everything else pales in comparison, even the Earth's natural resources. We are defined by our genes. But how do we treat this most precious wealth? We piss on it. As a race, we are drowning in the shallow end of the gene pool. It is the poorest people—and let's be blunt, the dumbest—that reproduce the most rapidly. Take for example California, where we are now. Fifty years ago it was ninety-percent Caucasian. Now it is fifty-percent Hispanic, and that half grows every day. Look at you, you are twenty-eight years old: young, strong, white and smart. But how many kids do you have? You have none. How many kids does your average Mexican your age have? Three, if not four. The situation with blacks is worse. They breed more rapidly, and they are even less intelligent. I am not being prejudiced here, I am being factual."

"Thank you for the speech, Hitler. I feel so much more enlightened now," David said.

"You mock me because you want to feel in your own mind that you are politically correct. That is all. Hitler was a fanatic and there is no reason to compare me to him. Yet he did have certain insights. The race has to be improved and the best way to do that is to have more intelligent people born than stupid people. Another way to improve it is to try to keep alive the best society has to offer. You think the men and women who came to us for organs were evildoers. That is not true—they were simply desperate, as all sick people are. They had exhausted the system and the system had turned its back on them. What we did was provide them with a service they could not get elsewhere."

David noticed his use of past tense, as if he was no longer providing the service, but another one, a new and improved service. Yet he acted bored as he said, "Are you trying to skip over the part where you bought young people in poor countries and cut out their hearts and put the hearts into rich people?"

"No. Remember, I was the one who brought it up. I am being frank with you. It is your weakness if you are unable to see the bigger picture. Hundreds of millions of souls are born in India and Africa every decade. The vast majority of these contribute nothing of substance to the human race. How many people from India or Africa win the Nobel Prize? Very few, and when they do it is almost always politically motivated. Yet if you look at my patients, you find some of the most brilliant and influential people on earth. Men and women who are giants in business, science and art. Please, for a few minutes, drop your emotions, set aside your conditioning, and you will have to admit that these people deserve life more than some mindless kid kicking rocks around in a dirty village."

"I do not admit that," David said. "Because any white person who is so corrupt as to take the heart out of a black or a brown person so he can stay alive does not deserve life. That person is a murderer—likewise, you are a murderer for helping them. So if all you have to feed me is neo-Nazi bullshit, then why don't you either let me go or else shoot me in the head. Because I am already sick and tired of listening to you."

Dr. Rean did not like his tone of voice. For an instant his emotions showed, and they were not so brilliant or rich. But then he collected himself, smiled again. "I didn't think you would understand," he said.

"I take that as a compliment. You are leading up to something. What is it? Just cut to the chase."

"Fine. If that is what you want. Let us go back not ten years, but five. Imagine, if you will, our successful transplant club. We are doing a thousand people a year—hearts, livers, kidneys—but it is still an exclusive club. No one who joins is allowed to talk about it. They don't want to talk about it. Through my partners and I, they have been given a new lease on life. Their health is better, they are still alive when they should be dead. But still they are not young people. They have postponed death but they have not escaped it. That is a problem that has faced everyone throughout time. And sitting out on our boat, alone on the sea at night, my partners and I began to discuss in earnest what we could do about that."

"Don't tell me you've discovered the secret of immortality?"

"In a sense, we have."

David chuckled. "You are nuts."

Dr. Rean was grave. "You laugh. But you will not be laughing in a few minutes."

David saw he was serious. "Tell me your big secret."

"Have you heard of the street drug, Special K?"

"Yes."

"Have you ever taken it?"

"No." David frowned. "That is ketamine. I remember now. I saw vials of that aboard the *Lazarus*."

"You saw more than we planned. You are right, Special K is ketamine. But the way we use it is not the same as the way your average junkie on the street uses it. Let me speak to you in scientific terms for a few minutes so that you have a full understanding of what this drug is and what its implications are for the future of humanity.

"Ketamine hydrochloride was not discovered in the darkest jungles of Africa, nor does it have a long history of traditional use among primitive tribes. Ketamine is a human creation. It was first synthesized by the Belgian chemist C. L. Stevens in 1963 and it was patented by Parke-Davis in '66. Not long after, the FDA approved it for use as a surgical anesthetic. But ketamine is not a general anesthetic. It is what is known as a 'dissociative' anesthetic. The anesthesia is the result of the patient being so dissociated from their body that it is possible to carry out surgical procedures. This is different from the unconsciousness produced by general anesthetics. You understand the difference? It is important."

"Yes," David said.

"Although ketamine was an effective anesthetic it soon became clear that it did have one unusual side effect. Twenty percent of all patients anesthetized with it reported having out-of-body experiences. This was before all the books on near-death experiences came along. Most of the early research on ketamine was done by medical doctors and veterinarians. They were the only ones who could get their hands on it. It wasn't seen as a street drug at first. It wasn't made in a dirty basement. No, ketamine was approved for human consumption by the sacred FDA. No one paid much attention while it was passed around for further study within the medical community. Frankly I don't know what these early guys discovered, no one published their results.

"Five years later the shit hit the fan. Almost overnight a ton of books appeared on near-death experiences. People were coming back from the dead left and right. They were on talk shows, in *Time* magazine—a few had their own TV programs. The reason was obvious. In the sixties resuscitation techniques made quantum leaps. People could be down ten minutes or more and be brought back.

"Of course, I exaggerate to make a point. Because they were eventually revived, these people had not been technically dead. But they sure talked like they had been dead. They had interesting things to say about their experiences. Things that happened to coincide with what people who were experimenting with ketamine had to say.

"There is not one classical near-death experience, but people do have similar experiences. Feelings of peace and contentment. A sense of detachment from the body. Feelings of entering a transitional world of darkness. Rapid movements through tunnels—the whole tunnel experience. Emerging into bright light. A sense that what is experienced is real and that one is truly dead. Transcendent mystical states are also common.

"Here is my point. The administration of fifty to a hundred milligrams of ketamine can reproduce *all* of the features which are associated with near-death experiences. It does not matter if a person takes the drug intramuscularly or intravenously. This is not a casual discovery. And there are significant neurochemical reasons why ketamine is able to do all these things.

"Say you are about to die. Either you are drowning or you are having a heart attack or someone is smothering you with a pillow. Or let's say you've been shot and you're bleeding to death. It doesn't matter. In all these cases your brain is starved for oxygen, and in that state it gets super excited and releases a powerful neurotransmitter called glutamate. You need glutamate to think clearly, but too much is toxic—it kills brain cells quickly. From a brain chemistry point of view it does this by overactivating the N-methyl-D-aspartate receptors—the NMDAs. Fortunately, the same conditions that trigger the glutamate also bring a flood of ketamine, which binds to the NMDAs and protects them. Do you follow?"

David was interested despite himself. "Yes. By taking ketamine you simulate one of the main chemical reactions that occurs in the brain at the moment of death."

"Exactly. It was the discovery of this link between near-death experiences and ketamine that led many doctors to dismiss near-death experiences. They said if a simple chemical can make you see dead relatives and golden angels, then the entire phenomena of 'glimpsing an afterlife' is a product of neurochemistry."

"That does not seem a fair deduction," David said. "The phenomena could still be real. The relationship to ketamine does not disprove it."

"I agree. I am merely telling you what most scientists say. But let us return to the *Lazarus* and my group. We knew about the effects of ketamine and decided to do experiments of our own. That figure I quoted earlier—that twenty percent of the people taking it as an anesthesia have an out-of-body experience—that is for a full dose. One-fifth that dose is much more effective if you want to remember what happens. Fifty to one hundred milligrams produces an out-of-body experience in eighty percent of people. It is quite remarkable. When we started to play with it, the majority of us found it easy to leave our bodies and float around the room."

"You are serious?" David asked.

"I am. Everything I am telling you is pure science. Others have done what we have done." Dr. Rean added, boasting, "Only no one has taken it as far as we have."

"Meaning?" David asked.

"As we experimented, we discovered that if two people were out of their bodies at the same time they were able to momentarily switch bodies. I mean that literally. They were able to will themselves into the body of the other.

The problem was they were not able to stay in the other person's body for any length of time. Something would snap them back—it was like an elastic band. We tried all types of variations on the drug dosage and altered the environment but we were unable to stop the whiplash effect.

"Then it occurred to me that the person was drawn back into their body because it was what the person knew, it was home. It was more than that— it was a big part of their sense of self. Naturally, spontaneously, they would have to return to it if it was alive. *But what, I asked myself, if their body was dead?* Could they then enter another body and stay there? Would the whiplash effect vanish?

"I had a patient, a successful businessman, he was very old. Let's call him Ralph. We had given him a new heart but then he developed complications from diabetes and there was not much we could do for him. But I spoke to him about my idea and he was very interested. By chance we had an Indian teenager aboard—Panda—who was there to help us out with another heart patient."

David had to interrupt. "Help you out? You mean he was going to unknowingly have his heart cut out of him. He was going to die. Is that what you mean?"

Dr. Rean was only mildly annoyed at his outburst. "Yes. But who gives a damn? Let me continue. At my urging, Ralph tried to project his Second Body—that's what we called it—into Panda's body. Ralph had already used the ketamine and was experienced at moving around the room after dosing up. But like all of us, he was whipped back into his own body after a few seconds. Even when we shot Panda up with a high dose and Ralph jumped inside him, he was yanked back." Dr. Rean paused. "So we decided to shoot up Panda one last time, drive his Second Body out of his physical body, and then kill Ralph."

"Ralph agreed to this?"

"Yes. He was in constant pain. We'd just amputated a part of his leg to stop a gangrene infection. He had nothing to live for. If it didn't work, he didn't care, he was going to die anyway."

"I don't believe this."

"Believe what you want, we did it. As soon as Panda had the ketamine in his system, we shot Ralph in the head with a thirty-eight revolver. Then something strange happened. When the drug wore off, Panda was confused and disoriented. He wasn't Ralph, though, he was not acting like Ralph. He was still an Indian teenager. We figured the experiment had failed. The other doctors recommended we use Panda for the purpose for which we had brought him on board. But something nagged at the back of my mind. Ketamine had not caused the rest of us to experience disorientation, not after it wore off. Why did it do that to Panda? I decided to keep him around for a while. I brought him back to Miami, let him stay at my house with Teresa." Dr. Rean paused and then added, "He was with us a month when he came into my room one morning and told me he was Ralph."

David shook his head. "No."

"Yes. He had all of Ralph's memories. He had all of Panda's memories for that matter. But in his essence he was Ralph. He identified with Ralph. The Indian teenager's memories were just a data file inside him. They were still hard-wired into his brain. They had not been erased with the transfer. This is an important point. Physically, memories are stored as strings of chemicals in the brain. They are made up largely of proteins. Science is only beginning to understand how these chemicals interact with consciousness, where the line between consciousness and matter falls. But what science does not even begin to suspect is that there is another manner in which memories are stored inside all of us. They are stored in the Second Body."

"How can you be sure?"

"After the transfer, Ralph was not attached to the life Panda had led. Oh, he remembered everything Panda had done. He remembered his childhood, his teenage years. He even had Panda's talents. For example, Panda had been able to play the flute, and now he could play the flute. That talent was *chemically* stored in his brain. But *he* was not Panda anymore. He no longer had Panda's desires. He wanted to do the things Ralph would have wanted to do if he was alive. And that was the crux of the matter—Ralph *was* still alive. He was inside Panda's body."

"How was it so easy to displace Panda from his body?"

"It wasn't easy. We had to use a high dose of ketamine."

"But how come Panda couldn't get back in his body once he was driven out? It was *his* body. To use your own phrase, it was hard-wired to him. Why would Ralph be able to push him aside so easily?"

"An insightful question. The host is not psychologically prepared for the transfer. We did not warn Panda what we were going to do. Then, when the host is driven out, he is disoriented. He does not know what is happening. It is during that period that the new person enters the host. And once he is inside, he is hard to get out."

"Why?" David asked. "Panda or Ralph or whoever we're talking about did not even know what was happening after he got *in*. How is this new person able to fight off the original person?"

Dr. Rean paused to smile. "*Fight off?* The way you word that might contain the answer you are searching for. You assume when the person is kicked out of their body, they *want* to come back."

"Of course they would want to come back."

"I agree. *I* would want to come back. I would do *anything* to keep living. But maybe, at that critical moment, there is something that draws them away."

"What are you talking about?"

"I don't know, it is just a theory."

"What is the theory?"

Dr. Rean spread his hands. "What can I say? Maybe they see God and they like the look of him and go running toward him. Maybe angels come and whisper in their ears. I don't know. Maybe that proverbial light draws them into its warm and loving bosom."

"Did you ever see that light when you used ketamine?"

"No. Then again, I didn't look for it."

David shook his head. "You are making this all up."

Dr. Rean spoke with firmness. "You are in denial. You know where all this is leading and you refuse to accept it."

"And where is that?"

Dr. Rean flashed his creepy bedside smile, the one he had shown on the plane. The smile that gave David the feeling he was screwed. He continued. "I will return to that in a minute. For now, this experiment with Ralph and Panda brought up deep philosophical questions. Who are we? That question stands behind all profound questions. Are we our memories? Are we our physical bodies? Or are we our Second Body? I am not sure the experiment answered these questions—to this day I am still not sure—but I do know it opened up a Pandora's box of possibilities I had hardly allowed myself to dream about."

"You did not begin to transfer old people's souls into young people's bodies?"

"Yes and no. We tried to replicate our success with Ralph and found in most cases the transference didn't take place. We decided one reason was the ketamine itself. It did not produce out-of-body experiences a hundred percent of the time. We began to tinker with it. Scientists are always tinkering with existing drugs, trying to improve them. Take for example codeine, the opiate. By attaching a hydrogen to its basic molecule and mixing it with ordinary Tylenol, you get Vicodin—or hydrocodone, probably the most-prescribed pain killer in hospitals. One that is much stronger than plain codeine. In the same way, we eventually discovered that by bubbling ozone through pure ketamine we could increase the potency of the solution. Brain cells have an affinity for oxygen. They have a much greater liking for ozone. When we mixed it with ketamine it seemed as if the ketamine molecule was able to piggyback onto the ozone and reach the brain faster and with more force. Our improved solution could bring about an out-of-body experience in almost a hundred percent of the cases.

"Still, transference seldom happened, and we began to see that a relationship between the dying patient—the one who was trying to transfer—and the new person—the body we were trying to use—was essential. In other words it helped if there was an emotional bond between the two. I did not mention this earlier but Ralph had not known Panda was on board to donate his heart. For that matter, Panda had not been aware of his ultimate role. Quite by chance, the two had struck up a relationship. They used to have dinner together sometimes. They were actually quite close, although Ralph was not above using Panda if it meant another chance at life." Dr. Rean paused to find the right words. "Reflecting on their relationship, I began to understand that a person was more readily able to enter and stay in another person's body if he or she cared for that person."

David snorted. "How can someone care for someone they are trying to destroy?"

Dr. Rean laughed. "You are so intelligent, and yet, in your own way, you are one of the most naive people I have ever met. Have you not heard the line that you can only truly hate those you love? Look at the state of marriage in our country. Have you ever visited a divorce court? We loathe what we have a passion for. Otherwise, if someone does something bad to us, we get angry, we might even sue them, but it seldom turns into an all-consuming emotion. There's no conflict between caring for someone and wanting to use them.

Couples use each other all the time. If not for sex, then for money, or else for position. It is the way of the world."

"It is the way of *your* world."

"My world is your world. You are still not listening to what I am saying. You are not reflecting on what it means to you."

"I don't know what you're talking about."

"Yes, you do. But let me go on. Taking this last clue to heart, we set it up so that patients seeking to transfer into another person's body first got involved with that person. It did not have to be a sexual involvement, although that helped. We found emotion to be the key. It helped if the intended *victim*—I use the word loosely—loved the would-be immortal."

"Stealing another person's body does not make you an immortal."

"Sure it does. Who's to say the transference cannot be achieved again and again? That's the plan, you know, to live in an endless succession of young and vital bodies. And I know what you are thinking—that I'm sick, that I should be locked up. It's not true, I'm an innovator. I'm ahead of my time. All the people who work with me are."

"Including Teresa?"

"Yes."

"So she knows about all this?"

"Of course."

"Then she lied to me in Miami."

"You were not ready for the truth. I wonder if you are ready now. You see the pattern I am describing and you refuse to accept what it means. Yet you have been given more than enough clues. People who've had their bodies taken over continue with their memories for some time. Then their memories begin to crack in places. Alien memories appear in their heads, from seemingly nowhere. They begin to suspect there is something wrong with their minds. They talk to their friends, they say, 'I don't know what is wrong with me. I am not myself.' They might go to a doctor, or visit a hypnotist. None of that helps, it does not help *them*, I should say, the old person who is no longer there."

"You speak gibberish," David interrupted.

"You know exactly what I am saying. Certain methods, however, can facilitate this transformation, make it smoother, which eventually leads to the breakthroughs I have mentioned. One thing that helps is to have the body of the person who has been freshly transferred hang out with an old lover. Of course, the new person does not recognize the lover. The person buried inside the new body doesn't have his or her memories back yet. But by hanging out with an old friend, the memories start to snowball." Dr. Rean paused. "That's why we put you together with Julie."

"I hardly know Julie."

"That is not true. You have known her for two years."

"I knew her in high school, ten years ago."

"That is not what I am talking about and you know it. We tried a few other tricks with you, to speed up the process. One was having you read Sienna's book. Thoughts can be visual or they can be purely emotional. But they are by and large verbal. You think in the language you grew up with, and you think in specific ways. My thoughts are not the same as yours. I am not talking so much about the content, more the tone, the rhythm. We had you read Sienna's book so that you could begin to think like her."

"That's dumb. When you read a book, you don't start to think like the author."

"To a small extent you do. But when you *are* the author, the effect is magnified many-fold. Another thing, smell is the most intimate of the senses. Studies have shown that people are attracted to their mates largely because of their odor. In a sense, smell is the most primitive of the senses. For that reason we gave Sienna a distinct smell. When you think of her, you think of lemons. She washed her hair with lemon-scented shampoo, she had a lemon tree outside. She went out of her way to create this smell you associate with her. Now, every time you smell lemons, you think of her, and that brings her that much closer to you. Do you understand?"

"No."

"Admit it. Everything I say rings true to you because it is true."

"Everything you say is nuts! You cannot transfer souls or Second Bodies or whatever you call it! None of this is real! You are not an innovator! You are a sicko doctor who is trying to justify stealing organs so you can make money!"

Dr. Rean spoke in a flat methodical tone. "A year and a half ago, Sienna's father was dying of multiple organ failure. No number of transplants could save him. He came to us asking for help and we transferred his Second Body into the body of a young gentleman you met—Rudy Turbel. Six months after that Sienna discovered she had incurable cancer and she asked for our help. We began a search for a suitable body for her to take over. She was involved with Julie at the time, and Julie suggested you. Sienna flew out to bond with you for one purpose only—to remove you from the scene. This fantasy you have of her, that she loved you and you loved her, is absurd. She just used you, everybody in this world uses each other."

"You don't know how I felt about her."

"Don't I? I know a hell of a lot more than you know. You don't even know who you are anymore."

"I am David Lennon."

"You are mistaken. She shot you up with ketamine that night. Your Second Body was forced out of your physical body, and she killed herself so that she could permanently take over your body. The transfer was a success, the proof is obvious. You're beginning to have Sienna's memories. You flew to Las Vegas to meet someone you didn't know, but someone that Sienna knew intimately. Last night, on the beach, for the first time, you saw through Sienna's eyes."

"How do you know what I saw?"

"Because Julie saw you. She saw Sienna." Dr. Rean stopped and put a hand on his knee. "Accept what has happened. You are not David Lennon. This part of you that fights us is merely a memory-based identification. Right now, I have not been talking to David. None of this conversation has been for his sake. I have been talking to Sienna, trying to help her understand what is going on. I am not worried, however; I know this amnesiac phase will not last. Partial breakthrough has been achieved. Full breakthrough will follow. It is inevitable."

David pushed away his hand. "If I am Sienna, then why do you keep me chained up? What are you afraid of?"

"I'm afraid of nothing. I'm an immortal, remember? But once partial breakthrough has been achieved, we have found it useful to slowly weaken the new host's body. It aids in the breaking down of false identification. For that reason, you are to be kept here until full breakthrough occurs. You will be allowed to drink water, bathe as often as you like, but you are to receive no food. After a week or two you will get so weak the remainder of the false identifications will drop off and you will know yourself to be Sienna."

"You did not do that with Panda."

"We have refined our technique since Panda." He added, "I mean, since Ralph."

"So you think I will starve in this house for a week or so and then one day I will magically transform into Sienna?"

"No. You do not listen. You are already Sienna. David is already dead. You will just realize the truth is all."

"You are full of shit."

"And you are full of nothing but false memory complexes."

A silence fell between them. David found it impossible to argue with a person who was convinced he was not there. Of course, what Dr. Rean was saying was absurd. The man was a megalomaniac. David would not have been surprised to learn that Dr. Rean was the one who had cut Sienna up.

Finally, though, he was having to accept that Sienna was dead.

"Did you kill Krane and his partner, Carol?" he asked.

"Associates of mine had them killed, yes. They were getting too close."

"Two dead FBI agents? You think that won't attract attention?"

"We have friends at the FBI. One person, rather high up, is already on our team."

"Why would an FBI employee join your team?"

Dr. Rean shrugged. "So he can live forever, what else?"

"You know you have not offered one shred of proof for what you are saying."

"Your mind is the proof. It is a mess. It has been a mess since that night. What did you do after your last date with Sienna? You immediately flew to New York. To her hometown. You wanted desperately to get away from anything that had to do with her and you ran off and rented a room in her old stomping ground. Odd, don't you think?"

"I paint book covers for a living. My work is in New York."

"I am not going to argue with you. Sienna knows what I am saying. She hears every word."

David mocked him. "So no proof, huh? Not even one little piece?"

Dr. Rean stared at him intensely, as if for the first time he was truly annoyed. "Are you sure you want proof?" he asked.

"Yes."

"It happened ten years ago. The first transfers."

"What? I thought you said you guys started five years ago."

"Not the first two. They happened here in Lompoc. A young woman was struck by a terrible tragedy. Her face was burned in a fire. She was badly scarred—she looked hideous. Even her boyfriend couldn't stand to look at her. She couldn't bear the thought of living the rest of her life as a freak. She searched everywhere for a cure. She prayed for help, if you know what I mean. Luckily she had a beautiful sister whose body she didn't mind stealing. Then there was her boyfriend, whom she still wanted to be with, and who still wanted to be with her. The only problem was her sister had recently married a famous doctor. It was not a major problem, though, because after she transferred into her sister's body she no longer loved her husband. She couldn't stand the guy, actually. But she liked his position and power, his money and knowledge. So she arranged to have her boyfriend go into him. She helped her boyfriend make the big leap. She held his hand at a critical time, so to speak. Do you understand?"

David had to strain to speak. "You are not Billy. Teresa is not Rachel."

Dr. Rean ignored him, just kept staring. "She told you in Miami how Billy saw you and Rachel making out. How he saw you trying to steal from him the one thing he loved the most in the whole world. You know, when your name came up as a possible host for Sienna, I supported it all the way. I thought, what karma. It's David Lennon's turn to experience a little payback."

"I would never have hurt Billy."

"You did hurt Billy."

David shook his head. "I was a kid, she was flirting with me. We stopped before it went anywhere."

"You stopped because I came over."

"You are not Billy! He would not have done this to me!"

Dr. Rean stood and patted him patiently on the head, as if he were a child or a pet. Taking a step toward the door, he spoke over his shoulder. "Julie will be by occasionally to check up on you. Seeing her will help speed up the process. Otherwise, don't bother trying to escape. We've had a lot of experience with people in your state. You won't get far, and besides, there is nowhere for you to go. You are already gone."

David spoke angrily. "Billy was the one who started that fire! He was the one who burned Rachel's face! He destroyed her life just because she made out with me!"

Dr. Rean stopped at the door, sighed and looked down at him. "I didn't hurt her. Someone else did," he said.

"Who?"

His gaze was suddenly far away. "That is the question, isn't it? Was it the chicken or was it the egg? Perhaps I should come back in two weeks and ask you. I read Sienna's book. It's possible she knows the answer."

"I loved Billy," David said softly.

"He did not love you."

Dr. Rean left. He left David alone.

TWENTY-NINE

He had nothing to do, he could only sit there. Well, he could stand up, he could lie down. He could even pace a few steps, the chains gave him some room to move around. He could use the toilet easily. They had left him plenty of toilet paper, and a stack of fresh towels. He tried all the faucets, in the sink and shower, and discovered he had hot water. That was good but it did not make up for the thinness of his mat. Every bone in his back could feel the linoleum floor. They had left him only one paper cup, no soap—maybe they were afraid he would poison himself with it. They had removed the mirror from the medicine cabinet so he could not slit his wrists with broken glass.

The boards on the bathroom window had been pounded in with a sledgehammer. The nails must have been eight inches long; they had badly splintered the window frame. Without a crowbar, there was no way he could pull off the boards. It was a pity—with a nail, even a bobby pin, he probably could have picked the locks on his handcuffs.

He suspected the landlady was in on their insanity. That, or she was away on an extended vacation. He tried shouting for help but quickly realized the uselessness of the effort. The guest house was far back in the hills. A person would have to be standing directly outside to hear him, and no one ever came back here.

He pondered their choice of jail cells. This bathroom was where he had shared his first intimate moment with Sienna. The infamous shower scene— it had meant a lot to him. Strange how, even with the window boarded up, he could still smell the lemon tree outside. He could still smell *her*. He tried not to think about it too much. The last time he had been in this bathroom, he had fainted.

He wanted a shower, but the cuffs prevented him from taking off his gown. He considered trying to work around it, maybe let it get wet. But in the end he ripped it off. The guest house was warm, a blanket came with the mat. If he needed to cover himself, he could always throw the gown over his front. Who was going to visit beside Julie? She had already seen him naked plenty, the fucking bitch.

After his shower he felt drowsy, so he laid down and took a nap. When he woke up it was still bright in the living room, still daytime. He could see his clothes folded nicely in the corner of the living room. His nap had made his back stiff and he paced to work out the kinks, did some stretching exercises. He drank plenty of water. He was hungry and it seemed to help him forget about food.

Finally, he sat down and thought seriously about his predicament. He did not believe Dr. Rean's story for a moment. Besides being utterly preposterous, the guy was a born liar. Yet the man could have mixed in truth with his lies. David had no doubt he had been injected with ketamine, perhaps more than once. A powerful dissociative like that could have played havoc with his mind, particularly when it had been administered by people who had a penchant for manipulation. For all he knew, Julie, Sienna's mother and even Teresa had shot him up without his knowledge. He suspected the drug could have made him susceptible to suggestions. They could have planted all kinds of shit in his head.

Of course, the big question was, why? If they wanted him dead, why not just kill him like they had Krane and Carol? Why all the games? They must want something else from him.

But he accepted that Sienna was almost certainly dead, and that she had been involved with them from the start. She had burned that CD for Julie— that was no small piece of evidence. He tried to face the fact that she had betrayed him, that she was that body he had found rotting on the beach. But his feelings refused to come into sync with his mind. It was almost as if he had pondered the mystery so long that the solution had no place left to fit inside him. He hated what she had done to him, and he hated what they had done to her. But at the same time he felt almost nothing, and that bothered him more than his handcuffs. He cared but his emotions were like a package. He worried if he unwrapped them he would find nothing inside.

But he was David Lennon, he told himself. No doubts there.

It grew dark outside. The bathroom lights had been removed. With the window blocked, the gloom grew so thick he could not see his hand in front of his face. He laid back down and tried to sleep but he was not tired. So he just laid there, hour after hour, and it was a slow form of torture. Because he knew he would have to do the same thing tomorrow, and the day after that, until he changed into Sienna, which was never going to happen.

"Maybe I can fake the transformation," he muttered.

Sometime during the night he passed out.

The next morning he got the idea to cannibalize the inner workings of the toilet and find himself a piece of wire. But the lid on the toilet tank was glued shut with superglue, and the sides were made of kick-proof plastic. He pounded on the damn thing for an hour and it did not crack open. They had thought of everything. He shouted for help again but all that did was make his throat hoarse.

He was much hungrier the second day. He drank extra water but all he could think about was food. He fantasized about stuff he did not normally eat: pizza and shrimp and tacos. He remembered that Sienna had liked all three.

Boredom was his worst enemy. He tried jogging in place so that he could get tired enough to pass out again. But he only ended up hot and sweaty, and the sound of the jingling chains began to grate on his nerves. The shower and the tub were connected, and he took a cold bath for variety. The guest house was hotter than the previous day. It was summer—they were at the start of a heat wave. The greenhouse effect from the sun streaming in through the living room windows overwhelmed the insulation. The house did not have air-conditioning, few places in Santa Barbara did.

The second day went slowly. To pass the time he sang Beatles songs. He had always liked the Beatles. Sienna had loved them. *If I fell in love with you, do you promise to be true. . . .*

The third day he awoke in terrible pain, deep in his guts. It felt like he had lava in his intestines and dwarves excavating his liver. He jumped up to take his medicine. He knew exactly what he needed—two white Demerol and four green Percocets. But then he realized he had no pills, that he was only a naked and starving prisoner, and the pain suddenly disappeared. He remembered he'd had a similar attack sleeping in Sienna's bed. He did not understand what brought it on.

His hunger got worse, and he was sick of water. To distract himself he mentally reviewed Sienna's novel, trying to find the clues in it she had purposely planted. He felt she had written it especially for him. Julie had said as much, and Sienna had gone out of her way to get it into his hands. But he ended up plotting alternative endings to the story. He came up with a version where Cleo did not cut herself, where she ended up begging Ash to leave their baby alone. Then he thought of a scenario where Ash blew his brains out just before the birth, while Cleo smothered the infant before bleeding to death. He wondered if Sienna had considered such endings, they each had their own charm.

The fourth day his hunger disappeared and he got violent attacks of diarrhea. He spent half his time on the toilet, in between taking showers. He hoped his body was just purifying from all the water, that he was not getting sick.

The fifth day his hunger was still gone and he felt more energy. He ended up pacing for several hours. The guest house was hotter than ever. He took long baths to stay cool.

The sixth day passed much like the fifth, except he had several attacks of dizziness. He worried about his blood sugar; he figured he didn't have any.

The seventh day he just laid there. He did not feel like doing anything.

He dozed frequently, spending a lot of time lost between waking and dreaming. A recurring mental video ran in his head. He was at the Metropolitan Museum, ten years old, enjoying the exotic paintings and the forbidding statues with younger versions of Sienna's parents. They lingered at the Egyptian exhibit, and the sight of the mummies and the carefully arranged stone blocks covered with hieroglyphics filled his head with wonder. He felt certain *those people* knew things about staying alive—secret potions and dark rites—even when you were supposed to be dead. He imagined a mummy coming back to life right before his eyes, rising out of one of the stone coffins and reaching out a bony hand to grab him. The fantasy was so vivid in his mind that he actually backed off and whimpered. Mr. Wither grabbed him by the ear.

"Don't make noise," the man snapped.

He had not been a nice man, David thought.

Then he pushed the entire fantasy out of his mind, and did not let it back in. He was not experiencing a memory from Sienna's childhood. That was not possible.

Julie came by on the eighth day.

She walked in without announcement, smiling cheerfully, wearing a white skirt, a tight-fitting blue blouse, her hair tied in a long ponytail. Her lips were painted dark red; she wore thick eye shadow. He was not sure what day it was. It was possible she had a date planned for that evening, not that he cared. He covered himself with his torn hospital gown and sat up, as she stood at the door of the bathroom like a nurse peering in on a patient. He could tell she was afraid to get too close.

"How are we doing today?" she asked.

"*We* are doing fine," he said.

She hesitated. "So have you made much progress?"

He laughed, and the weird thing was, he could not stop. His laughter filled the tiny room like moans surround the gallows. "*We* have made lots of progress," he said finally.

Julie frowned. "I'm not here to bother you. If you want me to leave, I'll leave."

"Okay. Leave."

"Don't you want to talk?"

"No."

She came closer, crouched on her knees. He could see her underwear. Yellow, with stripes—he thought he had seen it before. "I would like to talk to you," she said.

"You would like to talk to Sienna. But she hasn't moved in yet. Sorry."

"There's time." She added, "She did care about you, you know. It tortured her, what she was doing. She was just scared, she didn't want to die. You understand?"

"Sure. She wanted to steal my body. No problem."

Julie shook her head. "You won't feel that way soon."

"Tell me, is Stanton still searching for me?"

"Yes. But he didn't find anything to connect you to Krane's death. He won't be able to put you back in jail."

"Since I'm locked up here, that is not much consolation. Is he part of your gang?"

"No."

"Is Simpson, my lawyer?"

"He is not directly involved. It is my understanding he is an employee of people who are close to the Reans."

"Why did you guys choose a male body?"

"What?"

"If you believe all this shit, why did you and Sienna choose a male body? I mean, she was used to a sexy female form. I would have thought she would have gone after a famous model. Why did you choose me?"

"Because you seemed like a good candidate to get close to Sienna, and I knew you. You were sweet and innocent, sort of gullible." Julie added, "Also, we thought if she was in a male body, we could have more fun together."

David sighed, looked deeply troubled. "I am changing," he whispered.

She brightened. "Really? Tell me what you remember."

"Are you sure you want to hear?"

"Yes!"

He looked at her, kept a straight face. "I remember being her, and thinking about you. Thinking how when this was all over, I could get rid of you. How great you were at oral sex but not much else. How you were nothing more than a white trash ex-cheerleader who deserved your boring nine-to-five job selling cheap clothes at Macy's. And how the first chance I got I would fly back to New York and my high-class friends and my many millions and never think about you ever again."

Julie stood and stalked out the front door. He laughed at her back.

The next few days were a blur. The water stopped working its magic. His hunger returned and his dizziness increased. The guest house got so hot that even lying perfectly still, he still sweated. He continued to bathe frequently but he was losing the energy to dry off. Most of the time he just laid on his back and tried not to think. The bones in his spine were permanently bruised. He felt as if he was not transforming into Sally Wither or even changing back into David Lennon. No, he was becoming a sheet of linoleum. He smelled the floor as the hours crept by and it was the one thing in the whole bathroom that did not remind him of lemons.

Another week passed, he was not sure. Julie did not visit again. It got so it was difficult to stand. When he was awake he enjoyed thinking about Cleo and her baby. He decided that she was the one he loved.

His head ran another mental clip about himself and an even younger version of Mrs. Wither playing in Central Park together. They were flying kites, having a great time, only there was another man there that was not Mr. Wither. This man was tall and blond and much younger than Mr. Wither. But he kept grabbing and kissing Mrs. Wither like they were married. And he remembered thinking to himself, a little puzzled, that he must have two daddies.

It was nothing, he told himself. Just a dream.

Then one foggy Christmas Eve Santa came to say that the linoleum was not the original linoleum that had been there when he had been dating Sienna. That meant it had been changed, obviously. That meant it was possible there were scraps of her life hidden beneath it, maybe in the corners, tucked in the sides. Sienna had been fond of bobby pins. She used to pin her hair back all the time. It made him wonder—if he had the strength to pull up the floor—what would he find?

He set to work, without a single tool. The linoleum was not held in place by wooden strips. That would have been ideal—he could have popped the nails off the boards. The floor was gripped by glue alone. The linoleum had been expertly cut—it circled the toilet bowl like a line of bricks in the Great Pyramids. Yet there was one place, in the corner beside the tub, where he could see a crack of the original floor. It was there he dug in his fingers and nails and threw all caution to the wind and all pain down the sink. Boy, did it hurt; he was yanking at something that counted leverage in terms of millimeters.

It cost him an hour of hard labor and four broken nails to get the corner up. The rest was simple—the linoleum cracked like burning toast as he shoved it off the floor with the bottoms of his feet. It took him only three minutes to find two glue-stained bobby pins jammed beneath the outside of the tub.

Now what? In movies people always opened handcuffs the second they got their hands on that precious bobby pin. But he was not practiced at picking locks. He did not even know what the inside of a lock looked like. As a kid, he had not played with locks. He had played with dolls. No, Sienna had liked dolls, he had liked trains.

All he could do was fiddle with the damn things, hope for the best.

The handcuffs on his wrists popped open after one hour of trying.

The ones on his ankles took until dark. Finally they went.

"Cool," he whispered.

Using what little strength he had left, he stood and went into the living room and put on his clothes. They had even remembered his shoes—he was grateful. But he ran into a problem when he tried the front door. It was locked from the outside. He tried the back door, got the same results. Furious, he returned to the bathroom and grabbed the loose chains and headed for the main front window. There were no curtains. Inside and outside was dark, but he did not stop to consider if he should try a light switch. He just started whacking the window. Glass flew everywhere, in his hair and face, but he didn't stop until he had an unobstructed view of Sienna's front lawn. It was odd that he did not notice her approach.

The front door opened. Julie stepped inside, turned on the light.

She carried a gun. A small black revolver.

"What are you doing?" she asked.

He realized it was no coincidence she had shown up. She must have been living in the main house, another thing he had failed to think about. His brain needed a banana—some sugar—it felt like a pumpkin that had been carved out with a machete. He hoisted his chains in the air.

"What the fuck does it look like I'm doing?" he asked.

She raised her gun, pointed at his heart. "Put that down or I will kill you."

"Kill me and you kill your baby doll." He started to swing his chains as if he were Thor and they were a celestial hammer. "Get out of my way."

She cocked the revolver. "I'm not bluffing."

"You are bluffing. That is all you know how to do. But I am not bluffing. I am in a real bad mood. If you don't get out of my way, I'm going to kill you."

Her aim wavered, but she did not put down the gun. He kept swinging his chains. It was a standoff, one he believed he would have won, despite his frail condition. But just then headlights shone through the shattered window. There was a car coming up the long driveway.

David almost made a dash for it right then. The look on Julie's face stopped him. She was scared—the visitor was unexpected. That was good news, he thought. Yet he worried she might shoot anyone that was not a team player. He hoped it was Stanton, a guy who knew how to shoot back.

In that ridiculous position, not speaking, with her gun in her hand and his long chain twirling like a fan, they waited for the visitor to arrive.

The car parked, turned off the headlights. A slight figure in dark clothes got out and walked toward them. The distance from the main driveway to the guest house was fifty yards. The person appeared in no hurry. He or she could have been a spirit out for an evening stroll in a deserted cemetery. Although David struggled to make out who it was, all he could see was a pale face.

Mary Pomus entered the guest house.

She wore black leather pants, a red turtleneck. Her boots were black, and her eyelashes and eyebrows were painted the color of an asteroid. Yet her eyes sparkled with color and a dozen moods. He saw brown and bravura, violet and violence. She smiled as she entered the room, and her purple-coated lips pulled over her white teeth like flesh over an incision.

"Hello," she said.

Julie stared at her incredulously. "What the hell are you doing here?"

"Daddy wants to see him," she replied.

"What?"

"Daddy wants to see him now."

"You get out of here, you little creep!" Julie said, and with that she grabbed Mary by the back of the head and shoved her toward the door.

Mary's hand slid by the windowsill, beneath the broken window, and her fingers fastened on a large piece of jagged glass. In a blur too fast for him to follow, she reached up with her free hand, grabbed Julie's ponytail and yanked Julie's head back.

Fifteen-year-old Mary Pomus cut her throat—one quick slice. Julie lost her gun and dropped to her knees, and the blood began to form a puddle around her leaking neck as deep and dark as a wishing well. Only Julie Stevens had run out of pennies. Gasping for air, she tried to speak but all that came out was a garbled nightmare. Mary stood over her and watched her die as if Julie were nothing more than a roach that had been stepped on.

Julie stopped gasping and lay still.

"I never much liked her," Mary said, before turning to him and offering her hand. It was the hand she had killed Julie with and it was stained red. "Come along, David. My father wants to talk to you."

THIRTY

Mary had arrived in his car. She was the one who drove them back to Lompoc. He did not worry that she did not have a license, nor did he ask how she had obtained his keys. She appeared to be an excellent driver, and he was too weak to drive. The tussle with Julie had exhausted him. He slumped in the seat and tried to keep from passing out. But he did have the wherewithal to ask her to take him to the police station instead of to the church. She assured him that her father only needed a few minutes of his time.

They entered Lompoc after ten. He was not sure what day it was. The streets were relatively empty, as if everyone was inside and watching the final episode of a miniseries. Mary drove him straight to the church, the three-sided glass pyramid shining like an ancient monolith beneath the half moon. She parked near the front entrance.

"I'll stay here," she said.

"You'll wait for me?"

She leaned over and kissed him on the lips. "I always liked you," she said.

For a moment he saw her from the perspective of seven years ago, that day at the beach when he had rescued her from drowning. The riptides had been rough, the waves cruel. She had felt like a piece of soggy spaghetti in his hands. He had been sure he was saving a corpse for burial. She was nonresponsive, she was not breathing. Yet, when he finally got her to shore, even without CPR, she suddenly sat up and kissed him on the lips. *"Thank you for saving me,"* she said.

"We have to talk about what happened to Julie. We have to go to the police."

"Don't worry about that."

"You killed her. You cut her throat."

Mary shrugged. "So?"

He realized she was chewing something. A breath mint.

"Then, going up on her tiptoes, she leaned over and spoke in my ear. I felt her breath on the side of my face, and there was something familiar about it—the scent. It reminded me of peppermints, it was not a foul smell, but it was still a cold breath. And when she spoke I felt ice in my veins . . ."

She could not have been the one Krane had seen. Not that ghoul.

"Why did you rescue me right now?" he asked softly.

"I am not rescuing you."

David remembered what Krane had been told. "Am I going to die?" he asked.

Mary patted him on the back. "We all die. It's just a question of when and how horrible it's going to be."

His very own thoughts. Trembling, he got out of the car and entered the church.

The interior was warm, dim; the overhead lights were off. With the glass walls, the church was always hot in the summer. Pomus liked it that way. He was sitting alone in a pew close to the central altar. He had a Bible on his lap, and was looking at the huge wooden cross. There were six lit candles, three on each side. The light was magnified by a series of mirrors at the base of the cross, and their yellow reflections cast a ghastly hue over Christ's suffering.

Pomus stared at his savior's face as if he were trying to remember something important. He did not look up until David cleared his throat, even then he did not speak. He gestured for David to take a seat by his side, and they sat in silence for more than a minute. David felt he should have eaten something before coming. An apple, or even a cracker would have helped. He was seeing stars where there were only shadows.

"He said that there is no greater love than that a man layeth down his life for another. Do you think that is true?" Pomus asked.

"Yes."

"Do you think Christ has the power to wipe out all sins?"

"I don't know. Reverend, I have to talk to you. I have to tell you what is going on in this town and across the country. There's this group of people, they're harvesting organs and selling them to rich people. They're the ones who killed Sienna. They killed Krane and his partner and God only knows how many other people. They . . ."

Pomus held up his hand. "I know about them."

David blinked. "You do?"

"Yes."

"Who told you?"

For a moment it was as if they were back in that jail cell. Even before he spoke, David knew the minister was going to talk about his ex wife. His face looked the same as it had then, even in the light of the candles. He appeared gray, lifeless—his skin was as loose as a pocketful of change. His breathing was labored—he struggled against the weight of his bulk and his heavy suit. Yet, paradoxically, he did not appear frail. In this place, this church he had built largely with his own hands, he had power. It was as if he was surrounded by an aura of immense energy.

"I told you how I was young when I met Jane, and how I tormented her most of our married life. My self-righteousness, my judgments—they drove her to distraction. So that one afternoon when I was watching the ball game and she walked in and said she was leaving, I shouldn't have been surprised. But I was, it caught me totally off guard. I think I lost my mind right then. I told you how we started fighting, but I didn't just yell at her. I hit her, a few times. Then I locked her up in our room. I kept her in there a week. I didn't let her eat or drink. I wanted to make sure she was sorry for what she was thinking of doing." He added, "I punished her in the worst way."

"What did you do to her?"

Pomus glanced over, smiled briefly, then shook his head. "It doesn't matter, I crossed the line is all. I did what few human beings are capable of doing, and after that, I was a changed man. I told you how I changed back then, didn't I? How I saw that it did not matter what sins a man committed, that Jesus was always there, ready to forgive them. I saw sin in a whole new light after I tortured Jane."

"You tortured her?"

"Yeah."

"What exactly did you do to her?"

"I burned her."

"You what?"

Pomus shrugged. "I got carried away."

"You burned her hand or something?"

"Yeah. I burned her hand, maybe her arms and her back a little. She got these red blisters all over. Blood blisters, I think you call them. When they burst they gave off an awful smell, and her skin turned black and . . . well, it doesn't matter. It was not a pretty sight. I felt bad about it afterward, but then, when I saw that demon on the couch I told you about, I started to feel better. I didn't tell you this part earlier, but I went over and sat beside it, and it put its arm around me. It really wasn't so bad. It was actually exciting. I felt as if the power of the universe entered into me right then, and I completely changed. All my worries and doubts, they vanished. I was a new man, reborn in the spirit. I felt as if I could do anything, it didn't matter what. Jesus would be there, for all of time. In the end, he would forgive me because that is the kind of God he is. Do you understand?"

David stood. "I think it was a mistake for me to come here right now. Why don't I come back another time?"

Pomus looked up. "You're leaving? But you just got here."

"I think I better." He turned. "You have a nice night, Reverend."

Pomus grabbed David's hand, stopped him. "Don't go, we need to talk."

David tried to shake off his grip, discovered he couldn't. He must be weaker than he thought, or else Pomus was very strong. "I have to go home right now. But we can talk later." He added, "Let go of my hand."

Pomus did not let go. He gestured to the pew with his other hand. "Sit back down, we need to talk. You don't understand about LESS. What Dr. Rean told you—it's only half the story."

David felt cold. "How do you know about LESS?"

"I told you, I know all about that group. Sit, stop arguing with me and listen."

David sat back down. Pomus let go of his hand. But the minister moved closer, so near David could hear the air straining through his lungs. It sounded like bugs digging through the dirt, insects buzzing in their hives. He did not understand how Pomus could barely breathe and yet walk around like a powerhouse. The minister put his large fleshy hand on his knee.

"How are you feeling right now?" he asked.

"Not so good. I'd really like to go now. I want to go home."

"I'm afraid you can't do that. That's not an option anymore."

"Why not?"

"Dr. Rean told you what the deal is. What happened that night with Sienna."

"With Sienna. She . . . wait. Reverend, how do you know Dr. Rean?"

"He works for me. He's an employee."

"But . . . he's a doctor. How can he work for you? You're a minister."

Pomus shook his head. "It just seems that way from the outside. From the inside, things are a lot different. You know about the inside and the outside? They're like this side and the other side, life and death. Doctors are supposed to specialize in this side, and ministers are supposed to take care of the other side. But sometimes things get messed up. Dr. Rean wanted to work the other side. Or I should say Billy wanted to, Billy and Rachel. She was the first one in your gang to go there and come back. But that doesn't mean she understood everything when she was over there. I tell you, she understood very little. The two of them, Dr. Rean and Teresa, Billy and Rachel—call them what you wish—they think they have it all figured out. But they're arrogant, they don't know the half of it. They don't know their future obligations to certain folk on the other side. You follow me so far?"

"I don't know what the hell you're talking about."

"Funny you should use that word. Technically, it's not an accurate term. There are many levels, many places to go. But it is somewhat descriptive of certain places. It's the folk from those places that are really behind LESS. Oh, I know Dr. Rean fed you a long story about how he developed the ketamine technology, and I have to admit that he and his partners helped refine it. But he's arrogant, he wants all the credit for himself. In reality, it was my partners and I who first saw the drug's potential to draw in new recruits. You see what I am saying?"

"No."

"Sure you do. It's the chicken and the egg question. How did it all get started? From my point of view, it began with that preacher locking his wife in that room and tying her to the bed and lighting that candle. Telling her that she wasn't going anywhere. That no other man was going to touch her. That he was going to make damn sure of it. Did you know he burned her ears off? Just using a candle, that takes a while but he kept at it."

David felt sick. "You mean, *you* burned her ears off?"

Pomus patted him on the back. "Now you are asking the right questions! Who am I? Who are you? I remember everything that man did. You remember everything David did. But memory can be a tricky thing. It all depends on where you make your stand, and whether you're on this side or the other side. See what I mean?"

"Did they shoot you up with ketamine?"

Pomus chuckled. "No! I was the one who shot Rachel up, or, I should say, I shot Teresa up. She was the one who got the ketamine. She's the one who was driven out of her body. That's how this whole business got started. Wait, let me take that back. I was the one who burned Rachel's face, too, so I guess you could say that happened first. Herb helped me out there, by the way, although he didn't know what I was up to. He supplied the necessary drugs, especially the opium-laced pot that made the two of them fall asleep before I entered the house." Pomus paused. "You don't know where he is, do you?"

"Herb? No."

"You're sure about that? I need to find him. I need to talk to him."

"I don't know where he is."

Pomus nodded. "That's okay, sometimes they get away at the last second. You can't blame yourself, these things happen. That's what I told Mary when he disappeared. 'Don't beat yourself up,' I said. 'There's plenty of fish in the sea.' By the way, speaking of the sea, that was nice work on your part when you rescued her from drowning. But you almost ruined my plan that day. Did you know that?"

"How did I almost ruin your plan? What plan?"

"I was making a quick switch there. Letting another one of my partners come on over. You see, my daughter and I are not like these others who just want another body. We're at the management level. Rachel and Billy don't know anything about that level. They think their work is totally scientific. But that Rachel, she's got to be in denial. She should know better. When I spoke to her years ago and she was looking for a new face, she knew damn well that I was not your normal everyday minister."

"What did you do to Rachel?"

"I made her an offer, that's all. You just have to find the right lever and you can offer anybody anything and they'll take it. I was working on a deal with Charlie—what he could do to get his wife back—when he suddenly left town with Karen." Once more, Pomus paused. "You didn't have anything to do with that, did you?"

"Yeah. I told them to get the hell out of here. That this town was dangerous."

"You've been a busy bee, haven't you?"

"Does Stanton work with you?"

"No. But he will someday. His son is in bad shape, I am sure we can leverage that somehow. Maybe promise him a sudden recovery. We can work miracles, as well; we just don't go around bragging about it. Anyway, where was I? Oh yeah, after Rachel lost her good looks, I told her what was possible using the ketamine and she was all for it. She was amazing, she didn't hesitate a minute. I like a bold woman. I suppose that was a quality you liked in her as well. Did you know Billy was with me when you and Rachel started making out? I felt your passion, even at a distance. It was like a disturbance in the Force. I told Billy to hurry over to your house so he could see what he could see. When you think about it, that was a crucial element in the way everything has unfolded. It takes your breath away when you consider how the hand of God was right there, guiding events from the very start."

David felt furious. "How can you sit here and talk about all the suffering you have caused and then talk about God?"

Pomus gestured to the altar. "I told you, Jesus forgives everyone. He's got to forgive me. The number of sins I commit doesn't matter. I admire that about him. Yeah, I have no problem with him at all. A lot of people who go to church are confused on that point, but it is true. Without him I would be nothing."

"You are as crazy as Dr. Rean."

"No. You think about it. Without salvation, there could be no damnation. It just wouldn't be fair. Without people like Jesus who are ready to lay down their lives for a higher cause, there could not be people like Sienna who are eager to sacrifice their souls merely to extend their lives. I see I got your attention with that remark. Even though I am sitting here and acting like I am still talking to David, I know you are in there listening to me. Let's be frank, girl, you are the most sorry case of the whole lot. You were smart enough to see that there must be a penalty for engaging in this kind of exchange. You said as much in your novel—which was a good book by the way, I thoroughly enjoyed it. But your creative insight did not stop you. Then, you honestly fell in love with David—which was difficult to do given the circumstances—and still you betrayed him. Think about the synergy of those two faults. Think about who and what you are. While you're at it, think about the special places I am allowed to take you after this life is over.

The decisions you made, Sienna—they opened all kinds of doors for us. You're exactly what I was talking about when I mentioned new recruits."

"Shut up. I am not Sienna. You are not a demon."

Pomus grinned, his face gluttonous. "I sure as hell am not the Easter Bunny."

"What's that supposed to mean?"

"Just a little impish humor, don't get excited. By the way, did you ever sleep with my daughter? She told me you did but she has a nasty habit of lying. I don't really like that about her. She might need a little punishment herself, just to remind her who Daddy is."

"I did not sleep with her."

"I didn't think so. I appreciate you telling me."

"Are you the one who killed Sienna?"

"Yeah. I killed you, when you were supposed to kill yourself. Or do you forget how you chickened out at the end? You were just like Billy. He was lucky to have Teresa there that night. You were lucky to have me there. But that was silly of you to step in your own blood when the party was over. You got it all over his floor, and I was the one who had to clean it up. But I guess you were sort of out of it right then, after the switch."

"Why did you cut her up? Desecrate her body?"

"It was fun, and my partners on the other side like it. Some of the folk above me, they *need* sacrifices like that. It keeps them nourished. Also, it's kind of a requirement. I told you, Dr. Rean and Teresa are running around telling people that LESS is completely scientific. But these ritual killings serve as a signpost for others that there might be more to the organization than meets the eye. In a sense my partners and I are obligated to warn people what's what. That there could be a price to pay later. Also, it is *time* for such rituals to resurface. Sienna was smart to bring that up in her novel. You can call it what you want. The end of time, the age of Aquarius, the last days, Armageddon—it is all the same thing. It's simply a time in history when all kinds of new and exciting recruiting techniques are possible that were not possible before. The ketamine technology is just an excuse for my partners and me to solicit new workers."

David snickered. "If this is Armageddon, when does the Rapture start?"

Pomus was not offended. "The Bible provides a number of juicy hints, but it's only got a portion of the story. Actually, when my partners and I get rolling, we're going to set things up pretty much the opposite way the Bible says. That way no one will know what we're up to. We're not stupid, you know, most Christians haven't figured that out yet."

"This is all nonsense. LESS has nothing to do with biblical prophecies."

"You are not listening. It was *I* who created LESS. Dr. Rean did not start illegally transplanting organs until Billy was in his body. I had my eye on the real Dr. Rean from the time the real Teresa introduced me to him. I thought to myself, a guy like that, properly motivated, could take what I had to offer and run with it. As soon as Billy was on the inside, I made it a requirement that he do business with me. That's why I said at the start that he's an employee."

"He doesn't think you're a demon."

"He tries very hard not to think about me at all. So does his wife. But one day he is going to be like the proverbial mad scientist who realizes he has been conducting wild experiments that have a lot more consequences than he ever imagined. On that day he's going to come running to me, and after we chat a little, he's going to try to run the other way. But by then it will be much too late, for him and his wife."

"I don't believe any of it."

"Now you're lying to yourself. You believe all of it."

"It's not true. Stuff like this does not happen in the real world."

"We are not in the real world. We are in a church."

"Why do you pretend to be a minister?"

"I am a minister. What I preach is not much different than what Jesus taught. It is all a question of perspective. I told you, I'm a fan of grace and forgiveness. I believe in them, I have faith in Jesus. It is only my goal that is a little different. I see grace as a tool to allow me to do what I want. Really, I almost always get what I want." Pomus added, "But I could not get the real David Lennon."

He had to ask. "Why not?"

"Because he was a good man, he had genuine love for his fellow man. People like that are rare. It is difficult to get leverage on them, make deals with them. And to tell you the truth, I was not sorry to lose him. He deserved to leave when he did. He did not need all this shit."

He almost wept. "I have gone through nothing but shit since that night."

Pomus patted his knee kindly. "Well, don't worry, that will soon be over."

David stared at the minister, at the cross, tried to take in everything he was being told. He did not believe it, of course, but he did not disbelieve it either, and that crumb of doubt was enough to form a crack in what was left of his intellectual armor. A crack that was threatening to erupt into a gusher. He felt a pressure at the back of his head, a ringing in his ears. Listening to Pomus was not the same as listening to Dr. Rean. Dr. Rean had been an asshole, it was like Pomus was the real shit.

David shook his head. "Let's say just for a moment that you are telling me the truth. You are a demon and my best friends are working with you and Sienna stole my body. You are not going to get your way, not with her."

"Forgive me, I don't follow you."

"Because I love her. Because there is grace. You said it yourself, they are real. That means I can save her."

Pomus was puzzled. "Why would you want to save her? Really, she's no good."

"I don't care. That is the nature of love. It cares—it cares no matter what. You are not going to take her away to some cold hell. I swear, I will save her, and you can't stop me."

"How will you stop me?"

"I can always do what Cleo did in the story."

"Kill yourself? Sacrifice yourself?"

"Yes. Maybe that was what she was trying to tell me with her book. Maybe that was why she wrote it."

Pomus was impressed. "You know, if it was David who was talking to me right now, I think the plan would work. Sacrifice is a powerful tool—it can move mountains. Jesus himself might even step in and help out some. Unfortunately, David is gone and I don't think Jesus is interested in you. I know it's you who's in there, girl, who's trying to impress me with your talk of love and grace. Grace is for the grateful. When were you ever grateful? You were given everything life had to offer except a long life, and not once did you offer thanks. And love? You were given the love of a good man and you killed him. You do not deserve love or grace, and although you wrote about sacrifice, you do not have a clue what it means. It is just another plot device to you. No, trust me, it is not a cold hell you will go to when this body dies." Pomus came suddenly close; his breath was in David's face and it was so hot it felt like fire. He gripped his knee painfully, his voice raised to a shout—a preacher exorcising the demons, or else calling them down to Earth. "It will be a very hot hell! Because you deserve to burn, Sienna!"

The crack started to shatter. The ringing became a screech.

"No! You are not going to burn me!" David's voice came out loud and clear, terrified. Yet it was not his voice.

Sienna, he thought.

Pomus slowly grinned and grabbed his arm. Standing, the minister pulled David to his feet, and yanked him toward the altar, toward the candles. David dug in his heels, but it was hopeless. The minister had the strength of ten men. It was only then, at that very late hour, that David realized that Pomus could not be a man.

The minister dragged him onto the altar, close to the cross, and reached out and took down a burning candle. With his free hand, Pomus brought the flame near David's hand. The minister laughed as he did so, and David saw teeth inside his mouth that did not belong in a human body.

"Tell me your name," he ordered.

David continued to struggle. "No."

Pomus brought the flame to within an inch of his fingers. "Tell me your name!"

"My name is David!"

Pomus burned him. Not much, he just kept his fingers a few seconds in the small flame, but the pain was excruciating. It reached all the way inside and poked his deepest fear. Yet the terror gave him a burst of energy; he was momentarily able to pull free. The effort brought a whiplash, however, he kicked the cross and accidentally knocked off one of the mirrors that were arranged in a curve at its base. The row of mirrors were there to reflect back the ceiling lights, the different-colored bulbs, and create the impression that the small-town church was one giant celestial cathedral.

The mirror cracked as it fell on the floor, and when he looked down he saw his reflection scattered in many pieces. Each piece seemed to hold a part of him, but not a single one looked like him. His physical breath underwent a strange transmutation. He drew in a breath like any other breath, but when he exhaled a cold vapor filled the space. There were crystals in the midst of it, a lattice of memory and mind, but when he breathed in again the lattice shattered. Then he knew that he knew nothing, and the last breath of his illusion was destroyed. *He* felt himself leave, *he* felt himself die.

And then *he* felt nothing whatsoever.

Pomus stepped closer, his heavy feet cracking the glass. He continued to hold the candle ready, to burn again if necessary. "What is your name?" he asked quietly.

She lowered her head. "Sienna."

Pomus gave her the candle, nodded to the cross. "Put it back for me and clean up this mess. When you are done, you can light a candle of your own, if you want." As he turned away, he added, "But it won't help."

The minister left her alone, in the church, to think about her life.

1st DAY

HR Dept

8:30 ; 4:30

435 9th Street

f train   9th street

42nd

DATE DUE

NOV 1 2 2003	
DEC 3 - 2003	
JAN 6 2004	
2 6 2004	
FEB - 9 2004	
MAR 1 3 2004	
APR 3 0 2004	
JUL 1 0 2004	
OCT 1 2 2004	
APR 1 3 2006	
SEP 0 8 2016	
SEP 0 8 2016	

DEMCO, INC. 38-2931